"FAST-PACED, ORIGINAL, AND UTTERLY TERRIFYING—TRUE, TEETH-GRINDING TENSION. I LOST SLEEP READING THE NOVEL, AND THEN LOST EVEN MORE SLEEP THINKING ABOUT IT.

MARTIN FLETCHER IS THE MOST VIVIDLY DRAWN, MOST RESOURCEFUL, MOST HORRIFYING KILLER I HAVE ENCOUNTERED. HANNIBAL LECTER, EAT YOUR HEART OUT!"
—MICHAEL PALMER, AUTHOR OF *SILENT TREATMENT*

W9-BTA-245

**Praise for John Ramsey Miller's
terrifying debut thriller**
The Last Family

"The best suspense novel I've read in years!"
—Jack Olsen

"Martin Fletcher is one of the most unspeakably
evil characters in recent fiction. . . .
A compelling read."
—*Booklist*

"The author writes with a tough authority and
knows how to generate suspense."
—*Kirkus Reviews*

"Suspenseful. . . . Keeps readers guessing with
unexpected twists."
—*Publishers Weekly*

THE LAST FAMILY

John Ramsey Miller

BANTAM BOOKS

NEW YORK TORONTO

LONDON SYDNEY AUCKLAND

This novel is dedicated
to my wife of twenty years,
Susan Dedmon,
whose love is the rock my life stands on.
And to my sons,
Christian, Rush, and Adam
for their blind faith
and the joy they have brought me.

Acknowledgments

There are people who I wanted to thank personally, who deserve to be mentioned. Few readers will recognize the names listed below but if you enjoy this book at all you'll forgive me for thanking them. I owe them and others, no less significant but too numerous to mention.

My mother, Gene Ramsey Miller, Ph.D., 1924–1979, who died too young and unfortunately, and who taught me to bear disappointment and pain with grace, to trust my heart and to always follow my dreams. To my father, Rev. R. Glenn Miller of Oxford, Mississippi, whom I counted on for advice, understanding, and a sense of humor. My wonderful stepmother, JoAnn, who has always kept after me to write and rescued my earliest efforts from an attic cleaning.

To Andrew Morello, 1975–1992, of North Miami Beach, the son of our dear friends Joseph and Andrea, who taught me how truly devastating the death of a child at the hands of another can be. Andrew's death was a specific impetus toward creating the desire to write this book so I could share that through fictional characters.

My mother-in-law, Pearl Dedmon, who dreamed my first novel was in her hands.

My most trusted reader and champion, authoress Shirley Yarnell of Cabin John, Maryland, who saw something in my work and guided me.

My agent and dear friend, Kristin Lindstrom, of The Lindstrom Literary Group in Arlington, Virginia, who weathered 130 rejections with steadfast devotion.

My thoroughly remarkable and patient editor, Beverly Lewis, who saw something she wanted to work with and who put so much effort in guiding me to make this book what it is.

To Katie Hall, who passed this book to Beverly Lewis with a strong recommendation.

To all of the people at Bantam Books who have worked so hard to make sure this book had a chance to find an audience.

I thank my patient technical advisers, Dr. Steven Haynes, the nationally respected forensic pathologist in Rankin County, Mississippi; Cecil "Chip" Devilbiss of Nashville, my surveillance and security systems adviser; Jerry Cunningham, my Lake Pontchartrain and nautical adviser; Brooks Harris of the Nashville P.D., who has been my model for police officers who strive for excellence in fighting crime; Tom Austin, fellow writer and chief of police in Santaquin, Utah; and last but not least, U.S. Marshal David Crews of Oxford, Mississippi. God forbid, any technical mistakes are mine alone.

To Gene Weingarten, now with *The Washington Post*, Tom Shroder and Bill Rose, editors with *Tropic Magazine* at *The Miami Herald*. They gave me my first assignments and encouraged me to go to fiction.

Special thanks to my dearest friends and mentors Pup and Lee McCarty of Marigold, Mississippi, who showed me where the rest of the world was. My brother Rush G. Miller, Jr., and his wife, Johnnye, my dear friends Kerry Hamilton of Los Angeles, Nathan Hoffman of New Orleans, Mike Horton of Miami Beach, William Greiner of New Orleans and Jay and Lisa McSorley of Charlotte and the Netherlands.

And I want to thank the supportive friends and family members whom I have been blessed with. I so hope their faith and encouragement is rewarded by the following pages.

John Ramsey Miller

THE LAST FAMILY

1

A SOLITARY HAWK SHIFTED ITS WINGS AGAINST INVISIBLE CURRENTS and traced lazy circles in a blue ocean of sky. The shoulders of the mountain, like the soft contours of a sleeping woman, blazed bright yellow-green where fingers of sunlight caressed the features. Fog still hung in the cradles of valley. On the ribbon of trail that lay among the trees like a forgotten piece of twine, there was movement that caught the bird's attention. Flashes of yellow, blue, and flesh-white skittered to and fro in a space where the ground was open to the sky. Children.

The Cub Scouts who had run up the trail were headed for a rock that was roughly the size and attitude of a forty-foot sailing ship, a granite vessel that had lost its mast and was in the process of slipping beneath the waves. They had instructions to stay in a group at Schooner Rock and await the leaders, who followed with the stragglers. The immense slab of rock angled from the ground to a point twelve feet above the trail—a perfect ambush point. As the scouts erupted up the path toward the rock, they slowed at the sight of a man who stood leaning against the rock's wall with his arms crossed. He was watching them and smiled as they approached. The man was wearing a khaki uniform and mirrored sunglasses. He had red hair and a matching mustache. The boys crowded around him.

"Morning, Boy Scouts," he said.

"We're Cub Scouts," a small boy answered. "You a ranger?"

"I sure am," the man said, smiling. "Ranger Ron. You boys having fun in my woods?"

"Yes," they responded certainly.

"You boys know the difference between a white oak and a red oak?"

Silence.

He held out two large leaves. "See, one has pointy edges and the other has rounded ones. This one, the pointed one, looks like a fire if you hold it by the stem. Fire is red, that's how you remember. White-oak leaf has soft, curved sides like a soft-serve ice-cream cone, and that's white."

The closest boy took the leaves, and the others looked over his shoulder waiting their turns.

"I want all of you to go back down the trail and find me one of each. Then bring them back and you'll get woodsman merit badges."

The boys were excited by the prospect and all turned to run.

"Whoa!" he yelled. "Which one of you is George Lee?"

The boys went howling down the trail, leaving a small red-haired boy standing alone. The man knelt down and looked at him at eye level. The boy was staring at his own reflection in the glasses.

"Your daddy asked me to come get you and take you to meet him at the parking area. He's got some camping things for you, and he's waiting there about now." The man looked at the backs of the scouts as they disappeared. As George watched, the man opened a small brown bottle and poured some clear liquid over a handkerchief.

"Did he give you the code word?" George asked.

"He said for me to say . . ." He bent to put his lips to George's ear. "Crackerjacks." George tried to break and run, but the man had him in his arm and put the cloth over his mouth. George struggled, the sound of his screams muffled to a low roar by the kerchief.

As Ruth Tippet, the den leader, and Sarah Rodale, her assistant, arrived with the stragglers, they found the boys lined up on the rock against a brilliant sky like a victorious army, brandishing staffs and dark clubs looted from the forest floor.

"Lord of the flies," Sarah said as they approached the rock. "Think they'll attack?"

"Refrain from sudden moves and maybe they'll let us pass without scalping us," Ruth said. "And don't touch any of their uniforms if you're allergic to poison ivy," she added. She was allergic and just knew the boys had been off the trail and neck high in the stuff.

Ruth stopped to check her compass—even though there was only one possible trail—and to let the three straggler Cub Scouts take a break. The two women were dedicated and wore the uniform of den leaders. Short pants, official knee socks, and the short-sleeved shirts of summer. Wide yellow ribbons wrapped their epaulets, and colorful patches had been sewn all over the fronts of their uniforms. Patches. Ruth, the undisputed leader of Den Six, had four more patches than Sarah. The packed ground beneath their boots was as cold as a gravestone.

"You guys 'er actin' like idiot fools," said Andy Tippet, who had dropped to the ground and propped his considerable bulk against a fallen tree.

"Yew guuuys 'errrr actin' lack foools," a child said mockingly.

Ruth Tippet's son, Andy, had single-handedly slowed the scout leaders and two other children who didn't feel at all safe away from the adults. He was overweight and lazy and had kept sitting down, causing everyone to stop until the more vital of the young boys had been released to run ahead to Schooner Rock. Ruth had got involved in scouting so Andy wouldn't turn into the couch turnip his father was.

The fifteen boys were between the ages of seven and nine. The children were not even carrying packs on this early-morning hike. The trail above the rock was steeper, and there were places where a child could wander from it, slip, and fall. That was why they had been told to wait at the rock. The adults were no more than five minutes behind.

At the summit several other mothers and a couple of fathers waited with the tents, sleeping bags, clothes, scouting manuals, and food. Ruth carried an emergency pack that had, among scores of useful things, a first-aid box complete with a snakebite kit and bandages. She also carried one apple for each of them, flashlights, three canteens, spare batteries, NASA survival blankets, insect repellent, and on her belt she wore a massive chunk of a knife with every imaginable utensil attached, including a spoon and a saw blade that would cut through a branch the size of an adult python in seconds.

"Ten minutes, boys," Ruth said. "If you need to relieve yourselves, please do it now. I suggest a rest before we continue. So sit quietly and talk among yourselves. Drink in the natural splendor."

The two women sat and the boys split up into groups. Instead of resting they began to run about like escaped weasels; the blue uniforms and yellow kerchiefs seemed to be everywhere at once.

"Nothing will grow on that slope for a few years." She laughed and pointed to a ridge where two scouts had arched their backs and were crisscrossing yellow streams in the air and laughing.

"I figure we're about one mile away. This rock is the two-mile point. So figure six hours," Ruth said. She looked over at a fallen tree where her son was collapsed in a state of imagined heat exhaustion. "I don't know how to motivate Andy. Maybe I could tie his Nintendo to a stick and dangle it in front of him."

"Oh, we're not in a hurry," Sarah said. "It gives the others a chance to go slow and enjoy the trip."

"Up ahead maybe half a mile there's an overlook that is just mind-blowing," Ruth said. Sarah had never been on this particular trail before. Ruth seemed to know every trail in the Smokies, because those she had not walked she had read about and studied on her maps, some of which were three-dimensional.

"There's a guardrail but we'll have to be very careful to keep them back. With the drop I don't imagine any of them will get too close. It's a spine tingle to look off that cliff, I can tell you."

Ruth stood and blew the stainless-steel whistle that hung from a lanyard and rode between her breasts. The boys started wandering back up to the trail from three or four directions.

"We need to rest here awhile," Andy said. "What do we have to eat?"

"Roots and berries," Ruth said. She didn't plan to use the apples except in an emergency. Stopping to eat would kill an hour. The idea of the hike was to let the children burn off some excess energy and build an appetite for lunch.

"I ain't eating no roots and berries," he growled.

"Andrew, a double negative becomes the positive. So you just said you are going to eat roots and berries. Aren't you glad I didn't say roots and grubs?"

"Gross!" Teddy Barnes said. Teddy was wearing his cap pulled down so that his ears were at right angles to his head. His thick lenses made his eyes look like blue tennis balls. "Or cat poop," he said. Andy tried to strike Teddy with his worn Reeboks, but he was too slow.

"He said I eat cat poop!" Andy yelled.

"Well, you don't, do you?" his mother said. "Sticks and stones. All here?" she said, standing. She had been fat until she had started hiking and eating right. Now her thick legs were defined with muscle and well tanned. Her husband and sons could sit and watch television, but she had turned the garage into a gymnasium and spent her spare time on her program.

Ruth pointed at the little heads as they bobbed and weaved. "One, two, three, four, five, six, seven . . ." She stopped counting and held up two fingers to quiet the boys. "Be quiet. What's this? Silence," Ruth said.

"What's this? What's this sign?" Sarah added.

"Akela. The wolf!" several shouted. Soon the air was filled with small waving hands echoing the women's "V" signs.

"And it means what, everyone?"

"Shhhhhhhhh—" It sounded as though all of the children had sprung air leaks.

"Okay." Ruth started to count the heads again. "One, two, three, four, five, six, seven, eight, nine, ten, eleven, twelve, thirteen, fourteen."

"Fourteen?" Sarah said. "Who's out?"

"Who's missing?" Ruth asked. She turned 360 degrees, her eyes scanning the forest floor for a flash of yellow or a flesh tone amid the green, brown, and stone-gray.

"One, two, three, four," Sarah counted as she pointed at each head until she got to the last scout. "Oh, dear God—who's missing?" she said.

The children looked around at each other.

"George is," a child said.

"George!" Ruth yelled out. "George Lee!"

"He musta went with that ranger man," Timothy Buchanan said. Timothy was George's best friend. "He left his hat, though." The child pointed to a blue-and-yellow hat that was lying beside the rock.

"What man?" Sarah asked.

"He asked for George Lee," Timothy said.

Panic threatened to close Ruth's throat. She fought to maintain control in front of Sarah and the children.

"Yes," Timothy said. "He said George Lee. And he's gonna give us merit badges for these leaves. White oak and—"

"What in the world?" Ruth said.

"What did the man look like?" Sarah asked.

"He was big," Timothy said.

"And he had a gun . . . ," another child added. ". . . Like a cowboy. Silver with a black handle and silver diamond shapes on the handle."

"In a holster," the black child added. A slug's-trail of mucus, which ran from his nostril to his lip, glistened. He wiped it onto his sleeve and inspected it in a shaft of filtered sunlight.

"And cowboy boots," one said.

"But no spurs," offered someone else.

"Where is he? When did he come up here?" Sarah asked.

"He was already here when we got here," Timothy said.

"And was he wearing a uniform?" Ruth asked.

"Yes," Timothy said. "Brown with a Smokey the Bear hat and glasses that showed you your face back."

"He was tall like Michael Jordan," another child said.

"Was he black like Michael Jordan?" Ruth asked.

"No, he was a ranger with a red beard on his lip."

"They don't have black rangers," someone added.

The black scout objected. "They got African-American rangers, polices, cowboys, and silver war soldiers, too."

"They did not!" another child said. "They were just cooks and cleaners."

"Which way did they go?" Ruth asked.

"That way." A scout pointed up the trail. "To his Jeep."

"Well, no need to panic," Ruth decided. "He knew George's name and had a description and he was in uniform. It must have been some sort of emergency. It happens."

"Isn't his daddy a . . . ?" Sarah started.

"A government official would certainly know how to get to his son if he needed him. He's DSF, you know."

"DSF?"

"Drug Strike Force. It's a branch of the DEA or something," Ruth said. "I'm going to hurry on ahead—y'all can catch up."

"We can't go faster," Andy whined. "My feet hurt—I'll pass out—I'm starving—I'm all fuzzy-headed."

Several scouts began laughing. Someone was mimicking his whines.

"Ah'm fat. Ah'm mooshy-headed. Ah'm stupid."

"Uh-uh!" Sarah said. "We're all one team. All for one, and one for all. We pull together or we'll pull apart." The double entendre was wasted on the children.

"Very well," Ruth said as she lifted the pack. "Stay here all night, then. Come up at your own pace. And, remember, bears almost never attack if you simply play dead. Just lie up against a tree like you're doing now and close your eyes, and no peeping even if she does bite you."

"Den Six—line up!" Sarah yelled.

"Forget it!" Andy jumped to his feet. By the time the scouts were lined up, Ruth was already running far up the trail.

The ranger stopped at the overlook and placed George's limp body on the railing that had been made out of foot-wide stone cemented into a wall stretching between two large rock facings. He looked off at the scenery for a few seconds, drinking up the natural splendor. He picked up a coconut-sized rock, placed it on the rail near George's head, and shoved it out with a quick motion. It seemed as if four or five seconds passed before the canyon gave up the echoing sound of the missile landing on the rocks below. He contemplated the child for a few moments, as a man might stare at a car someone else owns, removed the hat and glasses so he could wipe his forehead with a handkerchief. "Well, George. Nothing personal," he said as he placed his hands under the body and lifted.

He caught a flash of something through the trees moving up the trail. It was a scout leader. He watched behind her for the others but saw no one except the lone woman jogging toward him. Quickly he took a metal tube with a threaded end from his pocket and screwed it into the barrel of a small black automatic, which he pulled from his right boot.

Ruth had run all the way to the overlook without stopping even once. She was thrilled when she saw the man leaning against the stone railing watching her over his right shoulder. She was trying to put a smile on when she realized that the man was alone.

"Sir, are you the ranger who came for George Lee?" She almost yelled it. *Maybe George was in the woods relieving himself or wandering ahead.*

The man straightened and his face softened in a smile. He had his right hand behind his back, the left propped on the top of the railing. There was something strange about his wearing dark glasses in such a shady place.

It's all right, he's a park ranger. She looked around, still expecting to see the child.

She was closing the last ten feet between them with her right arm extended. "I was worried sick—" she started.

Then she saw the gun.

2

NASHVILLE, TENNESSEE, WAS ORIGINALLY BUILT TO TAKE ADVANtage of the Cumberland River. It was established as Fort Nashboro and a reconstructed facsimile with ramparts stands as a tourist attraction, a few short blocks down the hill from Nashville's greater tourist attraction, the original Grand Ole Opry. That building is in turn a few blocks down the hill from the federal courthouse, where, sharing the floor with the federal prosecutor's offices, the Drug Enforcement Agency is located.

Special Agent in Charge, Rainey Lee, had been a DEA agent since just after leaving college and had led the DEA/DSF for four years. The DSF was an elite branch of the agency, and its cloak of secrecy was a large part of the appeal it held for men like Rainey Lee. He had gone straight to work at the DEA when it was formed from several branches of the Justice Department. At six feet five Rainey Lee was the tallest agent in the organization, and at forty-eight had packed sixty additional pounds around his basketball player's frame since college, when he had played for Duke University.

When he received the call from the sheriff's office in eastern Tennessee informing him that his son was missing, presumed abducted, he requisitioned an agency plane and was on site in the mountains ninety minutes later. He arrived still wearing his suit, though he had changed into a pair of boots he kept in the trunk of his car.

Forty searchers were already at Schooner Rock, where the scout and the leader had last been spotted. Twin bloodhounds and a small-framed German shepherd were dancing in place, twisting their nylon leads around each other. A deputy held George's scout cap to the animals so they could separate the boy's scent from the others'. After a few seconds the dogs circled wide and struck out up the trail.

The bloodhounds were kept on leads while the shepherd was allowed to run ahead, alone. They ran directly up the trail, often as not pulling the handler through dense brush beside the trail for half a mile, then stopped beside the shepherd, who was standing with his front paws on the railing of the overlook, barking at the sky. The bloodhounds moved a few feet on up the trail, then turned abruptly, agreeing with the shepherd, and sat shifting their gazes from the gathering of men to the open view and back.

Then the shepherd jumped back, looked around for a few seconds, investigated a large brown circle in the grass beside the path, and launched himself off into the woods. He stopped suddenly and barked. The rescue team ran toward the animal with Rainey leading, his gun drawn.

Ruth Tippet's body was on its back, her face aimed at the sky. The leaves had been pushed out of the way where she had been dragged. The single bullet had entered her forehead above the open left eye and exited through the back of her head.

Rainey turned and ran back to the railing where the

handler was holding the bloodhounds. He leaned out over the railing but couldn't see directly down because the overlook they were standing on formed a shelf out over the sheer rock wall.

"She smells the boy, all right," a deputy offered.

Rainey's heart dropped.

A thin deputy anchored himself by hooking a rope rig to a tree opposite the railing and extended, almost horizontally, out over the ledge. He gazed down at the large rocks piled at the base of the wall where something bright had been splashed in a wide circle. The emptied husk that had been George Lee was hardly more than the dark blue center of that stain.

"Sir," the deputy said, "I'm real sorry. We'll have to go in from below."

The sheriff said, "I think you might want to return to the camping area. We'll get him out. You can't do anything more."

Rainey Lee was among the first to scramble over the rocks to the body. After he had seen what lay there among the jagged edges and flat plates, he sat down on a nearby rock. He opened his mouth and, for what seemed to the deputies and rangers a long time, there was no sound. Then his scream dropped to a pitch they could hear. The noise was like the sound of an animal being eaten alive.

Doris Lee was in the kitchen thinking about her husband.

Rainey had been uncharacteristically silent since their daughter's funeral three months earlier and wouldn't speak to the minister or a psychologist no matter how Doris pleaded. She had done all she could. She had talked to her minister, the agency-approved psychologist, and a support group of grieving parents who met once a week at the Episcopal church. She was drinking half a fifth of vodka daily just to keep her nerves evened out. She planned to quit drinking soon. Rainey, never overly religious, blamed God, she thought.

Her mind was on her husband and George. Because there had been a rash of accidental deaths of family members in the DEA, Rainey had not wanted George to go on the trip, but she had insisted on it. She had learned from the other people in her survivors' support group that it was irrational to let fear and the projecting of possible disaster rob them of the future. You couldn't fold up your tent and hide from life, and it wasn't fair to George to keep him under virtual arrest. Until George had gone on the trip with the scouts, until he had actually stepped into Ruth's van and driven off down Maple, at least one of them had kept him in their sights at all times, except when they left him at school. She knew that it was because of the other deaths over the past few years. Accidents to other children. Wives of Rainey's old associates. Eleanor's death, surely an accident, had unleashed something in Rainey. He had changed in some basic way. It was as if someone different were possessing her husband's body.

Doris hated it when Rainey was late. She had game birds in the oven that would be ready in a few minutes, but once he knew he was late, he didn't seem able to hurry along. They both needed time away from the horror; the thought of her daughter running out of the garage—of the flames consuming Eleanor's clothing—of Rainey rolling her in the grass—her skin coming off in sheets—of the emergency room—the screams that went on and on for days. And Rainey's eyes as he sat beside the bed with his hands in his lap because there was no part of her either of them could touch. The thoughts took the breath out of her.

Doris stood, straightened her skirt, wiped the tears away with her fingers, and poured herself a glass of vodka. As it was, she'd had too much already, but, she rationalized, George was in the mountains and—then her mind seized an image of Eleanor's inflated face set against white hospital linen, looking as though she had been barbecued for a giant's dinner. Doris tipped the glass furiously, throwing several ounces of the clear liquid down her throat in one gulp, and gripped the edge of the sink as it burned back. She took a breath and decided that she had to stop drinking soon.

Rainey had a major bust about to come down, a bust he had worked on for two years, and after that pressure was off, she would stop. Now they'd get through their weekend, and George would be home with or without poison ivy, which he was highly allergic to, and they could finally get back to being a normal family.

They would get over the loss of Eleanor. Never completely—but they had to go on for George's sake. And they could have more children in time. *But we'll never forget you, Eleanor. We love you, baby—so much.* So much. She took another sip directly from the bottle and put it away in the cabinet. She heard the Cherokee stop in the driveway and took a lemon wedge from the refrigerator, chewing the bitter pulp from it to cleanse her breath.

She heard the front door close and familiar footsteps on the tile. She listened for the closet door to close after he'd hung up his shoulder rig and his jacket. Then he would . . . *That's strange*, she thought. *He didn't open the closet.*

She stopped and pushed her hair back and braced herself into a smile. "Honey? Rainey?" she called in a high chirp, feeling about as good as she could feel.

He was walking toward the kitchen, his boots against the parquet. *His boots are muddy—men!*

"Rainey, do you want a martini? Dinner will be ready in a few minutes," she said. When she looked up from the boots into his face, the breath escaped her in a low hiss.

Rainey's face might have been crafted from wet dough, his lips twisted in on themselves, the jaw quivering. The set of his mouth and his glazed eyes told her that some catastrophe had befallen him. The air around him was sour, malignant, charged with dark electricity. It was even money whether he'd collapse in a heap or put his fist through the wall.

"My mother?" she said. Her mother had suffered a stroke, and her blood pressure had been up and down on a seesaw for months.

He sat in the chair and stared at the table.

"Oh, God, not *your* mother," she said. His mother

was in good health, but who else could it be? Their fathers were both long buried.

"Sit down," he said, his voice without body, used up. His shoulders began to pitch and yaw, and tears started streaming down his cheeks. She put her hand on his shoulder and patted. The muscles that ran across it were like steel cable, unyielding.

"I can't believe it . . . don't know how to say it."

"Say what? Rainey, you're scaring me."

"George." He managed to say between whimpers. "Oh, my God," he wept.

"What's wrong with George?"

"Dead. He . . ."

The curtain that the vodka had closed over her nerves was jerked open, and Doris howled so loudly that the next-door neighbor, Ted Broom, a retired policeman dressed only in a strap T-shirt and boxer shorts, came running over with his .38 in hand. He came right into the kitchen with the gun in the air, his bare feet squeaking against the linoleum. The Lees stared at him through their tearstained eyes.

"Sorry, I thought it was a rapist . . . ," he said, apologizing. His face was English bulldog, his chest barreled, his arms too long and his legs too thin and rudely veined.

"Everything okay, Rainey?"

"No, George is gone."

"Camping. Aw, guys, he'll be back on Sunday. Boy has to get out."

"Dead!" Doris shrieked. "My babies are both dead!"

Doris's eyes rolled toward the back of her head, and some invisible magician jerked the skeleton out of her frame. It was Ted who dropped his gun and moved to catch her. Rainey never moved a muscle nor even looked at her. He didn't seem aware that his wife had fallen to the floor in a cold faint. Ted lifted her up like a sleeping baby, her arms and legs so much wet rope. He abandoned the pistol where it lay on the shiny antique-white floor tiles, and Rainey stared at it as though it might start spinning in place and playing music out through the barrel.

"Should I put her on the couch?"

Rainey looked up at Ted, his eyes clouded. "Bed, I think."

"Maybe you should call a doctor . . . ," Ted said. ". . . Minister or something?"

"She likes the Episcopal minister Hodges." Rainey stood and began looking out through the window, where birds were watching him, tilting their heads here and there and shuffling their feet.

"Which church is it?" Ted had returned.

"Something . . . ," he said. Two cardinals were trying to decide if they should go for some of the seed that Doris had put out or if Rainey might be about to pounce at them through the glass.

"Are you all right? I mean, is there anything I can do? Anything at all?"

"I don't . . ."

"What happened?"

"Happened?"

"To George."

"Murdered."

"Murdered? But he's on a camping trip—saw him leave myself."

Rainey looked at the old policeman. Rainey's eyes were moist from tears but dead as mica. "I have to go make the arrangements for my boy. He's coming . . . in a couple of hours."

"Shouldn't you and Doris go together? I mean, she's his mother, would she want to . . ."

"George fell into rocks. They picked him up with shovels. Nobody'll ever see him again because he doesn't exist." Rainey squeezed his eyes shut. "I wish to Christ I hadn't . . . seen him. Sweet Jesus, how could anybody hurt George?"

"I'll call Mary over here and I'll go with you. Drive you."

"Stay here for me. I'll call the preacher from the office. I just can't be here right now. I'll be back in a couple of hours. I appreciate . . ."

"Don't mention it, Rainey. We'd do anything to help. What's that smell?" Ted asked. He turned to the stove, shoved his hands into oven mitts, and opened the oven door. While Ted was pulling the blackened game hens from the oven and the kitchen was filling with angry smoke, Rainey stood and took his leave.

Special Agent Rainey Lee was stuck in a dream with walls of albumen, curtains of clouding. He felt no more substantial than a ring of cigar smoke as he floated out into the evening air, was absorbed by his Cherokee and . . . found himself at the office. The elevator delivered him up like Jonah to his floor, and then . . . he was in his office drinking bourbon and looking out the window. He found himself locked on to his children's faces, where they were fixed in the silver frame on his desk beside the image of their mother. The smile, Eleanor's missing front teeth, bright-blue eyes; George's face, the freckles, the elfin smirk. They seemed almost alive to him. He didn't cry again. He took his Smith & Wesson automatic from the shoulder holster, put the barrel into his mouth, cocked the hammer, and tasted the gun oil, but the fabric of his resolve had holes in it large enough to climb through. He fell back into the chair, alive and disappointed. He laid the pistol on the desk. He found the second pint of bourbon in the deep drawer among the files, resigned to screw up his courage with the bottle. A walk to the roof, a minute under the evening sky, and then he'd be out there in the stars. The idea was drawing at him, pulling him along as he spun the top from the bottle and turned it up so whiskey flowed into the cup that read "Daddy's Coffee."

3

TED BROOM, RETIRED, DRESSED NOW IN A KNIT SHIRT AND SAN-sabelt slacks, opened Rainey's front door to a distinguished older man in a navy blazer and a knit polo shirt. Ted's eyes ran over the steel crutches with the stainless bands that circled the man's forearms. Polio most likely, he thought. The crutches that had been so common at one time were now rare, and Ted hadn't thought about polio in decades, but his brother had a son who'd had it in the early fifties. The doctor carried his bag by hooking the handle with the tips of the fingers of the hand on the right crutch grip.

"Dr. Evans. Rainey sent me. To see after Doris."

"Come in," Ted said. "Please."

The doctor followed Ted like a shadow, the crutch tips chirping as the old man moved in fluid, one-way pendulum strides. Ted opened the bedroom door, where his wife, Mary, was sitting on the bed holding Doris's hand, cooing to her sobs. It had been less than half an hour since Rainey had abandoned the house.

"Tom Evans," the older man offered, his voice surprisingly vital.

"This is Dr. Evans," Ted said, introducing the man to the two women.

"Rainey sent me," he explained to Doris.

"Where is he?" she asked, the words trembling out. Doris was on her back with her hands over her eyes when the doctor sat on the side of the bed and propped his crutches against the wall.

"Please excuse us," the doctor said as he opened his bag. By the time he looked up from its depths, the door was closing behind the couple.

Doris stared up like a frightened fawn. The doctor smiled at her, his eyes soft through darkened lenses. Her own eyes were points of horror. *Get me out of here! Get me away from this place, now!*

His face floated above her, the peppermint breath washing her as he spoke. "I understand how you feel," he said. "I lost a child years ago."

Her hand flew to his forearm and was like a claw. "I want to go to him," she whimpered. "I'm his mother."

"Have you been drinking?"

"Some vodka—before." She started crying again. She knew drinking was a sin, and she a sinner. Her mind was running from one place to another and touched on the thought that God was perhaps punishing her for that sin among many. Or punishing Rainey for something she didn't even know about. *Hadn't Rainey cursed God, questioned his worth?*

"Now, now." The aged physician removed a syringe and filled it from a vial of clear liquid, the bottom pointed at the ceiling as he pulled back the plunger. "Doris, are you allergic to anything?"

"No," she said, "just dairy products."

"This'll sting a little, but it will help you get through the next few hours." He inserted the needle, but it didn't hurt at all. Doris was numb to the needle because she was overwhelmed by real pain. Immediately after the shot she closed her eyes.

"What's that?" her words slurred.

"It's succinylcholine. It'll force you to relax. I want you to close your eyes and remember a good time with your children. Imagine their smiles. They aren't in pain now. They're in a far better place. Do you believe that?"

She smiled. "Yes, I do."

"Now, imagine the two children together hugging somewhere far away, happy to have each other again. I imagine they're waiting for you."

Her head rolled gently to the side.

"Doris?"

She didn't move. Her eyes were open slightly. He put his hand to her neck, gently. Then he kissed his index finger and touched it to her nose. "Sleep now." He lifted her arm and felt for a pulse. "One more just to be safe."

He refilled the syringe and held it against the light. He took her arm in his hand, twisted it, and carefully inserted the needle into the artery, depressing the plunger until the liquid was gone. Then he dropped the syringe back into the valise, closed it with a snap, and placed it on the bed. He put his fingers to her neck and smiled at her.

"Go into the light," he said, snickering. Then he pulled a note from his pocket and placed it between Doris's breasts.

There were two telephones beside the bed, one for Lee family personal use and a secure one for agency business. He lifted one and removed small oblong pieces of plastic from the base. The microphone in his pocket, he dialed a number on the small Sony. It was answered on the third ring.

"Special Agent Lee?"

"Yeah." Rainey's voice was flat, his words slurred. "Who's this?"

"This is your family's doctor."

"Who?"

"Dr. Fletcher. Martin Fletcher. We haven't met in some years."

"Who?" Rainey demanded, his voice raised. "Martin Fletcher? Can't be."

"Check the caller ID readout on your desk. What do you see?"

"What?" Rainey was silent as he looked at the display on the machine. He didn't speak for the time it took for him to realize that the number Martin Fletcher was calling from was Rainey's own private line. The secure line. Rainey's mind flew in a thousand directions at once. "What . . . do you want?" he said, trembling.

"I want you to think about some things. Remember when I said . . . I forget the exact wording—that I would eat your hearts?"

"Martin . . . I didn't . . ." His mind raced to remember what it was Martin Fletcher was referring to.

"I want you to listen to me. I have a lot to say and not much time. Let me tell you first that I am the one who killed your little girl. It wasn't an accident . . . I designed it to look that way. If I live to be a hundred and fifty, I will never get over the horror of it. Fire is so ugly. And the way you tried so valiantly to save her. I watch the tape often late at night when I'm feeling nostalgic."

"Martin . . . ?"

"This morning your son, George. It is amazing how long a scream can last when it's echoing all around the rocks like that. What did he say in those last seconds? Secret. Five seconds. Sobering, I tell ya. Bet he was a mess. Hard to see over that railing. Thinking about how he must have looked? Did you look . . . course you did." He laughed.

Rainey began screaming into the receiver. The words were blurred together, and the counterfeit doctor placed his hand over the receiver and smiled.

"Calm down, Rainey. There's more, I'm afraid." He spoke just loud enough for Rainey to hear. "It's about Doris."

"Please, don't hurt Doris," Rainey pleaded. "I'll give you anything! Not Doris! Take *me*."

"She's right here. Want to speak to her?"

"Martin . . ."

Martin Fletcher put the phone to her mouth.

"She can't think of a thing to say. I'm not going to lie to you, Rainey. After all you've been through, I owe you the truth. She's dead as an oyster shell. But she didn't suffer. She'd suffered far too much already because of you. God, the guilt you must feel. But nothing to what Paul Masterson must feel. He's the one who did all this, you know."

The phone was silent as Rainey sat with his eyes unblinking.

"Are you still with me?"

"I'll kill you! You filthy bastard!"

"That's the spirit."

"I swear, as God is my witness . . ."

Martin laughed. It was a staccato metallic rattle, half beast, half machine. "But, Rainey, he isn't your witness. I want you and your pals to know that the old saying 'Every dog has his day' is the truth. Tell Paul all of this was for him. Tell him his true legacy is written in the hearts of his men. Do you love him now? Do you love your master, Rainey, knowing that he has killed your families? He still has his, Rainey. How does that make you feel?"

"Martin! I'll . . . get you . . ." Rainey began bellowing obscenities blindly into the phone.

The counterfeit doctor hung up. Then he disconnected both receivers and laid the handsets on the bed, blocking the line to incoming calls. He retrieved his crutches and left the room carrying his case, shutting the door behind him.

Ted stood when the doctor came into the living room. Mary looked at him anxiously. "Will she be all right?"

Dr. Evans took Mary Broom's hand and smiled. "She won't wake for quite a while. I've just spoken to Rainey, and he assures me that he will be right along."

"They've been through a lot," Ted said. "We're here for them."

"Well, I've done all I can here. I'll just see myself out."

Ted went to the window and watched the doctor move down the street with his bag swinging at his side as he worked the crutches. He was like a measure of music that kept repeating as he continued to the end of the block and turned without once glancing back.

"Guess he must live close by."

"How's that?" Mary said.

"Well, he's on foot, so to speak."

By the time Martin Fletcher reached the car, the sound of sirens was in the air. He climbed into the Range Rover that he had stolen two days earlier. It was parked just around the corner from the Lee house. He hadn't wanted anyone to get a description of the car just in case the cops got lucky. It was all he could do to keep the crutch tips touching the pavement. He fought the urge to throw them into the bushes and run. So Rainey had called 911.

When he got to the Rover, he tossed the physician's kit and the crutches onto the rear seat. He took a quick look around to see if he had attracted any attention, and satisfied no one was watching, he drove away. As the car gathered speed, he started to remove the disguise, which was the most realistic, and by far the most expensive, masquerade of his career. He peeled off the wig and hand makeup, which was complete with small liver spots. Then he pulled over against the curb, removed the gray wig, and peeled off the latex face and turkey neck. He took off the blazer and tossed it onto the backseat as he accelerated and moved back into the street. Then he put the sunglasses and cap on. Seconds later a pair of prowl cars flew past headed for the Maple Street address. Martin had laid his Browning .380 on the console.

At the next red light he slipped on a London Fog golf jacket and combed his dark hair so it looked as if it had been painted on his skull. He removed the remnants of spirit gum with a cloth soaked in acetone. Then he put on his round-lensed sunshades and admired himself in the lighted mirror set in the visor.

He amused himself by trying to picture the confusion, the pain and the rage, that the neighbors would witness. He tried to imagine Rainey's face when the Brooms told him that the killer was a seventy-year-old cripple. Rainey would know he had been disguised, but by then he'd be long gone.

He parked the Rover as close as possible to the DEA's "secret" airport operation offices on the ground floor of the airport's parking garage. The DEA airport operation posts were twin bunkers with darkly tinted windows built under the ramp that led to the upper-level parking deck. One had a chain-link fenced-in area for equipment storage. He climbed from the vehicle and removed a suitcase. Then he lifted the coat from the device on the floor behind the driver's seat. It looked like a small cigar box and had wires leading to a small plastic cylinder that lay on the floor between two gallon jars. As he removed the lid of both jars, the smell of gasoline and the thickening agent hit him. He poured the gellike contents from the jars over the carpeting and then placed the electronic match, or omni switch, so that it was an inch or so above the level of the stuff, where the vapor would be ignited. Then there was a metal box with six sticks of Olin dynamite and a slow-burning fuse for the finale. He walked away toward the airport, carrying his suitcase. As he walked, he reached into his jacket pocket and flipped a toggle, which started the bomb's liquid quartz watch timing device at 59:59.

Not more than a couple hundred yards away he opened the door to a battered Caprice and dropped the case onto the seat, crushing a park ranger's hat. He slid in and smiled at the man who was leaning against the driver's window with the bill of a baseball cap pulled down over his features. The man, who had been napping, stretched and looked at his watch.

"We should go," Martin said. "We've got a long drive ahead of us."

When the timer hit 00:00 a second short of one hour later, the battery in the cigar box made circuit and the omni switch created its first and last spark. There was a bright flash and then the flames leaped through the Rover's exploded windows and the homemade napalm spewed flame thirty feet in every direction. Within seconds the heat had caused the tanks of the automobiles on either side to explode, and a few seconds later another pair or three, until almost every car on the ground level was blazing, and thick smoke, colored black by burning rubber, poured from the open concrete structure. When the sticks of dynamite went off, they turned the windows of the vacant DEA bunkers to confetti.

4

To the tourists who flooded the Café du Monde in the French Quarter he might have been a local as he sat sipping coffee with his back to the levee, facing Jackson Square. He looked like anything other than what he was. He was dressed casually, but expensively, and was reading the newspaper account that detailed the search for a multiple-murder suspect who had killed three people in Tennessee and covered his escape with a bomb. One composite looked like a child's drawing of a man in a ranger's hat, and the second a bad rendition of an elderly physician named Evans. To Martin Fletcher it looked like a drag queen dressed up for Halloween. The crude drawings made him want to laugh.

The newspaper article quoted a fire official as saying it was a miracle no one had been killed by the incendiary device planted at the airport, which had destroyed seventy-eight vehicles. It had taken several hours for the

Nashville fire department to put out the fire. The bombing itself was relegated to page two, since the article detailing the abduction and murder of George Lee and scout leader Ruth Tippet, and the overdosing of Doris Lee, covered most of page one. The picture of Rainey Lee seated on his home's rear deck with his head buried in his hands warmed Martin's heart.

He laid the paper aside, sipped at his coffee, and watched a couple with a small child at the next table. The child's face and hands were covered in powdered sugar from the French doughnuts. The mother caught sight of him watching the child, so he smiled at the parents. "How old is she?" he asked.

"Four," the mother said.

"I like benyenays," the child giggled, holding a square with a perfect half-moon missing from one side.

"They're called ben-yeahs," her mother corrected.

"What's your name, my little beauty?" he asked.

"Molly!" she squealed.

"I once had one just like you at home," he said. "Children her age are so wonderful. But they can grow into troublesome adults."

"Where's home?" the man asked.

"Spain. Outside Madrid."

"You don't have a Latin accent," the man said.

"I am an actor," he replied, placing his fingers gingerly at his chest. "I have many accents and many languages. My grandfather was a Texan, my mother a saint—but aren't they all?" He winked at the wife, who blushed.

"Might we have seen you in anything?" the man asked.

"Possibly," he replied. "If you see Spanish or Italian cinema. I have yet to make it in Hollywood films. But I audition often enough, and who knows? Recently I played a doctor in a small production. A two-man play."

They showed Martin a "gee, that's too bad" smile and resumed their breakfast. "We'll be watching for you," the man said. The child made a pair of glasses with her index fingers and thumbs, peering at Martin through them.

Martin opened his paper and spent the next few minutes reminiscing over the series of kills he had made during the past four years. While he did so, he remained aware of the people parading past the open-air café. As was his habit, he made an appraisal of each in relation to himself. This hunter was also hunted, a fact of life he could never lose sight of. He laid the paper aside, happy that the couple and child had moved on. Then he peeled the wrapping from a large cigar and lit it with a wooden kitchen match from his pocket.

The two ex-Greers and three McLeans had been easy enough. Hardest for him had been the little Lee girl, Eleanor. He had discovered early in his surveillance that she kept her imaginary treasures, everyday-found objects, in the shed that doubled as her playhouse. He had rigged the explosion so that it would look like a child-playing-with-matches accident. He'd taken the matches from the Lee kitchen himself when they were out and put them beside the lawn mower. A simple device insured that when she opened the door, it would tip a can filled with gasoline, and when she closed it again, a match struck and *voom*. The evidence of the booby trap—the fishing line, a plastic paint bucket, a mousetrap, and a piece of tape—were destroyed by the fire. He had assumed she would die at once. It was both good and bad that she had lingered. Good because it gave Rainey a chance to twist in the horror of it, bad that the innocent child had suffered so long. But so it went. The innocent suffered for the sins of the parents.

The Green Team members from Miami were suffering hell, and now they'd blame Paul Masterson, as they should. He wished he could see the confrontation between the men and their old boss, and he tried to imagine Paul's reaction when he heard about the latest killings. *Surely he's been keeping up—so why hasn't he shown?* It was a perplexing question. Martin had challenged him openly now, and he would have to come. *Unless he's even more of a coward than I imagined.* He wanted to show Paul the cold hearts of his wife and children.

He put a set of earphones in place and switched on the Walkman in his pocket. He listened to the latest tapes he had retrieved, concentrating on the voices of the woman, Laura, and her two children, Adam and Erin. Soon the work would be done. He closed his eyes and thought sadly about his own wife and child and their deaths at the hands of hired killers. And then he let his creative side take over, and he freed his mind to dream of how he would deal with the last family.

5

THE TWO MEN WHO STEPPED INTO THE NARROW DIRT STREET FROM the Ford Explorer were trouble. Aaron Clark, alone in his general store, knew it as soon as he saw them. He watched as they looked the town over and then turned their attention to his store. They came inside with the demeanor of gunslingers, sweeping the store with cold, measuring eyes. Aaron, who had been sorting mail, cut his eyes to the short-barreled Wingmaster pump shotgun that lay under the counter. You just never know—he had learned that from years of living on the edge of nowhere. The men were wearing military-style eyeglasses, new hunting boots, and factory-stiff canvas game jackets. Aaron knew they weren't fly fishermen, and elk and mule deer weren't in season for a spell. Aaron assumed the coats were hiding handguns.

Aaron Clark had lived high in the clouds over Montana for sixty-eight years. His store, Clark's Reward General Merchandise, comprised six low log buildings built one into the other over the course of 120 years. The bulk of his business came from loggers, sportsmen, and the few full-time residents. Mountain people were clannish, but they could abide visiting sportsmen as long as they were well behaved—didn't shoot livestock, take too many trout, try to make the local women, and didn't overstay their welcome. Lumberjacks? Well, on the weekends you gave them elbow room and prayed they kept their knives folded and their motor-driven saws in their trucks. Years before Aaron had been forced to kill one who was attempting to saw off the head of the bartender with a knife for refusing to sell him a fifteenth glass of bourbon. Luckily the knife had been dull and there had been time for a barmaid to fetch Aaron. There were still nine buckshot holes in one wall of the saloon where the pattern overestimated the size of the man.

There was a constable who lived fifteen miles away, the county's sheriff three times that far. The killing of the lumberjack was ruled death by misadventure. The bartender's neck took sixty stitches but healed eventually, and the locals called him Frankenstein because it looked as if his head had been hastily added to his torso. The residents of Clark's Reward, Montana, were the serious sort, and even the drunkest of loggers would have to be mighty desperate to challenge any of them. The local axiom was, "If a boy can't shoot the heart out of a running deer by the time he's three, he's considered retarded."

Aaron Clark wasn't afraid of the two men he was watching. Hell, he had always stayed in shape and kept a gun handy. Regardless of what the movies might show, never once in the history of the West had any outlaw or gang of outlaws intimidated a town full of citizens into submission. The American West had always been populated by people with the grit and the means to defend their own. It might be different in the cities and towns, but in places like Clark's Reward, Montana, the law was still pretty much what you made it. Generally speaking, mountain people didn't run crying to the authorities ev-

ery time there was trouble; they handled it themselves, in
their own way, and usually it stayed handled.

Clark's Reward wasn't one of those places you drove
into accidentally. People came there on purpose or not at
all.

The Black Canyon Inn, down the street, was open
only during hunting season, and it had room for about
two dozen sportsmen at any given time. The local
guides, almost one-fourth of the resident total, bunked
clients there. The guides were responsible for attracting
most of the area's cash flow. There was a restaurant/
lounge where a line painted on the floor separated the
two enterprises. It got lively after the dinner crowd
thinned out and the jukebox was plugged in, but it was
rare that anyone crossed the line with a drink in hand;
the restaurant was a respectable establishment where
families could take meals. The bar served three kinds of
beer, all domestic, four brands of bourbon, one domestic
vodka, Beefeater gin, and a single malt Scotch for the
fancy-pants shooters and fly fishermen from the city. The
jukebox was filled with country tunes, the whinier the
better. A yodel here and there didn't hurt the chances of
a song staying on the menu.

Aaron's general store also served as the post office,
and he accepted payments for electricity from those few
who had it and used it. He, like his father and grandfather before him, took the "general store" title to heart.
He sold staples, hardware, knives of all manner, utility
clothing, Harley-Davidson T-shirts, sleeping bags, snuff,
sporting guns and ammunition, fishing rigs, and a thousand other items jammed onto shelves, packed into glass
display cases, hanging on the walls or from the ceilings,
and loaded into crannies. For people who wanted real
choice in groceries or tools, there was the town of Rusty
Nail, which had a grocery and hardware store in separate
buildings. Aaron ran the store alone because people that
far out at the edge of the earth were honest. The rule of
the mountain was "Never piss off the people you may
need to save your life down the line." Due to grudges,
hungry animals, the weather, and particularly unfriendly

geography, people who went out their doors didn't always manage to get back in.

Aaron watched the men out of the corner of his eye as he sorted the mail. The larger of the two had jet-black hair, a high forehead, and eyes the color of topsoil. The other was five seven or so and looked to Aaron to be wound up tight as a truck spring. They were physically different as a dime and a dollar, but they could have grown up sucking at the same hind tit for all the real difference there was between them. They were tough characters, no question about that, and IRS serious.

The big one ambled over, leaned against the counter, and smiled, showing a line of even teeth. *He must do the talking for the pair.* The shorter man was looking around, fingering the stock without seeming to take any interest. "Hello there," the big man said. "Nice place you got here."

"I help you fellows?" Aaron asked.

"Well, I hope so. We're looking for a man," he said. "An old friend of ours."

"Well, there ain't as many men around these parts as bears. Have a name, your friend?"

"Paul Masterson."

Aaron swallowed hard but kept on sorting without looking up. He remembered what Paul had said. A man might show up some day. He'll probably be alone. He might say he is an old friend. He might have an official vehicle or identification. He might not be armed, and he might seem friendly. He might ask nicely, or he might remove your skin with a straight razor while he asks. He'll be here to kill me.

Aaron tried to mask the reaction. In the past five years not but one person had asked for Paul Masterson, and the request had caught him off guard. "Paul Masterson, you say? Masterson's a common enough name. Lots of Mastersons in Montana. Fellow name of Henry Masterson founded this burg."

"Paul Masterson gets his mail here, doesn't he?" the larger man said.

"I sort a right smart amount a' mail. Paul Masterson, you say? What's he look like?"

The large man shifted against the counter and spread his hands apart, palms down. Aaron could almost feel his breath. "He's about five foot ten, hundred and seventy pounds give or take. Limps a bit favoring the left leg and has this nasty scar the shape of a horseshoe on the side of his face. He likely wears a patch over his right eye. Be hard to miss."

Aaron continued to sort through the letters. "Horseshoe shape you said? Horse kick him?"

"A nine-millimeter horse," the smaller man said.

"Sissy gun. Give me a two hundred forty grain forty-five, preferably long Colt. That's a bullet you can be proud of."

"Where is he?" the big man pressed.

Aaron said, "Blond-headed cuss, built like a boxer? Nasty-ass disposition? Hermit."

"Can you tell us how to find him?"

"I ain't certain that it's my place to sell maps to people's houses. He might not take to having company."

"Well," the man said, "can you tell me how often he gets his mail?"

"He comes in for it once a week. Sometimes every two to three weeks. You fellows have business with him or just want to be catching up?"

"Touching base. We're good friends, like I said."

"You can prove that?"

Aaron pressed his leg against the stock of the gun and measured in microseconds the time it would take to get it up. It was loaded and the safety was off. He made his hand tremble as he handled the mail. *Don't fret me, you stupid son of a bitch. . . . I'm old and I'm feeble. . . .* He figured they'd both be road stiff and wouldn't think the old man a danger. And they'd have to get their hands into the coats. If push came to shove, the men would eat up three to five seconds getting the handguns out and in operation. *By then they'll be stumbling around dead, looking for the gates a' hell.*

The big man sighed too loudly, lifted his right hand,

and slipped it toward the jacket. Aaron moved with the reflexes of a freshly wet cat, bringing the gun up and sticking it under the man's chin with enough force to draw blood and put him on his tiptoes. The man's face was pointed up at the rafters even though his eyes were still aimed at Aaron's. "Don't you pee on my floor, bub," Aaron said. *How's that for feeble?*

The shorter man froze, slowly brought his hands up, palms out, but Aaron didn't want him to think he could go for it. "You move and I'll turn his head to jelly," Aaron said.

"Take it easy," the smaller man pleaded.

"I was going in for my identification," the larger man said, speaking without moving his jaw. "Federal officer."

"Real slow I want you to pinch out whatever you were reaching for," Aaron said. "It's a gun, I want it held by the tip of the handle and dropped on this counter."

The man reached into his jacket slowly, pulled out a small black wallet, and flipped it open on the counter. There was an ID with the man's picture on it that identified him as a special agent of the Justice Department. Aaron relaxed the gun so the man could come down onto the flats of his feet. "Well, Joe McLean, why didn't you say? Paul's told me about a Joe McLean."

"We were in the DEA together," Joe McLean said.

"Justice," Aaron said as he inspected the ID. "DEA get too hot?"

"Left for Justice three years ago. That's Thorne Greer," Joe added, jerking his head at the shorter man behind him.

"Thorne Greer? Thorne Greer retired," Aaron said. "Minding Hollywood pussy, Paul said."

"We were with Paul in Miami," Thorne said. "He was our regional director."

"Then you'll know what happened to him? Exactly, I mean."

"We were both there."

"Tell me the story." Aaron maintained the grip on the shotgun.

"Man might want us to keep that to himself. If Paul Masterson wants to share the details . . ."

"I know Masterson's story. You tell me what happened and I'll get you to him. Warned me fellows might come after him carrying phony badges. How would I know it for real and true? I never met either of you, and I never saw a Justice Department ID before either."

Joe McLean looked over his shoulder at Thorne Greer, who nodded.

"Ambush on a Miami pier. There was a shipping container we were told was loaded with four tons of cocaine. It wasn't. It was loaded with three hundred pounds of plastic explosives, and three machine pistols held by three Colombian gentlemen who had pledged their own lives. In return their families would be looked after, so to speak, by their drug cartel."

"An ambush," Aaron added. "Go on."

"Two of our agents cracked the doors and were killed outright. Booby-trap detonator failed when the doors were forced. The killers were behind three tons of sandbagging. Paul was standing just behind the two agents who opened the doors. The Colombians fired armor-piercing KTW that passed through those boys like they weren't even there. Thorne here, a fellow by the name of Rainey Lee, seven locals, and I filled the container with holes and took the shooters out, but we were too late. Paul was hit . . . five times, I think it was. One bullet entered his right eye at the bridge of his nose and exited his temple. Took two in the leg that shattered the big bone—hence the limp. Two through his guts and one passed through his hip. Thorne drove him to the hospital while I held the brains in his head." Joe held a large palm up to Aaron's face. "This hand."

"Steel plate in his head?" Aaron asked.

"Yeah."

Aaron tensed, tightened his grip. "Stainless or carbon?"

"Plastic," Thorne corrected. "Some sort of space-age NASA junk. They were only planning to do the final cosmetics if he lived."

"Why don't he wear his glass eye?" Aaron asked, knowing the reason wasn't common knowledge.

"I heard it kept falling out. Socket was all wrong, but he left the hospital soon as he could stand up to get his pants on."

Aaron remembered well enough. His trip to Miami to see Paul had been the only time he had closed the store in decades. He could ask them how Laura and the kids took it, but he didn't need to. Reb, at three, had been horrified by the altered face. Erin as well. Laura . . . Well, they'd had problems they couldn't deal with. Or wouldn't. Aaron hadn't involved himself in the details of the split because Paul had never opened a discussion of it. Aaron believed in leaving people with their own private thoughts.

"That's pretty nigh on perfect. If you ain't who you say, I reckon I'm a goner." Aaron smiled and put the gun away under the counter. "He lives simple up here." Aaron reached down and placed a wire basket on the counter. "Don't be offended if he ain't dancing glad to see you. He don't always remember people, but I imagine he'll know you two. Leave your guns here. You'll find he's not the same Paul Masterson you used to know."

"I'm not carrying," Thorne said, opening his jacket to prove it. Joe McLean handed Aaron his shoulder rig, and Aaron put it in the basket and the basket under the counter.

"Can we drive to him?" Joe asked.

"You can walk. Go out this back door and follow the trail through the pines right on along. You'll run smack into the back door of the cabin. A half mile. Stay to the right forks or you'll be cougar food."

Thorne smiled. "You know him real well?"

"Raised him from a pup."

The two men went behind the store, where they found the trail. They took it through the woods. There were three forks in the trail and they followed Aaron's directions. A porcupine lumbered across the trail ahead of them, and the two men joked about being watched. They wound around the side of the mountain, and just about the time their ears picked up the sound of water moving, they came upon the rear of a cabin. It was a log affair set in a clearing. A sheer wall of dark rock curved out fifty feet above the roof and sheltered it from the sky. Smoke rolled up the wall from the chimney.

The view was staggering, a panorama of steep blue mountain walls under a cobalt sky and a stream of clear water turned to rapids where rocks broke the surface.

"My God," Thorne said. "Takes your breath."

"Do make a man feel small," Joe said.

They turned the corner, and as well as they knew Paul Masterson, they would not have recognized the man who stood on the porch in faded jeans, his right eye covered by a patch of black glove leather. The military buzz cut Masterson had always worn had grown into a flowing mane that cascaded helter-skelter over his shoulders. The unkempt beard was long and shot through with white hairs. The only thing that was familiar to the agents was the left, undamaged side of his face. The horseshoe-shaped scar that touched the edge of the eye patch looked like a piece of twine that had been stitched under the skin. Despite the surgeons' best efforts, the skull was indented on the side where the round had shattered the bone. His left arm hung at a strange angle, the hand trembling like a grounded fish.

"Hi, boys," Paul said. "You want to come in?"

"Paul. You've changed a little," Thorne said.

"You look like a mountain man," Joe said. *Grizzly Adams scrambling out from under a derailed train.*

"Don't get many visitors up here," Paul said.

The men shook hands.

Thorne said, "Wondering why?"

"First time I had a twelve-gauge tucked under my chin in years. Then we had to walk through the haunted forest unarmed. That old coot's some guard dog," Joe said.

"My uncle Aaron. I got some coffee on. Might as well warm up for the trip back out. And hope Aaron hasn't got an offer on your pistol. Said you were carrying a forty-five. That impressed him."

The cabin was larger than it looked from the outside, but the door was barely tall enough to allow Joe to pass without having his scalp nicked. It was built of square logs and hand-hewn beams with large windows in the kitchen and the den that framed the breathtaking view. The furniture was covered with Indian-style wool blankets. The walls presented dozens of Indian artifacts and antique weapons from the 1800s: bowie knives, skinning knives, a few Henry and Winchester rifles, twin Colt Peacemakers. There was a bow and a quiver of arrows with feathers that looked ready to disintegrate. The bedrooms were in a loft over the kitchen and the bathroom. The den's ceiling was vaulted, and one wall was covered by a bookcase, filled to bursting.

There were three coffee cups on the kitchen table, which Paul began to fill with black coffee from a fire-blackened coffeepot that looked as if it belonged on a Great Plains campfire.

"How'd you know we were coming?"

"Radio."

"How do you pass the time?" Thorne asked, sitting at the table.

"Read. I write a few articles on bear behavior, elk hunting, and fly fishing."

"I didn't know you were a hunter," Thorne said.

"I'm not a trout fisherman either. But I get exposed to a lot of sportsmen, and they talk a lot. I listen and write a lot down." Paul treated them to a ruined smile. The muscles moved slowly, testifying that it was a foreign maneuver. "Novel in progress . . . for three years."

"About the agency?" Thorne smiled.

"No, about a boy growing up in the mountains of Montana. Ought to try it sometime. Great for the soul. I write awhile and tear it up and write it again."

For a few minutes they made small conversation. Then Paul asked Joe McLean about his family.

"Dead," he replied. "All three."

"Jesus, Joe. I didn't know."

"My wife, Jessie, died of a heart attack almost four years back. . . . Least I thought heart attack then. My son Robert died the following spring wiring a two-twenty line. A month later my daughter Julie bled to death in her kitchen. Looked like she cut her ankle open with a jar she'd dropped. Looked to be a freak accident. Just sat there and died. It didn't make sense. Robert was a master electrician and Julie was a psychiatric nurse, trained for emergencies. I never believed they were accidents, but try and convince the cops of that unless there's a trail a four-year-old could follow. The FBI boys looked real hard but found nothing."

"Christ," Paul said, shaking his head slowly.

"Thorne's, too," Joe said.

"What?" Paul looked at Thorne Greer.

"Ellen and my boy Scott were killed when their car went into a canal in Deerfield Beach two years back. Drowned. Someone spotted a tire protruding from the canal next day," Thorne said.

Paul stared at the two men in turn. The color was a few seconds returning to his face. "God, I don't know what to say. It's terrible."

"Gets worse," Joe said. "Last week."

Thorne said, "Doris, George, and Eleanor Lee. Eleanor burned up four months ago. Other day George went off a cliff, and Doris was overdosed. Same day, same guy. Disguised professionally."

Paul felt a hot flash sweep over him. "I don't get it," he said. "How could"—he counted the passing faces in his head—"eight people die like that? Eight out of the one group. The odds of that happening are insane. Didn't anybody notice?"

"The agency should have caught it sooner, but we're all spread out since the Miami days, Paul. Thorne retired to Los Angeles doing bodyguard work. I'm with Justice as a field investigator," Joe said. "The deaths all took place over a period of time scattered across the country. We honestly thought the first couple were accidents. Couldn't prove anything at all until the killer showed his hand with Rainey. Then we knew . . . because he wanted us to know."

"He wanted you to know?" Paul repeated. "Some nutcase murdered eight innocent people and bragged about it? Why?"

"To punish us, obviously," Thorne said. "He hates us that much."

"We came all this way because we need you to help us get this guy, Paul," Joe said as he stood up and washed his cup in the sink using an ancient handle pump.

"You need to get the FBI involved. Come on, guys. This calls for a major effort by the authorities. If you have the proof . . ."

"We're dealing with different jurisdictions . . . be a red-tape nightmare," Thorne said. "No federal crimes involved unless we can prove state lines were crossed. By the time we get the deaths reclassified, if we can, and get the proper authorities working to solve this, it'll be too late. He knows that. In ten years we'll be on that *Unsolved Mysteries* program asking for people who might have seen someone driving away from the scene."

"So what's the plan?"

"We want to get this animal and we need your help."

"Want me to call someone and—"

"Physically, Paul," Thorne said. "We need you to be involved."

"Me? Jesus, guys." He laughed nervously as he shifted his head from one to the other slowly. "Look at me. I got one eye, I have epileptic seizures sometimes, and if I walk without my cane for long, I fall over and flail like a belly-up turtle. Half of my body is stainless steel or plastic, my left hand shakes like a Mixmaster, and I'm carrying an extra thirty pounds of flab from sitting here and watching that creek wear the rocks down. Plus there's things I can't remember at all, and I can't smell gun oil without breaking out in a cold sweat. There isn't a weapon in here that's been fired in my lifetime."

"It has to be you, Paul. No one else has got the thunder it would take. Senators and congressmen know you. If it hadn't been for the shooting, you'd be the DEA or FBI director by now, and they all know it."

Paul walked to the door, his shoulders rolling from side to side as he went. "I can make some calls. Think it's someone we hurt in Miami?"

"It's Fletcher," Joe McLean said.

"Martin Fletcher?" It was as if Paul had been kicked in the chest. He all but staggered back against the door-jamb. His lip quivered and he blinked rapidly. "God, I had hoped he was dead."

It all came to the surface in a flash of pain. Martin Fletcher was the man who had had him shot. Fletcher had escaped from federal custody and vanished even as Paul had fought for his life in a Miami hospital's trauma unit. He had masterminded the hit on Paul's team from his prison cell and then had escaped the same day, before anyone could put it together.

"Far as I can find out, nobody's ever come close to catching him," Joe said.

Thorne sighed. "The family killings started four years back. That gave him a good two years from his prison break to plan it."

"I don't remember all of it. It's kind of fuzzy. I remember he escaped. If he was retaken, I never heard about it."

"Remember when he said he'd eat our hearts out?"

"Sort of. Yes. I know he was berserk last time I saw him. At the trial."

"What is this if not a way to eat our hearts out?"

"I remember sitting on the stand and his eyes as I testified. And the outburst when he was sentenced."

"He set us up, remember?" Thorne turned and looked out at the stream. "You know what he did to you . . . tried to kill all of us."

"I know what he did to me." *Every time I look in a mirror or try to use my left hand or gauge depth.*

"It's retaliation, Paul," Joe said, breaking in. "The ultimate twisting of the blade. Better than blowing our brains out."

"I'll make some calls," Paul said. "Some people still owe me, I guess. Maybe I can do something."

"I'd trade my life for two minutes alone with him," Thorne Greer said. "Look what he did to you, for Christ's sake. How long has it been since you left this god-damned cabin? Look around. You're stuck in a calendar shot. The closest town is a cluster of log huts. He's already fuckin' killed you, you just ain't noticed yet."

Paul looked out the window. "Five years since I came back here. Month since I even went to Aaron's store. I'm no good outside here. I just can't . . . you got to understand . . ."

"Goddamn it," Joe exploded. "You owe us. He fuckin' did it because of what you did. You nailed his ass to the cross. You set him against us."

"Come on, Joe. Fletcher's nuts," Thorne said.

"What?" Paul stammered. "I just arrested him."

"Nobody bothered to tell Martin it was merely an arrest and that you didn't mean anything by it," Thorne said.

"Martin left a note on Doris's body. Wanted you to know it was him. Said he'd leave you alone if you'd leave him be." Joe realized Paul was confused and frightened. But they had to have Paul to get Fletcher. Paul was once powerful stuff at DEA. At the time of the ambush he had been a heroic figure in the agency, a leader who went into the field and faced danger with his men. The files bulged with citations and press clippings on his career.

"I'm sorry . . . God, I'm sorry. I was doing my job. If I had known—" Paul hung his head.

"Fletcher wants us to blame you. But we don't. Do we?" Thorne looked at Joe. Joe nodded slowly and slammed the flat of his hand against a beam. "Martin Fletcher's crazy as a shithouse rat."

"Crazy as a shithouse fox," Joe said.

"Couldn't it be anyone else? We made some people mighty unhappy. Maybe it's someone wanting us to think it's Martin. Hiding behind his mystique."

"The players we chased around after are mostly

washed up—kids who were in diapers then are leaders now. Ochoa, Lopez, Perez," Joe said. "The ones that are still alive are in hiding in Spain, in jail, dead, or so deep in the jungle they're making monkeys."

"He butchered our families. He has to be stopped. You have to come out and help us," Thorne said.

"I'm sorry," Paul said. He looked out the window and took a deep breath and exhaled it. "I can't . . . can't think about going out there again."

"What the hell do you mean?" Joe snapped. "Haven't you been listening? Our families have been fucking wiped out! What makes you think he's finished?"

"Finished?"

"There's only one family left, Paul. Yours." Thorne frowned.

Joe started. "You think because you left them and took up with the fucking trout they aren't targets? He may have disliked us, but, Paul, he hates your fucking guts. He said he was finished in the letter he left for you, but you believe for one second he'll let your family live?"

"Dear God," Paul said. "It didn't occur to me." *Laura, Erin and Adam—Reb.*

Thorne washed out the coffee cup. He watched as Paul tried to use the weakened left hand to get a cigarette from the pack, failed and used the right.

"It's better," Paul said defensively when he realized they were watching the hand. "I'm still doing my therapy. I'm supposed to squeeze a tennis ball. I forget."

"We've got people in New Orleans watching Laura and your children, but we can't keep them there long without T.C. getting wind of the expenditures. We've got a twenty-four seven in place, but we need cops and all sorts of help down there."

T. C. Robertson's face crossed Paul's mind. He was the acting director of DEA, and he and Paul had never been friends. They had been rivals for the position T.C. now held. He was acting director because the presidents couldn't find an excuse to push him out, but they didn't want to make him director either. The new president was no different. But T. C. Robertson was popular with the average man on the street because he was always showing up on the evening news making tough statements about drug cartels.

"Okay," Paul said after a long silence. "I'll think it over. In the meantime let's talk about what you'll need."

Thorne and Joe watched in surprise as Paul slowly began to pull himself together and take control again. In the few minutes they'd been in the cabin, Thorne had actually forgotten that Paul's face was so fiercely fucked up. Now he could see that under the ill-fitting flannel shirt and beneath the beard and scraggly hair, well, Paul Masterson was still in there after all. This was the man that he and the other men would have followed through the gates of hell. Now Thorne and Joe both had actually begun to believe they could take on Martin Fletcher. Believed that they would do it. And they could see in Paul's face that he knew it as well. After three cigarettes and a few cups of coffee he had written down an outline for capturing Martin Fletcher. Then he stood, stretched his arms, opened the refrigerator door, and stuck his head inside. "You guys up for elk steaks and bourbon?"

"I could eat a horse," Joe said.

"You choose, I got both," Paul said.

Paul was in Miami. He didn't know that because of anything he could see—the world was a seamless wall of white, thick fog—but from a feeling he had. But his face was healed and he was seeing out of both eyes. There were two men standing a few feet away in the fog, and as Paul approached them, they turned toward him, their movements jerky, machinelike. But he knew them. Paul turned at the sudden sounding of a freighter's horn, and when he looked back, the men had disappeared. He was alone. "Joe Barnett? Jeff Hill?" he called.

He walked after them, and the ground grew soft, spongelike. Then suddenly there was pressure on his ankle, and he looked down to see that skeletal hands were gripping his legs. He shrieked and awakened to the familiar dark of his bedroom. He listened and realized that the two men in the cabin were not awake. So he must not have called out in his sleep. He was thankful for that.

Paul was not often seized by the horror anymore, had few dreams at all, thanks to the pills he took before he went to sleep. But the combination of Irish whiskey and the thought of leaving the mountains and of his family's danger at the hands of Martin Fletcher, fell over him like a net. His mind froze in fear, his chest constricted, and the room seemed to enlarge. His life was an obvious mess held together by twisted, frayed threads, and he felt small and powerless. He wanted to roll under the table or the bed and make these men leave him alone. But he knew he couldn't. He had to be able to face his image in the mirror. He had to realize that leaving wasn't death, that he wasn't inadequate in the eyes of others. They didn't know how terrified he was, how his soul cried out in pain, and how fear had become something that he could taste and almost feel with his fingers. He would be vulnerable out there. He was afraid, so afraid. He began to breathe deep breaths. He didn't want the anxiety attack to continue, but it was beyond his control.

The grandfather clock chimed three times. Paul could hear either Thorne or Joe snoring. It was a bizarre feeling having people in his cabin, but he didn't dislike it. Aaron visited on rare occasions, usually on his way to fish Paul's stream, but had never spent the night. The men had stayed because Joe was too drunk to navigate the trail back to Aaron's.

Paul got out of bed and made his way quietly to the bathroom. He looked into the mirror above the sink, studying the hair and the beard. The familiar mountain man stared back at him. The hair didn't really hide the damage but certainly cut down on the number of people who engaged him in idle conversation when he was in town. He readied the scissors but hesitated before attacking the beard. It was like losing an old friend. A warm friend.

He had to go out there and help them. He hoped there hadn't ever been any real question of its being otherwise. Even if his own family had not been endangered, he hoped that he would have gone to help his friends find their tormentor. Martin would be all but impossible to find and even more impossible to take alive. That was just as well. Martin was the mad dog people spoke of when they used the term. Martin Fletcher had been taken alive once . . . and it hadn't panned out.

The fact that his family was threatened required his attention. How could he live knowing that he had turned his back on them and allowed harm to befall them? Maybe they were safe, maybe not. He couldn't gamble on it. He could protect them here, but they would not come to Clark's Reward. This way he could do what needed to be done from a distance and get back up on the mountain, and they wouldn't even have to know he had been down. He would insist that they not be told he had been out in their world. He loved them with everything he was, but he couldn't face them again. The very idea caused his chest to tighten.

He looked at the man in the mirror and tried to remember what that face had looked like before it had been altered. He had looked at this other face so long that it was Paul Masterson's smooth, unmarked face that was all wrong. His old face reminded him of another time, another life, and of Martin Fletcher. He realized that Fletcher had never been completely out of his mind.

He had met Fletcher because the expert on terrorism was training the DEA's elite force when Paul came into the organization from Justice. Fletcher was a corn-fed, military-trained CIA asset who enjoyed inflicting pain. He had remarked once to Paul that interrogation was rarely about gaining information. He had explained that it isn't what you learn that matters but what the person you're working on lives to tell others. Torture one, and let his contemporaries see what you're capable of.

Paul had never liked Martin Fletcher. Not that he wasn't charming when he chose to be. But there had been something missing from the man's personality that had bothered Paul from the get go. He lacked compassion, for one thing. He also lacked the ability to shoulder responsibility. But the main thing he lacked was real emotion. It was as if he mimicked emotions—acted them instead of felt them. And then there were the man's eyes. His eyes were flat, lifeless.

Fletcher had joined Paul's group as an adviser and had pulled strings to do that. Paul hadn't felt comfortable with it, but the argument was that the group needed an objective observer, someone who knew the ropes and had experience dealing with Latin American drug cartels. He had pulled his weight, certainly hadn't done anything overtly suspicious. But things started to happen. Deep-cover agents started disappearing. Most of them were working close to the two main cartels based in Colombia. Two had been in Mexico, working to uncover corrupt government officials.

Martin Fletcher had been getting sensitive intelligence somehow. Paul was certain he had purchased it, or possibly used blackmail to get it. Paul committed his theory to a report and passed the word upstairs. They knew that the cartels had a man on the inside of the DEA but couldn't seem to get hard evidence. Paul knew it was Martin. Knew it in his heart. But proof was never forthcoming. So word had come down that the leak had to be plugged. Paul had plugged it by having evidence planted. Martin had been arrested, tried, and convicted. Paul had somehow believed that would be the end of it. With most men it would have been.

So Martin Fletcher hated Paul because Paul had been personally responsible for his arrest, his fall from grace. Death was unimportant to Fletcher, because in the world Martin inhabited, death was always a choice, a slipup or a few seconds away. Martin was an animal who operated near the top of a complex feeding chain—eat or be eaten. It was a life that depended on knowledge, sharp reflexes, planning, lack of conscience, and flawless intuition. Paul had defeated him and humiliated him. Killing him, the alternative, would have been understandable, even forgivable, in Martin's mind.

Paul had known that Martin would come for him one day unless he was, as rumor had it, dead. He thought it was possible that the others had been killed first and the confession made so Paul would be forced to come out to play. Because the fact was Martin could have killed Paul at any time over the past years. Maybe he planned to kill the Masterson family while Paul watched from the sidelines, helplessly. He would enjoy that. If it was Martin, Paul was no match for him. A team might beat him, if it was the right group.

Paul closed his eyes and imagined Martin as he had known him. In Paul's mind Martin had grown to mythical proportions. He was ten feet tall, had the instincts of a cougar, and was as strong as something hydraulic. *Has a day ever passed that Marty didn't cross my mind, soil some pleasant thought?* Paul was afraid of him—deeply afraid. Maybe that, more than the other reasons, was why he had really hidden himself here. Paul felt as if Martin Fletcher were working the strings and they were leading from his hands to Paul's life.

Paul looked at the wild beard one last time. He pressed the scissors against the jawline and squeezed. The first cut is the deepest, he thought as a bird's-nest-sized clump of beard floated down to the basin.

Sunlight was just beginning to sear the bottom of the sky with a light crimson band. Aaron was dressed and standing in the kitchen brewing coffee in an electric aluminum percolator. Something moved in the window, and as the back door opened he turned and was face-to-face with a beardless Paul Masterson. His nephew's hair was combed back against his head, and the beard had been replaced with a large handlebar mustache. He opened the kitchen door and Paul stepped inside.

"Paul. Hell, son, I've seen happier faces in a proctology ward."

"Coffee smells good," Paul offered.

"I reckon you want some of it?" The old man frowned. "Never see you unless you want something. Bet you want the top of the brew?"

"Give me some of that burned syrupy stuff off the bottom, like you usually do."

"Where's your pals? Shit-faced I bet. Look like serious whiskey drinkers to me. Looks like you had a few yourself." The old man poured two cups of coffee, replaced the pot on the stove, and sat. "Now, that's hot."

"Good, the heat'll take the top layer off my tongue, cover some of the taste," Paul said, taking a tentative sip. "Joe McLean does a right good jig with the bottle. Thorne's a teetotaler. Alcohol doesn't agree with his personality."

They were silent for a long time as they sipped, steam rolling up over their cheeks.

"Never fails to amaze me what you can do to perfectly good coffee beans."

"It's free, ain't it? You can get a twenty-five-cent cup of muddy water down the street anytime."

"Too far to walk."

"So when you pullin' out?" The old man cocked his eyes up into Paul's and frowned.

"Because I cut that beard off? You think I'm leaving because I shaved?"

"Well, ain't you?"

"Couple of hours."

"Knew them fellows showing up was bad news. It's that guy you warned me might come looking for you, ain't it? He's up to somethin'?"

Paul took another swallow of coffee and nodded. "Killed eight women and children. The men who were in here—it was their families. Plus Rainey Lee's two kids and wife, too."

"Someone thinks you can catch him? Probably right."

"Fact is I don't think I can. But I have to try. He's gonna go for Laura and the kids."

"I see. Then there ain't nothin' else to say."

"I wanted to say—"

"Listen, Pauly. Don't get all teary-eyed like your mama used to. I'll watch your place. You go on down there and take care of your business without a worry. Not that you ever did much worryin' on my account. Old man with no one to leave the enterprise to. Go on. But I want your word that when that rat bastard is cold, you'll come home and bring those kids for a visit. Might be one of them might want to run this place. Never know."

"Never know." Paul smiled. "I don't imagine they want anything to do with me."

There was another period when the two men were lost in their individual thoughts. Then Aaron stood up. "I want you to take something with you." He started out into the store, came back five minutes later with a narrow walnut box about three feet long and a small cardboard one. He placed them on the table.

The old man removed the masking tape to free the flaps. He opened the cardboard box and pulled out a black leather shoulder-holster rig. The holster and the belting were hand-tooled in ivy leaves. Paul stared at it without comment. The gun was a Colt Combat Commander with stag grips.

"Remember this?" Aaron asked.

"Yes. I wasn't sure what happened to it."

"DEA sent it after you got here. I didn't know if you'd ever want it back."

"Thank you."

"For what?"

"For not selling it." He stared at the old man for a few seconds before his mouth turned up at the corners.

"Think I wasn't tempted. Rig like this is worth six or seven hundred to the right fool."

Paul picked up the weapon and looked at it. He dropped the magazine and inspected the chamber.

"It's clean!" the old man said defensively.

Aaron turned his attention to the wooden box. He removed a nail from an ancient hasp and slid the top back, revealing a burgundy velvet-lined interior. He lifted a long black cane from inside and handed it to Paul.

"I remember this. Haven't seen it since I was a kid."

Paul couldn't believe the heft of it. The hand grip was L-shaped and made of hand-carved ivory. The base of the cane was black and shone like dark glass all the way to the fancy filigree sterling tip.

"Take it with you," Aaron said.

"It's even more magnificent than I remembered," Paul said. "Must weigh ten pounds. You reckon I'm that cripple, do you?"

"It's weighty for a reason, and you don't have to be cripple to need it. Look at the tip."

Paul admired the cane. The handle told the story, in bas relief, of a gunfight, with one man standing tall and the other falling wounded. Paul flipped the cane and looked at the tip, where carved silver circled a black hole.

Aaron took the cane from Paul and twisted the handle. It opened, exposing a breech. He dropped in a brass shell and closed the breech. Then he raised the cane and pointed at a large wooden beam, and there was a deafening explosion. Paul stood and put his finger on the new hole in the wood.

"This old cane has an interesting history," Aaron said. "Can't recall exactly what it was, but it had to do with a gambler. Made by a famous gunsmith from a design the gambler worked out in a dream or some such. Had the handle carved in Frisco by a Chinese artist in 1880. Rod is ebony from Africa, covers a rifle barrel. Silver tip's from Mexican mines. I traded some stuff for this cane fifty years ago. In time of dire straits it'll give you the answer to one final prayer."

"I never knew it fired."

"No reason to tell you before. Forty-four forties are expensive rounds, so don't waste 'em. Open the breech and load it. A half twist back on the handle sets the pin and drops the trigger. I'm giving you six shells, and I just hope it don't blow up on you."

"I'll be careful."

"Don't shoot your fool foot off."

"I won't keep it loaded."

"Of course you'll keep it loaded! What the hell good is it gonna do unloaded? Just like your mama. Sayin' fool stuff."

Paul shook his head. "Thanks."

"Worth a fortune, too, I'd wager. I'm just loaning it to you. Give me your word you'll keep it with you. And that you'll bring it back to me . . . personally."

Paul stood and the two men embraced. "I'll be back, Uncle Aaron."

"With the kids? Bring 'em to see me before I die."

"We'll see."

The old man wiped his weathered eyes on the back of his sleeve. "I ever tell you how much you've meant to me all these years?"

"No, Uncle Aaron, you never have."

The old man slapped his nephew's shoulder. "And I ain't about to start now. Trim down that fool mustache, you look like a cattle rustler."

Paul finished his coffee with a swallow and stood. He leaned the cane against the wall. "I'll pick this up on the way out."

"Suit yourself," Aaron said, waving his nephew away with a flick of his ancient wrist. "You always do."

6

Laura Masterson stood at the far side of the ballroom where couples had once turned in elegant circles beneath a crystal chandelier imported from France. In this very room smooth-faced boys in dress gray bowed to giggling girls in sweeping hoop skirts, and string quartets played sweet waltzes. Meanwhile a nation divided against itself prepared to trade minié balls and cannon shot. This room had served as a hospice where yellow-fever victims had lain on mats, ministered to by a parish priest and women in white linen. Laura was surrounded by old ghosts, but she stared straight through them as she critiqued her latest painting.

She was leaning against the jamb of the tall pocket doors that were open to the home's wide hallway, called a gallery. From fifty feet away the face on the canvas looked as detailed as a Vermeer, while up close it was all tiny swirls, short slashes, and dots of oil. The face in the painting was partially destroyed, or partially incomplete, the right eye missing, plucked from the angry socket by an all but angelic vulture. She sipped her coffee and contemplated the image. In her mind the face, like all of her images, was a thing of beauty, but as one critic had said, her figures were "disturbing visages that haunt the viewer while seducing them."

"This one won't be seducing anyone," she said to the coffee. She was far from pleased with the image, but that was true of all of her paintings. If she was pleased, she might lose the edge, whatever that was. She had no idea where her gift—though she would never call it that—came from. She had never shown any more talent at art than friends who were involved in painting. She had come to it late, but it had consumed her with a passion that she had never dreamed possible. The brushes seemed to know what they were after. There was a surety of line and, as her mind commanded, her hand followed. Before she had discovered these images trapped inside her mind, she had been another person altogether. She had been called the Anne Rice of oils, and it had less to do with their shared hometown than with their perspective.

She thought of the reviews from her last show, which her daughter had insisted on reading aloud at the breakfast table. "The subjects get in close, mesmerize, and then tear you to pieces," Roger Wold had written in the *Times-Picayune*. . . . "They are images of angels . . . modern martyrs . . . exciting to some for that very reason. Classically erotic. . . . This is art that may just turn on you as time passes." Some people wanted art to move them, and if the work could keep moving them as time passed, all the better. That was worth money, and the flow of money allowed Laura to live in a house built in 1840 and paint in a ballroom where Jefferson Davis had once danced and refrain from dipping into her principal.

This particular painting was of Paul Masterson as he existed in her heart. Physically wounded, emotionally terrified, alone and packed to bursting with guilt. A lot of her work centered on Paul because he had left her filled with pain and confusion, and she was trying to resolve the conflicts in her heart on canvas. Even when she had other subjects in mind, when she began a painting he would often invade the work by appearing in part as he did in this large canvas. The set of Paul's jaw, the line of his ears, the bright blue of his single eye, the angle of the mouth, the attitude of the head, a shape, a frown or a ghost of a smile, might take form. Consciously she thought she had her feelings for him licked; subconsciously, every time she thought about him, it was as though someone stumbling around inside her head had kicked over a bucket of electric eels.

Some of the people who had purchased her early paintings had sold them to get rid of them, possibly because the owners had become irritated with them or had decided to change the style of their art as part of a redecoration. To their delight there had been a ready market for the pieces, and profits were made. The kind of people who enjoyed being bothered, or who wanted their walls to have personality and their collections to appreciate, snapped up Laura Masterson paintings as fast as they became available. She had been forced to hire an agent to compile a waiting list and negotiate prices. The bidding for the privilege of being seduced and disturbed had driven her prices from two thousand dollars for the first canvas, completed five years ago, to forty thousand in four short years. Now Laura showed at prestigious galleries in New York, Chicago, San Francisco, and in a few months' time would launch a show in Berlin. Her work was perfect for the German market, Lily Turner, her agent, had said. "The sausage eaters"—Lily called the Germans that—"will devour them happily at one hundred thou a pop."

Laura wandered back to the table, dropped a brush into the baby-food jar filled with thinner, and watched as it influenced the turpentine to a cloudy rose. She let the brush become saturated and then cleaned it carefully, squeezing the bristles in folds of soft cloth until the damp spots were clear of hue. After she had cleaned all of the brushes and her hands, she dropped the bits of turpentine-saturated cotton cloth into the lidded rubbish can. She looked at her watch. It was three A.M.

She glanced at the chair across the studio where Reid Dietrich, her boyfriend, often sat and either read or simply studied her as she worked. He was a perceptive critic, and having him there was always a comfort. Tonight he had gone off to her bed upstairs to await her retirement. Sometimes he did that; tonight he had not spoken but had simply disappeared from the studio. She had been so wrapped up in her painting that she hadn't taken direct notice of his disappearance—she couldn't recall the specific act of his leaving, but she knew that he had kissed her cheek; he always did that when he left her alone. Often when she worked she lost hours and sometimes an entire day. During those times she might agree to some request from her children and not recall having spoken to them at all.

Laura Masterson often worked well into the night, passing through the hour of the wolf. Sometimes the golden rays of morning sun would break through the tall windows as she worked—covered to the elbows in paint flecks. The rays would come through the beveled glass and echo the rainbow on the walls and burn long orange waves across the floorboards. But no matter what, she was the one who awakened her children in the mornings, fed them, watched over them, hugged and kissed them and put them to bed. For Laura the desire to be a mother to her children was far stronger and more important than the desire to paint. *I can paint after they are in their own lives and I am here alone.* She had not had to make a choice between her career or her family, as some did.

Laura's house had been constructed in a time when craftsmen bundled their hand tools in canvas bags and roamed the country like soldiers, spreading the doctrine of hand-carved moldings, bright murals that brought the wonders of nature indoors, decorative masonry, form-fitted and wood-pegged cypress-beam skeletons with oak floors as solid as chopping block. The house was located off St. Charles in the Garden District, built by people who had every reason to imagine the house would stand forever, a monument to grace, form, and function.

The structure had been mauled and divided in the 1950s when an owner's heir had decided the property had to generate capital. The house was made into seven separate apartments. It was all but abandoned to the elements when she had come across it.

Laura had never painted for money. She had inherited a lot of money from her father, who had been a tax attorney and had sat on the board of the Whitney Bank. She had used some of that money as leverage to buy and restore the house to its original floor plan, but she had taken her time furnishing it. The kitchen was large and open and modern, the rest of the house filled with antiques.

The lot on which the house sat was just under two acres, encased in a six-foot wall of stuccoed brick. Sections of the yard had been allowed to develop a will of their own, and at the rear of the property the paths had become a thick tangle of angry vegetation armed with cruel teeth, barbs, and razor edges that challenged passage of all but the most feral of varmints.

The house itself was two stories, and the first-floor joists stood four feet from the ground. Wide wooden steps led up to the wraparound porch with its large columns. Laura had added a swimming pool with living bamboo walls on three sides and liked to sit there by the water and think.

The dog, Wolf, shook his body and followed Laura up the wide staircase to the second floor. She always looked in on the children before she went to sleep, whatever the time.

Reb, who had selected the nickname himself at an early age, having decided that the name Adam lacked something crucial, was nine. He was slight of frame, with his mother's light-red hair and pale skin, and he slept twisted up in a yellow-and-red nylon sleeping bag winter, summer, spring, and fall. Laura referred to the bag as Reb's cocoon. His room was in constant turmoil, with toys scattered, a hamster cage with one occupant, a gray cockatiel named Biscuit, and comic books layering the rug like scales. Laura made a mental note to make him straighten up on Saturday. She didn't mind letting him express himself by living in disorder, but she wanted him to learn some discipline. The dog walked in, looked at the sleeping bundle of bird, sniffed the hamster, which was running inside the wheel, and then curled up beside the boy's bed. He would stay there unless Laura passed by going back downstairs.

Erin's room was the opposing camp in more ways than one. She was fifteen and had inherited her father's finely chiseled features, blond hair, and the single-minded drive he'd had before the infamous Miami massacre. Erin made straight A's, was businesslike and precise, and was at the age where she had no patience with her mother and most especially her little brother. She found her mother's art disconcerting and tasteless and objected to her leaving any of her paintings on any wall, outside the studio, for more than a couple of days. She called it showing off. Reb, on the other hand, loved his mother's work and often painted with her in her studio. For nine he was advanced and possessed a remarkable feel for color, balance, and design.

Laura loved both her children, equally if such is possible, but Erin could take care of herself, and usually did, so her son received the portion of his mother's affection that Erin turned back unused. Erin remembered her father as a flesh-and-blood reality. To Reb he was an album of pictures, two letters a year—tucked into the Christmas and birthday gifts that arrived in the mail. He dreamed about the man in the pictures, and sometimes in his mind they had a real relationship. He clipped photographs of Montana-looking mountains out of magazines and pasted them in a sketch book he kept under his bed. Casting a fly out into the rapids in the cold blue shadow of mountain walls was his fondest fantasy of all. Laura knew all about it and felt powerless to help either of them find the other. She had tried. She had tried and failed. When she thought of Paul hiding from his children, she bristled—a flame burned beside those feelings. It was the closest she could come to hating the man she had once loved more than anything on earth.

Laura's bedroom, with its fourteen-foot ceilings, was located directly over the ballroom and was half as long. She entered the room and crossed to the bed where Reid Dietrich slept curled in on himself, still in his clothing. The four-poster was shrouded in sheer netting, which made Reid look like someone stuck in a dream. She had thought long and hard some months earlier before she invited him into her bed with her children in residence. There had been no ill effects from it. She and Reid stayed private with their intimacy. He was never there before the children went to sleep and was always out of her bed and into his own, in the guest room, before they awoke, for appearances' sake. No one was fooled, but it made Laura feel better and the kids never mentioned it. They seemed to know that loneliness was worse than whatever else was involved.

The children had grown accustomed to Reid, and the influence of a man in their lives again had been positive. They never suggested including him but, on the other hand, never seemed to mind his inclusion either.

When Reid Dietrich was in town, he split his time between Laura's house, his own in the French Quarter, and his sailboat on the lakefront. He kept clothes in the closet of Laura's guest room and had a toothbrush in the bathroom.

Laura studied his face for a few moments and then kissed him on the cheek. He smiled and looked up at her through the fog of faraway dreams.

"You ran out on me," she said, a mocking chastisement. "You, sir, is a very bad boy."

"I got tired. What are you gonna do, spank me?" he said.

"Don't you wish?"

"What time is it?"

"After three."

"I came up just after midnight."

"I thought maybe you didn't like me anymore."

"Don't be silly. Who else would I let ignore me for hours at a time and then come to bed smelling like Pine Sol?"

"Turpentine." She creased her brow. "Poor baby, do I ignore you?" She undid his buttons and slid her hand down his smooth chest and over the solid stomach. Then she unzipped his pants, and her hand traveled farther down, into his pubic hair. She ran a fingertip the length of his member, which had stirred to life.

"Now look what you've done," he said. "You have to put him back to bed."

"Hold that thought," she said. "I'll be right back after a quick shower to get the Pine Sol off."

She moved a few feet, unzipped her baggy jeans and dropped them to the floor, removed her sweatshirt, and stopped in the door of the bathroom to allow him a side view. Laura was thirty-eight years old, had a perfect helmet of straight light-red hair in which veins of silver had lately appeared here and there, and a wholesome, beautifully balanced face. There were the faintest whispers of crow's-feet at the corners of her cornflower-blue eyes. Despite having two children, she had a well-toned body that caused men to smile to themselves as the fire of wickedness played behind their eyes. Then she peeled her panties off, twirled them in her hand, shot them out into the bedroom, and disappeared into the bathroom, laughing. She turned on the shower and climbed in, the granite floor cold under her feet, and let the needles of hot water wash over her. She was standing with her back to the nozzle and her hands against the wall, her head bowed, when the door to the shower opened and Reid entered. He moved up to her and put his arms around her, interrupting the spray.

"That striptease has my little friend wide-awake," he said, looking down.

"Up indeed," she said, laughing. "That's a *little* friend?"

She didn't mind the intrusion or the sudden pressure against her leg. She turned into him, pressing her body against his, and ran her hands down his back, stopping at the muscle-tight buttocks. He ran his tongue down her neck, over her breasts, pausing to tweak the rose nipples with his teeth, and then tracing a line through her belly button and down with his kisses. Using his tongue, he traced letters in the soft hair over the pubic cleft.

"Oh, Reid. That's good. Oh, and I really like that," she said playfully. He put his tongue through the patch of pubic hair to the place where the valley began. "Oh, but that's the best of all."

She threw her head back as he brought her to the slippery edge of an orgasm. She put her hands on either side of his head and pulled him up. Then she brought her right leg up until it was caught at the top of his pelvis, opening herself to him, and helped him inside with her hand. She brought the other leg up and locked her ankles behind him and, using him as a fulcrum, rocked them into an orgasm.

Later when they were lying in bed locked together like a pair of spoons, she studied the back of his head in the glow from the open bathroom door. She had always insisted on sleeping with a night light in the bathroom and that door cracked. She claimed it was so she could get to the children faster if they cried out, but the truth was she had always had a fear of the darkness. She ran her hand over the line of his shoulder, to the center of his chest, and hugged him tight. She felt safe and secure when they were together.

Laura was very fond of Reid—maybe she even loved him—but she hadn't felt the same release of control she had experienced with Paul. She reasoned that she was older now, more experienced—not the schoolgirl she'd been when she found Paul. But she never revealed herself, her deepest thoughts, to Reid. She'd done that once.

Found Paul—no, discovered Paul. She thought about that phrase. Yes, she had found him and savored every minute they'd been together in the early days. They had lived a perfect love in those early days of their relationship, and then they had fallen into complacency, routine. But she had remained in love with him, and there had always been electricity when he touched her. She could admit that he had been less giving, but given the whole of their relationship, he had been so much more. Why was that? Reid was more handsome—more her type. He loved the same things she loved and had a remarkable body that fit with hers as though they had been designed as a set. Paul, on the other hand, had been self-absorbed; he had made decisions that affected them both without discussing them with her. He had been a magnificent consuming soul as a lover, but outside the bedroom he had been pensive and distant and didn't need to be touched as she did. He had been dedicated to his work, often staying in the field weeks at a time, calling only sporadically. But they had been in love, and there was no doubting that. Even after the children were born and inhabited their lives, he had been like a lover at the beginning of a torrid affair. But that was then and this was . . .

Reid Dietrich was thirty-nine but looked ten years younger. Laura had met him at an opening of her work a year before at the Arthur Maxwell Gallery on Magazine Street. He had been staring at a particular painting when she arrived, and fifteen minutes later he was still staring at it. She had studied him as he studied her work. Reid was almost six feet tall, thin but muscular, and wore his light hair combed back over his ears. His features were delicate but masculine, sensual. His eyes were like children's marbles with light-gray circular swirls beneath the surface. She had never before seen eyes the shade of his. She had been mesmerized by them, lost in the absolute depth of them from the moment she saw them. It was artistic interest at the beginning.

"God, he's gorgeous." Lily had spotted him first and pointed him out. Laura had finally wandered over and stood beside him as he'd stared at the painting of St. Sebastian.

In the painting of Sebastian, the martyr had dark locks cascading over his shoulders, and a pale halo. His skin was translucent, the veins tracks of deep blue. Most of Sebastian's blood had been leeched out by the five arrows, which were all heeled with purple fletches. The blood that dribbled from the arrow shafts was being licked away by a pair of ewes. In the darkness of the tree limbs above there were sinister black birds watching, obviously waiting for their turn at the saint-to-be. Despite the inconvenience of being lashed to a tree, despite the arrows and the birds waiting for his eyes and sweetmeats, Sebastian was smiling at the sheep who cleansed his body. What Laura had thought she was painting had altered itself as she'd worked—a move of the brush, a moment when something unexpected happened, something outside her control, and St. Sebastian was at peace. Reb's comment had been, "I didn't know sheeps ate blood."

"Ouww, gross, Mother," Erin had added. "Like someone would stand still for that!"

"It's an amazing piece," Reid had said even before he turned to look at Laura. "A truly unique interpretation . . . of the death . . . of St. Sebastian. The degree of pain a man can feel and remain at peace with his inner self . . . his God, or his soul. It touches me in a place I've never been touched." Laura thought he was serious until he laughed. "Who did shoot St. Sebastian?"

"I should know," she said. "Martyr makers, I'd imagine."

"I am considering it for my house, but . . ."

"But?"

"It's a lot of money," he'd said. "Fourteen thousand for an unknown."

She had looked him over. A solid-gold Cartier, a designer suit with the cuffs breaking on a pair of obviously expensive loafers.

"Come, now, I'll bet you paid that much for your watch. What does any watch do but intrude on your thoughts and divide your day like a drill sergeant? 'It's ten-twenty—oh gosh, I have to go—it's almost time to shower. . . .' A slave driver in eighteen-carat gold. Attractive slave driver, but, still, the ticking is merely the cracking of the whip."

He had looked at her and studied her for a few seconds, his eyes crystal points of interest. "Maybe the artist would trade me for this watch?" He smiled. "I could kill two birds with one Cartier. I'd have the painting to keep me company, and I'd be free of this tyrant on my wrist."

She studied him for a few long seconds. "You'd trade your watch for that canvas?"

"In a moment," he said, smiling. "Do you work here?"

"No, but I know the owner." She had looked around and caught the gallery owner's eye. He walked over. "Arthur, this is . . ."

"Reid Dietrich," Arthur said, smiling his wolfish smile. "Mr. Dietrich is newly arrived in New Orleans and a client of the gallery."

"He wants to trade his watch for this painting," she said.

"Well, it's okay. But there's the question of how you'd pay me the gallery's commission." He stretched up on his tiptoes and crossed his arms. "Possibly the band?"

Reid had blushed. "Your painting? Oh, you're Laura Masterson? This is embarrassing."

"No relation to Bat."

"Dietrich. No relation to Marlene, either."

They'd both laughed.

"I'll just pay for the painting. Your husband must be terribly proud of you. Such work is truly amazing."

"I'm divorced."

"But the wedding band?"

"Keeps me from having to spend time being chased by men I'd rather avoid. Those awkward moments in the grocery store. I have two children."

"I'm a widower." He had fixed his eyes on hers and then touched her hand. "Please excuse me so I can conduct my business with Arthur before someone snatches my St. Sebastian from the wall."

"I could always paint you another," she'd said, surprising herself. She realized that she was flirting with Reid and was suddenly embarrassed. He had held her eyes for a few seconds longer and smiled what was, as far as she could discern, a perfect smile.

"Who was the model?" he had asked.

"My ex-husband," she said.

"Have you considered the subliminal implications?"

"Believe it."

Reid had written Arthur a check for the fourteen thousand dollars, and a red dot had appeared beside the title placard, signifying that the work had been purchased. Reid often commented that the painting had appreciated three hundred percent since he'd bought it, while the watch had not.

Laura had not been able to talk to him any more that evening because there were so many other people she had to greet, and he had disappeared shortly after writing the check. Later in the week she had quizzed Arthur about him. He told her that Reid, a recent New York transplant, was a partner in a company that sold high-tech, high-dollar diagnostic machines to hospitals. He was interested in Louisiana artists, came from an old Atlanta family, had a large sailboat on Lake Pontchartrain, and lived in the French Quarter. Most important, he wasn't gay, though Arthur deemed that a shame.

Weeks later Arthur called her to ask if she would accompany him to Reid's home and oversee the hanging of the painting, as Mr. Dietrich had requested. His house on Dumaine was four thousand square feet on three floors and filled with antiques and artwork. The house had a private courtyard protected by tall brick walls, and servants' quarters that he used strictly for storage. The art movers hung St. Sebastian over the carved-marble fireplace in the living room.

She and Arthur had been met at the door by a casually dressed Reid.

In the living room there was a haunting egg-tempera portrait of a woman, painted in a style similar to that of Andrew Wyeth. Arthur said she was the dead wife. "Car wreck," Arthur had whispered as they passed. "Decapitated," he added, raising his blond eyebrows for emphasis.

Reid had insisted they stay for sandwiches, but Arthur begged off. Laura had needed to go, too, but when she looked at her watch with the intention of making an excuse, Reid had looked into her eyes and said, "Your drill sergeant?"

They had reclined on the Oriental, eaten pastrami sandwiches, and sipped dry red wine. They had struck up a friendship almost at once, and as if to make a wonderful dinner perfect, the clouds had opened and driving rain had covered the courtyard. He had built a fire below St. Sebastian to chase the damp chill from the room.

They had all but lived together for the past six months, each assuming that they would spend nights in each other's company unless there was some reason not to. Reid, if not perfection, was as close as men came, to her way of thinking. And available just enough. *And love grows.*

Reid didn't talk about the details of his wife's death, and Laura didn't ask. He had a way of changing the subject with unequaled grace when conversation strolled too close to something he didn't care to discuss.

After five years of life without Paul she still dreamed sometimes that he was beside her in bed. She was very fond of Reid, but her soul had been pledged to Paul, and it remained with him despite her attempts to forget him and move forward. She knew she would never remarry strictly for love. Luckily there were enough other reasons so that she might decide to marry. But there was no hurry. Her life was full enough.

7

THE GEORGETOWN BROWNSTONE WAS SMALLER THAN MANY OF THE others on the tree-lined street. Paul smiled at the fact that there was nothing on the outside to offer evidence that the building was occupied by one of the most powerful men in America.

Paul Masterson pressed a white disk beside the outside door, and a short man with mean eyes dressed in a jogging suit opened it and frowned at Paul. "Yes?"

"I'm Paul Masterson," he said.

"I know who you are. Mr. McMillan is expecting you."

Paul stepped into the foyer. The floorboards were polished to a mirrorlike finish.

"Wait here and I'll see where he wishes to receive you." The man closed the door and slid a bolt into place.

Paul stood and admired a painting depicting several Indians on horseback riding amid a herd of buffalo. Two

minutes dragged by, feeling more like twenty, when a
door opened and a smiling Jack McMillan entered with
an apron on. He walked up and hugged Paul dramati-
cally. "Paul! Come in, boy! How the heck have you
been?"

Paul had once decided that if God were to take human form, he'd probably model his appearance on Jack
McMillan's. He looked like a cross between Santa Claus
without the facial hair and F.D.R. without the wheel-
chair. He was six feet tall and had wide shoulders, hands
like steel, and a belly that was as flat as sheetrock. Paul
knew Jack was in his sixties, but he could have passed
for ten years less.

"I need to talk to you," Paul said as he was released
from the grip. "Thank you for seeing me on such short
notice."

"I always have time for you, Paul. Let's talk inside. I
have something going in the kitchen. You eaten?"

"Yes. But I could use a drink."

Jack was cooking a casserole. He explained that he
was having the Speaker of the House for dinner. Jack
was married to Martha Hall, a retired actress whose B-
movie career comprised three completely forgettable
films. Jack had seen one of them, flew his plane out to
Hollywood, and three months later came back to Washington with Martha seated beside him. She had been
married to him for thirty-five years. Their sons, Terry and
Jackson, ran successful businesses. Paul had saved
Terry's life when, as a boy, he'd been swept down a rain-
swollen river in Montana. The event had made Paul, a
stranger to the McMillans, into a kind of honorary son in
Jack's eyes.

Jack patted the man in the jogging suit on the shoulder. "Artie, get Paul a Scotch and then go watch television while we talk. Martha's out of town—she's with
Terry in New York. He asks about you. You should call
him. How's Aaron?"

"Mean as a snake," Paul said. He took the glass of
single malt from Artie, and the personal assistant stared
blankly at him before he sulked his way out of the room.

The Scotch was dark amber, a signal that it had been aged in a sherry cask for seventeen years.

"That man of yours has never liked me," Paul said.

"Macklin's been real good to me," Jack said. "He's a lousy judge of character, though. If he doesn't like or trust someone, I know I'll like 'em. He's just jealous because I don't enjoy *his* company."

"I need a favor."

"You do?" Jack slipped the casserole into the oven and set the timer. "What's on your mind, Paul?"

Paul leaned against the counter while Jack stirred garlic into something he was sautéing over the flame. He told him what had happened to the families of the other agents. Jack asked no questions. In fact, it appeared that he wasn't paying the story any attention at all. But Paul knew he was listening and analyzing every word. He described what he wanted to do.

"You've never asked me for a favor before, Paul."

"I know. You're my only hope. Seems no one is returning my phone calls. I know the people I want to talk to are busy, but at one time they did return my calls."

"Politics is a twisted business, Paul. Guess people need reminding."

"I don't think T.C. will cooperate unless I can apply some measure of pressure."

"T.C. is a horse's ass."

Jack sat on a stool and took a sip of his Scotch. "Paul, I'm not saying I can do anything about this. But I got an idea. Let me call a couple of friends of mine. If I were you, I'd go on over to La Côte d'Or for a late lunch. Ask for Raymond, he's the owner. I'll call and arrange a nice meal. You'll love the food. Come back when I got some time, so we can sit down. You need anything else?" He put a hand on Paul's shoulder and squeezed lovingly.

"Thanks, Jack. Nothing else."

"If you need anything else, you call me." Jack was dismissing him.

Paul finished his drink and put the glass in the sink. "Tell Terry I said hello."

"I will."

"Thanks, Jack," Paul said.

Jack hugged him again at the door.

"Stay upright," Jack said as he opened the door.

Paul turned and walked down the street, and Jack watched him to the end of the block. Then he shook his head. The thought that Paul was probably going to get killed this time out made him sad. He closed the door and went back to his kitchen.

Paul took Lee Highway to the restaurant. The owner of La Côte d'Or was expecting him and showed him to a table in the rear. It was early afternoon, and there were only three people dining in the front by the bar. Paul had the entire dining room to himself.

He sipped a glass of wine, which the owner had personally delivered to him, and lit a cigarette. As he turned his head, he recognized the short, round man who was entering the dining room as the aide of a well-known senator. He strolled to Paul's table and sat down.

"Mr. Masterson, it's been a long time. How delightful to have run into you here."

"Mr. Palmer. Would you care for a drink?" Paul asked.

"That would be great. I understand you called the senator's office. I'm sorry he was out of pocket."

"No problem," Paul said. "No problem at all. I know how busy the senator is with elections looming."

The aide stared at Paul as though he were the most important man on earth.

Paul looked around at his bedroom in the Willard Hotel, drinking in the decor. As he gazed out of the closest window, he could see the sharpened top of the Washington Monument glowing golden in the early-morning sunlight. After six years in the cabin the suite's elegance was sobering. *I could get used to this again*, he decided after inspecting the well-stocked honor bar and refrigerator. Paul had called T. C. Robertson, acting director of the DEA, and asked for a face-to-face, and Robertson had agreed. T.C. owed him, and Paul meant to collect.

Paul looked at the Rolex Submariner that he was wearing for the first time in six years. He was pleased that all it had needed was a winding. In Montana the only clock he'd paid attention to had been his own body's. The suite he was in was leased by the government and used for visiting VIPs. It was a multiroomed affair with lush carpeting, silk walls, expensive furniture, and views of the capital's more impressive buildings. There was a living room, a kitchenette and dining area, two bedrooms with large bathrooms, and an office complete with computer, fax, and a secure line. He was impressed by the hospitality of the DEA under T. C. Robertson.

Thorne Greer and Joe McLean were putting the preliminary plans he had given them into operation, approaching the men that he wanted for his team. Most of the names on the list were old-line pros, and Paul had been out of touch with them for years. The talent search was not going that well. They had talked with some old friends, but six years changes people's priorities. A volunteer mission without funds, which could involve days, weeks, and maybe months of work around the clock, wasn't a great lead-in. Then add the constant risk to life and limb and the fact that to join might cost a career and pension if anything went wrong, and it didn't exactly make for a great close on the offer, either.

His idea of a team had changed out of necessity. The team would be young and would have to make up in enthusiasm what they lacked in experience. Paul would rather have seasoned pros, but he had no choice. Now he had to get T. C. Robertson's approval and support.

As Paul checked his new haircut in the mirror and adjusted the eye patch, his thoughts moved to Laura, Reb, and Erin sitting like clay targets in New Orleans. They were under close surveillance by a fairly good team, but "fairly good" was just a low wall for Martin to step over on his way inside.

Paul had just slipped his left hand into the pocket of his navy blazer when there was a light tapping at the door. He opened it to find T. C. Robertson standing there with two aides who looked like young, successful attorneys. *These guys wouldn't know a kilo of coke from a sack of flour.* They averted their eyes when Paul stared at them. T.C. looked right into Paul's eye, pumped his hand like a long-lost brother, and swept into the room with the two men in his wake.

Paul had learned from Joe McLean that T.C. was having problems with ATF and FBI. The FBI's director, George Sharpe, wanted to absorb the other two agencies into the Bureau, and he had the ear of the President. T.C. was fighting him but for the wrong reasons. He wanted to do the same thing Sharpe wanted to do but with T. C. Robertson ruling the roost. A flight of fantasy as far as Joe could tell. But in D.C. nothing was impossible. . . . It was all information, timing, and alliance.

Thackery Carlisle Robertson had more gray in his hair, and his eyebrows had whitened. He looked vastly more distinguished than the last time Paul had seen him. He had been assistant to the director when Paul was shot and had moved up only when it was clear that Paul wasn't after the post. He stood taller than the five seven he had been before, thanks to lifts, no doubt. He looked like a senator or a judge, which was surely his aim.

He slapped Paul on the shoulder and smiled his best "God, it's great to see you" smile. "Paul, it's been *too* long." He seemed earnest, which was his real talent. Paul knew the man had all but danced naked around his desk when Paul had chosen to leave DEA.

Paul motioned T.C. to a chair. "Please," he said.

T.C. tucked the tail of his coat under his buttocks as he sat. He crossed his leg, right over left, tugged at his cuffs as though he were sitting for a formal portrait. The other two men sat on the couch, as Paul had seized the only remaining chair for himself. He and T.C. were eye to eye, and the other two seated slightly lower. *Perfect.*

"Well, well. Boys," T.C. said grandly, "this man here is an honest-to-God national hero." His teeth looked as if they had never been used. "Highest-ranking DEA officer ever wounded in the field."

The men, who hadn't been introduced, nodded their heads in thoughtful unison.

"Drinks, sodas, coffee?" Paul asked.

"No, Paul, I for one have a full day ahead of me. Please, help yourself. Scotch drinker of some ability, if memory serves."

The two yes-men showed Paul the palms of their hands and grand smiles.

"I was hoping we could talk in private," Paul said. "No offense, fellows."

"These men are my most trusted confidants," Robertson replied. "Surely we don't have anything that secret to discuss, do we?" T.C. said, smiling broadly.

"This meeting has to be completely off the record," Paul said. "Some of what I want to discuss concerns our mutual past and might prove . . . delicate. Things we have yet to discuss in front of anyone. But if you want them in, it's no discomfort to me. I'm retired."

T.C. searched Paul's face and turned toward the men seated on the couch. "Go have a cup of coffee and I'll see you in the café downstairs after the meeting. We wouldn't want to bore you men with old war stories." Paul saw that one of them tensed, and though the man tried to look unconcerned, it was clear he was. *There's the tape recorder*. Paul might have smiled but didn't. He had known T.C. would tape the meeting in case there was something he could put in the safe for leverage later. T.C. wouldn't want any witnesses to this meeting, though.

Paul watched them leave. T.C. looked slightly uncomfortable. He loved an audience to play to and looked smaller after the other men left the room. He couldn't pretend with Paul now.

Paul sat and lit a cigarette and took two large draws on it before he spoke. "Mind if I smoke?"

"Actually, I believe this is a nonsmoking suite," T.C. said. "But you're our guest. We can air out the room after you're gone."

"It's strange being back in D.C.," Paul said. "Couldn't imagine being back in all of this again." He watched T.C.'s eyes following the cigarette. "You used to smoke, didn't you? Let's see . . . those Dorals in the green package, wasn't it? Low tar. Safe."

T.C. waved at the air. "I believe you're right. Foul habit, Paul. Times have changed. You could probably get ten years at hard labor for lighting that outside this room. Nobody who is anybody smokes anymore. The days of cigar-sucking senators sitting about plotting mass destruction and filling their pork barrels is about at an end. And good riddance."

Paul took another pull. "I should quit."

"So how have you been? Living a quiet life? We have a medal that belongs to you somewhere. You should take it back home when you go. When will that be?"

"How have I been? Not bad, considering I've been practicing to become a monk. I have the silence and celibacy down, and I'm working on getting used to the sackcloth."

T.C. looked at him and then laughed out loud. "Well said," he roared. "Very good. Still have that sense of humor." T.C. picked at an imaginary lint speck on his knee. "Have you seen Jack?"

"Jack?" Paul knew exactly whom T.C. was referring to. "Which Jack, T.C.?"

"Ah, same Paul, I see." T.C.'s smile flat-lined. "If you're thinking about coming back into the world you left, I should caution you that things have changed. Six or seven years is an eternity, career-wise."

Paul crushed out the Camel, taking his time. "T.C., let's cut to the chase and save the small talk for cocktail parties. I want to come back into DEA like I want a hubcap shoved up my ass pipe. I don't want to live in this town again with the brand of creatures who inhabit it. Present company aside, naturally. I don't ever want to command anyone again. I lost whatever it was I had that made me want to be responsible for other people's actions, and I am truly sorry I was ever where I was. Things would have been so different had I gone to State instead of Justice."

"Save that for the hicks. You love commanding. We all know you'll be back unless someone buries you."

"It takes self-confidence and a certain inner moral outrage that I can't muster. Plus I don't believe it, any of it, anymore. The old Paul is dead and buried. My days of believing the company line are over. That's the first point."

"Well, Paul—"

"Hear me out," Paul said. "By now you know that Martin Fletcher has killed eight of your people's family members."

"Two were *ex*-agents," T.C. corrected, holding up his hand. "I am aware. Just the other day . . . the Rainey incident. God, anyone who would kill children like that. . . . If it was Martin, he will be caught and punished. Rainey said Martin, of course, but Rainey isn't exactly reliable right now—suffered a complete breakdown. He'll be out for months. Maybe for good. I've been looking at replacements just in case."

"T.C., Rainey heard Martin's voice. He left that note for me."

"Martin probably had someone else do it. He would never return to the States. Too much to lose. Besides, the killer was an old man. Martin Fletcher's my age."

"Hear me out."

"What do you suggest?"

"Let me assemble a team under the DEA umbrella to go after him. Give me carte blanche for a period of time and reasonable funds. Reactivate me as a special-team leader. If anyone fails, it can be me."

T.C.'s eyes went cold as old steel. He crossed his arms. Paul was losing him. "You don't want to return? Doesn't sound that way from here."

"One shot, T.C. You'll get one hundred percent of the credit when we find him. He won't be alive to remember the past. Anyone's past."

T.C. seemed to be weighing the proposition. "We're not talking about a sanction here? Breaking and entering, shooting things up, rampant muscle? Keeping the man healthy was your calling in life."

"We both know the DEA doesn't plan deaths. Even

planning the deaths of monsters like Martin Fletcher would have been illegal."

T.C. looked uncomfortable. "Of course. I'd like to help you. But I really can't see any advantage. And our budget is limited. Bastard senators on the Appropriations Committee have clipped my wings. They're destroying this country, Paul. Drugs pouring in from everywhere. They don't want them stopped because it would be bad for the law-enforcement business."

"You don't see a political advantage to letting me get Martin?"

"I'll be frank. If Martin Fletcher is fool enough to be back in the country, we can find him without you. The FBI can deal with him, it's their job. If you are back in the administrative saddle, you pose a political threat because people liked you—hell, they probably still do. There are a few people in high places who would do anything to help you."

"Physically, T.C."—Paul pulled the wounded hand from the pocket, and it trembled visibly until he returned it to the pocket—"I can't do what I could."

"Your apparent handicaps aren't enough to keep you inactive. I've read your meds. The hand'll get better. Besides, look at Bob Dole. Never one hundred percent, but who the hell is? A little plastic surgery and you'll be good as new. And with Jack McMillan behind you—"

"I told you, Jack isn't."

"There are people who'd help you on the off chance it might please Jack McMillan. Frankly, Paul, I can see nothing but a downside for me, politically speaking, and I'm a political animal. Maybe if you could get Jack to help me be appointed director once and for all? That isn't much for the man to do. One phone call to the right cigar-chomping dinosaur, and I'm a shoo-in."

Paul sat up on the edge of his chair. "Jack McMillan is a friend of mine, and I don't use my friends. If I did, he wouldn't be a friend."

"Jack McMillan is probably the most powerful man in this town." He smiled. "If you'll talk to him about me and swear you won't come back into the DEA, I'll give

you my American Express card and my wife, and you
can cut Martin Fletcher's throat at high noon on the
White House lawn with Robert E. Lee's sword."

Paul shrugged.

"You can do that, Masterson. McMillan owes you a
life. Surely you haven't used up that favor. Favorite son.
I'm sure a word from you and—"

"I wouldn't ask him for that."

"Because he wouldn't do it?"

"No, T.C. He would do it. Fact is I don't need his
help for this. You are going to do what I'm asking."

"Why do you imagine that? You need to have the
rocks in your head changed. Why would I?"

"It's the only thing you can do."

T.C.'s face grew red as his anger built. "You
wouldn't have him drop weight on me? I have my
friends, too, Paul."

Paul leaned in toward T.C.'s chair. "Normally I
wouldn't see him or speak to him for any favor, and neither would I ask him to use his power against anyone on
my behalf. But don't forget that we're talking about my
family's safety. This is one hundred percent personal. If
anything, and I do mean anything, happens to my family, you won't have to worry about what Jack McMillan
does. There won't be enough of you left to do anything
to."

T.C. stood, his face ablaze in vein-popping fury.
"You're threatening me? You fuckin' asshole. Don't you
dare threaten me, you one-eyed, hobbling son of a bitch!"

"You're right. Don't give it to me because Jack can
have you sweeping the Capitol steps with a toothbrush.
Do it because you owe me this much as an ex-agent. Do
it because you owe your agents loyalty and retribution
for this loss. And do it because you can't let any man
hold your agency hostage. Think up your own reason—
you're creative. But you will do it."

T.C. exhaled slowly and cracked his knuckles
thoughtfully. "I'm sorry, Paul, but I can't. I will promise
you that I'll deal with Martin—with assistance from the
Bureau." T.C. smoothed his jacket and turned toward the

door. "Enjoy your visit, Paul. See some monuments. Get yourself laid." T.C. winked at Paul. "Must have quite a load built up after living on that mountain all this time."

"Just a second, T.C.," Paul said as he crossed over to the door to the second bedroom and opened it wider. A distinguished-looking man in his seventies entered the living room and took a seat on the couch. T. C. Robertson's face went as white as his teeth. "I'm sure you know Senator Stanton."

"Well, this is a surprise." T.C. was fighting to recover, but the realization that the man had been listening to the conversation was devastating.

"I bet," Senator Abe Stanton said as he lit a cigar the size of a small log and exhaled a plume of smoke that covered the well-known face from T.C.'s view. "Now, we're here to discuss what Paul wants," the head of the Senate Appropriations Committee said. "And if it's all the same to you, Thackery, we'll just keep this between the three of us. It's my opinion that mentioning this to Mr. McMillan, or anyone else, would be completely unnecessary and might have unpleasant consequences for one of us. Sit," the senator commanded.

T.C. sat and smiled nervously, his face hardly darker than a sheet of typing paper.

"Interesting conversation you were having," Senator Stanton said. "I for one am thrilled you've agreed to help Paul."

"Paul makes a lot of sense, as usual," T.C. said, nervously wiping at his brow with a napkin he lifted from the coffee table.

The senator blew a spinning smoke ring toward the television set and fixed his eaglelike eyes on T.C. "Have one of mine. It's Cuban. What Castro smoked before his bout of throat cancer, I understand." He reached into his pocket and removed a case, opened it, and held it out to T.C. T.C. took a cigar, sniffed it, and chewed the tip off, picked it from his tongue and placed it into the ashtray beside him. He lit the cigar using a lighter that was beside Paul's cigarettes and inhaled the first puff.

"God, that's excellent!" he said grandly. "I love a good cigar." He was beginning to recover.

"I like to imagine I'm putting the torch to Castro's crops." Senator Stanton laughed and winked at T.C. "I bet I could get ten years for lighting this outside the room here."

T.C. puffed on the cigar and listened to the inevitable.

8

Paul had spent the following day meeting with members of the DEA and poring over the files of agents whom T.C.'s personnel manager had deemed fit for the team and available. He had finally narrowed it to ten possibles. That evening he had dined at La Côte d'Or again, this time with the owner of the restaurant. They had sat and sampled wines for several hours, and a taxi had delivered a rubber-legged Paul to the Willard at one A.M. Paul staggered to the elevator, maneuvering among the ghosts of U. S. Grant, Robert E. Lee, Abe Lincoln, and George Armstrong Custer, all of whom had walked through this same lobby. Paul opened his door and dropped his clothes, like a trail of bread crumbs, as he meandered to the bedroom and fell headlong toward the mattress, asleep almost before he hit the bed.

Paul awoke certain that he was not alone in the suite's master bedroom. There was the faint scent of cologne in the air, a difference in the patterns of air flow. Just enough that a man who had slept alone, and in the absence of commercial fragrances, for several years would pick it up. Just enough for an alarm as he fought toward consciousness. He didn't move but lay still and let his eye take in the fact that the door was open and he had closed it before he went to sleep. Then he heard the breathing of someone beside the bed, and he was trying to decide how to move when the presence sat down in the armchair by the window.

"You're awake," the unfamiliar voice said. "If I planned to harm you, you'd surely be in the hereafter by now."

The man in the chair twisted the knob on the floor lamp and was illuminated against the dark walls.

Paul rolled over and felt on the table for his eye patch. He located it and put it over the right socket as he sat up. "Who the hell are you?"

The man seated in the chair was tiny, no larger than a ten-year-old child with fifty extra pounds, and skin the pallor of the recently deceased. He had a round, bald head, and his features were remarkable only for their blandness. The eyebrows were light hints of hair above the washed-out blue eyes. He wore heavy framed glasses with lenses that seemed to suggest the body was being piloted by a far smaller being. The face, except where the glasses compressed, was almost perfectly round, and the mouth was a thin line between pink, fleshy lips. He was dressed in a green V-neck sweater and bright-blue pants. He wore twin golf gloves over remarkably small, round hands. There was a battered and old-fashioned briefcase beside him on the floor. The shoes were canvas Converse high-tops that were in no danger of touching the floor.

"Who are you?" Paul demanded. "How did you get in here?"

"My name is Tod Peoples. I picked the lock on the outside door."

"You picked the electronic lock?"

"Well, no, actually I had a pass key. But I can pick locks."

"Are you armed?"

"No, but I certainly could be if I chose," he countered. He locked his small hands to the arms of the chair. "My man outside is."

Paul couldn't tell if the dwarf was kidding or not.

"What can I do for you, Mr. Peoples?" Paul asked.

"I'm here to help you."

"Not to help me sleep."

"No, you were sleeping fine on your own. Call me Tod." He crossed his ankles and let his legs swing a few times.

Paul lit a cigarette. "Was I snoring?"

"Cigarettes," Tod said, like a disapproving teacher.

"They'll stunt my growth?"

"They'll kill you. Ever heard of free radicals?"

"Stop, you'll scare me. Doesn't anyone worry about themselves anymore?" Paul inhaled and expelled a plume of smoke. Then he crushed out the cigarette. "Lighten up, Tod Peoples, it's my room, remember? You're one sight to wake up to."

Tod frowned. "I'm not sensitive about my height or my appearance. I am aware of what I look like."

"That's good. I figure my appearance, much like my breath, is other people's problem."

The little man smiled for the first time. "Yes, we share something there. That's true, isn't it? I mean, we look fine to ourselves. Amazing how often people are shocked that a man with my power isn't a ringer for Clark Cable or Cary Grant."

"So what is it you plan to do for me?"

"I am a friend of friends of yours."

"What kind of friend are you, Tod?"

"The best kind of all. The kind with information and other friends who possess talents you will need. I was made to understand that you are having trouble finding the right personnel for the job."

"I can get help just fine. Information on whom?"

"Oh, on everyone. But I think you are interested in one man in particular."

"And that would be?"

"Martin Fletcher."

"CIA, right?"

"Me? Goodness no. Let's say my role is multilateral data collection and interpretation, and dissemination of information. My little group coordinates that information with those who need or deserve it. I might take information to the very top, or I might give a tidbit to some sheriff in a county. Depends. But I have access to information that rarely makes the computers."

"Pentagon?"

"Let's not dwell on where I'm from. You can reach me through the DEA switchboard. Just ask for Special Agent Peoples."

"DEA?"

"I am not DEA, never even been inside the offices, never been inside FBI's headquarters, either. I meet very few people, Paul, and fewer still meet me."

"I stand in awe."

"Your calls will be patched to my office. Give your name to the person who answers and a number where you can be reached and for how long. If you can't stay by the telephone, tell them it's an emergency and they'll find me. But don't do that if you can help it, because they'll call my mobile, and that is an unnecessary expense that the taxpayers will have to pick up."

"You're shitting me! They don't make you pay for your mobile phone calls, do they?" Paul laughed.

Tod Peoples frowned. "Unnecessary records of the call. Just follow the instructions," Tod said.

"That's fine." He was enjoying Tod Peoples. If the man meant any harm, he'd have already killed Paul or drugged him, and he figured Martin Fletcher was their mutual target.

Tod lifted the briefcase to his lap and opened the top. He took out a file several inches thick and held it out to Paul. Paul opened it and removed a stack of pictures. The first was of a child smiling into the camera. The front teeth were missing from his cocky grin.

"That's my earliest picture of your Martin Fletcher. I

will furnish you copies of whatever you require for your purposes."

"I could use a set of slides for team briefing."

"The pictures won't actually do you much good. Martin's had extensive surgery on his face, possibly even his body. He stayed at a plastic surgeon's clinic in Madrid for five months, five years ago."

"The surgeon has no after pictures?"

"The surgeon and his nurses are after pictures themselves. They were killed in an unfortunate accident involving a large amount of plastic explosive. Fuse was—"

"Remote radio trigger?"

Tod smiled. "A hands-on sort of guy. I understand that specific, and unnamed, elements of an organization want Martin turned into axle grease worse than you do. The three-letter wonder agencies of this country who might have any interest in Martin Fletcher will stay out of your way unless asked for help. If you need help, the FBI would be my personal choice."

"You have access to CIA files?"

Tod giggled. "We control the influx of certain information. My people see everything that comes in. We decide who else gets access. Very complicated affair. Also totally nonpolitical. I'd rather confine this discussion to Mr. Fletcher. You only knew Martin a short time, while I have known him, or of him, for two decades. I know his strengths, his favorite foods, the beverages he drinks, his sexual tastes, and most important, what you don't know—his only weakness."

"Do you know why he's killing the families?" Paul said as he flipped through the file.

"Yes, possibly."

Paul looked up into Peoples's smug face.

"Well? Are you going to tell me, or do you want me to guess?"

"His only weakness is his mother. He has seen her every year of his life, on or near his birthday, with one exception six years ago."

"Not that. Why he's killing the families."

"You don't know already? On some level it's all

about the unfortunate attraction of opposites, coupled with the sociopath's inability to accept any blame for his own misfortune. Don't you think it interesting that the perpetrator of a horror never forgives his victims? On another level he blames you directly for his troubles. You are his overall scapegoat."

"Who broke him out of prison?" Paul wanted to see what this critter would allow. He might know more than Paul did.

There was no hesitation. "Two men in suits entered the prison using forged credentials. They were CIA-hired freelance, one brought in from Houston and the other from Seattle. Martin was far too valuable to be allowed to fall into a position where he might trade information for his freedom. The information he has might be classified as embarrassing and destructive to some powerful entities. They flew him south with a promise of life in paradise. Then they tried to kill him."

"They planned to kill him?"

"They did, indeed. Oh, that's right, you were in a coma when all of that happened. And it wasn't a story that received wide circulation through channels you would have had access to, anyway. You haven't kept up at all, have you?"

"You'll tell me, though. Tell me what I missed."

"Certainly. You *should* know, since it's surely the main reason he's back. Well, three young and brutally minded men met him and his wife and child at a small strip in the jungle of Guatemala. They should have sent ten times that many or killed him on the spot while he was unarmed. They struck at night and Martin dispatched them as you would expect. In the hoopla Martin's wife, technically his girlfriend, Angela something . . ." He snapped his tiny fingers twice.

"Lopez." Paul remembered Angela Lopez. She was the kind of woman you noticed and didn't forget.

"Yes. Miss Lopez and their small child were killed. He blames you, and to some lesser degree your team members."

"That's crazy. I had nothing at all to do with it. I was in a coma, doesn't he know that?"

"Well, Martin Fletcher *is* stomping-the-ground nuts, *and* guilty of untold horrors." Tod Peoples nodded and interlocked his small fingers. "He's also brilliant. The best example of what a twisted background and our finest brain-and-brawn trainers are capable of producing."

Paul lit another cigarette. "A bull-goose nightmare."

"A bull-goose nightmare you could have rid the world of."

"I wasn't authorized to order or condone murders. I thought the way I handled it was the right way."

"But we all know there's authorization and . . . there's authorization."

Tod Peoples reached over and pulled the cane to him. He ran his hands, as fragile looking as bird eggs, over the length of it and examined the handle.

"Some people seem to think you can take him. Not man on man, naturally. But the feeling is that you're every bit his equal. Well, you were once, anyway. It is a friend's opinion that you may not be able to take him due to mental and physical . . ."

"Shortcomings? I've thought about that."

"I am prepared to offer you a team you can utilize, deploy as you see fit. I have files on all the professionals in the group. They will undoubtedly suit your needs."

Tod lifted another folder from his valise and passed it to Paul. "These are the men I have chosen for you. If for any reason one of them is not to your liking . . . I can make substitutes."

Paul looked at the sheets and photographs. "Rangers, SEALs, and freelance goons," he said.

"No, sir. Not one goon in the crowd. Each of these pros is capable of taking orders in a team, thinking independently, and staying on task. They will not quit until Martin is stopped cold. They aren't kids. The sort of people you need aren't on the DEA payroll."

Paul leafed through the personnel records. "I'll think about it. Let you know."

"Do! No skin off my teeth. There is *one* long, unbreakable string attached to your little expedition, though."

"One string?"

"One I know of."

"I'm listening."

"A member of your team has been preselected. A young man by the name of Woodrow S. Poole."

"One member. I see." Paul started flipping through the file.

"He isn't in there."

"If I refuse?"

"You could refuse him, but I'm afraid that without him you'll find the going much rougher. Red tape tends to ruin everything, and as interference goes, it's almost impossible to see where it's coming from."

"One of yours?"

Tod Peoples shrugged in reply.

Paul crushed out his cigarette, locked his fingers behind his neck, and exhaled the smoke at Tod Peoples. "So, Mr. Peoples, tell me about this Woodrow Poole."

"As nice a young man as you'll meet."

"Nice."

"I like you, so I'm going to tell you something. There are others after Martin. There is a great deal more at stake than your family. A lot of ebbs and flows under the seemingly calm surface. Crisscrossing interests. And where there is a big interest in something, there is money invested. Investments have to be covered."

"I see. Martin has friends. Ex-friends."

"There's something else I'm going to tell you, but you must never breathe a word of it to anyone."

"Do I cross my heart and hope to die?"

"Precisely put, Mr. Masterson. Most precisely put."

PAUL MASTERSON HAD COME BY HIS DISLIKE OF HOSPITALS HON-
estly. In his mind those institutions represented pain beyond description. As he walked the carpeted hallways of
Nashville's Vanderbilt Hospital, his heart hammered and
a swallow lodged in his throat as fragments of memory
slammed into him like flying shrapnel. Ancient memories, recent memories, were sliding around together in his
mind.

As a child he had been brought by his mother again
and again to a small hospital, where he had been required to sit and watch some poorly constructed, yellow-
skinned effigy of his father wither away by degrees.
Finally all that was left was an empty hull connected to
life by plastic tubes, each hard-fought breath measured
by whirring and throbbing machines. He remembered
the face he had been held up to to kiss good-bye. He
remembered how the skin was drumhead-taut over the

skull, how the hollowed bones felt under his hands. He remembered the dry half eyes, the black holes of his nostrils, packed around the breath that smelled of decaying tissue. Paul's young dreams had been haunted by his father's corpse floating through at inappropriate moments. No matter how deeply he tried to bury him in his mind, he surfaced. He could not locate one moment of his loving father as a living man. *Death is evil, blind, and cruel.*

Paul was away from his Montana nest for the first time in five years, and the world he had found beyond the mountains was alien, the smells focused and sharp, the colors garish and liquid, and the faces filled with fear, angst, suspicion, and disapproval.

Six years earlier he had almost died in a hospital not dissimilar to this one and had had to be taught again a few basic human skills, like walking. It had taken all the king's horses and all the king's men a year to put him together again.

Paul had no memory of being gunned down, but he remembered the before and after well enough. He knew from the accounts of others that he had been shot while trying to open a room-sized container reportedly filled with tons of cocaine. Two agents, Joe Barnett and Jeff Hill, both street virgins dressed in black assault suits with clammy palms and infinite trust in Paul, had perished. Sometimes he still saw them in his dreams. In the dreams the two agents were opening the doors to hell.

The KTW rounds, solid brass coated with Teflon to dissuade friction, passed through the agents' Kevlar vests, vitals, and bone like hornets through cigarette smoke. There was instant retribution as the other agents and locals fired clip after clip into the container from the sides, turning the enclosed assassins into wet confetti. By some miracle no round had hit the detonator, nor had any been able to touch off the plastic explosives. Otherwise, the story would have ended there for all the troops.

Barnett and Hill stopped breathing before they hit the boards, and Paul's heart had stopped beating in the operating room because the pump ran dry. A good measure of his right frontal lobe had become gull food.

He'd lain there day after day staring at a gallery of friends and family, most of whose faces didn't register through the veil of morphine and damaged tissue. There had been nothing between his brain and the wind but bandages.

An army of physicians had used their skills and constructed a modern Frankenstein from used blood, shifted tissue, suture, formulas from NASA and Du Pont, and finished it with a glass eye that didn't fit. They had wanted to finish the job, but other things had interfered—the ghosts of Barnett and Hill, the pity of old friends, and the feeling of being a stranger who frightened his children shitless. The shaking hands and blind unreasonable fear. The uncertainty. He had bolted to his mountain and stayed there. He had been paralyzed and unable to make even the smallest of decisions ever since.

Paul realized he was lost in the maze of look-alike hallways and stopped at a nurses' station, an empty balloon of human skin with a piece of paper wadded up in his hand. They seemed to know there was nothing inside the suit but bone. The horseshoe scar that started at the top of the right ear and curved back around to the bottom of the same ear by way of his right temple, the patch, and the slightly misshapen skull marked him as the undisputed property of medical science, and worse, work interrupted while in progress. A coward, probably. The doctor who wandered by had eyes that measured him for a bed.

"Wrong floor," one of the nurses said after looking at the paper.

"Elevator. Two floors up," said another whose face he didn't see because she was on his dead side.

The elevator ride was remarkable for the black orderly in his early fifties who smelled of disinfectant and soap and who stared openly at him. "In country?" he asked, possibly hoping he'd spotted a kindred soul who had seen the rockets' red glare in Vietnamese skies. Wounds like Paul's came from few known places.

"Miami," Paul had answered.

"Hell of a war, that one," the black man said, shaking his head and snapping his gum at Paul's back as the door closed, leaving Paul on another floor that might have been the same as the others but for different-colored carpeting. He seemed to float down the hall through clouds of antiseptic odors.

When Paul saw the object of his visit, he almost wished he had not come. Rainey Lee sat in a rocking chair staring out the window at golden treetops and slices of redbrick building with dark windows. He was much changed. Old flowers, kept beyond their endurance, had scattered petals across the surface of the lap table. The window ledge was cluttered with cards offering condolences, coupons, and other junk mail surely hand delivered by some well-meaning friend. Household bills were stacked and bound with a red rubber band. The bed with its hard sheets was aimed at a dead television affixed to the wall beside a poster of a schooner in a steel frame.

Rainey Lee had lost weight and substance. He seemed fragile, far older than possible; his hair, which had been an uncertain shade of auburn, was streaked with white. The skin was pallid. There was an open Bible in his lap.

Rainey looked up when Paul entered but seemed not to recognize him. Paul walked over and looked down into his face. Then Rainey's eyes focused, sparked recognition, sadness, and embarrassment, and he stood slowly, like a man underwater. He laid the Bible on a table beside him and embraced Paul. Rainey hugged him a little too long, and Paul felt awkward and single-sided and flimsy, but he returned the hug and patted at Rainey's back with both hands. He was pleased that the left hand was working pretty much as it should, since he had been squeezing the tennis ball he carried in his pocket.

"Paul, long time," Rainey said.

"Didn't expect to see me?" Paul asked.

"I didn't expect to see you . . . and to see you so changed. Truthfully, Paul, I didn't recognize you. I thought you had come into the wrong room."

Paul changed the cane from his right to the left hand

and touched Rainey's shoulder to let him know that he was glad to see him and shared his grief.

"I can't tell you how deeply sorry I am," Paul said. "There are no words to express what I'm feeling. How are you doing?"

"This is a nice room. See my flowers?" Rainey's voice was like gravel. "Looked better yesterday . . . day before." He stared at Paul as he stood the cane against the wall. "I'm real glad you came. I was pissed at you. That note."

The note. Paul remembered the note Martin had left on the bed beside Doris's body. It had been put into an evidence locker, so he had yet to read it.

"I heard."

"Martin wanted to set me against you—all of us."

Paul said, "You thought any about going home? The future?"

"Why?" Rainey sat down and looked out the window. His eyes filled with tears. His body shook with sobs. "There's nothing at home, Paul. I got no mountains to hide behind."

Paul was unsettled by the reference to his exile.

"What are you doing here?" Rainey asked. "I'm flattered, but what brings you all the way here?"

"I'm going after Martin Fletcher," Paul said. "I've been in D.C. ironing out the details. The agency is pledged—within reason."

"Robertson? T.C. authorized *you* to find Martin? How?" Rainey looked up at him and his eyes cleared.

"T.C. has three solid reasons. First, because his agents have to feel like he'll go to the wall for them and move heaven and hell to protect their families. Second, because he knows that for any number of reasons the normal authorities who would be in control would never get Martin Fletcher in custody. And, finally, because a senator who oversees the DEA's budget requests told him it was a capital idea."

Rainey's eyes refocused far outside the room. "That makes perfect sense."

"We're going to get him, Rainey."

"Who's 'we'?"

"Thorne, Joe, and some newbies."

"I am ready to get out of here," Rainey said. "I'll get dressed."

"Wait a minute, Rainey. You need some R and R."

"I have to come."

"We'll have to get you released. It'll take time." Paul didn't plan to have Rainey anywhere but here. He wasn't fit for mowing a lawn, much less what had to be done.

Rainey looked out the window. "Let me come, Paul. You owe me that much."

Paul was shocked into silence.

"It's out of the question, Rainey. This . . . you just aren't up for it yet. Stay and rest."

"What do you know about me?"

"I'm sorry, Rainey." There was a flicker in Paul's eyes that Rainey seized on. And before Paul knew what was happening, Rainey was carrying his suitcase toward the elevators.

They didn't speak again until Paul was winding through Nashville's heavy traffic on Broad toward the office building across from the post office where the local DEA offices were located. The logical place to gather the team was Nashville, because that was where Martin's trail had ended. There was investigating to be done, and Paul would stay in Nashville long enough to see what they could discover that the police might have missed.

"The Tennessee bureau thinks there were two of them, the ranger and the old doctor," Paul said. "Don't think he could have done what was accomplished by himself."

"They don't know Martin," Rainey said. "I don't think there were two. Martin was always a loner. He would want to have the pleasure of killing, himself. Sharing was never his thing. It's not like he'd trust or need anyone to watch his back."

"The Rover at the airport had what remained of the polio crutches inside. I understand the old doctor wasn't on any of the airport tapes." Paul shook his head. He stared at the yellow stains between his fingers as he spoke. "Fletcher left the country after he escaped from prison, and he had his face changed in Spain."

"How's agency intelligence on Martin?"

"We're getting files on him from the Navy, FBI, and the CIA but the CIA may not be as cooperative as the others. They certainly won't open any of the Black Operations files. They may, in fact, still be protecting him. The agency'll ship what they compile to us as soon as it's assembled," Paul said. "We need to check for other possible suspects. We know the ranger had red hair, mirrored glasses, and a fancy pistol on his hip. He used a three-eighty on the scout leader—silenced, maybe. Nobody heard a shot."

"Why did you come? He told you he would stop if you didn't come after him."

"I don't believe it for a minute."

Rainey looked at Paul and seemed to be measuring him. "Gonna poke the snake with a stick?"

"He has to be stopped, Rainey. Doesn't matter what he said, even if I believed him. Can't walk after what he's already done."

"Once on stakeout he dressed up like a derelict and called himself Willie the wino," Rainey said. "He disguised his voice and had this pair of pants that he'd pissed on days before. Smelled like a truck-stop bathroom. Trained to do makeup by one of those Hollywood experts. And got the government to pay for it. So tell me what Robertson said. Pissed, right?"

"I think he saw the wisdom of my idea."

"T.C. wouldn't give you green dog shit he scraped off his shoe."

"I talked to Senator Stanton's aide the day before I saw T.C. An informal dinner in Arlington. He passed my request for help on to the senator."

"And the senator was receptive?"

"Absolutely."

"He agreed?" Rainey slowly shook his head.

"Thorne and I have been reinstated as special agents to apprehend Fletcher, who is also a fleeing felon. He is to be returned forthwith to Marion, Illinois, where a cell awaits him. If he resists capture, we are to use whatever force appears necessary."

"Great!" Rainey's eyes glazed over and lost their focus for a few seconds.

"T.C. was very cooperative. Postal inspectors, U.S. marshals, Secret Service, FBI, and the CIA are to cooperate in whatever manner we see fit, if we need 'em. Thorne and McLean have been reassigned to me."

"And I'm on your team. Not going back to what I was."

Paul didn't answer. Rainey was on extended leave, and Paul didn't want him activated yet, if at all. Paul said, "Look, I know we'll get Martin. But the reality is that we may or may not get him before he moves against Laura and the kids. Logically, they have to be his next target. I have to know that someone I can depend on will make sure he doesn't get them. Otherwise, I'll have to go myself."

Rainey couldn't conceal how ridiculous the idea of Paul pitted one on one against Martin Fletcher was to him. "And see if maybe he'd just kill you and go away?"

"We're roughly the same size," Paul said in self-defense. They both knew it was a ludicrous statement.

"Me. I'll go because I'm the best choice," Rainey said.

Naturally, Paul knew that Rainey wanted to sit and wait for Martin to show up. His own hatred would give him infinite patience and the courage to face him.

"Rainey, who out of the agency or any other agency I've mentioned would be best suited to watch over my family? Aside from you. You've been around while I've been out of circulation. I need for you to be my right hand on this. Who besides you?"

Rainey looked down into his lap and contemplated the request. "Thorne Greer," he said finally. "Thorne Greer is the best guy for that. He has the patience of a rock, he's a crack shot, and he always had great reflexes."

Paul didn't speak the rest of the way to the office. He had said more in the space of the past few days than he had in six years, and it had tired him. Rainey spent the rest of the time in traffic drumming his fingers against the Bible on his lap and humming to himself. Paul hoped the operation would give Rainey a chance to regain some balance. It was obvious to him that the deaths had altered him in some fundamental way—how could they not have? Of all three agents who had lost their families, Rainey was the one most likely to spin out of control when he got the scent of Martin Fletcher.

Paul had to keep the operation as quiet as possible. Powerful people trusted Paul to see that all the *i*'s were dotted and the bodies, if any, were buried quietly. Rainey Lee's addition to the team wasn't a good idea, but Paul wanted to help his old friend.

The operation was a hunting party staffed with people who were conflicted by circumstance and driven by revenge. And there were the others in the mix, the new guys. Then there was Tod Peoples's wild card, Woodrow Poole. Paul hadn't been able to get any background information on him through his sources at DEA or Justice. The CIA had no one listed with that name, nor did FBI, Secret Service, marshals or anyone else tied into the government-employee database he had access to. So Woody Poole was either an alias for a known agent, deep cover, Black Operational, or freelance.

Paul eyed the people passing in their cars and trucks and wondered what they were thinking as he and Rainey were planning the destruction of a mad killer. A man Paul now knew he should have killed years earlier. Paul tried not to dwell on the fact that he was responsible for letting Fletcher live. He knew that it was his moral stance, his refusal to allow the man to be taken out, that had paved the way for innocent deaths, the destruction of lives, and his own downfall. There was no moral element to the equation now. Martin Fletcher would die.

10

JOE MCLEAN HAD BEEN CHAIN SMOKING CIGARETTES, AND THE small ashtray leaked gray ash onto the conference table's laminated wood surface. He looked across at Thorne Greer, who rolled his eyes at the ceiling to let McLean know how he felt, working with kids again. Rookies for a job that clearly called for hard-core pros.

There were seven people sitting in the small conference room awaiting Paul's arrival. The five younger agents were making small talk, sipping sodas or mineral water, and trading the war stories they had heard since they'd joined the DEA. Stories Thorne and Joe had told at the same stage in their own careers. Two of the five were women. McLean pegged all of them at between twenty-three and thirty tops; thirty-four was cutoff age for joining the DEA. A couple still had Quantico, Virginia, soil on their shoes. Only one of the women was attractive, to Joe's way of measuring, the other looked like a lesbian to him.

Rainey's secretary, Sherry Lander, had made sure everyone was offered coffee, soda, or mineral water. The agents fresh from the training academy or backwater outposts were excited. McLean and Greer were beyond being excited. The old pros were both wishing Paul had pulled in some freelance or dark-angel pros who'd run Martin to the ground and eat the meat off his bones.

The agents' eyes followed as Paul appeared in the doorway, then limped to the table, carrying the cane like a shotgun in the crook of his left arm and a valise filled with files in the right. Rainey Lee followed like a tall shadow, carrying the slide projector and a box containing a carousel. Paul's appearance brought the room to immediate silence. He could almost hear the smoke roll off the cigarette in Joe's hand. Thorne and Joe got up and shook Rainey's hand.

"Rainey!" Joe said. "God, it's great to see you."

"Hey, Rainey," Thorne added. "We were planning to get out to see you this afternoon."

Rainey nodded and smiled weakly. The two agents exchanged glances and took their seats.

"My name's Paul Masterson. You new troops don't know me, but I know all of you." He reached into the valise, pulled six files and tossed them onto the table in front of him. "I wasn't always this handsome," he said, unsmiling. He pointed at his eye patch. "This is what can happen to you if you don't stay on your toes. I assume you've heard the story of what happened in Miami a few years back. I understand you studied it at the academy under 'don't let this happen to you' or something similar."

He saw a flash of recognition in their eyes. Greer and McLean were smiling. He wished they had discussed his appearance with the new agents before he'd come in. He hated looking into the virgin mirrors of other people's eyes.

"You weren't briefed in any depth on this operation because I plan to keep everything I say within this group. Our quarry may have sources in the CIA, DEA, and other groups that give, trade, or sell him information. I have selected each of you from over fifty possible candidates recommended by Mason Anderson in personnel. You five are all fairly new, but enthusiasm and energy are as important as experience." Paul saw the light go on in the older agents' eyes. He had said it without saying it. He made the inexperience seem a plus instead of the minus it was.

"The man with me is Rainey Lee, who has been in Nashville for the past four years. He's providing this conference room."

Rainey nodded without looking them in the eyes.

"You should know that the four of us were together on that dock in Miami when this happened to me. We four have known each other for at least fifteen years, so forgive us our shorthand. Hopefully you'll all catch up before we're finished."

Paul counted heads. "We're missing someone."

Thorne nodded. "A guy named Woodrow Poole is coming in any second from the airport."

As if on cue the door opened and a baby-faced young man with white-blond hair bolted into the room. He was holding an overnight case. His hair was combed back over his ears, and he was built like a middleweight. He sat beside Sean Merrin, who was a dead ringer for the host of *Wheel of Fortune*, though a foot taller.

"Sorry I'm late," the newcomer said nervously.

"Woodrow Poole?" Paul asked.

The man nodded and shook Paul's hand.

"Your timing is perfect."

"Flight was late, sorry." He took a seat and nodded at the people around the table.

Paul opened a file. He had been prepared for someone who looked like Arnold Schwarzenegger and picked his teeth with a tenpenny nail. Woody would fit in. In fact, he didn't look like much. But looks were often deceptive. Martin Fletcher himself had originally been nothing special to look at.

"Most of you don't know each other. Hands up as I mention your names, please. Agents Stephanie Martin,

Sierra Ross, Walter Davidson, and Larry Burrows . . ."
The hands rose and fell. "You four will make up team
Nighthawk under the command of Joe McLean. Each of
you has surveillance training, and you will be able to put
those skills to use."

Joe straightened and looked at Paul. There was a
smirk on his face.

Doesn't like the idea of teaching, Paul thought to himself. "Your objective will be to conduct surveillance on
the sole occupant of three twenty-one Tucker Court in
Charlotte, North Carolina."

Paul looked around the room. "Woodrow Poole and
Sean Merrin." Paul looked at each as they raised their
hands. "You will accompany Thorne Greer to New Orleans, where you will be responsible for protecting three
civilian family members. You will have the services of the
local police and DEA agents to help, but each of you will
be responsible for maintaining constant cover on the
principals. If you need help, you will have contacts to call
on. Need ten cops or fifty, they'll be there."

"Sorry, sir, but might I ask why this family is so important?" Sean Merrin asked.

"The family in New Orleans is our best and possibly
only means of capturing the person responsible for mur-
dering eight people. Those eight were family members of
the three strike-force agents in this room. They were slain
in the most cold-blooded fashion imaginable. We have
every reason to believe the three people in New Orleans
will receive the same treatment unless we can prevent
it."

Paul's voice cracked under the sudden emotion.
"The man responsible, one Martin Fletcher, is possibly
the most dangerous individual any of you will ever face.
He may not be working alone, and if he has an associate,
that man or woman will also be extremely dangerous—and unknown, unless we can get lucky with our
investigation here in Nashville."

"Will we be bunking in with three civilians?" Sean
asked.

There was nervous laughter scattered about the room.

"I mean, will we be with them twenty-four hours a day?"

"Yes and no," Paul said. "They are not to be aware that you are there at all."

"Why?" Sean asked. "I mean, how? Protect people from outside their house?"

"Stealth. I won't risk the team being uncovered by the target. Everything has to appear normal. If the family knows you are there, they might telegraph it in their behavior. Under no circumstances are you to be seen by the family. Also, we will take for a given that they are under surveillance by the target. So you have to avoid being seen by them *and* Martin Fletcher."

Sean Merrin shook his head slowly. "I'm new, but according to what I know, it's not . . . I mean we can protect them better if . . ."

Paul's hand stopped the agent's voice. "I have thought this through. The family in New Orleans you're protecting is mine. Believe me, if I could protect them from the inside, I would. If I could spirit them away to a safe place, I would. But I have to do this knowing that we will have *one* shot at Martin. We believe he will go to New Orleans to kill them. He might eventually come for them wherever we put them, but whatever plan he has in place is more than likely already in motion."

"But won't he assume there'll be people watching your family?"

"Good thinking, Sean. Keep that up." Paul nodded at Rainey, who switched the lights off. The slide projector came to life, blazing a white rectangle on the wall. The first image was of a man in a tough-guy pose wearing fatigues and a black beret cocked over one eye. He had dark hair cut against his skull, and dulled eyes.

"Ladies and gentlemen, meet Martin Fletcher. Martin was born in 1947. His father, Milton, was an eyeglass grinder in Charlotte, North Carolina. The father was a suicide—blew his head off with a shotgun. Martin was educated in public school in Charlotte, and in 1965 he went straight into the Marine Corps from high school. He was channeled to the SEALs after boot camp because of his special interests and obvious talents. In Vietnam he was decorated for valor on three separate occasions. Martin is cool under fire and fearless to the point of craziness. He's an expert marksman, a whiz with demolition, and he has few equals at electronic surveillance. He has the conscience of a flashlight and the acting and cloaking skills of a professional performer."

Paul changed to a shot of Martin in a suit and dark glasses taken in some pigeon-packed Italian plaza.

"Martin's skills were such that he became a cleaner. He was involved in especially delicate work. He took difficult government assignments where his particular talents were needed. He worked with the Central Intelligence Agency and several other groups who won't be named. He was what we call a dark angel. Dark by nature of deed, but an angel because they're on the right side, our side."

Paul looked around the room. "Factually speaking, this government does not, outside of national emergency or war, employ people like Martin Fletcher. I will say this once and never again. Martin Fletcher is one of a double handful of men we could accurately refer to as antipersonnel weapons."

"Wet work?" Stephanie said. "A hit person?"

"Let's just say he was a soldier under exclusive contract to certain of Uncle Sam's representatives until ten years ago, when he was retired from the field and put into a training position. Normally people in Martin's field do not retire as we think of retirement. They stay commissioned until they die. Sometimes they die at a rate well beyond the actuarial tables. Accidents without witnesses are not uncommon. Neither are mysterious disappearances. Martin Fletcher was made an instructor at the Democratic College at Fort Benning, Georgia, where he made good friends among some of the future leaders of Central and South America. Those connections have served him well."

He lit another cigarette and inhaled twice before he went on.

"Let's assume for a minute that Martin Fletcher was helping certain elements of the CIA move heroin from the Golden Triangle while he served in Nam. Let's imagine he made some important friends and possibly millions of dollars toward his retirement. While he was working at Fort Benning, let's say he made contacts within another set of important people. People who were interested in what the DEA knew. So Martin may have used his contacts to attach himself to the DEA in Miami as a member of the Green Team in the guise of field study and evaluation of our troops. He may well have used his position and clearances to sell certain drug lords information and a measure of protection. Let's say he did help intelligence just to cover his bases."

"In short," Thorne added, "he played all sides against the middle with little regard for what tragedy befell anyone."

"So he's a real scumbag," Sierra said.

"Rich scumbag," Joe added.

"Would be if it were true, but we're merely supposing here."

"Why is he killing families?" Stephanie asked.

Paul lit a cigarette and paused while he thought.

"Martin was caught with stolen cocaine secreted in his house, and convicted of possession with intent to distribute. Stolen cash and drugs and a fifty-year sentence of which he would do every single day. Fletcher insisted he was framed."

"He thinks we, the DEA, sold him out?" Sean Merrin said.

"We're going to always tell the truth in this unit, and anything said between us is privileged information. Agreed?"

The heads nodded almost in unison.

"The agency suspected him of selling DEA field agents for cash and favors and taking drug profits through a network of Latin bank accounts."

"Was he framed?" Sean asked.

Thorne's eye met Paul's for a split second. Nothing had ever been committed to paper on the operation designed to put Martin away.

"Of course not. He's just crazy," Thorne said. "Paranoia is his reality."

Paul wanted to come clean, but that wasn't the way it worked. Need to know. Fewer mouths to worry about down the road.

He cleared his throat. "Don't ever make the mistake of thinking of our target as a human being. Martin Fletcher is an animal just as surely as a mountain lion is an animal. I arrested him and testified against him. I regret not putting one behind his ear and burying the carcass in a swamp. If I had, at least eight innocent people would be alive right now."

Paul looked each of the new agents in the eye. "Martin, not being the forgiving sort, swore revenge and he has been getting it."

"How did he get out of prison?" Stephanie asked.

"Friends of friends broke him out."

"Broke him out?" Sierra said.

He nodded. "It was well planned and executed flawlessly. Out of prison and out of the country within hours. It is my understanding that he had a direct flight. Accompanied by his common-law wife and son."

Rainey slammed his hand on the table, and all eyes went to him. He smiled nervously.

Paul cleared his throat and looked at Thorne and Joe. "There was an incident with renegade soldiers in the jungle in Guatemala. His wife, Angela, and his son were killed. Martin went off the deep end. We think elements of the CIA set him up."

Thorne shook his head sadly.

"The attack on us in Miami happened a few days before he escaped." Paul ran his hand along the side of his head, the bristles of hair foreign to his fingers. He had cut his hair back into a modified GI, and he felt naked without the additional cover. He reached up to twist his mustache and realized that he was clean shaven. "He left a note at the scene of his last killing with his fingerprints

on it." Paul triggered the remote control, and a photocopy of a note appeared on the white wall.

> Masterson,
>   We are even for Angela and Macon.
>   It's over if you let it lay, and I am nothing more than
> a lingering aftertaste.
>   Come after me and I will present you with Laura,
> Adam, and Erin's hearts in a bowl.

"What if he does know we're there?" Sean repeated.
"He'll know you're after him."

"I expect him to know," Paul said. "He knew I
would come before he wrote that note. We're going after
Martin with everything we have, run him into a corner
and neutralize him."

They all understood.

Paul looked at the young agents, who were in turn
looking at the older men.

"Sir, this all seems highly unusual," Stephanie Martin said.

Thorne put his head in his hands and sighed loudly.

Paul said, "None of you should stay if you have any
reservations about this effort. Although it has been authorized, I assure you that if anything goes wrong, if one
innocent civilian goes down under any of our weapons,
we will not find a roof over our heads or a net below us. I
have no career to consider. You do."

"But this is a murder investigation. We're DEA," she
said. "How do we . . . I mean, what's the cover?"

Paul smiled. "Officially, the agency is investigating
someone dealing massive amounts of drugs, and we're
trying to gather evidence on that if possible. Our cover
includes the capture of a federal fugitive if we run across
him. In our capacity as bounty hunters our powers are
expanded. We may pursue Martin Fletcher wherever we
have reason to believe he has gone. We may search any
premises where we think he may be hiding. We may use
any necessary force to achieve our goals."

The agents' faces were hard to read, but Paul was

prepared to replace the whole group if he had to. He sipped from a cup of coffee that had cooled. "This is not a training exercise. This is the real thing, and lives depend on your accuracy, stealth, and speed. You are all to follow my orders, and the orders of these men, to the letter. If you have a creative idea, they'll want to hear it."

"Are you . . . we going to kill him?" Stephanie asked.

Paul frowned as he weighed what he should tell them. He didn't want to be haunted by the answer. "First off, you people on surveillance in Charlotte shouldn't fret that one too much. It isn't likely that your team will ever be faced with that decision. There is another group assigned to follow your target once she has left Charlotte and lands someplace else. They will be faced with that dilemma."

Paul was aware of Thorne and Joe shifting in their seats and exchanging glances.

"You'll be following her, monitoring her until she is off the plane at her destination," he said.

She looked confused by his answer.

Don't leave it there. "Ms. Martin, Stephanie, if we do somehow capture him, he'll never make it to prison again. Kill him? Let me say this for all of you. If you can kill him and don't, you will almost certainly be sentencing others to death. He *cannot* get away. Think of our Martin Fletcher as a mad dog who's going to enter a playground filled with children unless you stop him. He will see you as a bug standing between him and freedom."

Thorne Greer cleared his throat sharply before speaking.

"Do not engage Martin Fletcher one on one under any circumstances. Do not allow him to engage you in conversation. He is a master, and whatever you think of your own skills, remember that he can use anything at hand as a weapon. He has never been seriously hurt, but his adversaries have been—those who lived. Unlike imaginary monsters, however, he is as vulnerable to a lead bullet as any of us." Thorne said.

Paul scanned the faces of the new agents. For a brief couple of seconds his mind flashed a clear memory of the faces of Hill and Barnett, the two agents who had been standing with him in Miami when the container was opened. He turned away and took a deep breath.

Paul remembered the two dead agents, the wives, the children of Joe Barnett, a Mississippi boy with an accent as thick as a gambler's flash roll. Jeff Hill's young wife had sent Paul the flag that had been taken off Jeff's casket. Paul believed he knew what her message was: You killed those two boys. *Did I? Maybe I did. I must have. Else why do they haunt me, wander about in my dreams?*

Paul's mind went back to the Miami office that had been, and still was, the nation's epicenter of drug activity and the springboard for his promotion to deputy director of the DSF. God, he had been driven in those days. The dealers with their big houses, expensive cars, and women, the glitz and glamour—he had gone after them like a hellhound.

He realized that Thorne had finished his speech pertaining to the technology they would be using in the field. His eye met Woodrow Poole's, and for a split second he read something disquieting in them.

"I'm sorry. Sometimes I . . . ." He looked around the table. "I'm delighted with the team we have here. I asked for the best and brightest and most enthusiastic agents. There isn't anything for me to add about Martin. Except one last bit of advice. If you have him identified, shoot to kill. You get a chance during a moment of weakness or vulnerability on his part, use it. I promise you . . . God will smile."

The projector clicked, and the next picture on the wall was of a large, awkward-looking woman watering a bush.

"This is the surveillance team's target in Charlotte, Eve Fletcher. This woman is Martin's mother and his only known weakness. Learn this face."

"How could you forget it?" Sierra said.

Laughter.

"Looks like Rod Steiger," Thorne said. "I met him once."

"I doubt that she knows where her son is most of the time. She may know where he is at the moment and surely where he will be in the near future, but she will never tell of her own free will, and we are not authorized to beat it out of her."

Nervous laughter.

"This woman is an emotional anchor for Martin, and whatever has happened, or wherever he is, he contacts her and sees her on or around his birthday. We're banking on it. The year after he escaped from prison, she made reservations for four separate flights and then flew to Heathrow. She was followed to her hotel but somehow got out of the hotel and disappeared. Interpol picked her up when she surfaced in Madrid four days later. That was how they knew Martin was in Europe. We believe he had reconstructive surgery and no one has a picture of the new Martin Fletcher. Intelligence is that every year they get together. Last year she took a bus tour through Mexico. The surveillance team, a group of professionals, lost her for an afternoon."

He crushed out a cigarette and lit another.

"This time we will not lose her." He held up a small plastic box with something that looked like dark nails inside. "These are the latest thing from the technological whiz kids. They are transmitters capable of sending a continuous signal that can be picked up for a range of fifty miles. By utilizing a plane or a helicopter the pick-up team can triangulate her whereabouts. Once she lands, we will be able to follow her without having to be on her tail."

"Do we put them in her pockets?" Stephanie asked.

"We have decided that the most effective place to plant them is in the heels of her shoes. There's a gun that fires them in so the transmitter head is just below the surface. No matter what else she sheds, she'll most likely keep her shoes on. She wears custom-made orthopedic shoes."

"How are we going to get to her shoes?" Stephanie asked.

"Simple. She wears slippers unless she goes out, which is rare. So they'll be in her closet or under her bed. One in each heel."

"And how do we get into the closet?" Sierra asked.

"We have that worked out," Joe said.

Paul took a tennis ball from a small black bag and began squeezing it in his left hand.

"Martin's birthday, our target date, is October third. That is seven days from today. Now, he may meet her on the first or the fifth. So far, according to intelligence, these yearly visits have all fallen within two days of the third. The one variation was a missed visit six years ago."

"Did he at least send a card?" a voice asked. There was more nervous laughter from the young agents.

Paul turned his eye on the source of the words. It was the female agent named Sierra. She shifted uncomfortably beneath his frosty gaze.

"McLean's team is to be in place in Charlotte by seven hundred hours tomorrow. As unlikely as it seems, my sources believe Martin will arrange a rendezvous with her in spite of the murders hanging over his head. His psychological profile targets her as his one compulsion, and she may provide our only shot at isolating or at least identifying him before he strikes."

Joe McLean stood. "Okay, if Larry Burrows, Stephanie Martin, Sierra Ross, and Walter Davidson will follow me, I'll finish the briefing down the hall."

Thorne, Rainey, Sean, and Woodrow sat until the others were gone. Paul leaned against the edge of the table and looked at the two young agents.

"You two were selected for your skills. There will be others in support positions when you get there, but I am charging you to protect the family at any cost. Is that clear?"

They nodded.

Paul opened a file. "Sean, you had the highest score in your self-defense classes—marksmanship was exceptional. Whatever you have to do, you do. Of all the team members you two have the greatest chance of meeting Martin Fletcher face-to-face. Thorne and the two of you are best prepared to handle him. You know what I expect. Stay alert at all times. Rainey, you and Thorne take Sean to get something to eat. I'd like a word with Woodrow about his late arrival."

Paul waited until the two had left the room. He stepped to the window, turned, and looked at Woodrow.

The agent returned the look. His hands were on the table, the fingers interlocked. "You were pressed on me," Paul said. "Tod Peoples referred—make that insisted—that I use you."

"I'm not familiar with anyone named Tod Peoples, sir."

"No matter. Tod Peoples isn't your boss on this. You will not report to *anyone* else while you are on this operation. The success of this operation is your one loyalty. Is that understood?"

"My orders were to that effect, sir."

"I'm not going to ask what you did or who you did it for before you came here. As of now you are mine alone. There had better not be a hidden agenda."

"Sir," Woodrow started, "I'd like to . . . the truth is that I was asked to join your people because someone felt I'd be useful if it comes down to having to defend your family. I am, by trade and preference, a baby-sitter. It's what I do. In my immediate group we have never lost a client, though there have been attempts to spoil the record. My word to you is that I will protect your family first and neutralize Mr. Fletcher secondarily only if it doesn't compromise the family's security. If I fail, it will be because I am dead. My loyalty to your family is absolute."

Paul stared into the deep-set blue eyes, protected by light eyebrows. Despite the smile on the young man's lips, his eyes were all business. Woodrow was there as someone else's backup boy. He was the chief pit bull, the dog backed by the real money, and Paul suddenly felt comforted to have him on their side. He offered his hand,

and Woodrow's grip was remarkably gentle, though the tissue under the tight skin was as unyielding as ivory.

Paul showed the soldier his warmest crooked smile. "I believe you. You'll go to New Orleans tonight with Thorne Greer and Sean Merrin. Your cover is . . ."

"DEA L.A." Woodrow Poole smiled a goofy, child-like smile that beamed California free-wheeling beach boy.

"Good luck in New Orleans," Paul said. "You'll take orders from Thorne. If you find an order . . . well, if you have reason to disobey . . . I'll back you. Don't put me in a switch. Thorne knows that you are a specialist. That's all he knows." He smiled. "It's all he needs to know."

"No problemo."

"Good."

Woodrow got up. He lifted his suitcase and walked to the door. He started to say something but didn't. He left abruptly as Rainey Lee stepped in.

"So, Chief, what do you and I do?" Rainey asked.

"You and I are going to track Martin from the other flank. Starting here because he was here last. We're gonna try and pick up his trail. See if we can discover who's helping him, if anyone is."

"I want to be there, to be in on the kill," Rainey said. "I'll play detective, I'll crawl through mountains of paper and wear out the soles of my shoes, but when it goes down, I have to be there." Rainey's lip quivered. "I have to see it ended."

"That's out of the question."

"I can't be there when he's stopped?"

"It isn't a good idea."

"What do you mean?"

"I mean you are still listed as suspended until further notice. T.C. would have to reassign you. He won't. This is too delicate. You can stay with me and help behind the scenes. Or you can go back into—"

Rainey turned and started out the door. "Then I resign. From all of it. Neither you or T. C. Robertson can keep me out of this. I'm gonna be there whether you like it or not. Martin is mine."

"Fine," Paul barked in irritation. "Find him on your own. If I see you, or if Thorne or Joe see you, you'll be arrested and warehoused until it's over."

"My way or the . . . highway?" Rainey said, dropping the volume on the word highway. "This is a revenge exercise, Paul. Nobody deserves revenge like I do. Dammit, I paid for my ticket to the execution!" Rainey's eyes lit up like bulbs, and he squeezed his fingers into a fist and rapped the conference table so hard, an electric pencil sharpener flew off and bounced on the floor. "This was all your doing. Just stay away from me, or I'll kill you." Rainey slammed the door as he left the room.

Off the fuckin' wall. Rainey had no business whatever being out of the hospital, and the prospect of his running around with a loaded weapon sent a wave of chills up Paul's neck. He ran a finger over his scar where the bullet had travelled. He *knew* what the promise of revenge tasted like. He couldn't even force himself to think of taking Martin alive. . . . *It ain't going to happen.* Anyhow, Martin Fletcher would never allow himself to be captured by Paul—or by anyone else, for that matter. He would be carried off the field. They might all be carried off the field.

Paul walked to the elevator, and as he waited, he looked at his face reflected in the mirrored wall. He pushed his cigarette into the sand in the ashtray beside the elevator door and stepped in, fresh anger radiating in waves, his eye filling with hot tears.

Rainey's Cherokee was gone from his slot. Paul climbed into his rented Taurus and drove out West End Boulevard. He ate a cheeseburger on French bread at a place near the replica of the Parthenon. It was a student hangout, and Paul took a booth with his wound toward the wall.

After he finished, around eight-thirty, he drove to Rainey's house, parked across the street, and settled against the car door to wait. He hadn't felt tired, but he went out almost immediately.

When Paul woke, the sun was coloring the bottom edge of the night sky, and every muscle in his body felt as if it had been chewed on. He got out, stretched, and tried to put himself in Rainey's head. *Where would I go if I was Rainey Lee?* Suddenly he knew. He started the car.

Paul sat in the car and watched his old friend perched like a vulture on a gravestone, reading his Bible. Rainey was facing the twin mounds of dirt that covered the caskets of his wife and son. Paul finished his cigarette and pressed the remains into the bottom of the ashtray. Then he stepped out, slammed the door, walked up, and stood beside him. Rainey didn't turn his head so much as an inch from the Old Testament text he was open to.

The Bible was open in his lap. There was a third grave where the grass had grown over the remains of his daughter. Eleanor's grave had a dark granite stone. The inscription said:

ELEANOR ANN LEE
OCT. 17, 1987–DEC. 12, 1995
SLEEP WITH THE ANGELS

Rainey closed the book and looked out over the graveyard and then turned back toward Paul.

"I came to a funeral here a few years back, and I liked the way this place felt. I could have buried them in the graveyard back home where my father is, but I decided we should all be here. You believe in heaven, Paul?"

"Did once, I guess."

Rainey looked over at the graves. "I guess most deaths are senseless to someone. But none are as senseless as these three. I feel . . . I keep thinking if I had just paid closer attention."

"You didn't know," Paul said. "Any man who could murder a child is a demon."

"I'd feel better about it all if I could kill Martin myself. I know I would."

"For a few minutes. Maybe like you'd been underwater struggling to get to the surface with your lungs about to explode and you get there and you take that breath. Then you look around and you're in the middle of the ocean and for three hundred sixty degrees there's nothing but the horizon and a few fins circling. No wind and no birds. You're lost. Would you remember how good that breath felt for very long?"

Rainey smiled. "Christ, Paul. I'd forgotten. Where do you get those . . . analogies? You got a book somewhere with 'em listed out?" He looked at Paul. "Man wants to take revenge, see shark story page twelve. Man wants to poke the baby-sitter, page eight. God, I hate him," Rainey said. "I hate him so . . . I didn't know my emotions ran so deep. It's like a fire in my chest."

"I'm no grief counselor, Rainey. I've hated him because of what he did to me, and I realize it's a speck of nothing compared to what he's done to you and Greer and McLean."

"The day George was killed, I just wanted to die myself. After Martin called, I forgot all about that. I started burning after that. All I could think about was my hands digging into his chest and jerking his heart out before his eyes went dark. I could take him. God would help me do it."

"That's no answer, Rainey. It won't stop the pain."

"I don't think I can live without them, Paul. I can, maybe, but I just don't know as I want to." He looked at Paul, and tears ran down his cheeks. He nodded his head and wiped at his eyes. "The Bible says God will punish Martin—but I can't be sure."

"Help me, Rainey. I need you. The reason I agreed to let you in was the thought that the four of us are the only people who won't mess up the chase—won't give up until we have him in our hands. It'll be four hundred percent with us. But I need you solid. I can't do this if I have to keep my eyes on you, too. You've got to maintain."

Rainey was silent for a long moment, and then he

said, "Okay, Coach, it's your game. You put me where you want me. God'll make sure I get to see what I need to see."

Paul looked at the three graves and wondered if three like them were in his future. The thought struck hard, making him shudder.

Then Rainey looked back down at the graves and smiled. "I believe in heaven. I know what heaven will look like." He looked out over the cemetery as though he were seeing something beautiful in the distance.

11

Laura found a stopping place around six as the shadows of the foliage outside were softening. Her eyes were tired of looking at paint strokes, her arm was tired from holding a brush, and her mind was tired from thinking about what her arm was tired of executing. She put the brush in the cleaner, and because she never abandoned a dirty brush, she cleared it of color and then went out to the kitchen. Her children were there waiting; Erin in the glassed-in miniden, lying across the couch with the phone receiver against her ear, and Reb reading a book. They reminded her of cows responding to the inner voice that whispers to them to stand at the gate until the farmer comes.

Reb lost interest in the book when his mother entered the room. He went over to sit at the counter on a director's stool, watching as she removed the skins of spicy Italian sausage and began to brown them in a skillet. Then she added a can of spaghetti sauce, sprinkled in a few spices, and started the flame under the stainless steel pot of water at the rear of the stove. Erin was still talking on the telephone with her hand cupped around the mouthpiece for privacy. She giggled and rolled her eyes. Laura was warmed by having her well-growing children in sight. She thought about how Erin would be going to college in three years and how Reb would be joining her in nine more. It made her feel a twang of guilt that she was painting while they were growing. What had she missed while she was locked in her studio and they were fresh from a day at school? They had grown to the point where they usually didn't disturb her. Once they had come to her with questions whenever the telephone rang, but they had stopped that after a thousand discussions. They had just wanted attention, and it bothered them that they couldn't get her attention when she was working, while anyone who had use of a telephone could.

"Talking to a new boy at school—Eric something," Reb said, explaining Erin's behavior. "Doesn't know what a jerk she is yet." He leaned on the counter with his chin in his hands, watching his mother. The bird perched on Reb's shoulder whistled.

"Time twelve minutes, Reb," she said as she snapped a bundle of pasta in half and dropped it into the now boiling water. "Put Biscuit in his cage before you eat. That bird's unsanitary."

Reb set his Casio for twelve minutes and pressed the button. He watched the numbers fly in reverse for a couple of seconds and then turned his attention to his mother, who was adjusting the tomato sauce with creole seasoning.

"This is going to be grrrreat," she said, pulling the last word through time like taffy.

"Mama," he said. "Know what?"

"No, what?"

"Why do people follow me around?"

"Because you're cute. You having young female admirer trouble?"

"There was this plumber van out there across the

street when I got on the bus Monday, and when I got out of school, he followed the bus home." Reb reached up, and the cockatiel stepped onto his finger. He brought the bird to his face, and the small beak nibbled at his lip. "Kiss the bird," he said.

"That's nice," she said absently as she worked.

"And he stayed outside in front of Mrs. Walters's house for a long time."

"Who?"

"The plumber in the van with pipes on top."

"It was probably a different van, Reb. Some companies have lots of trucks. Erin, get off the phone and set the table."

"Yesterday it was a plumber van in the morning on the way, and in the afternoon all the way back, but then today it was a plumber van on the way and a red car back home. Do plumbers drive red cars sometimes?"

What Reb had said finally began to filter through her thoughts. "What are you talking about?" She stopped and looked at him.

"A car with two men in it at the school. And when I got off the bus, it stopped in front of Alice's house. Isn't that weird?"

Weird? "What did the men look like?"

"I dunno. Just one was kinda white-headed. Sunglasses and a cap. The other was older, I think."

"Was it the same man? The plumber and the man in the red car?"

"I don't know. Couldn't see inside the van on account of the dark windows."

"Would you know the man if you saw him again?"

"If he was in that car. I didn't really see him face-to-face."

Laura stared at Reb. Reb stared back. It had been years since she had considered her family vulnerable to danger from the sort of people . . . *What sort of people?* "Erin, watch the spaghetti for a minute," Laura said. "Off the phone. Now." The sudden authority in her mother's voice shocked Erin and she sat up.

Erin said good-bye to the person on the line and

crossed to the counter. "What?" she said, obviously irritated.

"When Reb's watch goes off, remove the pasta from the heat and pour it into the colander. Then turn the stove off and serve your plates, okay?"

"Sure, why?"

"Because I have to take Wolf out for a few minutes."

Erin frowned and tilted her head. "How about I do that and you drain the noodles and stuff?" Erin leaned on the counter beside Reb. "I mean, it's just so Little Betty Homemaker, I could hurl."

"Women have to know how to cook, Erin," Reb said. He stepped to the cage in the corner of the nook and put the bird inside. Then he washed his hands in the sink.

"Women lawyers don't. I'm going to eat every meal at really fine restaurants. Except when I'm in court dazzling the jury."

"I'll be back in a few minutes," Laura said. She picked up Wolf's red nylon lead from the sideboard. Seeing his leash, Wolf started spinning in place and stopped only so she could clip it onto his collar. "Erin, have you noticed any strange men around lately?"

"What man isn't strange?"

"No, like strangers. Hanging around. Following you." Laura tried to seem casual, but the question registered some concern in Erin's eyes.

"You mean like winos? Sure, they're everywhere."

"She means like plumbers," Reb said. "And men in cars watching buses."

"Plumbers!" Erin said, laughing away the seriousness that had existed a split second before. "Oh, like I run around watching for plumbers."

Laura went out the front door, followed the dog down the walkway, and paused at the front gate. She looked through the wrought-iron bars toward Alice Walters's house, which was across the street at an angle. Alice was in the Bahamas for two months. There was no red car on the street and no plumbing van. Not that she had expected there would be. But, still, Reb wasn't given to an overactive imagination. Laura opened the gate and followed Wolf down the street. As she passed the house, she cut her eyes toward the bedroom on the second floor and thought she saw—no, "saw" was the wrong word, for she didn't see anything—she felt as though eyes were following her. She stopped and looked up. Then she stared at Alice's front door where the blinking red light showed that the alarm system was armed. While she watched the house, Wolf saluted the wisteria bush at the edge of Laura's wall.

Alice Walters, although she was sixty, was a friend of Laura's and visited once a week or so. She was the possessor of strong opinions on everything, but these opinions were carefully thought out and then mixed with emotion and served piping hot. Laura got a kick out of her. She hadn't asked Laura to keep an eye on her house, but Laura was afraid that Alice's art, furniture, and other valuables might draw burglars. Alice had never married and was fond of Reb and Erin, giving them presents on Christmas and allowing them to stay at her house when Laura had to go out of town.

Laura stared up at the second-floor windows and then followed Wolf back to the house. As she was about to open her gate, a red Volvo sedan with two men in the front seat turned the corner and slowed as if they planned to pull over. But the driver didn't stop. In fact, the car gathered speed, and as it passed Laura, she thought the passenger turned his head to avoid her stare. The car kept going and turned a few blocks away without using the blinker.

Laura thought about Allen White, a police homicide detective, who lived down the street. He was Reb's little-league baseball coach. He had said, "If there's ever anything I can do, call me." Maybe there was and maybe she would.

12

Eve Fletcher stood like a warden at her front door watching the spot of a dog on her lawn through the storm door's dingy safety glass. The animal, which was being bathed in the early-morning North Carolina sunshine, was an ancient, gray-faced Chihuahua, hardly larger than a hood ornament. He was possessed of a forehead shaped like a tennis ball, batlike ears, and bulging eyes filled with the milk of blindness. The animal was arching its backbone and trembling like a cheap vibrator. She cracked the door so he could hear her.

"Hurry, Mr. Puzzle," Eve said. "Toodatoo for Mommy. Yessireesir, it's a good boy that does his little toodatoo." Her voice had the quality of a hacksaw against mutton bone.

The dog turned its head toward the door, and as if by his mistress's command something that resembled a burned-up chili pepper issued forth, swung as if at the end of a string, and then fell into the tall grass. This accomplished, Mr. Puzzle shook himself, took a feeble shot at kicking grass over the refuse, and headed for the door, following his earlier scent or his mistress's voice. As he reached the stoop, Eve opened the door, waltzed down the three steps, and scooped him to her bosom, kissing him on the domed head. She was rewarded with a wet sneeze and a weakly wagging twig of a tail that might have been sectioned from a rat.

Eve shuffled toward the den on her stovepipe legs with the animal clutched to her chest like a treasure. Eve was almost six feet tall, a wide-shouldered woman of sixty-eight. She had large hands with thick wrists and huge breasts that hung from her chest like water balloons tied together and draped over a clothesline. Heavy prescription reading glasses balanced precariously on the tip of her wide nose.

The entire den was hardly more than a nest. It was littered with a confusion of accumulated clutter, including boxes in a wide range of sizes and states of disgorgement. There was an open sewing basket, a pink Easter basket filled with balls of yarn, stacks upon stacks of *National Geographic*, paperbacks, *Soap Opera Digest*, and other magazines. There were bundles of mail tied with string, paper grocery bags with newspapers tightly packed inside. There were also little black ruins of dog flop where the animal had sneaked a crap when Eve Fletcher wasn't paying attention.

Eve had smoked Pall Malls at the rate of two cartons a week for most of her adult life. As a consequence her teeth looked like kernels of corn. Her world, the interior rooms of the small house, had yellowed as well over the years. A beanbag with a green aluminum bowl of ashtray was perched like a sleeping pigeon on the arm of her BarcaLounger. When each cigarette was no more than one-half its original length, she would crush and fold the butt unmercifully and, once certain it was dead, pour the contents into the ash can beside the chair, wiping the ashtray out with a facial tissue. *It's the last half of a cigarette has almost all the tar in it*, she always told herself.

Then she would replace the cleaned ashtray on the chair's arm, where it would wait to receive the next offering. There was seldom much of a wait. She held her cigarettes between the wrong side of her middle finger and the next to last, so that if she fell asleep with one active, it would burn her awake and not fall to the bed or chair to smolder and ignite.

The walls in the den were papered in a nicotine-dulled floral and spotted with her favorite art. There was a textured reproduction of Van Gogh's *Sunflowers*, a painted-by-numbers *Last Supper*, and hanging over the television set, a large photograph of a thin-necked, bleak-eyed boy in his graduation cap. The color photograph had faded to a light-blue whisper, and noncritical sections of it had bubbled and adhered to the glass. A framed photograph of the same boy, though beefier, in Marine Corps dress blues, was perched on top of the television set beside a pot of orange plastic flowers held aloft by impossibly green stems.

Eve had seen herself as a beauty before she'd been married and forever lost her snappy figure to her sole pregnancy. During the Second World War she had worked in a factory making eyeglasses for soldiers and sailors. That was where she had met Martin's father, a quiet man sidelined from the army due to flat feet. Milton Fletcher had passed away in 1954.

Eve shifted her legs, the stubble catching against the pink sheeny polyfibered nightgown, and studied the *TV Guide* carefully. She stared at the Big Ben clock on the tray.

"Nine thirty-three! They promised me the cable would be back on before my stories start. Can't trust anybody."

She closed the housecoat over her knees and rubbed the dog's neck somewhat vigorously. After she'd located the remote control on the dinner tray and switched on the television, she watched the static for a few seconds, a deep frown embedded in her face.

"God-dangit, where the hell's those TV people?" she wondered aloud. "I bet I'll just deduct these hours from the bill if they don't get a move on!" she told the dog. She did the applicable math in her head but had a pencil in her hand just in case she needed to figure on paper. It was a talent she had. "Cable's thirty-two a month. Kill the extra dollar and, say, a dollar a day, and at twenty-four hours a dollar that's four cents an hour. Now. From seven-thirty to . . ."

She heard a car door close, then another, and the dog began growling. She scratched under her wig, which sat on her head like a gray turban, with the eraser end of the pencil. Then she stood and carried the barking dog toward the door. The buzzer sounded just as she got there. She had the pencil in her hand in case she needed a weapon. *You never know,* she thought. *Martin says anything can be a weapon.*

"Yes?" she said loudly so the people on the porch might hear her through the storm door.

"Cable trouble, Miss Fletcher?"

She opened the door a crack and looked at the people in matching coveralls standing on the porch and at the white pickup truck with *CABLE VISION* painted on the door. Mr. Puzzle, who could hear the voices, began having a conniption fit. Eve tried to quiet him by gripping his muzzle, and he bit her so hard it broke the skin above the ragged pink nail on her thick trigger finger. The closest one was a woman with her thumbs hooked into her tool belt. Behind her was a thin younger man with round-lensed, gold-frame glasses. There was a cigarette dangling from the girl's lips. Eve managed to get a grip on the dog's mouth and clamp it, whereupon the dog's cheeks inflated. He sounded like a motorboat.

"Pocket hound," the girl said cheerily. "My mama has one of them handheld attack dogs. Gotta get in close to use 'em." She laughed. Eve stared at her, her drawn face announcing that she was not a woman easily amused.

"Miss Fletcher?" the man said.

"Mizzus Fletcher," she corrected. "I'm a widow."

"You reported your cable out?"

"I most certainly did. Last night at eight twenty-one

on that answering machine, and this morning first thing they opened, to the lady that answered. I didn't think you would get to it before my stories. I have to keep up every day. It's Monday, and they leave you in the lurch on Fridays. If you miss Monday, you're just swimmy-headed about what's happening the rest of the week. I hope my bill will show an adjustment for the inconvenience. The money I pay for this is criminal!"

"That so?" the cable woman said, taking over from the man. "Never watch it. We'll need to come in. The trouble is most likely inside. Must be an old hookup."

"Well, I've had cable since seventy-seven. Don't ever watch the first story or you'll be hooked. I like that HBO sometimes, too." Mrs. Fletcher opened the door wide so they could enter. "Go about your business. TV's in the den."

"We'll need to get in the attic," the man said.

"They didn't need to get in the attic when they installed it," she said suspiciously.

"They probably snaked it in from the eaves, but we'll have to look at running new cable. The early cable was coaxial three, and it gets brittle with age. I'll probably have to replace it with this new finer gauge." He held up a piece of fiber-optic line for her inspection. "This stuff lasts forever and doubles your reception quality."

"I can't see the picture too good. But there's nothing wrong with my ears. Door to the attic is in the hallway. Just pull the chain and the stairs come down. Do you adjust color?"

Eve watched as the two checked the cable box on her set, and then the man went out in the hallway and climbed up into the attic with the roll of cable and a silver toolbox. The woman looked at the picture on the wall.

"He's a looker," she said.

"That's my boy, Martin," she said.

"Nice looking," the woman said. "Married?"

"Goodness no!" Eve said. "Hasn't found the right girl."

"What does he do?"

Eve shifted closer and confided, "He was in law enforcement. He's a police consultant to governments and such. He knows lots of very important individuals like you see on the news."

"Where is he these days?"

"How long is this going to take?" Eve asked nervously. She didn't want to discuss her son, what with the communists always trying to get revenge on him and doing things like framing him up and all that.

"Not long. What's the dog's name?"

"Puzzle. I call him Mr. Puzzle."

"Cute."

"Martin named him. He said it was a puzzle how come the breed even survived." She laughed out loud, and her foul breath staggered Sierra. "Why the rattlesnakes and Mexicans didn't eat them all up, he says, is man's greatest puzzle. Martin has a well-developed sense of humor. Gets his personality from my side. We moved in here in fifty-four, and first thing you know Milton's gone across the river. Well, I—"

The man yelled down. "Sierra, I'm gonna have to rewire."

"How long?" Eve asked, feeling the stories were in the pipe somewhere on their way to the TV set from the station, like water heading toward a shower nozzle from a reservoir.

"Half hour to an hour," Sierra said. "I better help him. He's a bit slow unless you work him. You know how men are."

"I should say I do! I had to stay on my Milton day and night."

Sierra slipped into Eve's bedroom and, being as quiet as possible, fired the small nail gun, placing a transmitter in each heel of the four pairs of orthopedic shoes in Eve's closet. Then she sneaked back to the ladder and climbed up so she could look in on her partner's progress.

The attic was one shallow space that ran the length and width of the narrow house, peaking at four feet and sloping to inches at the outside edges. Agent Walter Davidson moved like a snake to avoid hitting his head on the roof beams, and within a half hour he had installed the fiber-optic lenses so the team could view the activity in any room in the house at will from the mobile observation van. The lenses at the end of the cable would have fit into the barrel of a cheap ballpoint pen. Each had been positioned in a corner, up where the walls met the ceiling. Even in the bathroom and hallway. The microphones for each room were so sensitive, they "would pick up a mouse breaking wind between the mattresses," Walter had said. After he finished, he and Sierra climbed down, and she went outside to reconnect the cable to the house. That was easy, since it had been disconnected the night before. Eve's calls to the cable company had been fed to a cellular phone in the step van parked a block away.

As soon as the people had left the house, Eve settled down to watch her first story. Mr. Puzzle, unused to such excitement and physical exertion, fell fast asleep in her lap, the small beast rattling loudly as he exhaled.

Sierra and Walter returned to the long motor home and went into a rear room illuminated by a cluster of nine-inch screens. The German coach was the agency's best-equipped surveillance van. The front of the van looked as if it should be filled with tourists from Iowa. The driver's and passenger's seats fronted a dining area, the kitchen, and a door that would seem to lead to the bed and bathroom. Behind that door there was a large open area that held a network of sophisticated electronics, with two swivel chairs at the console. Beyond that room were four bunk beds, which folded into the wall, and a bathroom, which had a shower head in the wall over the toilet. Water drained down from a large tank on the roof, and electricity was supplied by means of a diesel generator. Agents could remain in the van, in relative comfort, until a job was over, ideally in a few days.

Eve Fletcher's post-office branch was located in a strip mall beside a large grocery store less than a quarter mile from Eve's house. McLean's assortment of federal warrants guaranteed access to mail addressed to three hundred twenty-one Tucker and allowed phone taps for the same address, and entry and search for the house and grounds at Joe McLean's discretion. He even had a pair of warrants signed by a federal judge but not yet filled in as to specifics of the search.

Joe led the young agents through the sorting room to the rear office door. Larry Burrows carried an aluminum case the size of an orange crate, and Joe was lugging a pair of small cases. Stephanie had been given responsibility for the thermos of hot coffee. Joe tapped at the door, which was opened almost immediately by a short, wide man with a stiff toupee set on his head like a beanie. He was dressed in a crumpled seersucker suit, and his shiny black wing-tip loafers looked as wide as they were long. His face seemed too red, his hands trembled slightly, and his breath smelled of fresh peppermint over old bourbon.

"Andy Lustiv," he said as he shook Joe's hand. "Come on in, and Ed'll get you whatever you need here. You have any problems, call my beeper. Day or night."

The postal clerk, a man who looked like a thin Burl Ives, opened an office door for them and handed the inspector a nine-by-eleven-inch manila envelope.

"This is to be delivered to the house tomorrow. Only Ed here is aware that you're working the address. He's a valued employee. His lips are sealed as tight as a frog's asshole, and that's waterproof," Andy said. Ed was a man who had just been threatened into silence and looked it. If he was the sort of man to drop hints at the water fountain, letting his co-workers know he was important enough to be trusted with classified information, he understood that to do so would mean the loss of his job. He was close enough to retirement to hear the fish jumping.

The office was government issue. The Steelcase desk and chair were in matching olive drab. There were two four-drawer file cabinets in olive and a calendar depicting three identical, undoubtedly playful, kittens in and around a basket with several balls of colorful yarn in it. The bulletin board was layered with official announcements. Agent Andy Lustiv might have been in the employ of the Soviet Union rather than the U.S. government.

The nervous clerk left, and Andy leaned against the wall. As soon as the door closed, Larry and Stephanie cleared the desk surface and began unpacking the cases.

"What sort of setup is that?" Andy asked. He gestured at the cases.

"Larry?" Joe said.

"This is a print recovery and identification kit."

Andy looked at Larry, ran the name through his personal filter, and smiled. "It's a Prick!" he laughed. "The initials. P-R-I-K. That's rich! I swear it is."

Stephanie rolled her eyes. Joe smiled. He wouldn't have imagined Andy for a brain that worked so well. Looks could be deceiving.

Larry ignored the remark and said, "It consists of a laser-beam scanner that isolates any body oils. It's from Lawrence Livermore research and development. The print scanner isolates and scans, the fingerprint is digitized and fed into this computer. The computer is armed with a complete set of fingerprints belonging to our subject."

"I'll be dogged," Andy said. "It works?"

"It sure does. One of only four in existence."

"We're field-testing it," Stephanie added as she pulled on a pair of white cotton gloves.

"Mind if I watch?" Andy said.

"No," Joe said. Stephanie cut her eyes toward Larry, who frowned.

Stephanie opened two bottles, and the small room filled with the odor of solvent. She selected a piece of mail and began dabbing the two solvents on the back edge of the envelope. Within seconds the flap popped open.

"I'll be dipped in shit," Andy said. "Dries fast."

"Four to five seconds and doesn't leave a water mark," she said as she slipped out and opened the letter using steel tongs with rubber tips. She placed it on the glass plate of the scanner. Suddenly a copy of the document appeared on the computer screen, and two blue swirls appeared at one edge of the latter. "Folded by hand," Larry said hopefully.

Larry tapped on buttons creating a black border around the individual prints, and the blue swirls grew in size until they filled the screen, one at a time. After a few seconds the words "No Match" appeared at the top of the screen.

"Sheeeit," Larry said.

"Junk mail is usually printed, folded, and stuffed by machines," Stephanie said.

"We know the subject stays in touch with the target. We suspect that the subject is contacting by mail. He's too bright to call her, and she's a shut-in," Joe said.

Andy nodded.

The room was silent as the process was repeated over and over again until all ten pieces of mail had been thoroughly scanned. After each failed to turn up Martin's finger tracks, Andy clucked his disappointment, but he was impressed.

"You boys always get the best toys," he said.

Stephanie began the task of resealing the envelopes. It was a slow process because it was of the utmost importance that none of the seams appeared to have been tampered with. A chemical reanimated the original glue strip, and she closed the envelopes one at a time.

For one and a half hours Andy and Joe leaned against the wall and watched closely. After each envelope was resealed, Larry would look at the seams through a powerful lighted pocket loupe to make sure there were no visible marks left by the tampering.

"What if he—the subject . . . target—already wrote her?" Andy said. "What if she got the letter yesterday? They haven't got a time machine for you to test yet, do they?" Andy said.

Joe laughed. "It's coming. Soon as they get those crashed UFOs figured out."

After they had completed the search, Joe handed Andy the manila envelope and they packed the kits. Andy handed the envelope of cleared mail in turn to Ed, who had fallen asleep in a chair outside in the sorting

room and had to be awakened. Then they filed out into
the alley where the cars waited. Ed stood in the open
door, watching them leave.

Andy paused with his car door open and his arm on
the roof. He spoke over the gleaming expanse of govern-
ment-standard white. "Remember, if we can be of any
assistance, call. Ed'll let you in from now on. Thanks for
showing me your *Prick*!" He laughed loudly and slid into
the Taurus.

"Can I ask what y'all are looking for?" Ed asked
from the doorway.

"Sure you can," Joe said as he and the rookies
climbed into the rental car and rolled away, leaving a
confused-looking postal employee standing in the doorway.

13

Paul was on edge as he paced back and forth smoking cigarettes. The coffee, always in good supply, didn't help calm him. He tried to stay busy and not think about the clock that was ticking away toward October 3. He had selected the final group of seven men from Tod's files, the ones he would use to cover Eve's arrival at her destination and the taking of Martin Fletcher. They would be in the air as soon as Paul figured out where she was going when she left the house in Charlotte. They were all resourceful, proven professionals. When Paul thought about them, he got a mental picture of a pack of lion dogs. And he couldn't help but think about what often happened to such a pack when they were successful and cornered a lion.

He wouldn't need them until Eve flew out, but they were sitting on an air base in east Texas. He had also been on the telephone to the chiefs of police in New Orleans and Charlotte to make sure they would be ready at a moment's notice to sweep in officers to help Thorne's or Joe's teams. The chiefs had no idea who the teams were after, and Paul hadn't let them ask but once. Although he had also been hoping to track Martin from the information he had to sift through, he didn't hold out any real hope that he would be able to work that angle. Martin wasn't big on leaving a trail.

His mind was whirring with logistics and angles, and the conference-room table was covered in a layer of paper, photographs, composites, and manila folders in varying thicknesses. He had also tried to wait at least an hour between calls to Joe and Thorne, but he could usually find a valid reason to call more often than that. The fact that he knew they would call him if anything came up was irrelevant. He decided to lay off, and the only way to do that was to stay busier himself. Otherwise, they would begin to see his calls as intrusive, or worse, decide that he mistrusted their ability to make decisions.

He could see Sherry Lander seated at her desk in the anteroom. He imagined she was worn-out, but she had eagerly agreed to work on his schedule for the next few days. He told her to feel free to stretch out on a couch if she needed rest, but he doubted she would.

He felt more comfortable in the conference room, where he could spread out on the long table's surface, than in Rainey's office. Rainey had been replaced by his assistant agent in charge, a young up-and-comer. Without an office Rainey seemed content to sit in a corner of the conference room and stare out the window or read his Bible or pore over files. He was waiting calmly. He stayed right with Paul; nothing interested him beyond the chase.

Paul told himself he should be moving faster, getting to New Orleans sooner, but he felt overwhelmed by the size of the task. He had work to do here, but wasn't it really work someone else could be doing? He tried not to think about Laura and the kids. He tried to concentrate on keeping the teams sharp while he pulled up the rear.

He knew there was more to his fear than he wanted to admit.

"Sherry," he said, loudly enough to get her attention.

She stood and came into the room.

"Hungry?" he asked.

"No," she said. "I can run out if you are." She smiled patiently. "I really wouldn't mind."

"I'm not," he assured her. "How long since I asked you that?"

She looked at her watch. "Ten minutes?"

"Rainey?"

Rainey shook his head without looking up.

Paul opened a hole in the files on the desk and placed the composites of Ranger Ron and the old doctor across the surface of the table for the tenth or eleventh time in so many hours.

"Could be anyone," he said as he shifted the twelve composites.

Sherry exhaled a bit too loudly but smiled when he looked up.

"They're just children, Paul," Rainey said. "They saw the Smokey the Bear hat, the gun, the mirrored glasses, and the mustache."

"The composites from the Brooms and the kids share a general facial structure, but they don't look anything like Martin looked before the surgery. The eyes might help, but they were covered both times. The face remake in Spain must have been remarkable."

"Extensive enough to make spotting him in airport films all but impossible," Rainey said. "He must have been confident of that."

Sherry made a note on the stenographer's pad, ready to go through the familiar territory as often as he wanted.

"So let's say it's Martin alone. He grabs . . ." Paul stopped, not wanting to mention the death of George Lee. "He leaves the mountains and drives here in three hours. That's pushing it, running at seventy-five or eighty. Taking a chance of being busted for speeding. We should check the speeding tickets issued between here and there at the time he had to be on the interstate."

Sherry scribbled. "How do you know he took the interstate?" she asked.

"No time for him to have taken back roads, and he wasn't driving the Rover, because the vehicle was hot and he's a professional. And the doctor makeup was very complicated. It had to age him and fool the witnesses in daylight. Face-to-face."

"Okay," Sherry agreed. "It took time to apply."

"Right. He would have been rushing all the time."

Rainey rubbed his eyes. He gazed out at the traffic on Broad Street. "If he had been putting on makeup and someone had been driving . . . that would explain it. It's the most likely scenario."

"So I think we should assume Martin had an accomplice until there is proof otherwise." Paul stretched. "Sherry, now, where was the Rover stolen from?" he said.

"Twenty-third just off Hillsboro Road. Sometime after Thursday afternoon. The owners were out of town Thursday night through Monday afternoon," she said.

"Okay, let's check to see if there were any cars in that neighborhood that were towed or reported derelict between then and now. Say a ten-block area from the Hillsboro address. If he came by car alone, that car might still be there. Either he would have parked near there when he stole the car, or he had an accomplice. We've assumed he took a flight out because of the damage at the airport, but maybe he wanted us to assume that. Maybe he doubled back. Why would he trigger a bomb out there? That doesn't make any particular sense. It was a crude bomb, too. Something else to throw us off?"

"Maybe he wanted to make a bold statement?" Sherry offered. Paul looked at her. "Maybe he wanted them to find the Rover at once."

"With the crutches in it," Rainey said.

"Maybe he took a cab from the airport," Sherry said. "When he arrived in town."

"Maybe," Paul said. "But I imagine he was here a good while. It wouldn't be his style not to know the ground and players like the back of his hand. We can't very well check every cab that was at the airport, because we don't have a description of him and we can't be sure when he arrived, or if he even arrived by air." Paul lit a cigarette. "Just to cover the bases, we could check back the night before the killings and see if any cabs ran from the airport to the immediate area near the Rover's address—cabby might be able to give us a description. Long shot, though."

"Course, he could have been disguised," Sherry said. "Maybe he's always disguised."

Paul looked up at her and frowned. There was a lot of effort going into chasing leads that were probably a waste of time and money. "Worth a try."

Rainey cracked his knuckles. "On the accomplice. Would Martin trust anyone else with his true identity? It isn't like Martin to leave a loose end dangling."

"Maybe an accomplice who doesn't know his true identity?" Sherry asked.

"Freelance," Paul said. "Possible, but not likely. Hired people are iffy, and they can be made to talk. Money doesn't buy the sort of loyalty Martin would need. Martin's accomplice is someone he knows he can trust. Someone he has a history with, or who is terrified of something Martin can do."

"To him or the accomplice's own family, maybe," Sherry added.

"This is nuts," Rainey said, suddenly agitated. "We should be in Charlotte. Or New Orleans. His mother will lead us to him, or he'll move on Laura and . . . we'll be sitting here with our thumbs jammed up our butts." He looked at Sherry and blushed. "Tails."

"Maybe we should call it a night and get a start early in the morning," Paul said.

Rainey stood and stretched.

Sherry went into the other room. She was packing her purse when Rainey passed through and lifted a hand in salute. She turned and looked at Paul, who was opening another file. She knew he'd be there in the morning in the same clothes after having catnapped on the couch. He had so much to lose—or to prove. She wasn't sure yet. He was a driven man, but who could blame him? Even in the midst of the unbelievable activity he generated, he was all alone, wrestling with unimaginable demons. She felt silly worrying about a man she hardly knew, a man who would be no more than a memory in a few short days. She found herself wishing she could offer him something, some comfort. But that wasn't her job.

She put the notepad aside. Fatigue was blurring her vision.

"Good night, Mr. Masterson," she called as she lifted her purse.

She decided he hadn't heard her.

14

THE MARTIN FLETCHER WHO SAT ALONE IN A BOURBON STREET strip club, nursing a drink, was nothing like the cocky lad with ears like open car doors. That young man was long gone. A lot of the old Martin had been incinerated in an oven behind a clinic in Madrid along with the blood-soaked sponges, disposable dressings, and slivers of bone and tissue. Martin Fletcher's old face had been erased, and an artist in a bloody white smock had designed him a new one that bore no resemblance to its predecessor. Only three things about Martin were unchanged: he had the same mother, the same fingerprints, and exactly the same dark thoughts.

He hadn't altered his fingerprints because he didn't plan to be fingerprinted. Ever. Altered prints would send an immediate alarm through the system. Because of his many identities it was doubtful that he would ever be placed in jail long enough to have his prints run. If he

was apprehended while committing a murder or selling a
bomb or anything of like seriousness, he would kill to
escape or he would die. Let them try. Martin Fletcher
was not of a mind to be caged ever again, period. In any
case there was no real resemblance between the man who
sat at the small table in Big Daddy's Strip Club and the
man who had escaped from prison.

Martin looked around and was comforted that there
were so few people in the place. The girl on stage, a thin
redhead with the slightest hint of a pooch belly, was
dancing to an old rock-and-roll number. Her bare breasts
were medium-sized, and the nipples were almost certainly accented with rouge. She did her steps and moves
on a stage that was an island in the center of the space.
The bar circled the stage and in effect acted as a moat to
separate the performers from the customers. The forty
tables were scattered about in a horseshoe around the
bar. The music was loud and had the scratchy quality of
a poor recording robbed from vinyl disks. The girl might
have been standing behind a cosmetics counter somewhere for all the emotion she was showing.

Martin Fletcher shifted in his chair, conscious of the
padded clothes that hid his well-maintained muscles. He
had always loved disguises, a holdover from his days of
playing masquerade to entertain himself. Halloween had
been his favorite. As a child he'd spent months preparing
for the holiday. The old Martin Fletcher had been five
foot ten, but lifts could make the new Martin six feet tall
in a second. Often Martin walked with a limp aided by
the difference in height of the soles of his shoes. Sometimes he carried a small knife, the blade filmed with a
potassium cyanide grease. Any cut, no matter how small,
would bring unconsciousness and death in seconds. Martin Fletcher was an intimate of death. He had looked at it
from angles most people could never imagine possible.

Martin's perfect white teeth could be covered by one
of several prosthetic sets he owned—from rotten and broken to discolored and overlapping. He owned contact
lenses in four colors and a dozen different wigs and fa-
cial-hair rigs. He had a suitcase full of stage makeup and

latex for molding complex masks. Everything in the kit was strictly first-class, Hollywood quality.

During the months he had studied Joe McLean's family, he had been Alex Potter, a traveling salesman who wore Brooks Brothers suits, drove a Lexus, lived in a condominium three blocks from Joe McLean's home, and listened to classical music.

In Deerfield Beach, while he had stalked the Greers, he had endured country music, lived three months in a narrow house trailer, and driven a Jeep Cherokee with a great circle of the bronze-colored paint peeling off the hood. He had made friends with her new husband, a witless cop, and had had a few meals with them. He had started an affair with her easily because her cop was not much in bed. He could have killed them any way he chose. He liked the idea of water, and drowning her and her son had turned out to be a breeze. After the woman and child were down, he had moved on to Nashville.

In Nashville, during the time he had studied Rainey Lee's family, he had worked for an alarm company as a salesman-technician and had spent almost a year designing alarm systems. As Wendell Jackson of ADC, he had met with Doris Lee and, under the guise of trying to sell her an updated alarm system, had gotten a look at her existing security and had been able to plant the bugs in the bedroom.

Martin Fletcher was worth three and a half million dollars. That was enough money to live out his life in comfort. He had a million dollars invested in Latin institutions, two million in Spain, and a half million spread around in hiding holes. There was also a hundred thousand and change his mother was holding for him. He had enough to last him if he lived to be seventy, though he doubted he would ever get close to that age.

Death was no big deal to Martin Fletcher, because old age held no attraction. He believed that he could survive in any world beyond this one, and the closer that world was to the classical image of hell, the better he figured he would do.

Martin ate healthy foods, drank fruit juices, and exercised for three hours every other day. On the off days he ran, often through the woods, staying off the beaten path. He did that so that if he ever had to escape through unfamiliar territory, he could move like a scared rabbit, depending on his reflexes to get him over logs or whatever. It was reflexes and timing that mattered in all things, especially in killing.

Martin took amphetamines to maintain his edge, and like a cat, he never slept the same hours two days in a row, nor for more than two or three hours at a time. He spent the majority of his waking hours staying ahead of the people he knew had been hunting him, knew because he had outsmarted them.

He was haunted by the fact that his mother was his one missing piece of armor plating—and if the right bowman caught sight of the spot, a single well-aimed arrow would finish him. And he knew that they knew. He was, however, confident that he had devised a plan that no one could anticipate. He had sworn to her that he would see her at least once a year, and he never broke a vow.

"Promise, Marty? Each year until I'm dead?" she'd pleaded.

"I promise, Mother," he'd replied. "I swear it. Until you are dead and gone."

He had maintained a relationship with some of the cocaine-cartel honchos, and it had always been good for some traveling cash for a hit here, a bomb delivered there, or information he could buy and resell. Martin had been able to make a few hundred thousand a year on contract hits alone. He kept twenty to thirty thousand in ready cash for emergencies, but he used a lot of money. Too much.

Now so much was happening at once. Perez, a man who had made use of his services for two decades, was double-crossing him. Martin understood what the cartel thought—that he was on the run and in hiding and could be put off. Martin believed that the deal he was owed for had been negotiated in good faith and the Colombian had reneged. It wasn't the money, though he wanted it.

He could not allow anyone to stiff him, or he was through. The money, which was to have been delivered to a numbered account, hadn't arrived. Lallo Estevez, the cartel's American-based money collector, who moved cocaine funds through his network of companies, had been making excuses over the telephone. Martin had to let other potential clients know that business was business and collections had to be made. Normally he would have killed the Colombian in his jungle hideout to make the point, but he couldn't exactly run all over Central America beating the foliage, and the debtors knew it.

Lallo had always been a friend to him, having smuggled him into Spain with forged papers. Things change. Martin planned to see Lallo face-to-face and try to reason with him.

Martin's thought train was derailed by a loud voice a few tables away, where three men, probably tourists from some place like Ohio, were whooping it up. The dancer, the bored-looking girl with jaws that worked chewing gum to the beat of the music, seemed not to notice the catcalls. Martin watched as a large, muscle-jammed man, almost certainly the bouncer, stepped over to the table and spoke to the men sternly. One of the men handed the bouncer a bill that had been rolled into a small cylinder and patted him on his back as he unrolled it and tucked it into his pocket. As soon as the bouncer was out of sight, the men began making even more noise.

Martin might have finished the drink and left quietly, but the amphetamines had his teeth clenched, and something about the men at the table a few yards away made him angry, sickened him. Not overtly angry—quietly angry. It was a smoldering resentment that seemed almost comfortable to Martin. He needed to do something. Not that he minded that the girl on the stage was being used as a verbal punching bag by these men. Not that they were making lewd suggestions or that they were drunk. The thing that angered him was the fact that they thought their money was a shield. These were men who used their wallets to insulate themselves from their surroundings. They were slumming and felt they could do whatever they chose here. Martin realized that these men were looking down their noses at the girl, the bouncer, the surroundings, and at him. One of the men glanced at Martin and dismissed him with his porcine, intoxicated eyes. Martin was the man seated alone by the wall, dressed in a leisure suit and worn cowboy boots, with hair reminiscent of Elvis. A tourist disguise he had worn all day to wander the French Quarter.

"Father, forgive them, for they know not what they do," he said to himself as he stood and made a show of finishing his drink and placing the glass on the table. He staggered a bit as he passed the men's table, and as he lost his balance, he bumped the table, sending the drinking glasses horizontal and the contents cascading over the table's surface and waterfalling into a man's lap. The men stood as one, their faces reflecting horror that would give way to anger. Martin staggered again and fell into the largest of the men, then righted himself, apologized, and as the man cursed him loudly, made uncertainly for the door.

"You *Hee Haw* motherfucker," the man called after him. "You dress like a goddamn pimp."

The other two laughed.

At the door Martin turned to see the men taking over another table and raising their hands to get a fresh round.

Martin smiled as the man he had bumped into made a face of alarm, started to stand, and then fell over onto the floor and went into violent convulsions as his friends moved to offer aid. As he watched, Martin carefully slid the small knife from the sleeve of his jacket and put it back into the holster under his right armpit. He was satisfied that the man hadn't even noticed the scratch of the blade in the excitement of the moment, the chill of the cold drink. Martin wasn't a man easily impressed, but he was always impressed by the speed of the toxin that coated the tip of his blade.

Martin stepped out into the bright sunlight and slipped on his large sunglasses. Then he strode off down the street, cheerfully whistling a Patsy Cline standard.

15

Laura Masterson liked the adolescent German shepherd, Wolf. She had let Reid present the animal to Reb for his birthday. Even though he was hardly more than a puppy, he made her feel more secure, lying there on the floor of the ballroom while she painted. He lay with his face between his overlarge paws, watching her work as though he could judge the results. Big brown eyes and pointed ears that stood, when he listened, like raised wings.

Laura had started the day by getting Reb ready for school. It would be easier to herd ferrets through a chicken ranch than to get Reb to do anything. He had the annoying habit of becoming sidetracked. You could leave the room with him pulling on his pants and return thirty minutes later to find him drawing with his pants still half-on. Plus, he hadn't looked well lately; in fact, he looked frail. She hoped it was just another phase, like bed-wetting. He ate so little. The doctor had said that he would eat what his body needed, so she wasn't going to worry yet. No, he'd said, it is not an eating disorder, it's a growth spurt readying itself for a go.

She thought about Paul as she painted. She remembered how handsome he had been and how she had fallen in love with him and decided she was going to marry him before they had spoken their first words. It was in a psychology class at Tulane. He had taken a seat two rows from her. He had traded looks with her—they had engaged in a game of eyeball cat and mouse for two weeks. She would turn to sneak a peek at him, and he would turn away as soon as she did, so that their eyes rarely met. It had been painfully obvious that he was shy and so was she. Finally he had stopped in the hallway to pick up the books she had dropped in front of his feet.

"You dropped these," he had said as he'd handed them back to her. She had handed him a paper and said, "I believe this is yours." Then she had turned and walked away, knowing he was watching her. She had been praying that he couldn't see how red her face was.

The note that she had agonized over for days had said: "So, are you going to ask me out, or am I going to have to swallow my pride and ask you out? Laura Hillary, 382-6677."

He had called that night and asked her father if he could speak to her.

"Laura?" he'd said, as if he had never heard of the girl he'd raised. "So who is this—Paul Masterson? You calling from Mount Olympus with all the other gods?"

"*Daddy!*" she'd yelled. She'd laughed but was embarrassed.

Then the old man had handed her the telephone. "Paul?" she'd said. "Excuse my father. He's insane but utterly harmless, as far as we can tell."

"So. I was just calling to see if you want to maybe go to a movie Saturday night?"

"A movie?"

"Yeah. Or dinner, if you'd rather."

"A movie would be good. Which one?"

"You could pick it," he'd said. "I like everything."

"There's a German film at the Prytania."

"A German film. I don't speak German."

"It's subtitled in English."

"I was making a joke," he'd said.

She'd laughed. "I see. Or we could see something in English."

"The German thing sounds fine. We'll see what you want. I'll pick a restaurant."

"Well, I'm not much for foreign films," she'd said. "I was just trying to impress you, actually."

"Really?"

"Yeah. If we are going to have a relationship, I think we should start by being honest."

"A relationship. That would be good."

"So I'll make a deal with you. Always level with me. Don't tell white lies to make me feel better, because I hate that. If you have a date with someone else, just say so, and if it isn't going to work, I mean, if the chemistry is wrong, tell me, and let's not get all deep into something that one of us will be hurt over."

"Okay," he'd said. "I'll do it if you will. No games."

And there hadn't been any games. They had married when the term had ended. After the first date they had been inseparable. He had kissed her on the second date, and they had made love on the fourth in her bed while her parents were out of town. It had been the first time for both of them, and neither could imagine wanting anything but each other. They had honeymooned in the cabin he owned in Clark's Reward, Montana. They had planned to have children as soon as they could afford it and then decided that they would never be in that position and had Erin anyway. Then they had made Reb and planned to have at least one more. But before they could, Paul had been shot.

The bullet that had passed through Paul's eye had killed them both. The doctors had assured her that the problem could be repaired. But he had changed. He just wasn't the same person after he was shot. His career was over because he'd willed it over. One more successful bust, and he would have been appointed the deputy director of the DEA. But the shooting sucked his ambition.

His injury had given him epilepsy and blinded him in the right eye by destroying the socket. The operations had been painful, and he'd suffered unimaginably. Another operation and he would have looked close to normal, down to a smooth patch of skin where the horseshoe-shaped scar was. But he had refused, though as far as she could see, he'd had no reason to. The worst was behind him.

After the accident he wouldn't talk to a psychiatrist. He would stay alone in his room for weeks at a time. He had bathed irregularly, didn't speak, and avoided his children. Erin had been terrified of him, as much because of his fits of rage as because of the disfigurement. He would go off like a pipe bomb at the slightest problem, throwing things through walls or smashing the television set with a crutch. It had been frightening for all of them. Then there had been the night when things had come to a head in the bedroom, and they had had a terrible fight. She had said some things she shouldn't have said.

The following day Laura had returned home to discover that Paul had packed a few things and was gone. He didn't even leave a note. She had followed him to Montana, but he wouldn't talk to her. She had sat on the cabin's porch begging and pleading and then yelling at him for hours. But he had refused to acknowledge her presence. He didn't even look out the window. *"Well, then, screw you!"*

She had gone home to Arlington, packed, and moved back to New Orleans. No matter how busy she stayed, her heart ached and ached.

Laura looked down at Wolf. He was sound asleep on his side, his feet jerking—dreaming of chasing or being pursued. She looked at her watch. It was two-thirty. She had been painting since seven that morning. She turned off the radio, which was tuned to a classical station, and the dog rolled to his feet and yawned.

"The silence wake you up, Wolf?"

He padded over to her and nudged her leg for a rub.

She scratched behind his ears, and his rear leg started scratching at his side but the claws were hitting the floor.

"Oh, no, Wolf, you'll ruin the floor," she said.

She went to the front door and out on the porch to see if the mail had arrived, but it hadn't. She looked down the street but saw no suspicious vehicles.

Reid was in New York at a sales meeting. All morning Wolf had kept Laura in sight. When she had gone to check the mail, he had accompanied her, and while she had studied the street, he had sniffed the air and marked the bushes and beds in front of the porch with his scent.

Thirty minutes before Reb's classes were dismissed, Laura piled Wolf into the car and headed to his school. She parked on the street two blocks away and watched the line of buses. Just before the children poured out, she saw a red Volvo pull up across the street from the bus yard and stop.

She wished she had thought to bring her binoculars. After ten minutes the bell rang, and a few minutes later the children lined up outside for the buses. When the buses pulled out, Laura watched the car. As Reb's bus passed the car, it made a U-turn and shadowed the bus. Laura followed the car and, being careful to keep a few vehicles between them, dialed a number on her mobile phone, calling Allen White, the policeman she had spoken to the evening before.

"Allen, it's Laura. The car, a red Volvo sedan, is following the bus."

"Just trail behind. Don't let them see you. I'll be waiting," Allen's voice coached.

When the bus stopped to let Reb out, the red car pulled over against the curb almost directly in front of Alice Walters's house. It stopped under the canopy of a live oak that covered the sidewalk. Laura angled in behind a VW van, stopping a half block behind the car. She stepped out and pulled a smiling Wolf to the grass. He stayed close enough to her side that there was slack in the leash. After watching Reb inside the gate she walked toward the Volvo. A lone figure turned the far corner and was jogging toward the red sedan.

NOPD detective Allen White was dressed in a gray sweat suit, and as he drew even with the automobile, he slowed, then bent in a motion that made it look as though he were going to tie his shoe. He knelt, pulled a pistol from an ankle holster, and aimed his gun at the head of the driver. Laura moved toward the car with Wolf beside her, his ears erect. She could hear what Allen was saying.

"Okay, pal, just keep the hands on the wheel where I can see them."

Wolf turned and barked, and Laura was aware of armed men running down Alice's drive, toward the car, with their pistols aimed at the detective. Allen White turned his head for a split second toward the driveway, and the Volvo's driver disarmed him and was out of the car in a second. The air was filled with the sound of running feet and loud voices.

"Freeze, DEA!" someone yelled.

"Lose the piece!"

"Gun on the ground! Now!" an armed man yelled. "Do it now!"

After the shock started wearing off, Laura realized that there was something very familiar about the man who was walking down the driveway from the back of Alice's house.

"He's a policeman, Thorne," Laura yelled. "Pull them back."

"Hello, Laura," Thorne said, smiling at her. He waved a hand, and the men stepped back from the prone detective.

"Why in the hell was he tailing Reb, Thorne?" Laura demanded, pointing at Woody Poole.

The agents replaced their automatics in their holsters, and Allen stood. The agent from the car reached down and handed him back his Chief, butt first. "What the hell's going on here?" the young detective asked as he replaced the pistol in the ankle holster and dropped the right leg of his sweat pants to cover it.

Thorne turned to Allen White. "Sorry. We're running a protective surveillance on Laura and her children."

"On me?" she asked. "What for, Thorne?"

"We're all DEA." Thorne pointed down the street at a car that had just parked behind Laura's. An agent in casual clothes stepped from the car and moved to the group on the street. "He was following you, but you—"

"I lost you in traffic," the man finished.

Laura stared at the agent without speaking to him. She turned to Allen White. "I'm so sorry, Allen, I had no idea."

"Don't mention it," the detective said. "I'm glad it was good guys."

"Don't be so sure," Laura quipped. "Good guys don't spy on citizens who're minding their own business. And calling it protective surveillance doesn't make it so. I want some answers really fast, Thorne. If Paul put you up to spying on us . . ."

"I'll explain everything later." Thorne looked at the detective as he spoke.

"I'm down the street if you need me, Laura," Allen said as he turned and walked away.

"I'll make coffee," Laura offered, but her eyes were flashing with anger. "And you can explain all this, Thorne Greer."

The two local agents went back into Alice's house. Laura tossed her car keys to Woody. "You with the reflexes . . . make yourself useful. Put my car in the garage and come in through the kitchen door, if you can find it."

Woody turned his hard eyes on Laura, smiled for a split second, and nodded.

Thorne and Laura crossed the street behind Wolf. As they neared the gate, Wolf barked excitedly. Laura looked up to see Erin turn the corner and come running up with a backpack hanging from a shoulder. There was a can of Mace locked in her grip.

"Mama, there's a man following me!"

Sean Merrin turned the corner. He seemed more embarrassed at being discovered than pained for the chemical he had captured in his eyes.

"Never mind, Sean," Thorne said. "Looks like we're all blown."

"Erin, this is Thorne Greer. I don't know the man you've just Maced."

"Agent Merrin," Thorne said. "Sean Merrin."

"She turned a corner and I followed and she was waiting behind a tree." Sean's eyes were red, and he was sweating.

"I friggin' Maced your short ass," Erin said proudly.

Sean nodded sadly.

"You should wear a uniform if you're gonna follow people around in this town."

"They're friends of your father's," Laura said.

"What are they doing scaring people? Shouldn't they be busting drug dealers or something?"

"We're headed in for coffee," Laura said. "Agent Merrin, join us inside and we'll run some water over your eyes."

Erin pointed her finger at Sean. "And you owe me a can of this," she said, handing him the empty can of Mace. "It was eight dollars at K and B." Then she added, "I was hoping it'd work better, though."

"Let's let the men run through the house for a moment," Thorne said. He spoke into his radio, and an agent appeared from Alice's house with a small black case and disappeared into Laura's front door.

After the agent had allowed them in from the porch, Laura made a pot of coffee while the three agents and two children watched from the counter. Sean held a wet cloth to his eyes, but he wasn't damaged much beyond the humiliation.

"Reb, Erin," she started, "this is Thorne Greer. He's a DEA agent who . . ." She thought for a second. "Wait a minute, didn't you retire? Weren't you bodyguarding some actor?"

"Arnold Murphy for the last three years."

"Really?" Erin said. "You know Arnie Murphy? Jesus H. Christ!"

"Erin!" Laura snapped.

"What does he need bodyguards for?" Reb wondered. "He's tough as rubber snakes."

Thorne smiled. "Not in real life. He's as scared as anybody else. People are always wanting to see how tough he really is." He looked at Laura. "The entire Green Team has been recommissioned."

"Not . . . Paul, too?"

Thorne nodded.

"My daddy?" Erin said, disbelief cracking her voice. "He's in the DEA again? Where is he?"

Reb leaned against the counter. "He couldn't do that. He never leaves his place in Montana. He's got brain problems and stuff."

Thorne smiled at Reb. "Just this one time," he said. "Temporary assignment."

"Why?" Reb asked. "How come?"

"Because there is a very, very mean person who is hurting people. Your father has agreed to help find him because we can't do it without him."

"The man who shot him?" Reb asked.

Laura straightened. "Reb, the men who shot your father were . . ." She was reluctant to say "were killed" because Thorne and Joe McLean were among the ones who had killed them. "Darling, Thorne was there. Tell him, Thorne. Tell him why that's impossible."

"Actually, Laura, he's right. Reb, it's not the men who shot your father, it's the man who told them to."

"See," Erin said. "You don't have any idea. You were tiny. You don't even remember Daddy's being in the hospital."

Laura turned her back on the agent so her children wouldn't see the panic in her eyes. *We are in danger.*

"Is my daddy coming here?" Reb asked, the excitement rising to his eyes.

"Is he?" Erin echoed. "Mother, is Daddy coming?" The excitement was contagious.

"We'll see. . . . I don't know. . . . Thorne?" Laura said. In light of what she had run into in Montana, the idea of Paul's walking through the door of her house seemed no more likely than Wolf's being invited to sing at the Met. "You kids have homework to do," she said. "First, Erin, clean the leaves out of the pool."

"I want to hear—" Erin started.

Laura's voice cut her off, startling the agents. "The leaves, Erin! Reb, you help her. We can talk about all this later!" The kids didn't argue. Laura was on the edge, and they knew better than to press.

Laura and Thorne watched them leave. She poured them another cup of coffee and led Thorne to her studio. He sat at the table that held Laura's paints and brushes and stared at the paintings on the wall.

"Nice work," Thorne said. "Is that Paul?"

"I've only got a few minutes." She crossed her arms and leaned against the window frame. "Why don't you cut the crap and tell me exactly what's going on. Who're we in danger from?"

Thorne began with the deaths of his divorced wife and their son. Then he told her about Joe's family. By the time he told her about what had happened to the Lees, she was crying.

"Who? You said the man who set Paul up?" she asked.

"Martin Fletcher," he said.

"Martin Fletcher! You people haven't found him yet?"

"He's back in the country."

"Oh, dear God," she said. "So did Paul send you?"

"Not initially. The local DEA has been watching the house for two weeks since the Lee hits. The infrared sensors and the laser listening post went up a week ago. Paul only came in a few days ago. He opened the doors in D.C. to allow us to . . . work the case."

" 'Us' as in you and . . ."

"Rainey and Joe."

"The very people he has sinned against. That seems a little unusual, Thorne."

He averted his eyes.

"And you're watching us from Alice's house?"

"She gave us permission. She's extending her vacation a couple of days to accommodate us. We needed to be close. We thought you might be bugged."

"Am I?"

"Not anymore."

"How do you know?"

"My man got them all."

"Bugs? Martin was in here? He was sneaking around in *this* house?" She covered her mouth for a few seconds, her eyes saucers of horror.

Thorne shifted his weight. "Martin knew all about our families' personal schedules. He planned George Lee's hit to the point of intercepting him on a scout trip in the Smokies. He knew where the boys were going to be and when; he was waiting on the trail in a uniform. If he had followed the car with George in it, he couldn't have been ready with a uniform. He had to have scouted the trail. It was smooth . . . excuse the term. Somehow he got their confidence . . . the targets never knew what hit them. Course, none of them knew Martin. He had to have had bugs in the house to know what he had to have known."

"Why didn't you warn us?" Her eyes were cold, accusatory.

"It was for your own good."

"Our own good? We're bait!" Laura was suddenly angry. "You're waving my family in front of that psychopath!"

"No. Well, actually, I suppose that's one interpretation."

"One interpretation? What's another?"

"You weren't in any danger. We've been monitoring the house. We've been listening to every . . ." He stopped, realizing what he had said.

"You have your own bugs in my *house*?" Laura was horrified. "You just swept to see if he did, too? You have a court order?"

"No. We use laser devices aimed at the windows. Like drumheads, windows."

"This is America, Thorne. We have rights just like everyone else out there. So the government will let people exact revenge on killers and tap the lives of innocent people to further those aims, and it's okay? Because Paul can pull a few strings?"

"Our devices are strictly to monitor for any unusual activity or panic situations, lasers, cameras watching the perimeters. We aren't taping except for the loop, which is two hours. Then it records over the last . . . it's a . . . loop." He realized that he was spinning his finger in a circle and stopped.

She seemed to calm. "How well can you hear what's going on in here?"

"I'd rather not say."

"I want to know to what extent . . . my family is being protected."

"Well, when it's quiet, we can pick up your brush strokes. We know Reid snores and there's a bird that whistles and something that squeaks like a hamster running in a wheel that needs oiling."

Laura blushed and put her hand to her mouth. "My God, Thorne! My bedroom?"

"The devices pick up the entire house."

"But he was listening to us? What did you find?"

"Several functioning transmitters. Two in the kitchen area, one in the phone and another in the light fixture, one here in the studio and two in the bedroom, one in the telephone again. The telephone devices pick up whatever is going on in the rooms. We weren't able to locate the receiver. Could be anywhere."

"Why in the receiver *and* the base?" she asked.

"Redundancy, maybe. Different kinds of transmitters."

"Martin Fletcher has been in my house?" Fear silenced her for a moment; then her anger came surging back. "Christ, I feel like I was raped once and then raped again by the cops when they showed up. I must be the most watched woman in America."

"Well, you're clean now," he said. "He'll know we found them when he checks the listening post."

"Great," she said. "So Paul's out. Where is he now?"

"He's heading this investigation. He's on the ninth

floor of the U.S. Courthouse building annex in Nashville. The DEA has offices with the federal prosecuting attorney. He's using Rainey's office."

"I didn't think anything short of dynamite could blast him out of his hole," she said, aware of the bitterness that filled her words.

"He's really changed," Thorne said. "He's not the same man. I suppose I shouldn't be surprised. After what happened and all."

"He didn't want me to know, did he?"

Thorne looked down. "Laura, it's . . ."

"Of course he didn't."

"He only agreed to come out when he knew you and those children were in danger. That was the only reason. He cares."

"Oh, I know how much he cares. Enough to send people to protect us . . . but not enough to actually visit his children. Enough to use us to lure Martin."

"That isn't fair, Laura."

"Do you know that he hasn't laid eyes on Reb or Erin in all these years, except for the photos I send? I don't care for myself. Really, I don't. But he has hurt those children. He was never around when they were little. Always chasing a drug lord or flying raids in Bolivia or someplace. We never saw him. Then he ran out on us completely. He didn't even try. So, fine. But I'm not going to let that son of a bitch tell me what to do. Don't tell me he cares—don't you *ever* tell me he cares about us. This is about him. All of you are using us. Fine, there's nothing I can do. But I don't have to like it. If it weren't for the kids, I'd take my chances with Martin Fletcher. At least Martin Fletcher is honest. He says he wants to hurt us, but Paul says he wants to protect us. Only trouble is he's the one who has hurt us."

"That isn't true."

"What do you mean?"

"I shouldn't be telling you this, but he's . . . the local agents say that he asks them to check on you every so often and report to him."

"When? When was the last time?"

"Reb had his school play last year—they took pictures of the thing and sent the prints to Paul."

"Why?"

"I'd guess he wanted to make sure you're all okay. Laura, when we first saw him in the mountains, he was like a wounded animal, defeated, frightened. But you should have seen him in Nashville. He was like the old Paul. In charge, surefooted—he seemed strong as a bull."

"Thorne, I can't tell you how sorry I am to hear about your family. I wish I had kept in closer touch. And Doris Lee and I were friends once. I've never been good about staying in touch with anyone, especially Paul's friends. You know how it is. People take sides or feel disloyal somehow."

She looked at Thorne and seemed to be figuring something out, weighing her words. "Promise me something?"

"If I can."

"Tell him I want to see him face-to-face. I need to have some closure so I can get on with my life. If he doesn't want to see the children, I'll understand, even though they won't. He has devastated Erin and Reb by hiding from them. It's plain rejection to them. I told them it's because of his face, the incident, and the brain damage, but now that they know he's back, all that is changed. No. On second thought he has to see them. He has to let us say good-bye so we can go on. I can't give Reid what he needs until I know Paul doesn't want it. I owe him that." *After what I did.*

"I'll try. You know Paul."

"Try hard."

16

"THE CAR THING'S A WASH," SHERRY SAID AS SHE PLACED A FOLDER on the conference-room table. She drummed her nails on the table surface for emphasis. "No abandoned or towed cars near where the Rover was taken. No speeding tickets we can connect. Nothing on surveillance tapes of outgoing air travelers we can connect."

Paul opened the report cover and grazed over the information. "So he probably had an assistant," Paul said. "You did a thorough job, Sherry." He smiled at her, memorizing details about her the way he committed a favorite view to memory. She was a beautiful woman, and more intelligent than he had figured at first. Not that brains and beauty couldn't reside in the same place. Laura had proved they did.

Paul had studied the surveillance pictures from the Nashville airport's cameras until they had become teasingly familiar, yet he hadn't seen anyone who looked like a newer model of Martin based on the old Martin Fletcher frame. It was an impossible task, though. Paul's mind had wandered as he'd scanned the shots for something familiar, waiting for a bell to ring.

"Martin's game on Martin's turf in Martin's time," Paul said out loud.

"Vengeance is mine thinketh Martin," Rainey said.

"Why leave the opening for you to thwart him? Why didn't he get Laura and the kids sooner?" Sherry asked. "The challenge?"

"I'm afraid he is saving the best for last," Paul said.

"Why don't you . . . I mean, why did you decide to stay here instead of being in New Orleans?" she asked.

"I've got a good team in New Orleans. They'll know what to do if Martin comes."

"Sure, but what I was really asking—wouldn't you rather be there? In New Orleans?"

Paul noticed Rainey turn to look at him, waiting to hear what Paul would say.

"Look, we need to try to get a description of Martin, hopefully to track him from where he was last seen. Maybe we'll narrow the variables somehow. I'm better off doing that here. Also, Martin believes he's superior to the rest of us. He'll want his final action to gain him maximum satisfaction. He wants to kill . . ." Paul stopped for a second and took a deep breath. "Unless our intelligence and mental profiles are way off, he'll want to kill the family while I'm on the scene. We know he'll meet his mother somewhere around the third of October to get his mind retwisted, or whatever the visits do for him, and go for the family after, when he thinks we aren't paying attention. So it's imperative we get him with Eve."

Paul thought about the A team, his carefully selected hunting team sitting at an East Texas air base, anxiously waiting for a direction to run in. Freelancers, and expensive ones at that. T. C. Robertson had agreed that he needed men like that to meet Martin. He hadn't quibbled about costs.

"There's no room for error," Paul added, more to himself than to her.

"I see," she said. And she did. Paul's family was meant to lure Martin Fletcher to strike, and Paul wasn't ready yet. The question was, Would he ever be?

Rainey turned away.

Paul thought about Martin's plan. Or plans, more likely; he'd have alternatives. He had had years to think and rethink his options. There was a trigger, and Paul wanted to keep from hitting it as long as he could. Being in Nashville was a way of playing for time. Maybe it was futile. Was he fooling himself? Was he wasting his time? Was he just afraid to get closer to the action, to Martin or the family?

Paul had never been consciously self-analytical until he had taken to the cabin. He knew now that he had suffered an emotional breakdown, a collapse of his self-esteem, a loss of his sense of place in the universe. His emotions, the strings that held his being together, were not something he had needed to, or cared to, inspect in the years before the Miami incident. Everything had just seemed to fall into place for him. He couldn't recall ever having asked himself what made him the way he was. Then he had become haunted by himself, a stranger.

After the accident he had felt overpowered with the darkness of guilt. For the first time in his life he had failed others and himself. He had been plagued with self-doubt until his fears finally spiraled out of control. As he had explored his own depths, he had been consumed by the thought that he was less than others thought he was; that he was just an illusion, a man behind a curtain, playing a wizard. No one else, not even his wife, had been allowed to have a naked look-see inside him. It was more than the fact that he had never been able to vocalize his inner feelings. Laura had said he sold himself short. Maybe, maybe not.

Laura. The name was a powerful emotional wedge. He had been in love only once in his life, and if he had had the ability to open up to her, maybe it all would have been different. Maybe he could have told her what he felt after he was shot and she would have helped him deal with his demons. Or maybe not, for he had been raised in a world of people who didn't touch each other much physically nor open up emotionally. So much was left unsaid or hinted at rather than attacked from the front. His role was to be strong, to shield his family from the unpleasant realities he saw every day in the world. Now he had to live with the fact that his weakness had put Laura and his children in the worst sort of peril. He had never loved her more than at this moment, had never missed her more. And she had never been further away.

He refocused on Sherry, took in Rainey.

"Martin had an accomplice in the mountains, so I assume he or she was supposed to check on the kids—follow the van. Martin was in place when the scouts got to the rock, and the parents didn't see him come out at the upper parking area. Maybe one of the kids saw someone else. It is a fairly isolated area, isn't it?"

"Very," Rainey said.

"We need to go see the kids ourselves," he said. "Contact the parents of the Cub Scouts who were in the van with George. We'll need to interview those few again. Rainey?"

"I can do that," Rainey said.

"Get on it. You want Sherry to help you?"

"I can handle it," he said.

Paul watched Sherry as she wrote. A shaft of sunlight bisected her, illuminated her left side. She was like a delicate porcelain doll with jet-black hair that cascaded to her shoulders, and red lips that looked as if they had been painted on by a Japanese artisan. He felt himself becoming aroused as he watched her. He thought about the way she was always staring at him when his face was turned away from her. It didn't just happen every once in a while, but with great regularity, and it made him nervous. He was a freak, and he couldn't imagine a woman like her finding him anything but repulsive. It made him uncomfortable and was distracting, and he would have asked for another secretary, but time was growing short—Martin's birthday was a few days off. Then there was the other thing. She was a thinker, a self-starter, and he was growing to appreciate her abilities. So what if she stared at him?

He had been impressed with how efficiently she had put together the report on the car search in a very short time. The report had covered all the bases Paul had wanted covered, and a few he hadn't thought of. A cab driver had picked up a fare at the airport and dropped him within two blocks of the house where the Rover was stolen, but he thought the passenger had been a one-armed man with white hair. Probably in his fifties. Paul thought the missing arm might well be a misdirection device, like the crutches. Paul wondered how Martin Fletcher had known the Rover would not be missed for the two days he had needed it. That was one of the loose ends that might never be tied up. "Sherry, where are we with the Rover info?"

Rainey stood. "I'll call the parents and set up interviews."

Sherry didn't move until after Rainey had closed the door. Then she looked out the window and turned and sat on the edge of the table.

"Something on your mind?" Paul asked.

"He's better," she said. "It's good he's getting to work on this. Gives him something to occupy his mind. It's all he can think about anyhow."

"We're all thinking about the one thing."

"It's different. Because Rainey is totally obsessed and channeling every thought toward the end of this, stopping Martin Fletcher. I don't think he sees *anything* beyond that. I think Joe and Thorne lost people they loved and they want revenge, but what Martin did to them is in the past, and they see a future after next week."

Paul nodded his agreement.

"How long have you been with Rainey?" he asked.

"A month before Eleanor . . . you know. I took the job out of school until I could find a job in my field. But I'm getting hooked on the atmosphere. The excitement. Think he'll ever be the same?"

Paul shrugged. "What's your field?"

"Anthropology," she said.

"That's interesting."

"That's why I studied it. Forensics and social science rolled into one."

"No, I meant it's interesting that you studied it. You don't look like an anthropologist."

"Oh?" She smiled. "Not the Margaret Mead type, you mean."

Paul searched his memory for a picture of Margaret Mead and remembered a small woman in gold-rimmed glasses seated behind a desk cluttered with tribal masks and other African artifacts. "Not at all."

Sherry was flipping through the file folders on the table, searching for the information on the Rover's owner. "Well, my father is a biologist. Teaches at Memphis State. I hate slimy things, but I've always liked antiques and trying to put puzzles together. Finding out how people did things before they could do them the way we do. And learning by finding clues—a pot here, a utensil there, something you have to identify, then figure out how it was used. And all the pieces of the puzzle put together tell a story about things that happened in the past."

Paul was pleased to discover this previously unknown side of Sherry. "Did you know Rainey's family well?"

"I just saw George once and Doris twice. George was a sweet kid. Bright eyes. Would have been handsome and tall, like Rainey. They were all very close, you know. He was a good father, worshiped his family. I never met Eleanor, but I understand they were all very happy before Martin Fletcher."

I wasn't, Paul thought. *I was in limbo.*

Sherry found the name and number of the vehicle's owner and dialed it.

"Mr. Theodore Reardon owned the Land Rover," she told him after she had hung up the phone. "He won a free trip from Discover card to Epcot."

"A fraud."

"Some man called and told him he had won a five-thousand-dollar prize. The cash was credited to Reardon's Discover card, and airplane tickets were delivered." She arched her eyebrows. "Four first-class tickets delivered overnight express. He had to take the trip during those four days."

"Sounds like Martin made sure he'd have those wheels ready and waiting."

"Seems a lot of trouble to go to for a car."

"No trouble for Martin," Paul said. "Planning is just part of the game. Another layer for us to have to unravel, waste time on. Obviously he studied the Reardons, and there may be no reason at all for the selection. Knew the guy had kids, knew he could take the vacation when Martin said he had to. Reardon is likely the sort of man who would win a prize and not look a gift horse in the mouth. Martin sent a five-thousand-dollar payment to Discover in Reardon's name, bought some tickets, and sent them. He probably knew Reardon, but Reardon almost certainly didn't know him. We're not going to play his game, chase this ball into the thicket of how he did what. We can't waste time looking back at his techniques. Fact is he's moving forward, we have to do the same thing. At some point either we pull even and pass him or . . ." *We bury my family.*

Rainey rushed in, an angry expression on his face. Paul looked at him questioningly; then he turned to Sherry and dismissed her with a nod.

"I spoke to Ed Buchanan. Timothy Buchanan—George's best friend—was there that day. His parents don't want him disturbed further."

"Where's Timothy's composite?" Paul asked as he opened that file and flipped pages. "I don't remember seeing it."

"It seems nobody had Timothy do a composite. His parents said he didn't see the man. The Buchanans are . . . they have big money. And they're acting really funny. Might be they don't believe we can protect the kid."

"Was he with George on the way up?"

"Yes. In the van and by his side from the lower lot until—"

"Then we get a court order and bring him in."

"I'll drop over and reason with Buchanan," Rainey said. "Court orders take time, and Buchanan could tie it up if he has warning."

"Okay, Rainey. You do it your way. But do it."

17

Reb stood at the hall mirror, appraising himself. He looked around to make sure neither Erin nor his mother was watching, and then he did a few muscle poses. He imagined a crowd being driven wild by the rippling of his pectoral and biceps muscles. Reb knew he was thin, but in the mirror he could be a well-oiled weight lifter with steellike tissue, a rock-and-roll superstar with a flowing mane of hair, or a movie star. Wolf sat and smiled at him as he posed. Reb was allergic to Wolf, and his nose ran some and his head was often stuffy, but a stuffy head was a small enough price to pay for such good and devoted company.

As Reb stared at his own face, he tried to formulate a picture of his father chasing bad guys around the country. He knew from photographs what his father had looked like before he'd been shot through the eye, but he couldn't imagine him with his eye out and a big hunk of his skull blown off. In his mind his father's eye socket was a black hole, and the side of his skull was open to the elements, with the brains visible like the anatomical illustration in his encyclopedia. Now he was trying to turn that image into one of a superhero who had covered his brains with bulletproof Plexiglas. It was hard to imagine a man whose brains were open to the air being taken seriously by bad guys.

Adam Masterson had no complete memories of life with his father. What he had were bits and snatches of dreamlike memory. He could imagine being on the shoulders of a man, feeling safe and protected, being lifted into strong arms, the sandpaperlike surface of a warm cheek, the smell of cologne or flowers . . . the feel of something like soft flannel against his face. And there was the phantom voice he heard in his dreams. The voice of someone who cared.

Reb didn't know exactly why the agents were guarding them and the house, but knowing they were there was nice and comforting, and it was sort of like starring in a movie. He liked the younger agents, Sean and Woody, but the older man bothered him a little because the man knew them and he didn't know the man, whose eyes were like leftover coals in the grill. He thought he might want to be an agent like Woody and Sean, to have a gun and to protect people, as they did. *One thing*, he thought, *nobody at school is gonna mess with me.*

Reb looked into the mirror and imagined himself walking down the halls with Woody on one side and Sean on the other, waving the other kids out of his way and maybe shooting a few bad guys who sprang in through the classroom windows. Maybe the agents would be wounded and he would have to use one of their big guns to save them. And he would be on television and get medals for bravery.

Reb sat on the bottom step and rubbed Wolf. Biscuit called from the kitchen, "Kiss pretty bird."

Wolf turned his head, erected his ears and barked.

"Don't encourage him," Reb said.

• • •

Erin sat on the floor of her bedroom amid a scattering of photographs. She was illuminated by a slanting shaft of sunlight as she stared at a picture of her father walking across the yard with her, a toddler, seated on his shoulders. Paul Masterson's arms were crossed, pinning her tiny legs against his chest for balance—her arms were cinched around his neck. It was a pre-Reb day in Washington, and the cherry-blossom trees were in full bloom behind them. She wished she could remember that day. Of course, her mother had taken the picture. She wondered what Laura had been wearing as she'd snapped the shutter. Was there a picnic lunch just out of the frame? It must have smelled wonderful, crisp and sunny as it had been.

Erin had been crying as she went through the album, but she all but had it out of her system now. She had remembered Mr. Greer from before, and it was comforting to see him but strangely disturbing at the same time. She could picture him with her father, standing at the grill in the yard, turning hamburgers. Sipping golden liquid from glasses and laughing. She had memories of Reb as a baby and her father's patience with him—with both of them. She had loved Arlington; looking back, it seemed to her those days had all been warm and positive. She thought back to the way news of the shooting had sent Laura into shock. Erin recalled how frightened she had been when her mother had explained what was happening. She had stayed with a baby-sitter while her mother went to Miami for several weeks to be with her father.

She had stood at the door as her mother had readied herself to go with the agency driver to the waiting jet.

"I'll call as soon as I get to Miami." The word "Miami" had terrified the nine-year-old. *Daddy went to Miami and look what happened.*

"Will he die?"

"They say he'll be fine. In time. His head is hurt, but they're going to make it all better."

"Honor bright?"

"Honor bright." Her mother had crossed her heart.

"If your father can get well and come back to us, he will. That I can promise."

When her father came home, though, everything was different. She thought about how he flew into rages—how angry he seemed to be all the time. She would never forget how his left hand seemed stuck at the end of his limp arm, trembling, all but useless. She would always wonder whether he would have stayed if she hadn't been so terribly scared of him. She felt guilty and she missed him. She missed having his arms around her, missed him tickling her, tossing her to the bed and walking with her feet on top of his. Now he was out there, just when she had finally begun to accept his sitting in his cabin in the mountains. *If he isn't there alone and isolated anymore, why isn't he here? If he wants to protect us, where is he?*

Erin told herself that she didn't care that he was disfigured, and she told herself that she had never cared. But if her mother's presence, when her friends were around, embarrassed her, she could imagine how the sight of her father would have made her feel. She hated herself for the thought. Now she was out of that phase. *Now . . .* she thought. *I could handle it now.* Or could she? *God, Erin, you're such a shit!*

Laura had told her that Paul had left because he wasn't right in the head from the wound. Erin had believed that; she had wanted to believe it. Now he was out there and evidently he was together enough to work a case. *His brain couldn't be too screwed up,* she reasoned.

Her parents had had a fight the night before he'd left, and she remembered the policemen coming and her mother begging her father to calm down. And she remembered that her mother had had a bruise on her chin, or maybe she had imagined that part. The policemen's faces had made her feel very frightened. They looked as if they wanted to hurt her father.

Erin believed she would see him again. *Someday he'll understand,* she told herself. *And he'll come back and love us again.* And maybe she believed it . . . a little.

18

Rainey was taking Halcion at night because if he didn't, he dreamed dark, haunting dreams. He dreamed of his family, and each time he dreamed of them, he woke up screaming, drenched in sweat. He had decided it was far better to close his eyes as he lay down on the bed and then open them to a new day than go through such hell. It was bad enough to live with it through the days.

And then there was Paul Masterson. He slept just fine for someone who had brought the man from hell down on them. Rainey knew that Martin was crazy, but Martin would be fixated on other enemies had Paul not put him away. Could it be that the injuries Martin's gunners had given Paul might be sufficient to allow him relief from further vengeance? A worthless left hand, one eye, a permanent limp? *Not hardly*.

Paul should have killed Martin, Rainey thought, or at least gone along with letting the DEA do it. But Paul

had refused for reasons of his own. Perhaps he simply
hadn't had the courage. It was cowardly to let the law
handle it—put Martin in jail. As if a jail might hold the
man! *Fuck!* When Rainey allowed his mind to run this
trail, it became dark, and he was truly haunted, enraged
that Paul was alive while his own family wasn't. He
would trade Paul's troubles for his own in a heartbeat, he
decided. Even given the pains Paul had suffered, he was
the luckiest man alive. Such tormenting thoughts made
Rainey have to fight to keep from seeing Paul and Martin
in the same light.

He thought a great deal about the message he had
received the night after Doris and George's funeral. He
had been staying in a motel room because he'd had no
intention of sleeping in an empty house. Two of his
agents had insisted on guarding his room. That night he
had let the agency's real doctor give him a shot, but sleep
was slow in coming. Before he'd dozed off, the Episcopal
minister who had performed the funeral service had
talked the agents into allowing him into the room, and
he'd tried to talk to Rainey about God's plan. Rainey had
known the minister meant well, but he had exploded.
"Fuckin' get out before I kill you!" he'd railed at the
frightened man in the collar. "No God who lets a madman slaughter my wife and children is worth talking
about! *Get out!*" Then he had grabbed up the minister
and thrown him into the hallway, where he'd hit the opposite wall and landed on all fours. The two agents
standing there outside the door had been shocked beyond words, seemingly frozen in midthought like depart-
ment-store mannequins. The minister had cowered,
covering his face with the sleeve of his coat.

"No more visitors," he had said matter-of-factly. Inside he'd been boiling, but at the height of his rage he
would, as often as not, calm outwardly even as the tem-
perature inside him soared. Had he been armed, he
might well have emptied the gun into the preacher.

The minister had not returned, nor had the guards
tried to gain entrance. Rainey had taken the Bible, which
the preacher had dropped onto the bed, and hurled it

against the wall. "Give me back my family, God. Or leave me alone!" he had yelled. Then, remembering how much religion, and that poor minister, had meant to Doris, he had cried himself to sleep.

Later, after sleep had enveloped him, he had distinctly heard Doris calling, and he had awakened from the first sleep since the night before George and Doris had died. Doris had been standing beside the motel room's bed in her gown, and she'd been crying luminous tears.

"Rainey. I can't find them," she had said. "Where are our babies?"

Rainey had felt a great conflict of emotions. Fear was not among them. He had held out his arms and Doris had slipped into them, and the great void of emptiness had been lifted from his heart and he had wept tears of joy. He had felt her moist face against his chest, and he had tried to console her by rubbing her hair. "It'll be all right, baby," he'd said through the free-flowing tears. "You'll see, we'll find them. We'll get them back."

She had cried. "There's nothing out there, Rainey. Nothing but voices in the dark. Rainey, I'm so afraid and it's so cold."

"We just have to keep looking. Want me to come with you?"

"Rainey. The voices say that none of us can be together until the circle is closed."

"Until what? I don't understand."

"The book will tell you," she'd said. "Please, I need my babies."

Then she was gone, and his arms had closed around nothing. She had been there, he had smelled her perfume, her breath had been warm against his chest. He was wide-awake and had not imagined it. It had been as real as anything he had ever experienced.

He had turned on the light, and the Bible had been opened on the floor. He had slid from the bed and crawled to the book. He'd touched it, and it had been hot as a coal. He'd withdrawn his hand and then touched it again. Pages had turned slowly and then stopped at a place where the minister had drawn a box about a series of lines. Numbers 35:18–19. Rainey's blood had frozen as he'd read.

". . . the murderer shall be put to death. The avenger of blood, when he meets the murderer of his own, shall put him to death."

It was God's judgment. There was no forgiveness for Rainey, nor would his family's souls be joined, until Martin was dead.

And while Rainey had studied the Bible, he'd had another verse stick in his mind. It had dealt with Paul's allowing a man like Martin to live with a hate burning inside him. A hate that would have to come back a thousand times stronger and blacker when it fermented.

Exodus 22:6.

"When fire breaks out and catches in thorns so that the stacked grain or the standing grain or the neighboring field is consumed, he who kindled the original fire must pay for the damage."

19

The cougar stood contemplating Paul, her big brown eyes locked on his. Then she sprang, leaping easily over his head and hitting the steep trail ten feet behind him. Paul turned and watched her lope off, disappearing into a wall of thick mist. He didn't feel fear; he was instead filled with an overwhelming sense of sadness and loss.

Paul awoke disoriented and encased in that sadness. He lay frozen in the hotel room's bed until reality set in. It was after four A.M. according to his Rolex, and even though he had been asleep for only three hours he knew he wouldn't be going back to sleep. He climbed out of bed and sat naked in the chair nearby while he thought. The weight of the past few days and the days ahead were overwhelming him.

Paul stood up and looked at his body, which was lit by the small amount of light that found its way in from the street through the sheers.

What if I fail? The answer was easy. *If I fail, they will die. If I am wrong on any assumption, misjudge one piece of evidence, or misinterpret any action by this lunatic, they will die as surely as the sun will rise tomorrow. Martin doesn't care about anything except punishing me. I can't ever lose track of that. This is only about Martin and me. The rest, including Thorne's, Joe's, and Rainey's dead families, is all window dressing.*

Paul was plagued by doubt. He knew he was too far from the action, but he was afraid to move closer for now. He wished he knew if it was fear of his family's rejection, of their judgment, or fear that he would fail because he wasn't up to the task. He hadn't had one night's uninterrupted sleep since he had left the mountain.

He even worried that he was not as worried as he should be, or not about the right things. For instance, he didn't want to face a decision on Rainey's mental state, in particular his ability to make judgments—his grasp on reality. It was entirely possible that Rainey's mind was a deep and dark place filled with twisting serpents. Sometimes Paul saw things reflected in Rainey's eyes that alarmed him. A shallowness to them, a lack of emotion that didn't make sense; he had to be boiling inside. And he was turning into something of a religious fanatic, reading the Bible constantly. On the other hand, he rarely mentioned what he was reading. What was the man thinking?

Problems demanded decisions, and he hoped he was making them as fast as he needed to. He didn't feel the conviction that he had found so natural before the Miami incident. Oddly, no one seemed to notice what a mess he was inside. Maybe the mask was holding up, or maybe that just spoke volumes about other people's needs.

The man in the mirror held his attention as the light and shadow acted in concert to take his body back six years. The diffused light softened and hid the scars; the light defined the bulk, outlined the body. His face, the right side deep in shadow, appeared normal. But he knew that if he turned on the lamp, he would see the mutilated stranger he had faced every day for six years. *Martin did this to me.* He knew that he should blame Martin for what he had lost, but he didn't. He had thought he hated the man. He had spent a lot of the past six years brooding over Martin. But no matter how he tried, he did not hate Martin. Despite everything the man had done, what he felt was more pity than hatred.

Paul remembered dreaming of the cougar. He had been climbing up the side of a mountain and had come face-to-face with her. He should have been afraid but wasn't. Awake, he knew where the dream had come from. As a boy of eight or ten, Paul had accompanied Aaron and a hunting party of some neighbors who had set out to kill a marauding lion who threatened their livestock. The female cougar, though fatally wounded by a rifle bullet, had gotten away but then had turned and moved slowly back down a rock face to meet the pack of baying dogs that had been trailing her. She had managed to seriously maul two of the fierce dogs, but the relentlessly circling pack had proved too much for the weakened lioness. The dogs had had her down before the hunters had arrived and fired a bullet into her head, stilling her. Later the men, who were trying to understand her return down the rock face, had discovered that she had made her stand between the hunters' dogs and her den. The dogs had found the den, and the men would have let the animals kill her twin cubs except that Paul had raised such a fuss, the lion hunters had spared them. Aaron and Paul had turned them over to the game warden a few days later. Paul had never discovered their fate.

Paul's subconscious had conjured up the big cat. An Indian, having the same dream, might have thought the cat was a spirit guide appearing to give him warning or to show him the way to a victory over an adversary. Paul supposed that, figuratively speaking, he was the cat standing between his own den and the dogs—Martin Fletcher.

He moved to the window, parted the curtains, and looked out at the traffic on the street. He lit a cigarette, inhaled deeply, and stood there in the dark waiting for the first inkling of daylight that would put him one sunrise closer to Martin Fletcher.

20

Reid Dietrich arrived in Laura's driveway a few minutes after midnight. He opened the garage door with the remote as he approached the back of Laura's house from the alley. The door rolled open, the light came on, and he entered, closing the gate behind his Jaguar. He parked it beside Laura's Jeep and locked it.

He didn't switch on the light but instead used his penlight as he passed a wall where there was a workbench. He moved a piece of plywood, slid a short pile of bricks out from the wall, and pulled out a pair of tape recorders that were joined together. He popped them open, removed the tapes, and put them in his pocket. He reloaded the recorders and dropped the tapes into a compartment in the flight bag.

Then he walked through the rear gate to the kitchen door carrying his flight bag. He set the case down and tried to insert his key in the lock, but it wouldn't fit.

Upon inspection he saw that the lock was newly installed and looked far more substantial than the other one. He stepped back from the door and looked at the key, then peered around the corner of the house to the windows of the ballroom studio. The lights were on, so Laura was working. He went to the first window and rapped at the glass with a key.

"Laura, it's me!" he yelled at the ghostlike shape that appeared on the other side of the sheer curtains covering the glass. Laura opened them and looked out, and when she saw him, her face lit up. "Reid, come around," she yelled, and pointed toward the front of the house. "Front door."

She opened the kitchen to him standing there holding his suitcase in one hand and his suit coat in the other. She kissed him and pulled him inside.

"Key didn't work. Just wanted to check in before I head home."

"The locks were changed," she said.

He walked into the kitchen and poured himself half a glass of red wine and sipped it. "That's better," he said. "I'd imagine it would take a very skilled burglar to pick the old one, wouldn't you? You weren't trying to give me a message, were you?"

"I've got a lot to tell you."

Wolf ran down the stairs and jumped up on Reid. "Okay, boy. Down." Reid pushed him to the floor. His tail ticked off the measure of his excitement.

"So I'm listening," he said as he poured another half glass.

"The DEA found out the house was bugged. They got two in this room. Five in all. In the phones and in the lights."

The glass fell out of his hand and shattered against the marble countertop. Wine ran across and cascaded off, dripping onto the floor. He grabbed a towel, and Laura joined him in the cleanup.

"You mean they're listening to us right now?" he said after she told him everything she knew.

"Yes," she said.

"Even in the bedroom?"

She reached over to his ear and whispered. "Not the bathroom. Especially with the water running."

"That's something, I guess," he whispered. "I hope I can," he added. "I've never performed for an audience. And they found two listening devices in this room?"

She nodded. "And one in the studio. They're going to try to find the receiver but don't want to draw attention to their presence by searching wholesale. Besides, it might be anywhere. I'll make it up to you."

"Don't be silly. The important thing is that you're all safe. A little inconvenience is a small price to pay for that."

Reid was seated on a bar stool. She put her arms around his neck and kissed him softly. "Sorry I shocked you with the news."

"Thank God they didn't jump out of the bushes with their guns drawn. I might have ruined a perfectly good pair of pants. Cops make me nervous. I know it's irrational, but—guns and all that."

"They know you already. They've been watching us since the first of September."

"How did the kids take all the excitement?"

"The agents don't show themselves. We know they're there and the house is covered. I really hadn't thought about it all day. Remind me to give you a new key. So how was your trip?"

"Nothing compared to yours. I looked at a lot of new equipment and listened to a lot of boring discussions about digital imaging and other tiresome claptrap."

"I wasn't expecting you back until tomorrow."

"Early flight out. No reason to stay."

"You look tired."

"A shower would fix me right up." He raised his eyebrows and smiled suggestively. "But I don't have the energy. I should go over to my place. I have some paperwork to do and my plants to water."

"Another time?" she said.

"No problem," he said, kissing her. "You want me to sleep over—to protect you with my life?"

"No. I'm perfectly safe," she said, smiling. "There's heavy firepower two seconds away."

"Yes, I imagine you're safe as milk. So I'll stay."

She giggled. "Fine. Water your plants tomorrow. I'd like company."

"I'll just get that shower," he said, picking up his bags.

She hooked her arm under his and they went up together.

21

LATER LAURA TRIED TO SLEEP. HAVING THE PROTECTIVE RING around the outside and Wolf in the house should have made her feel perfectly safe, but it didn't. She wasn't just afraid Martin Fletcher would get them if he put his mind to it—she was dead certain he would. Her instinct said run and hide. But Martin would find them, and he might find them when they were alone. Besides, how long could they hide from a man like that, who was driven by hate and a thirst for revenge? It was far better to wait here and pray Thorne was as good as Paul had always said he was. She stood and checked in the closet for her gun and found it in an old purse where it had been for five years. Paul had given it to her fourteen or fifteen years earlier. For protection. She was relieved that it was loaded. She didn't know what had happened to the box of bullets he had given her. She had fired the weapon once. One shot at a can. Paul had fired the other four rounds. Then he had cleaned it, and she had never picked it up again except to transfer it from one closet to another each time they moved.

Martin Fletcher was a terrifying man. She remembered the first time she had met him at a DEA function. Something about him had felt wrong. The way he had kissed her hand when Paul had introduced her to Martin. Something lecherous in the smile—a flatness in his eyes. He had stared at her all evening, and the stare had put ice in her blood. She tensed as she remembered the meeting in the DEA parking lot in Arlington two weeks or so after that party. She had been sitting in her car near the front door at DEA headquarters reading a novel. It had been a beautiful day, and the car window had been down. She had felt a hand on her face, initially thought it was Paul, but she had been startled to find Martin Fletcher leaning against the side of the vehicle smiling in at her. Leering.

"You want to take up where we left off the other night? I presume you've been thinking about me. What I could give you?"

"You presume completely wrong," she had snapped.

He had reached in and gripped her upper leg where the shorts were cuffed. He had pushed his fingers up her leg and into the crease in her panties. She had recoiled but was belted into her seat. "Laura, let me tell you something. I would give this little pussy the fucking of its life, and you'd have to keep bringing it back for more. In fact, you'd leave that faggot you're married to and follow me around on your hands and knees."

She hadn't been able to budge his hand no matter how she tried. She'd tried to slap him, but he'd caught her hand in midswing and kissed it, pressing his wet tongue between her fingers. Then he had turned and laughed—a laugh she would never forget. It had taken her ten minutes to stop crying.

She had never mentioned the incident to Paul because she feared the consequences to him. Paul wasn't a physical person, and this Martin Fletcher was. A few months later Martin had been arrested, tried, and sentenced to federal prison.

Martin Fletcher had said at the trial that he had been

framed by Paul and his team. He was even more dangerous than she had imagined. Eight innocent people. Children and wives. The thought of waking up looking into
those cold, dead eyes honestly terrified her. Just the idea
of violence made her ill. How could she fight him? He was
a monster.

She climbed out of bed, put on an old cotton button-
down that had been Paul's. The tail covered her almost to
the knees. She rolled up the sleeves and went downstairs,
with Wolf close at her heels. She had a lot of work to do to
get ready for the German show. She had assured the gallery twenty large paintings, and only sixteen were completed. She would have to work on four at one time to
meet the deadline.

Lily had insisted on bringing potential clients into the
studio to visit and see the work in progress, but Laura had
refused, saying the visits would intrude on her concentration. That was before she had federal agents in the trees,
ears taking in every conversation in the house, Paul off the
mountain, and the constant fear of Martin Fletcher running free. She turned on the studio lights and studied the
three paintings that were hanging on the work-in-progress
wall. She was amazed at how much better they seemed to
be. Maybe the pressure would work to her advantage, she
thought to herself. Wolf dropped to the floor by the table,
then seemed to remember something, got up, and went
ambling down the hall toward the kitchen. The sounds of
his lapping at his bowl of water filtered down the hall.

Laura sat on her stool and began mixing a flesh tone
on the pallet. She was planning to work on the canvas on
which she had sketched a woman standing at the edge of
a cliff, wrapped mummylike in barbed wire. The skin between the strands was protruding in fleshy pink bands.
She began painting in the skin between the strands of
wire. It was a self-portrait.

As she painted, she tried to lose herself in memories
so she could dredge up intense moments from her past.
That was easy. She simply tried to remember the last full
day and night she had spent with Paul.

22

Lallo Estevez was sound asleep. He was normally a heavy sleeper, but the gentle chirping of his personal cellular phone, tucked beneath his pillow, awakened him as a shotgun blast fired over the bed might have awakened another man. His wife, unaware, was lying flat on her back with her head aimed at the ceiling, snoring loudly beside him. Her eyes were covered with a white blindfold trimmed with burgundy lace, and her face shone from a coating of moisturizing cream. There were clear wax plugs in her ears to insure uninterrupted sleep. Lallo opened the telephone and put it to his ear.

"Yes?" he said, trying to sound alert.

"This is Spivey. Your office. Now. Alone."

"Now?"

"Well, take twenty minutes."

●　　●　　●

Lallo tossed the covers back and stepped into his room-sized closet. He dressed hurriedly, brushed his silver hair carefully, and put on his overcoat. He opened a drawer and removed a small automatic. He contemplated the handgun, started to slip it into his waistband, and then decided not to. If Spivey or any of his CIA dark-operations pros wanted to kill him, the gun would be useless.

Lallo slipped on his dark topcoat and went out to the garage. He opened the door to his wife's Mercedes wagon, climbed inside, and was about to close the door when the overhead fluorescent went dead and a man moved toward the car with a flashlight pointed at Lallo's eyes. He caught the door before Lallo could close it. Lallo looked up, then winced. The man's face was hidden behind the light, and he didn't try to look. To see the face, whether it belonged to friend or foe, could be dangerous.

"Mr. Estevez. Nice to see you again."

"Mr. Spivey," Lallo answered. "A surprise."

"Why didn't you tell me that Fletcher had contacted you?"

"I was . . . I haven't had time. . . . Tomorrow I . . ." Lallo realized that his hands were trembling.

"Then he has. When?"

Lallo could hear the smile in the man's voice and cursed himself for not contacting Spivey as he had been instructed—warned. *He tricked me. He didn't know!* "Today," he lied. "Earlier this evening. He called in saying that he was someone else, but I recognized his voice."

"You were supposed to call me."

"I got sidetracked."

"The meeting—when?"

"He wants the money that's owed to him. See, you people will get me killed yet."

"We hoped he'd want the debt settled. So I do know what I'm talking about, after all."

"Holding back the money I owed him was dangerous. He might have gone to Perez, who had already paid it to me. Then what do you imagine would have happened to me? My intestines would be on the carpeting. Perez pays me and I do not pay Martin . . . either of them could kill me. I am lucky he called me. He could just as easily have appeared in my bedroom." Lallo knew it wasn't the money that Fletcher measured, but the apparent disrespect that holding the money back represented. Martin's ego would be his downfall. Lallo knew that Martin had paid the doctor in Spain a fortune for the face alteration and had then killed the man after he had banked the cash. Lallo would have killed him before he'd paid him. That would have been a prudent business maneuver.

"Look, Lallo. You like doing business in this country? You don't want to end up out of our favor, do you? Be out of favor and into Marion or Fort Leavenworth for enough years so you'd be over one hundred when you got out. We don't want that, do we?"

"You don't know this man like I do. Martin is like a viper. He might not bite this time, but the next time he might, or the time after."

"When do you meet him?"

"Tomorrow night. Eleven P.M. at my pier. Beside the *Vasquez*, which is presently at the dock to unload."

"Meet with him. We have someone to go along with you. Ramon Chavez. You know him."

"Ramon?" He shrugged, wrinkling his brow, remembering the fierce Indian. "A good man. But, between us, he makes me very uneasy." Lallo crossed himself. Lallo had made use of Ramon to cover meetings and to instill a healthy fear in his business associates. That had been years before. He was aware that Ramon had left the cartel and had gone freelance. Only a man of remarkable talent could make a career move like that and not be killed by his ex-bosses. Ramon would not turn on his employers, because he had a large family to think of.

"Ramon remembers and likes you. We asked him to come up for a visit. He'll take care of this problem. Also, our best marksman will be watching from the roof."

"I am sure Martin knows Ramon. Martin . . . what if he sees Ramon?" Lallo was starting to panic at the thought of being in a cross-fire situation. Ramon was indeed a terrifying sight. A stony-eyed Indian with a deeply pocked, pie-shaped face and muscles a bull would envy.

"It won't matter. We will end this problem. As soon as Martin shows himself, get him to the car, open the car door, and step back. Between my two men there'll be nothing left to chance."

George Spivey made it sound as though facing Martin on the dock would be no more dangerous than a walk in Jackson Square at high noon. Even given Martin's demise, it was always possible that Spivey might decide to bury everything in one big hole. In that case . . . what could he do anyway? Nada.

"You know I am not used to this sort of—"

The man outside the car put a hand on Lallo's shoulder and applied too much pressure, the way a schoolyard bully would—measured for discomfort but not pain. A promise. "And for a bonus you get to keep the money you shorted him. No one will know Martin is gone but us."

"What about the police? They could hear the rifle."

"There will be no noise and no police. Just make sure you step out of the way after you open the door."

"*Sí.*" Lallo shook his head. *Bullets have no eyes.*

"Lallo, when all is said and done, Martin Fletcher is just another nickel-and-dime cleaner gone off the deep end. He's been lucky, that's all. Besides"—he patted the man's cheek—"he's an old man now."

Lallo shook his head. "And you are young. Never underestimate your elders and the experience that comes only to those who live to see the next sunrise. This old man has been evading you people for, what, five years? You should have sent experienced men to kill him in the jungle when you had the chance. Not boys."

There was no answer. The man who called himself George Spivey was gone. How George Spivey had got the information he had on Lallo was a question Lallo could not fathom. He was a professional. A cold man. Surely he was working for the CIA. Maybe freelance; there didn't appear to be any red tape wrapping Spivey. He was officially tied in, at any rate. How long would these *federales* keep making Lallo do their will? Maybe it would continue until they killed him themselves, or leaked word to the cartel that Lallo was playing games on the wrong side.

Lallo stepped from the car and went back into the house. But there was no question of trying to sleep, so Lallo used his key to let himself into the maid's bedroom off the kitchen, where he could lose himself in her soft, fragrant embrace until morning.

George Spivey sat in his car, opened his cellular phone, and hooked a small black box onto the telephone's mouthpiece to scramble his voice. He dialed a number in New Orleans that was a relay extension and sent the signal to some receiver in a location unknown to Spivey. The man who answered the telephone spoke in a flat, monotonous drone.

"Nature Center," he said.

"It's Terrence," George Spivey said. "We're about to tag the purple martin. The Amazonian parrot should be migrating north immediately."

"I have that," the voice answered. "Another thing."

"I'm listening."

"That one-eyed eagle from up in the mountains?"

"Yeah, I know the one."

"He's no longer on the endangered-species list. He's out of his nest in the sanctuary, and it seems he's circling the farm."

"I know."

"If he flies over the henhouse, he's fair game."

"If he interferes?"

"As long as he flies, an eagle's a threat."

"So he's not protected."

"The checkbook wants him brought down."

"Under what circumstances?"

"If there is a clean shot."

"That wasn't part of the arrangement. The deal was to tag the martin."

"There's a new grant that should cover the additional fieldwork. The deposit is already in your account."

"That's a go."

"Happy hunting, Terrence."

George Spivey ended the call and unhooked the box from the telephone.

He thought about Paul Masterson. It was a shame he had decided to get involved, but so went the world. Things were never easy. He made a note to check with the bank in Switzerland. Just to make sure. He understood that this was all in the interests of national security, but he wasn't an employee with a retirement plan. He was a nice guy, but he'd be damned if he'd do Masterson for nothing, national-security risk or not.

23

Stephanie thought that time was against the mail search's success. After the first night Andy Lustiv started delivering Eve's mail to the van so they wouldn't have to show up at the post office during office hours. She placed Eve's mail on the table and began by opening a gas bill and running the scanner over it. A few partials, no matches. She looked at Larry Burrows, who was yawning, a midafternoon slump. She took the next piece, an envelope with a condominium-development return address, and placed it onto the scanner plate. There were several prints, but none of them Martin's. She opened the envelope, and on the cover of the enclosed brochure she isolated three good prints. As she rubbed her eyes, the computer beeped, and when she looked up, there was a message on the screen. Her heart felt as if it had stopped beating, her throat closed.

Martin Fletcher . . . Left index . . . Left middle . . . Left thumb.

"Bingo!" she shouted.

Larry straightened up and turned his gaze onto the screen.

"I'll get McLean," he said.

"No, I'll tell Joe McLean," she said. "This is one announcement I want to make personally."

So what does this say? Where's the message?" Joe checked each of the faces in the van's radio-control room. He was holding a photocopy of the condo brochure and asking a rhetorical question for the tenth time. "We need to figure this out, people. We have to make sure we don't miss anything. Anything." He had just got off the telephone, having told Paul they had struck pay dirt on the prints.

Sierra was keeping an eye on the screen, which showed Eve sitting in her chair, clipping her toenails, and watching television. "Maybe he's going to meet her in Colorado?" she said. "I mean, really meet her there."

"Too obvious," Joe said.

"It's a code for another destination," Stephanie said. "Given the level of paranoia Martin Fletcher exhibits, I'd imagine there's a system of messages they worked out in advance."

Joe nodded. He seemed to be really listening to Stephanie for a change. "That's a fair assumption. Whatever the message, we have to stay with her from the second she leaves the house. She's lost every tail she's ever had on her. Maybe they weren't trying very hard, but if we lose her, it won't be due to lack of effort or manpower. Look at her, for Christ's sake, she can't be that smart. He plans all her moves. The lost tails were flawless. I imagine he set down the location last time they met. I'm sure the brochure just means it's a go."

Stephanie hated the way he had taken her thoughts as his own. Or maybe he had thought it all out before. It made sense. "We keep watching the Eve Fletcher show. And if it looks like she's going to get away from us, we grab her and hope Martin moves to take her back from us. He'll be close by, watching when she gets to her destination."

Walter said, "This surveillance is like bad BBC in freeze-frame. The most exciting thing that happens is when she gets her bowels to turn over."

Joe spoke without turning his head. "Stephanie, check all the travel agencies and airlines on the off chance that she's already made reservations or he's made some for her."

"Sure," she said, her voice barely over a whisper.

"When she moves, we have to be ahead of her," Joe said. "And, Stephanie, run any tickets in names that might be obvious aliases," Joe said.

Stephanie did a slow burn. *Stephanie, please do some shit work for me while Larry and Walter sit on their asses.*

"Eve hasn't seen Stephanie or Larry yet. They'll provide close cover. She's seen you other two, but if we alter you enough, we should be okay. She's almost blind. Martin would recognize me. We're closing in on E day, kids—let's stay alert," Joe said.

An hour later Stephanie came into the room and held up the pad she had been writing on. "I have it. In two days." Stephanie put her notes down on the table. "She's flying to Dallas/Fort Worth with a change for Denver."

"That was *too* easy," Joe said, frowning.

"That's what I thought, so I looked closer. There's a suspicious reservation on a flight to Miami on a different airline one concourse over, a few minutes later. And I called the charter services, and there's a private charter booked under that same name from Miami to Orlando. To be paid for in cash. And there's a reservation at one of the hotels at Disney World for two days and three nights."

"Too close for coincidence?" Joe said.

"Well, I didn't give up there. Seems the Evelyn St. Martin return is back here, Charlotte," Stephanie said proudly. "Also, while I was checking, I discovered mirror reservations exist in remarkably similar names over the three days following." She looked at the paper in her hand. "E. Martindale, Milton Martin, and Eve Farming-dale. The others have charters scheduled at different services at Miami International. Haven't checked the hotel reservations on those yet."

"All right!" Joe slapped his hands together. "She's planning to ditch the tail at Dallas/Fort Worth and double back to Miami. Figures we can't follow the charter. And she could change the destination in the air, I imagine. God, we're good," Joe said. "Do the hotels, but once she's on the ground, she may change all that. Besides, she'll be transmitting."

Aren't we good, Stephanie thought to herself. *You're welcome, asshole.*

Then Joe did something out of character: he hugged her and spun her around in the small room. "You are brilliant, Stephanie," he said. "With minds like yours on our side, the bad guys don't have a fuckin' chance."

Until that moment Stephanie had felt as though she had been doing the lion's share of the work on the team and that he'd take the credit as most of the superiors in the agency did. It was part of paying dues, she'd been told. Now she knew he was using her so much for the detail work because he thought she was the one who'd get results. His motives were simple—he just wanted Martin Fletcher's blood on the floor, and he loved anyone who could help him draw it.

24

As soon as Reb stepped down off the bus and passed through the gate, the agents watching him could relax. But he didn't climb down from the bus and go into the house as he was supposed to. Instead he stood beside a large oak, holding his backpack, and stared at Alice Walters's house across the street. Thorne Greer trained the binoculars on him and waited. As Thorne watched, Reb began walking toward the Walters house. Woody sat up from the monitors and stood behind Thorne.

"Shit!" Thorne said. "What in hell's he up to?"

Reb crossed the street and didn't stop until he was halfway across the lawn. When he stopped, he looked up at Thorne and yelled, "Hey, Mr. Greer, I want to talk to you!"

"What's going on?" the local agent, Alton Vance, who had been following the bus, asked over the radio. He was down the street watching from the Volvo.

"I don't know," Thorne said. "He's yelling that he wants to see me."

"Better do something," Woody said, entertained.

"Wish I was in on your joke. This is shit. With my luck Martin will drive by and see—"

"A boy talking to a house?" Woody laughed again.

"I'll open the front door," Thorne said.

"Do you imagine that Martin doesn't know we're here? I assumed he was supposed to see us," Woody said.

"What do you mean?"

Woody shrugged. "I assumed you wanted him to know we're here. That it's just supposed to *look* like we're trying to stay secret."

"What are you saying?"

"We did everything but take out billboards. We could have stayed invisible, but you had us doing close cover. Hell, we were spotted by kids! You're too good to be that sloppy."

Thorne walked to the door. "Orders shouldn't be questioned. I don't know exactly what Paul's thinking, but I trust his judgment."

"So did what's their names—Hill and Barnett, was it?"

Thorne was in the hallway, but he whirled and cast a look of pure fury back into the room.

Woody opened his hands and shrugged. Then, when Thorne was clear, he smiled.

Thorne stormed down the stairs to the front door. He waved Reb inside. Reb stepped to the edge of the front steps and no farther.

"Reb. You aren't supposed to know we're here. Remember? See, if you don't know we're here, then you can't be yelling at me or standing in the yard. Because someone could see us. Remember?"

The boy stood firm and fixed his eyes on Thorne. "I want to see my father."

"Reb, that isn't something I can control. I mean—"

"Then I won't cooperate. I'm going to wave at Woody and Sean and you, too. Every day I am going to stand here until I get to talk to him. He's in there, isn't he?''

"No, he isn't. Come on in," Thorne said. "We can talk."

"After I see him."

"After you satisfy yourself that he isn't here."

25

Rainey Lee seated himself across from Paul and locked his long fingers together on the conference table. "The Buchanans will be at home tomorrow night. I told them I'd call them then to see if they'd changed their minds. I'll pop over then."

Paul started to tell Rainey about the hit on the brochure when the telephone rang. Before Paul could pick it up, Sherry did. She lifted the receiver to her ear. "Yes?" She listened for a second and then held the receiver in the air. "It's Agent McLean in Charlotte."

Paul lifted his receiver. Rainey sat forward. "Joe. What is it?" Paul listened, smiled, and stuck his thumb up in the air so Sherry could see it from her desk. "Just now? Great. Miami to Orlando. Okay, that's possible. Don't close any doors unless you're two hundred percent sure. By the way, I've been thinking about the other prints on the brochure." He listened for a moment. "For-

ward them all to D.C. Sherry has the address for someone I want to take a look at them."

Paul had thought maybe Tod Peoples could find out
if any of the other prints belonged to a possible accomplice. A lot of people Martin knew from the old days
might not have prints in the normal files, but might have
prints in files Tod Peoples was in a unique position to
index.

"Fax me a copy of the brochure and start working on
Eve's travel options. We need to get ahead on her itiner-
ary." He turned. "Sherry. Give Joe the address in D.C. of
the Lux lab from the Rolodex." He waited until she lifted
the phone. "Great work and keep me posted," he said
before he hung up.

"What is it?" Rainey asked, standing. "Martin?"

Paul slapped his hands together. "They got three
Martin Fletcher prints—two partials and one complete."

"So where is he?"

"The prints were on a brochure. Junk mail."

"You were right. How did you know?"

"It was what I would have done. What maniacs
would fingerprint junk mail? Watch FedEx and UPS,
sure—but junkers? Prints were in a pamphlet from a condominium development in Colorado. Denver office says
the development has been sold out for two years, so he
picked up the brochure and envelope at least two years
ago."

"What a fox," Sherry said, the admiration evident in
her voice.

Paul cocked his head and stared at her.

She blushed again. "I meant 'fox' as in 'smart.' "

"It was mailed from Pueblo, Colorado. Three days
ago."

"Government information center's there, isn't it?"
Sherry asked.

"So we go to Colorado?" Rainey asked. "Wait for
Eve to come. Get into position."

"No," Paul said. "We wait. There was no message
they could see in the brochure."

"Maybe that's what he wants you to think," Sherry said.

Paul nodded. He had already considered that possibility. He would have helicopters and vehicles ready for his A team in both places. He would handle the logistics no matter how many cities might be thrown into the mix by Martin and the old lady.

"That just means the signal was a prearranged one. I doubt very seriously that he was in Pueblo long, if he was there at all. He might have paid someone to do that, or he may have been passing through. He wouldn't mail it from a home base. When Eve Fletcher moves, we'll be there. In the meantime we do what we've been doing and ignore the confetti he's throwing. We're running out of time."

Paul rubbed his hands together and opened a box of pictures. The first one illustrated the magnitude of the task. The photo showed a grainy TV-screen image of fifteen people carrying briefcases and suitcases, moving into the airport lobby. The faces were hardly larger than an infant's fingernails. "Great," Paul said as he thumbed through the stack of pictures and looked at the other boxes yet unopened. A twist of his wrist sent the stack across the table in a fan. "Fuckin' great."

Then he had a thought. "Get the airport tapes overnighted to Tod Peoples. Let his people look and see if they can identify anyone they know."

"This guy, Peoples. Do his guys know what everybody in America looks like?" Sherry laughed at the absurdity.

Paul looked at her. "Don't tell me you think that's not possible." Then he laughed and shook his head. "We're cooking with gas," Paul said.

Sherry left the room.

Rainey was staring at the back of Paul's head. "It's coming down," he said. "I can feel it."

Sherry opened the door and stuck her head back into the room. "Paul, there's a call for you. You might want to take it."

"I've got a lot to do," he said. "Ask them to call back later?"

"It's Reb Masterson."

The color drained from Paul's face as he stared at the telephone.

"Later, Paul," Rainey said as he hurriedly left the room.

As Sherry left, she saw that Paul, although he had a hand on the receiver, seemed to be studying the telephone's blinking light. When she pulled the door closed, he still hadn't taken the call. As she sat at her desk, she saw the blinking light go solid, indicating that he had opened the line.

Paul lifted the receiver to his ear and pressed the button opening the line. "Yeah?" he said. His ears felt as if they were burning; his stomach was hollow.

"Paul, it's Thorne. Reb's here in the watch room. He insists on speaking to you. I told him how—"

"Put him on." Paul didn't want Thorne to miss the displeasure in his voice.

After a second had passed, the small voice came on. "Hello?"

"Hello," Paul said.

"Is this my daddy?"

There was a long silence before Paul could speak. "Adam?"

"It's *Reb*," he said. "Don't you remember? *Reb*. Nobody still calls me that."

"Sure, son. What do you need?"

"I want you to tell me why you have these people watching us."

"Because a very dangerous man is—"

"Killing people. I know all that."

"Well, Mr. Greer can tell you. This man is very dangerous. You have to do what Thorne says. And everything will be all right."

"I have a question."

"Okay," Paul said. He put a cigarette in his mouth

and lighted it nervously, conscious that his right hand was trembling.

"If we're in danger, why aren't you here in New Orleans?"

"I'm in Nashville, Reb. I have a lot to do here. Really. It's important for me to be here."

"Why don't you love us? Is it because of Mama and Reid?"

"No, Reb. You don't have any idea how much I love you guys. Don't I always remember your birthday and Christmas?" Paul's voice was wavering slightly.

"Mama says words are cheap. You can't say things if you don't show 'em. And two things a year don't mean anything, 'specially if you send things we don't even need. And you don't even write or call ever. I know kids whose parents are divorced and they see them a lot."

"This isn't about love and this isn't the time for this discussion. Afterward we can—"

"After what? Erin and me are growing up without you, and you don't even know how hard it is not to have a father. If it was you in danger, we would be there to help you and not get strangers to watch you."

"I would be there if it was best," Paul said slowly. "What I'm doing here is more important to the whole operation."

"How're you gonna feel if we get shot dead and you're far away someplace? What if it was only you that could have saved us? You took a love-and-cherish oath with Mama. Death do you part, and you aren't dead! And you made a deal with God to get us . . . children. Mama told me. You swore to God you'd love us and protect us and make sure we were raised right. Did you lie to us or to God?"

"Adam, that isn't fair."

Paul was startled when Reb screamed into the telephone. "It's Reb, dangit! It's Reb, and if you weren't so stupid selfish, you'd know it! You don't know us! You're my daddy and you're just like nothing at all!"

"Adam . . . Reb. I can't come right now. Someday soon . . ."

"Don't come, then. If I die, I'm gonna haunt you till you never sleep again!" The child seemed to calm a bit. "You come here right now, or you just stay away from us for good and ever. That man wants to kill us, and it's you he oughta be trying to kill! We don't even know him. What did you do to him?"

Paul fought to keep his voice level, to remain calm. Inside it was as though his internal organs were being twisted. "Reb . . . it's more complicated than that. Listen to me for a minute."

"You listen to me. I hate you, and I won't let anybody say your name to me again, ever! You've always hurt us, and we never did any stuff to hurt you."

Paul's frustration and insecurity were replaced by anger, and he exploded. "Dammit, Adam Masterson, what the hell do you know about it? You're a child and you'll do what you're told!" Paul felt a strange tingling in the roof of his head, and then the room disappeared as though an aperture in his eye were being closed.

Sherry heard Paul's voice raised in anger. She couldn't make out what he was saying, but then he quieted. She started checking through some notes he had asked her to type up and fax to Mr. Peoples. She heard a loud thump, and after a few seconds she tapped at the door. There was no answer and the line was still lit, but she had a strange, uncomfortable feeling. She opened the door into the conference room.

Paul was sprawled beside the conference table in the throes of a seizure, his mouth oozing white froth, his body jerking as though he were being electrocuted. "Somebody get a doctor!" she yelled. Within seconds the doorway from her office was filled with the faces of DEA agents and secretaries from the offices down the hall. Rainey Lee knelt beside Paul.

"Seizure," he said. "Epilepsy. He takes medication for it."

"What do we do?" she pleaded.

"Just keep doing what you're doing. Just keep him from hitting anything and try to keep him on his side."

Rainey went into the bathroom and brought her a wet washcloth, pausing to close the door on the onlookers.

"Aren't you supposed to do something with his tongue?" she asked.

Rainey shook his head. "No. He'll be fine on his own," he said as he rolled his coat into a pillow and tucked it between Sherry's lap and Paul's head. "It's from the brain damage. He said this might happen, and that if it did, he'd come around and to just make sure he didn't bang his head against anything. He forgets to take the pills sometimes. I'll cancel the ambulance—it'll just embarrass him."

Sherry Lander was aware of Rainey closing the door as he left. After the trembling slowed, she took the opportunity to study the man she had been working with, up close. She put her finger on the scar on the side of his head and traced it slowly from the starting point to the finish. The indentation in the skull wasn't as deep as she had thought. She picked up the patch, which had come unplaced, and covered the red, raw-looking, empty socket.

Sherry turned Paul's head so that the right side was against her lap, his profile standing out against the black skirt as though lit from within. Aside from the damage the bullet had done, Paul Masterson was a very handsome man. The affected side did take some getting used to, but Sherry had liked something about Paul Masterson from the very first time she had laid eyes on him, heard his rocky voice. She could feel a shaft of sorrow in him that reached to a great depth. She had seen fleeting glimpses of a warm, caring person with a sense of humor buried beneath the serious mask of command. Somehow she felt that he had doubts about his abilities. It was just a sense she got when she caught him staring out the window, deep in thought. He was playing a game of life and death, and his own flesh and blood was the wager. How could he not be insecure beneath the facade?

Sherry wiped his face gently, and the eye showed its pupil again. Somewhere inside her a tension spring relaxed, and she was filled with a warm glow that he was coming back. She tried to imagine what it must be like to live with what he had to live with. Loss of blocks of memory, loss of physical abilities he had taken for granted, the constant pain. Rainey had described the rages that had taken control of him during his rehabilitation. That he had run away from the world and hidden alone for years. She felt sorry for him but not because of his injuries. She felt sorry for him because he still had a long way to go before he could begin to live again. She tried to imagine him relaxing but couldn't conjure the image. She tried to imagine him at the height of his ability—a man with the self-assurance of an alley cat. That she saw. She could imagine herself in his arms.

Paul tried to smile as the room came filtering back into his consciousness. She knew he must be embarrassed. He sat, rubbed the back of his head, and stood uncertainly before seating himself in the conference chair closest to him. He put his fingers to the patch reflexively, to make sure it was in place.

"Thank you," he said. "I guess I fell."

"Happen often?"

"No. Not really. Anger, frustration . . . I'm not sure of the triggers. I guess frustration and anger this time."

"You didn't miss a few pills, perhaps?" she asked.

"Yes. I suppose I must have." He stood and then sat behind the desk. He hung up the telephone.

Sherry stood and patted her skirt back into place. "You know, I saw on TV where there are dogs that can spot the signs of a seizure and get you to sit down before you fall."

Paul dropped the smile. "I don't like dogs," he said.

"Sorry. I didn't mean to presume."

"I don't exactly dislike them. I'm just sort of allergic to them."

"A poodle," she said. "They're hypoallergenic or nonallergenic, or whichever it is. And Chihuahuas, and there's some Japanese one."

"Poodles I hate," he said. "And Chihuahuas?" He

laughed. "I'd rather fall a thousand times than tolerate company like that."

Sherry frowned. "Standard poodles are like normal dogs—my mother has one. And my aunt Grace has a pair of Chihuahuas. Yin and Yang. I know . . . Chinese names for Mexican dogs?"

Paul laughed, bent down, and started picking up the files he had scattered over the carpet when he fell. Sherry helped him, gathering them in her hands. When she handed him the files, her hand wrapped his, and she held it in place for a long couple of seconds. Then she smiled at him. He averted his eye and turned.

"You okay?" she asked as professionally as possible.

"Thanks for everything. Sorry about the trouble I caused. Mind if I ask you a personal question?"

"If I do, I just won't answer it."

"Are you single?"

"Yes. I ask you one?"

"I guess so," Paul said. He shifted and put his arms behind his neck, enjoying the prospect of his first pleasant conversation in a week.

"Why didn't you ever get your face fixed?"

Paul laughed out loud as he jerked his hands from the chair's armrests to the desk. It was a laugh of surprise and embarrassment, more like a dog's bark. He stared at her, trying to decide whether he was hurt or angry or exactly what he was. "Why would you ask that?"

Paul started squeezing down on the tennis ball with his left hand.

"Well, you said I could. And because you would be a remarkably handsome man. I mean the left side of your face is really nice to look at. I just wondered if you didn't get plastic surgery because you wanted to punish yourself."

Paul turned and opened the file closest to him. He tried to read it, but he was shaking. "If that's all," he said.

"I didn't mean to upset you, Mr. Masterson. Really I didn't."

"I have work to do—I imagine you do, too."

She went to the door and stopped and turned. "Should I leave? Am I fired?"

"No, you aren't fired. Do something constructive. You shouldn't waste your time wondering about . . . me." He almost swallowed the last word.

"I'm sorry," she said, "if I offended you. Sometimes I let my curiosity get me in trouble."

"It's all right. I opened the door but let's close it." He looked up and slammed the file closed. "Two things. One, don't ever try to analyze me, because you don't have any idea what's gone on in my life or what I think or how I feel. And keep up the good work."

She smiled. "Thanks," she added. "Sorry." She stood still and stared at him.

He knew what he wanted to say. *I'm lonely right now. I need company. Companionship for a little while. I want to* . . . After Sherry left the room, he spent a half hour staring out the window at downtown Nashville, thinking about what had happened before the seizure had struck. *How many days since I took the antiseizure medicine?* Paul thought about the medicine and knew that because he was back in the saddle, he had almost unconsciously decided he wouldn't need it.

Paul had been in a rage when the seizure had taken him down. He regretted what he had said and how he'd said it. But he decided that his instincts had been fine. It was better that the child forget him. Better they all do. Even if he wanted to, he could not go to New Orleans until the time was right. *You'll see me soon enough, Martin.*

26

"He did what?" Laura shrieked. She studied her son, who was angry and not about to listen to anything she had to say. His face was bright red, his eyes seemed to be on fire.

"Nothing I could do," Thorne said. "He insisted he had to speak to Paul. Threatened to blow the whole surveillance."

Reb's bottom lip was extended in anger. "If he's not in the mountains like you said, I wanted to talk to him. He has a telephone now. What's so special about him that I can't talk to him? He's my father, isn't he?"

"You go upstairs," she said. She didn't move until she heard his bedroom door slam.

"What on earth did he say to Paul?" she asked.

Erin stood in a nearby doorway, listening with her head cocked.

"Reb told him that he should come here. He told Paul that he was selfish. He told him that growing up without a father was a hardship. He basically said that Paul was a selfish asshole and to come now or never."

"He said that?"

"Oh, more than that. But that was the gist of it—the high points. He spoke to Paul like Paul was the child."

Laura smiled. "Good," she said. "What did Paul say?"

"I've no idea. I think he hung up."

Reb was lying on the bed when Laura came up a few minutes later. Wolf put his head on Reb's leg, and his mother sat on the edge of the bed.

"Reb. You want to talk about it?"

"No."

"You know what you did was wrong?"

Reb fought to control his quivering lip. "He doesn't love us, Mama. Why?" He sat up, and she hugged him as he sobbed against her shoulder. "What did we ever do to him? Were we bad? Cause we were just little . . . we didn't mean to make him mad."

"Reb, you didn't do anything, and it isn't that your father doesn't love you. He does."

"But he yelled at me like he hates me. He said I should be turned over someone's knee and that my behavior could cost us all our lives and that this wasn't a game. He yelled some other stuff, but I wasn't listening. He's a horrible, mean man. I wish I hadn't called him. I wish he was dead. I wish those bad men had killed him dead and dead."

Laura did the best she could, but Reb would not be consoled. His face was like a mass of tight cables all pulling in different directions. Laura had never seen him in such a state. She left his room and ran into Erin in the hall.

"Just who the hell does he think he is?" Erin yelled.

"Erin!" she said. "Language!"

"The hell with him!"

"Erin, please."

"Just because he looks like a damned scarecrow doesn't give him the right to treat Reb like that! I don't care how he treats me, but I do care how he treats my little brother. How dare he?"

"Erin, I'm sure it's more complicated than that."

"Oh, so just keep on taking up for Mr. Slime Varmint. I'm sorry he got shot in his precious face." She looked directly into her mother's eyes. "I'm sorry it didn't kill him, too."

"Erin!"

"Oh, Mother, you're as bad as he is." Erin ran to her bedroom and slammed the door. The noise echoed through the hallway like a shotgun blast.

Laura went to the kitchen, poured herself a large glass of red wine, and drained it. "Thorne," she said, speaking to the window, which was like talking directly into his earphones, "do us all a favor and tell him we don't need to see him ever again. Tell him he can go straight back to his mountain. Tell him if he hurts my children again, I'll kill him myself."

Then Laura took her bottle of wine into the studio and turned up the stereo so she could cry in privacy.

Erin was furious. Her father had turned her family's lives upside down, put her social life on hold, and she didn't appreciate it a bit. She thought about the new boy in school, who might be the most beautiful boy she had ever laid eyes on. Eric Garcia had told a friend of hers that he had a crush on her. Earlier that day he had spoken to her while she'd been eating lunch. He had asked Erin out, and normally she would have jumped on it in an instant. Her friends had been sick, they were so jealous. But with everything that was happening she had had to put him off by saying that she was busy, although she had been careful to leave the door open for the week after. *I mean, how long can it take all these experts to nail one old creep?* After school that agent, Sean Merrin, had been waiting and had shadowed her, even on the streetcar from her high school. It made her feel like an idiot, a small child.

She decided that she would show them. She'd slip Eric a note arranging to meet him, and then she'd slip Sean Merrin. *Fuck 'em.*

27

GRAVEL CRUNCHED UNDER THE DARK CADILLAC BROUGHAM, ITS running lights burning orange, as it floated out of the fog like a manta ray. It slid up the truck ramp, swung out onto the dock, and pulled into the shadow of a rusting freighter. The freighter was a ghost vessel, abandoned for the evening, its crew scattered about the bars of the upper French Quarter. The car stopped, and after a few minutes the rear door opened as a single figure got out.

Lallo Estevez carried himself with the aplomb of an aristocrat. He wore his hair in a rolling silver mane. He had a pencil-thin mustache and wore heavy black-framed glasses. The all-weather coat hung shroudlike from his shoulders, and the gold signet ring with his ancient family crest had doubled as a sealing-wax stamp two hundred years before. He thought he heard something behind him and gave the Cadillac a proprietary glance, lit a blond Dominican cigar with his gold Dunhill lighter, then turned and walked up the gangplank to the deck. He thought the vantage point might be more advantageous from that altitude. The thin soles of his loafers slid against the damp boards, slick leather against the light coating of oil and beads of condensation. He stood at the top of the walk and looked up and down the deck. The broker could barely make out the window to the pilot-house through the fog. Not that anyone was in there. Privacy had been arranged with a word to the captain. The ship belonged to Lallo's coffee company. He looked around trying to spot the man with his rifle. No matter.

Lallo spent ten minutes standing and puffing on the cigar and listening for any foreign sound. As usual he wasn't armed. He had never liked weapons personally, though he had fenced at college in England, and he was a fair clay-target shot. He had never had to handle a weapon in violence. As long as there was poverty, there would be those willing to do anything for a TV set and a few dollars. He checked his Omega. Ten past the time Martin had set for the meeting.

Lallo wasn't nervous about the shooter, except he hoped the shot was clean. Sometimes these men weren't as concerned with what was behind the target as the target itself. And he hoped the CIA hadn't decided to end their uneasy partnership after all these years. He could describe Spivey's build and his voice but had never looked into his eyes. It was better not to see too much. The only other time he had met with him, Spivey had been wearing a baseball cap and dark glasses, a thick mustache and matching wig, neither of which looked convincing or had meant to be.

"Marty, where the fucking hell are you?" he whispered to himself.

"Such language." The voice shocked him like a cup of cold water tossed in his face, and Lallo was frightened to find himself standing two feet away from the author of the words. A stranger. He thought he heard the car door close, and he prayed the men in the car behind him would stay put. "Martin? Is this you?" Lallo had not seen Martin face-to-face since the operation.

"Not hardly," the man said, raising his chin. "Behind you."

Martin was indeed there when Lallo turned. The Latin broker almost had trouble drawing a steady breath. How Martin had come up the gangplank without rocking it, and so soundlessly, Lallo couldn't imagine. He was dressed in a black turtleneck and jeans. His face was smeared with something dark and moist. Lallo didn't recognize him at first. And not because of the face paint—the face was vastly altered from the one he had last seen, years before.

"How did you do that?" he said, trying to inject levity in his tone. "You took ten years off my life. And this one"—he nodded at the other man—"who looks strangely familiar to me, I must say." He made the sign of the cross and put his hands on Martin's shoulders.

"You've met before," Martin said. "Years ago. In our training facility in Colombia."

"I see. Now, Marty, we meet and speak face-to-face again like old friends."

"Well, my friend, I delivered my end on schedule, and we agreed on a price up front," Martin said in flawless Spanish. "Weren't you pleased with the quality of the merchandise? All you had to do was connect the Semtex and set the clocks. Sweet as it gets, and so any fool becomes a professional bomber. Pablo is having a cash-flow problem, you said?"

"Sí," Lallo said. Then he reverted to English, looking from Martin to the other man as he spoke. In his mind he prayed that the shooter waited and got both of them. The additional man was a problem, but one Ramon could handle easily. "A small problem getting his money moved around. Very temporary, he assures me. He moves from Guatemala to Colombia, and he is never where I look for him. Communication is a terrible problem, but as history has shown us, he is always good for it."

"I saw where his cousin and brother met with an accident."

"Police bullets, very bad for the digestion." Lallo

shrugged and laughed. "And that didn't help with these troubles."

"That was just a few weeks ago. I've been owed my money for six months now. Am I some worrisome dog who sneaked under the table?"

Lallo opened his arms expansively. "Oh, no! You are like my own family! I never thought that!"

"Still, Uncle Lallo, I haven't been paid. In the old days I was always paid, and well. Information I gave saved many lives in Pablo's organization. And millions upon millions of dollars in merchandise that would have been lost to seizure."

Martin smiled, but the smile was not a pleasant thing to see.

"But, my friend," Lallo said, "I have brought you your money, after all. That is why I wanted to meet out here this time of night. To pay you what Pablo owes you. He told me to wait . . . but I said no, Martin Fletcher is my dear friend, and I will pay him. If he doesn't like that"—Lallo put his fingers to his chest—"too bad. It's not your problem. I'm paying you out of my pocket, and I must collect later. You have changed so much! You look so many years younger. Handsome!" Lallo's eyes related that the familiar voice coming from this stranger was disconcerting. He tried not to look at the warehouse roofline, but he did, just fleetingly.

"Oh, Lallo, you make me feel guilty." Martin smiled sheepishly. "And I wasn't certain I could trust you any longer."

Lallo patted him on the shoulders, and the nervous smile grew larger. "It's nothing."

"Where is it? The money?"

"In the car. You come and I will pay you now. All this fog is like vampire movie, no?" Lallo laughed.

Martin smiled. "Blood from the neck." He laughed. "In the car, you say?"

"Yes. Come."

Martin walked behind Lallo until they made the dock and on to the car. Lallo was nervous. *What about the other man? Will he be shot at the same time?*

He opened the door slowly and said, "Your money is in there, Marty."

As he pulled the door open, he stepped back so Ramon, the man in the rear seat, would have a clean shot with the double-barreled shotgun—and the other man a shot from the warehouse roof. But as he stood there braced for the explosions, nothing happened. Martin Fletcher stared at Lallo, who stood holding the door handle with his left hand. Martin waited a full thirty seconds, eye to eye with Lallo, before he bent down and reached into the open door, grabbed an ankle, and tugged a limp body from the car to the dock, where it landed with a squishing sound not unlike that of a foot being pulled from the mud. The left side of the man's face had exploded out. There was a small hole in his left temple, and the window he had been seated against was perforated with tiny cracks that formed a spiderweb of shattered lens radiating from a small hole.

"Imagine my surprise when I found Ramon here! Was this sorry sack of shit supposed to give me my money, Lallo? Or was he supposed to give me something else? I have to tell you the money wasn't inside the car—only this." Marty reached behind him, under his jacket, and pulled a pistol complete with a silencer from his belt. "And a shotgun. So is the money in the trunk? All I see in there is two dead pieces of shit, your driver and a dead *pistolero* of dubious lineage. But money? No, I don't see my money." Martin's face was twitching, the anger floating from him. Lallo prayed for the man on the roof to shoot and end this. He scanned the roofline of his warehouse.

"The man up there had to leave early," Martin said.

Lallo's face melted toward his tie, and his lips trembled like his knees. "Marty, they made me do this! They threatened my family!" Lallo beat at his chest. *Don't give up the spooks unless you have to.* "This was Ramon's order from Pablo! That evil man was his personal assassin. I'm glad you killed this pig, because he was forcing me into this. They threatened my family. Even my grandbabies."

Martin pulled a knife from his ankle and reached

down and worked on the dead hit man with the blade. Lallo retched deeply when he saw what Martin was doing.

Martin finished, stood, and Lallo was horrified at the sight of his blood-covered hands, the knife reduced to a darkly wet conical shape extending from the right fist. "I knew this man Ramon, Lallo. A student as poor as this shouldn't be sent against his teacher. He looks awfully good in a tie, though."

Lallo could hardly breathe. He hoped his heart wouldn't explode.

"What do I smell?" Martin said as he sniffed at the air loudly. "Shit? You ruined a thousand-dollar suit? Are you so afraid of me, who is like your own son? I thought we were friends. What, fifteen years I've known you? We have had some times, Lallo. You introduced me to my love, Angela. You were to be godfather to my baby, Macon. You know," he said softly, "the anniversary of his death is coming up very soon."

"Please, Marty. I can help you. I can get you almost a million dollars. Now, tonight. I wanted to bring you your money, but they would not allow it. I swear."

"Who put you up to this? Perez?"

"Not Perez. A man named Spivey."

"Spivey? Who is he?"

"A company man, I think. He got Ramon and the man on the roof."

"Lallo, I find it difficult to trust you in light of all this." He spread his bloody hands eloquently. "Someone who forgets who I am . . . what I do? I can't be killed by fools like these. I'm bulletproof, Lallo. I can smell the breath of my enemies at a thousand yards. I can see their nostrils flare, their eyes move. I can hear their thoughts, I can feel them, Lallo."

"There is a million dollars in my office—in the place under my desk. You pull the rug back and there it is. I give it to you. Just let me go. We forget this and stay friends. For Angela and Macon's sake."

"Angela is with the dead, Lallo. Don't speak of her here among this shit." With the dripping blade he indicated the *pistolero*. "Here's the deal, Lallo. You are right that we are good friends. So climb into the trunk, and I'll send my pal to your office to get the cash. If the money is there, we can say good-bye as friends."

"Excellent," Lallo said, nodding rapidly. "Combination is three-two-four-four-five-oh. Here are the keys to my office in Place St. Charles." Lallo pulled a set of keys from his pocket and handed them to Martin.

"Security?" Martin asked.

"The system has a forty-second delay after the door opens. Keypad is on the other side of the door, and it is set for one-one-one-one. Then we say it's even?" Lallo's face was running with sweat. "I will explain these bodies."

"We'll just toss them into the river. So I can forgive you for the money. The other cash in your safe I will put to good use. Fund an orphanage, maybe. You know how much I love children."

"I deserve your disdain because I am a weakling." Lallo frowned. "I trust you, Marty. You have always been a man of your word. The money is there. I swear on my mother's eyes."

"All we have is our honor, my friend," Martin said as he opened the driver's door and reached over the dead man for the keys. He walked around and opened the trunk and Lallo climbed in. He looked up at Martin, a frightened bird in a dark nest. "I trust you, Martin. I trust you," he said. He watched as the other man joined Martin and stood just behind him.

"And I trust you. Haven't you seen my face? You are the only man on earth, aside from my compatriot there, who knows what I look like. We must trust each other. Watch your hands, Lallo. Will you be comfortable in there?"

"Yes." He nodded rapidly. "I will be just fine, Martin. And your friend—Steiner, Kurt Steiner. Of course," Lallo said. "Now I remember him. It was nice to see you again, Mr. Steiner." Lallo stared at the other man.

Kurt Steiner nodded formally. "My pleasure, Senor

Estevez. Maybe we will meet again under more pleasant circumstances."

"I'll put in some holes so you can breathe better," Martin said, taking the shotgun from Kurt and swinging it up to his shoulder. He aimed it at Lallo's chest. Lallo jerked his arm up and covered his eyes. Martin shrugged, raised the barrel to the open trunk lid, and fired both barrels, the pellets punching through the sheet metal and shattering both the rear and front windshields en route. The short gun's discharges sounded like dynamite going off; the sound overflowed the small trunk. Lallo was sure his ears were bleeding as he pulled his arm away from his eyes. There might have been some relief in his expression, but very little. He was a man separated from his Maker by the thinnest of threads, and they were being held by a psychopath.

"Sorry about your pants," Martin said as he closed the trunk gently until the hydraulic mechanism caught and sealed it tight. Martin put the shotgun on top of the car, grabbed the *pistolero*'s legs, and dragged him to the side of the dock, leaving a wide, dark trail. The body of the short, thin sniper from the roof was now lying beside the Cadillac, having been recovered by Kurt Steiner. The rifle he had been carrying was tossed into the water without a second thought. The sniper's throat was opened like a mouth. Martin reached into the slit in the man's throat and pulled his tongue out as he had the *pistolero*'s. Then, after admiring the thick purple necktie, he rolled the would-be assassin off into the Mississippi River. Martin and Kurt maneuvered Ramon to the side and pushed him in as well. They watched him float away, shoulders above the waterline, for a few seconds before he sank.

"See that, Kurt? Proves a very important point."

"What point, Marty?"

"Shit doesn't always float."

Martin walked back to the driver's open door, reached inside, started it, and then put the Cadillac into drive. He cocked his head slightly and watched the car roll slowly toward the ship's stern, gathering speed as it went. It rolled off the pier at an angle, the front passenger quarter hitting first, and sank in a fury of bubbles. Lallo's muted screams escaped the holes in the trunk as the car bobbed and the rear end moved along the pier, pulled along by the current. Then it slipped under for good, leaving a momentary churning of bubbles that moved downriver.

"I didn't touch you, Lallo, old friend," he said. Then he tilted his head back and filled the night with his deep, black laughter.

Martin changed into clothes he had in the trunk of the Caprice. He strolled out of the parking garage off Canal Place, crossed Canal Street, and walked to St. Charles Avenue, where he stopped to look at the displays in the windows of Rubenstein Bros. He slowed to savor the elegance of Italian suits, linen shirts, and sports coats as he walked toward Lallo's building. The expensive clothes appealed to Martin. He wondered why he had not worn such suits before now. He thought he would adopt a personality with a sense of style and taste. After the smoke cleared on this deal, if he was still alive, he'd come back to this store and outfit himself for just such a life—a new identity. Maybe he would rent an elegant house here for a few months and relax.

By the time Martin passed the final shop window, his thoughts were back to his business. His reflections on fine clothing and a house uptown no longer existed; they were as completely forgotten as the bodies he had slipped into the Mississippi River an hour earlier. His mind had locked on his errand again.

Lallo's office was located on one of the top floors of Place St. Charles on St. Charles Avenue, a block uptown from the French Quarter. His family owned coffee plantations, and he was officially a coffee broker. Lallo's brother had introduced him to the money to be made in the powder trade on the cleaning end, and with the friendship of certain American-government accommodations it had seemed perfectly safe. Money shuffling for both ends meant a percentage of the gross. A nice pad for a man with so many businesses set up all around the world and so many accounts in so many places. Lallo had banking relationships in the Bahamas, New Orleans, Miami, New York, Panama, Peru, Argentina, Bolivia, Honduras, London, Tokyo, and Paris.

Martin slipped easily into the building and up the stairs without being seen. He used Lallo's keys to open first the receptionist's office and then Lallo's. There was an alarm, but it wasn't on.

The office was large and expensively decorated. The desk, the entertainment center complete with leather couches, and the conference table were set on a carpeted platform—a platform built expressly to hide the floor safe under Lallo's desk. The combination worked perfectly. Martin stared in at the blocks of cash. He roughly counted the money, using the desk to stack the bundles.

Pablo would know Martin had killed his most valuable money man and taken many times what was owed him. And the drug king would spend the time when he wasn't looking over his shoulder for the Colombian army, instead looking over his shoulder for Martin. Martin knew he would haunt Pablo's dreams, because Pablo had seen him at work, had hired him for the wettest jobs he'd had—work where sophistication was necessary, where the target was covered over in security. The trouble with Latin muscle was that there was no finesse. Cut throats, sloppy torture, like the raping of proud, macho men by lesser men, machine guns, bombs, and chain saws. Martin believed that the Colombians and the Peruvians were pie-faced Indians without the imagination God gave frogs. Inferior beings. Martin knew this because he had trained them—or tried to—but they were, for the most part, ruled by their emotions. Most men were inferior to Martin. Most men had emotions to deal with. Martin had exorcised all but a few.

Martin put the money into a plastic garbage bag he had brought along and went back out into the night with the cash slung over his shoulder.

Back in the parking garage he handed blocks of the

money to his comrade. "One more big job before we close this one, Kurt."

"No sweat," Steiner said.

"There can be no mistakes. You have everything you need. The package is waiting for you."

"I understand, Martin. I've done lots of shit harder than this cakewalk."

"You have never had a more important job in your life. The absence of danger may give you a false sense of safety. Remember, you are the only one I would trust with this."

Martin embraced the man and hugged him tightly. The killers put their heads together.

"I won't fail you," Steiner said.

"Go," Martin whispered. "Go, now, and make me proud."

Martin watched as Kurt stepped from the car and made his way to the elevator. He knew that the younger man was in awe of him. It wasn't a physical love, but a worshipful love, a reverence of the student for the master. Martin put two pills on his tongue and swallowed them without water. "Of course he won't fail me. Because I'd cut out his fucking heart if he did." He smiled at the thought that soon he would be traveling lighter than he ever had before. After this was done, he would have no further use for Kurt Steiner.

28

Kurt Steiner drove up Magazine toward the Garden District. The rain stopped as suddenly as it had started, the windshield clearing the final drops of water. He thought about the money in the trunk, and for a split second he fantasized that he would leave for the airport and simply be gone. He could be home early with a king's ransom. Then he dismissed the thought and cursed himself for such a treacherous idea.

He turned his mind back to the airport in Dallas, where he had been dispatched on an errand by Martin. As usual he had no idea why the trip was important, because Martin never told him more than he absolutely had to know. Kurt didn't blame Martin; secrecy kept him alive.

Martin put seemingly unrelated pieces of an operation into play at different times. The envelope affair a month before had been another mission that had made sense only to Martin. Kurt had been dispatched to Pueblo, Colorado, armed with an address that matched a barren-looking, garbage-strewn, and junk-stacked piece of land in the middle of nowhere with a distressed-looking trailer parked on it. Martin had given him an unsealed business envelope that held ten crisp ten-dollar bills, and a separate manila envelope with what appeared to be an advertising brochure for a condominium project. There was no vehicle in evidence, and no shade, except for a few small trees with a minimal amount of leaves on them.

He had tapped at the door, and an elderly man holding a shotgun had appeared behind the torn screen. The old man, dressed in baggy jeans, didn't allow Kurt inside but placed the shotgun against the wall. He opened the door slightly, held out his hand, took the envelope with the cash, and opened it to count the bills. Then he took the manila envelope and peeked inside, nodded to himself, and closed the door in Kurt's face. They had not exchanged a single word.

He was sure he wasn't being followed, but he glanced in the rearview mirror, watching the faces and mannerisms of the people moving through, and thinking about Martin. He had met Martin while he'd been at Fort Benning learning counterinsurgency techniques as a representative of the police from a South American country. Kurt's father was a retired diplomat and had vast cattle holdings in Argentina.

From the moment the two men had met, Kurt had felt drawn to the older man, the instructor. In Martin Fletcher he saw the kind of man one could give loyalty to. Martin was a man who deserved loyalty; he was a master of his own mind, spirit, and body—a born leader. In short, Martin was someone to swear an oath to. *My loyalty is my life.* Martin had taught him so much that no one, not his schools, his grandfather, his father, nor the army, had. He had learned to ignore pain, to kill without compassion, to create multiple identities and disguises, and to live dual lives comfortably. His lives were like little compartments, each with a different story, different feelings, and different motivations.

Kurt Steiner had grown up in awe of his grandfather, worshiping him as only a small child can. Kurt Rudolph Steiner was a German national who had relocated in Paraguay directly after World War II, and then in Argentina. He had been a colonel in the Waffen SS, charged with special handling of prisoners prior to the collapse of his homeland. His namesake had grown up with the stories of the leadership of Germany and of the conquests and glory that were to be found in soldiering for the right commander. In Martin, Kurt found a commander like the ones the old man had spoken of in worshipful terms. The Aryan sympathies had been drilled into the lad. Pure-blooded knights whose destiny was to rule the earth.

Martin had taught him well and had appreciated the younger man's intensity and self-discipline. Kurt had learned lessons his grandfather hadn't taught him, the practical day-to-day methods of survival and the ways of the modern warrior. Under Martin he had been armed and hardened. Since his country had been at war with its rebel elements, he found himself immersed in learning a useful trade. He could watch the most grotesque forms of torture and feel nothing at all for the subject. He could execute his enemies with the same detached professionalism his grandfather had described to him. Life and death were hardly more than applied mathematics. A place where honor was loyalty, and loyalty was a man's life.

Kurt was in phenomenal physical condition thanks to constant workouts in swimming, running, martial arts, mountain climbing, bicycling, weight lifting, boxing and calisthenics.

Martin had stayed in touch with Kurt over the years. He had enlisted Kurt to be his aide while he trained troops for a cocaine cartel's war against the Colombian government. Kurt had been charged with teaching groups on his own, using knowledge Martin had given him. It was his training that had allowed him to figure out where a sniper, if one was used, would set up to cover the dock in New Orleans.

Kurt entered the Garden District through the back door, coming down Napoleon Avenue from Tchoupoulas Street, which was the road that ran its curving path alongside the Mississippi River's loading docks. Kurt looked at his watch. It was early yet.

Paul had not fired a pistol since a few months before he had been shot, and he wanted to see how rusty he really was. He went down through the doors and into the indoor range located in the basement of Gun City. He was happy that he and Rainey were the only customers there. On the table in front of him were three boxes of forty-five hardball ammo, which he had purchased upstairs. He loaded seven rounds into each of his three clips and put on the earphones. Paul clipped a target on the pulley and ran it back seventeen or eighteen yards. The gun felt alien in his hand as he jacked a shell into the chamber, aimed at the target, and pulled the trigger over and over until the slide locked open. Paul didn't see any holes in the black of the paper target. Rainey flipped the switch, the motor engaged, and the target came back.

"I missed seven times?"

"Haven't shot in a while."

"Six years," he said, smiling. "I was pretty good once."

Rainey pulled his Smith & Wesson .40 and aimed down the range at Paul's target. The explosions were almost intertwined, they were so close together. Then Rainey hit the switch, and the target rolled slowly forward, stopping a yard away. There was a swarm of holes centered on the target's face.

Paul removed the target and replaced it with a fresh one.

"Not *that* good," Paul said.

"You used to fire with both eyes open, and you're primarily right-eyed."

"Yeah," Paul said. "That's how I was taught."

"It's depth perception. Think of this barrel as your right eye. Use it like that, parallel to the other. Adjust for distance best you can. Just keep going and it'll come. We can put a laser aiming device on it the size of a double-A battery."

"Nope. I better get used to it with what I got." Paul was silent for a few seconds. "Nothing at all from the kids." It was a statement of fact.

Rainey was reloading his magazine from a new box of shells he had bought at the retail store upstairs from the range. "I still think Tim Buchanan might remember something."

"Maybe I should go with you," Paul said.

"You're busy," Rainey said.

"That's silly," Paul said. "How long could it take?"

"I'll deal with it. I don't think they'll be able to deny me in person." Rainey met his eye. "Besides, I hope you won't take this wrong, but he's a kid. Don't you think your battle scars might sort of put him off?"

Paul thought about it and nodded. "Scare the shit outta him, you mean."

Paul's second clip was better. Three hits, one in the center of the head. Rainey clapped him on the shoulder. Next clip, there were seven hits in the target's center mass border. Paul stopped when he still had a half box of ammo left. "I still got it," he said, laughing. For the first time in a long time he thought things might be breaking in his direction, after all.

He turned around to say something else to Rainey, but he was gone. Paul was alone in the range. Rainey had left his box of shells on the counter. Paul folded the targets and pressed them into the trash can behind his station. Then he picked up his and Rainey's shells before he went upstairs.

29

Eve Fletcher flung open the front door as soon as the mail carrier lifted the squeaky lid on her mailbox.

"Gimme that," she said, snatching the envelopes from his hand and slamming the door in his face.

The postman stepped down from the porch shaking his head. It was the first time he had laid eyes on her in a year, and then it had been the same deal. She had sprung the door open as if she had been there coiled and ready with her hand on the knob, pouncing when he opened the mailbox. Last year she had done it three days running, and then nothing until today. Totally wacky shit, he decided as he stepped onto the next porch. He would be ready for her tomorrow. "I'll just toss her shit up on the porch and walk off," he said out loud. "I don't have to take this mess from anybody."

Two blocks away agent Larry Burrows had been sitting at the console, where he had watched an overhead view of Eve standing at the door waiting for her mail. "Missing *General Hospital*? She's waiting for the mail with that anxious face we love so much."

He had watched as she had paced the hallway for half an hour before the postman showed. Agent Burrows looked around at the four faces illuminated by the monitors. It was close inside the trailer, but from here on out, except for double-checking the post office at night, they would not leave except to follow Eve to her son. After she closed the door, she scurried back to the den and sat in her chair while she thumbed through the letters. When she got to the condominium brochure, she dropped the others into her lap and looked at the envelope. She held it with her left hand while she fumbled around on the tray for her glasses with the right. She put the glasses on and examined the envelope carefully. She seemed to inspect the flap before opening the brochure and thumbing through it from front to back. Then she removed her glasses and tossed the brochure into the trash box on the floor.

"I wonder what it means?" Joe said. "What's the message? It has to be an all-clear signal. There's nothing there."

"Maybe it had something on it that only her glasses picked up," Sierra said.

"I doubt it," Joe said. He looked at the brochure photocopies and the copy of the outside of the envelope. The envelope said:

OCCUPANT
321 TUCKER COURT
CHARLOTTE, NC 28209

Joe looked at the return. "Motherlode Condominiums, on Madigan Street in Denver. *Motherlode.* Jesus, the man is amazing."

Larry snickered.

Eve's heart soared as she made her way to the den with the bundle of junk mail. Mr. Puzzle trailed behind her, following her form, scent, or through some other instinct, his tiny nails ticking the steps against the wood floor. When the animal arrived at the base of the chair and barked to be picked up, he was ignored. Eve had more important things on her mind than a yappy dog.

She had lifted the message from the brochure in an instant, as a billboard with a single word might be absorbed. She smiled at the thought that the instructions were invisible to anyone except two people on the entire planet. She was pleased with how clever her Martin was. First off, the brochure's arrival meant that her Martin was safe. It also told her where to go and how. It was a puzzle based on things they had discussed years before and she had memorized. Eve and Martin had always shared a love of games. When Martin was a child, they had started with Candyland and gone on to Sorry, Monopoly, checkers, backgammon, and finally chess.

She remembered the instructions. Where to go and where to get the key to the locker that would hold the new instructions. Instructions that would insure she would escape her tail and meet him in safety. By creasing the rear corner of the pamphlet he had signaled her to switch to the other identity at the airport in Dallas.

Eve was well aware that the intricately planned precautions were necessary. Martin's enemies had unlimited resources. Martin had said, "It's okay to be paranoid when there is good reason." Since he had escaped prison, she had lived her life assuming they were watching, as well as listening to, her every move. Martin had explained how they could use technology, secret beams and the like, to spy on people. Martin was an expert in that. The Fletchers were surrounded by the enemy and had been since Martin had worked against the international drug conspirators in Vietnam and later with the DEA. But the conspiracy had corrupted the DEA, and they had framed Martin. The dark cabal was made up of Jews mainly, but other international businessmen as well. Once Martin was eliminated, they would have a free reign. Luckily, she had taught Martin all about the Jews early on.

Eve hadn't actually seen any enemy agents lurking outside her house, but Martin had told her that they would follow her to him, and she believed him. In fact, she had been aware that she was being followed on several occasions. He was a noble soldier for his country, having even gone to prison as part of his plan to fight crime. He had been aided in his escape by other agents. And he had changed his face and identity to continue the fight. She knew that corrupted elements of the DEA, FBI, and CIA would find him and kill him if she made mistakes.

Eve dropped the brochure into the trash box along with the other mail from the day's delivery. The yearly visits with him were the only thing she had to look forward to, except for her stories and Mr. Puzzle's company, which grew less rewarding every day. The animal was seventeen and couldn't last much longer, what with one part of him failing, seemed like, every week or two. She sat gazing at the screen where two actors embraced even though they were married to other people. Normally scenes of adulterous behavior would get Eve's blood up, but today she wasn't thinking about people's shameless behavior.

She lifted Mr. Puzzle to her lap, stroked his head, and contemplated the trip. She would leave Mr. Puzzle with the veterinarian, who would take care of him. "He's a sweet nummins," she murmured. She wouldn't be coming back, ever. She wondered what would happen to her things, but it was a fleeting curiosity. She would be with Martin on a beach in South America, where they would live in peace. They had discussed it every year during their visit. It would be paradise. Eve and Martin. Son and mother.

Eve reached onto the TV tray, found a small tin, pulled it open by hooking the ring on the top. As the five agents looked on, Eve dug a wet Vienna sausage from the can by using a knitting needle and then held it like a carrot while the little dog greedily nibbled sharp furrows into the end.

30

THE TWIN-MASTED, WOODEN-HULLED SAILBOAT MOTORED ACROSS
the harbor, between the rock-encrusted sloping walls of
the channel. Once past the Coast Guard station, the
Shadowfax sailed out onto Lake Pontchartrain, a gently
rolling liquid prairie. To the south the lights of New Orleans burned yellow against the night sky. The moon was
almost full and illuminated the sails of a few other boats
against the dark sweep of lake. The wind was steady and
from the east. Reid Dietrich unfurled the mainsails by
moving levers on the cockpit's console as he held course
by maintaining a left-hand grip on the large polished-
mahogany wheel.

"*Shadowfax* is an odd name," Thorne Greer said.
"What's it mean?"

"It's named for a character in a book," Laura said.
"The wizard's horse in a fantasy novel, I think."

"She came already named," Reid added. "I might

have named her *Reb's Nightmare*—which she is. But a
wizard's horse is appropriate, since sailing has a mysti-
cal, magical side. Look at the lights of the city, feel the
breeze in your hair. Drink in the fresh air. Sailing her at
night is as close to heaven as you can get with your
clothes on."

"Boats scare Reb. Always have. He's like his father,
he prefers solid ground beneath him," Laura said.

"Beautiful night," Thorne said. He turned away and
yawned into his hand. "Peaceful."

"We're lucky we got the boat back while it was still
warm enough to sail her in shirtsleeves," Laura said.
"Reid travels so much we don't get out on it very often."

"All that travel sounds exotic."

"Not as exotic as hanging around with celebrities,"
Reid said. "I live in motel rooms and on airplanes. But
it's the business I chose, and where doctors have money
to spend, competition is fierce." Thorne checked the taut-
ness of a line. "Maybe that's what keeps the romance
fresh," Reid said. "The absences."

"Maybe," she said. "I wish you weren't leaving
again until this is over."

"She's safe with you at the gate, isn't she? I mean,
you're still listening to every creaking bedspring?" Reid
asked mockingly.

Laura slapped his shoulder.

"She is a beauty," Thorne said, changing the subject.

"She's been in dry dock getting a new coat of paint,
some cabin alterations, new navigation equipment," Reid
said. "Few more years and I'm going to retire, and then
maybe I'll live on her."

"I hear boats are holes in the water to throw money
into," Thorne said. "My present Hollywood employer
has one of those power racing boats—a Cigarette boat.
Goes like thunder."

"Bales and bales," Reid said, laughing. "But it's okay
to enjoy a sail on someone else's boat."

"Appreciate the invitation," he said. "I'm getting a
little stir-crazy watching TV screens all day and half the
night."

"Well, the thought of your sitting on the pier waiting for us to return would have displaced some of the pleasure. Besides, you guys are the best baby-sitters we've ever had," Reid said. "We can sail without a worry in the world."

"We try," Thorne said as he sipped the cola Laura had handed him.

Reid was standing at the wheel, the wind pressing his hair against his head, the nylon windbreaker flapping in time with the sail as the boat came around. He looked to Thorne like a model in a Rolex ad.

"You make sailing this monster look easy," Thorne said.

"It's the way it's rigged, so I can sail it alone from the bridge. It'll literally sail itself on autopilot. Set it once, and it'll go till it slams into the coast of Scotland."

"Or right into a ship," Laura said.

"The autopilot doesn't have eyes or a brain. It just holds a set compass course."

"Nice," Thorne said. "How deep's the lake?"

"This lake is man-made. About twelve feet deep in most places. Twenty-five miles across, and I'd say about the same wide. You can head out to the river and from there sail to anywhere water touches. This is a safe port unless a hurricane ever comes up the river, pushing water into the lake and into the city. New Orleans is eight to ten feet below sea level."

"Great," Thorne said. "Can't wait to get out of here."

"Back to the safety of earthquakes, mudslides, and fires?" Laura said, laughing.

"According to statistics New Orleans is the most dangerous city in the country. But it is also the most charming. How's that for a paradox?" Reid said. "The Pontchartrain Bridge there is the longest on earth."

Thorne looked up at the twin spans, which seemed to go from the south shore to the end of the earth. The lights from cars streaked along a good forty feet off the water. He had always thought being trapped in a car underwater would be the worst way to die. The way his baby had died.

"You don't have to worry about how shallow it is? This is a big boat."

"Boat only draws six feet of water."

"Ever thought of sailing across the ocean?" Thorne asked.

"In fact, I was thinking of a sail to the Caribbean in a couple of weeks."

"Be careful down there. There are dangerous people on the seas."

"I heard there used to be."

"Still are. Pirates will steal a boat that's large enough to fill up with drugs, or loot it. Then, after they take everything of value or run their drugs, they scuttle or just abandon it. But they like powerboats these days. Big powerboats."

"They always kill the occupants?"

"Oh, Reid, that's horrible," Laura said.

"It's reality in some parts of the world," Thorne said.

Laura said, "It's so peaceful spending the night with the waves caressing the boat. It's the most restful way to sleep there is. Like being rocked in your mother's arms." She was trying to change the subject.

"Keep an AK-47, M-15, or something. Might want a twelve-gauge too."

"A shotgun?" Reid asked.

"Perfect if you aren't much of a shot."

"Can we talk about something else?" Laura showed them a frown.

"I'm sorry," Reid said. "I'm afraid I don't know much about guns. The idea of shooting someone . . ." He let the thought hang.

"I'm gonna shoot the next person that talks about shooting, guns, or violence of any sort." Laura looked toward the bow and let the wind push the hair out of her face.

"It's like old times," Thorne said.

"Too much like old times," she said.

"I'd give anything to get 'em back," Thorne said. "Back to the days before my hair was gray and my belly looked like an Easter egg."

"Your belly is almost perfectly flat, and you know it." Laura smiled at Thorne. "And gray is in. Don't you keep up? Have a beer—or is it still bourbon?" Laura put a hand on his shoulder.

"No. I don't care for anything."

"The fridge is full," she said. "Make yourself at home."

"You sure have all the comforts," Thorne said.

"We try," Reid said. "Sure you don't want a beer? On duty and all that?" he asked.

"I'd love a beer. But AA frowns on drinking."

"Married, Thorne?" Reid asked.

Laura looked at Reid in disbelief. "Thorne's wife was one of Martin's victims, Reid."

Reid smiled the slightly bleary smile of someone who had not been paying close attention to the conversation. Thorne decided his mind was on the boat.

Thorne sipped at the cola. He had been through the Alcoholics Anonymous twelve-step program, and the fourth step had required that he take a searching moral inventory of his life. He had done that and because of it had left his younger wife and infant son. He had come to realize that Ellen was truly comfortable with him only when he was drunk, and that was because drunk, he was dependent on her. He had loved her and his son, but had left her for the sake of his own survival. He had left their small son with her because a judge thought it better for the boy than living with an admitted alcoholic, even given Thorne's year of sobriety. She'd married another addict—a cop who would snort cocaine on duty for a pick-me-up, snort for recreation at home, and probably snort any time he had the opportunity. For a cop the supply side was never a problem.

The couple had moved to Deerfield Beach. When Thorne was told his wife and baby had both died in the canal, he had blamed her, and it occurred to him that the deaths were a perfect excuse to drink again. But in the end the thought of starting over at step one after five years had kept him sober. He kept a sealed half pint of bourbon, which he had bought the day he'd learned of the tragedy, to remind him how easy it would have been to go back. How easy it would always be.

He started to take Reid through his history, but what was the point?

"What kind of electrical system does the *Shadowfax* have?" Thorne said.

"Twelve volt," Reid said. "When the generator is running, we have a hundred twenty for the fridge, microwave, central unit, and the lights. When we're moored, we're hooked up to the land line and the telephone line."

"That'd be a big help if you wanted to live aboard, I guess. It must be hell down there in the summer without AC."

"How is the search going?" Reid asked. "Close to an arrest of this nutcase, Fletcher?"

"This job is segmented. We guard, watch. Others read clues and search high and low."

"Makes selling CAT scanners seem dull," Reid said.

"This is dull. I don't mean now. But usually babysitting is just sitting in a room sipping coffee or sitting in a car trying to stay awake. Normally the stakes are smaller, of course."

"Maybe things will pick up for you," Reid said.

"I hope not," Laura said.

"Maybe Fletcher tucked tail and ran when he discovered he'd have to come through you, Reid," Thorne said, laughing.

Reid laughed, too.

Thorne helped tie the *Shadowfax* to the pier. After Reid locked the cabin doors, the three walked along to a space where a lone fisherman sat on a locker and watched his red-and-white cork floating between two moored sailboats. The trio slowed and watched him cast for a few seconds.

"Biting?" Thorne asked.

The man looked around at them and smiled, showing a mouth filled with gold caps and one milk-coated eye. He mumbled something incoherent that sounded like a few words about warm water, gave a generalized wave at the bay, and laughed like an idiot.

"I love fishing," Reid said.

"See ya," Thorne said to the fisherman, who grumbled something, bobbed his head, and snickered.

The fisherman was certain that he had not been recognized. He turned to watch the trio disappear into the parking lot. Then he twisted around for a better look at the boat parked at the end of the pier.

"*Shadowfax*," Martin Fletcher said as he cranked in the line. Then he propped his back against the closest upright post, closed his eyes, and let the baitless hook dangle beneath the red-and-white float.

31

"Shadow one, everything's locked down?" Sean said into the radio.

"It's calm," the voice of one of the local agents, Alton Vance, came back. "Thorne's package is ten minutes away."

The young agent turned and discovered that Erin and Reb were staring at him. The boy seemed wide-eyed, excited; the girl seemed as though she was being inconvenienced beyond reason. Sean looked over her shoulder to the television set, where a clown was offering a balloon to a child.

Sean looked at the other agent in the room. He hadn't been able to get close to Woody, but they hadn't actually spent much time in anything more than superficial conversation. Woody was like a closed book. Sean didn't know why Woody alone was allowed to leave the stakeout when he wasn't officially on duty. The red

Volvo was an agency car but was Woody's when he decided to take off for a few hours. Sean knew Woody wasn't DEA. He had made a comment about assholes, and Woody had asked him why he always called people, even the elderly owner of the house whom they had never met, assholes. When Sean had said that *all* civilians were assholes, Woody had smiled a strange smile and had shaken his head, dismissing him. "Asshole" was standard DEA lingo. Any cop would know that. He also knew that Woody hadn't participated in the agents' discussions of well-known operations like Condor, Leyenda, and Snowcap. Any DEA agent couldn't help but be familiar with the three—they were classic operations. That would be like an FBI agent not knowing who the last attorney general had been. Wherever Woody had been trained, it hadn't been at Quantico.

"What kinda gun you got?" Reb said, breaking Sean's thoughts.

"A black one," he replied.

Reb laughed.

"Wowie kazowie," Erin said flatly. "Can I go upstairs?"

"Sure," Woody said. "Sean, take her up."

"Want to see me do a double flip off the couch?" Reb asked.

"Sure," Sean said.

"You can't climb on the couch, Reb," Erin said.

"Just kidding," Reb said.

Erin thumped the top of his head.

"Shouldn't you get one of those lady agents to be with me?" she said. "Since I can't have any friends over, I mean."

"Orders," Woody said.

"Two are enough to watch over," Sean said. "Can't have our attention split in too many directions. Sorry about your friends."

"You guys are too cool to breathe," she said.

"Can I shoot it?" Reb asked.

"What?" Woody said.

"Your gun," Reb answered.

"Sure, anytime," Woody said.

Erin watched Woody take the gun from his holster and hold it out to Reb. "Fire it into the cushions so it doesn't bring people running."

"*Really?*" Erin said.

Reb's face was lit like a lamp as he reached for the proffered Glock.

Woody waited until Reb's hand was inches from the handle, then twirled the gun and flipped his wrist, ending the maneuver with the gun restored to the holster.

He pointed his finger at Reb and cocked his thumb. "Just kidding!" he said.

"I want to go out," Erin said. "This is boring."

"Where to?" Sean asked.

"Wouldn't *you* like to know?" she said.

"Would I?" Woody said. He pulled a chair from the kitchen table and sat with his elbows on the back, his legs crossed. "What's your idea of a perfect place?"

"Well, it depends." She smiled coyly.

"On what?" Woody said.

"Well, with a boy or my friends?"

"A *boy* with *Erin*?" Reb yelled.

She cut her eyes at him and frowned at the intrusion. "Well, if you're with a boy, you go to the French Quarter," she said.

"Why?" Woody looked at his watch.

"Well, it's romantic. The old buildings and all that stuff."

"You mean like the Hard Rock Café?"

She laughed. "Maybe. But there's Roscoe's Tavern, where they serve you if you can order with a straight face."

"I'm telling Mom," Reb said certainly.

"I'll crush your little thorax," she said.

"Okay, guys," Sean said, putting his finger to his earpiece, "your mother's home."

"Good," Erin said. "Now you can go back across the street."

Sean looked up to find Woody staring at him with a complete lack of expression.

32

PAUL STEPPED FROM HIS RENTAL CAR AND SCOOPED UP THE FILES HE had brought along. Sherry had called and asked him to drop by because she had had some ideas she wanted to toss around with him. She said she didn't want to stay at the office late because she had things to do at home. He knew she had been mirroring his long hours, so he had agreed, and here he was, standing before her door and tapping lightly. He checked over his mental list again as he waited; he had been on and off the phone with Thorne and Joe all day, as usual, and he had been assured that nothing was happening that warranted his attention. Rainey, he hoped, was interviewing the Buchanan child and getting some new information.

Paul could hear music inside. A ten-speed bike was chained to the railing with a lock he decided could be violated in seconds by any crack addict worth his stuff. He shuffled the files into his left hand and was pleased that the hand had developed so much strength over the past few days of vigorous tennis-ball squeezing. He could drum the fingers on a tabletop with relative ease and surprising dexterity.

Sherry opened the door and smiled out at him.

"Any trouble finding the place?" she said.

"No. I followed the opera music."

"Come in. I'm cooking us a snack."

Sherry lived in a cozy one-bedroom apartment near Vanderbilt University. In the space of thirty feet the living room became the dining room, which became the kitchen. From what Paul could see from the living room, the bedroom was large enough only for the double bed, covered by a thin Indian-print cotton throw, a dresser, a trunk painted sky-blue with white trim, and a bookshelf filled with books. The living room held two matching shelf units also loaded with books in all sizes and of all ages.

"We're having lasagna. I hope you like Italian. I guess opera seems highbrow, but it helps me cook Italian to hear Italian."

"I love Italian," he said. "I'd have picked up a bottle of wine if I'd known we were eating."

"You haven't? Eaten, I mean?"

"No."

"I've got the perfect bottle of red—Chianti with the little black rooster on the label. A friend who knows Italy says you should look for the rooster on a Chianti bottle because the rooster stands for the region where the best Chianti comes from."

He was silent.

She turned and looked at him and cocked her head. "You brought the files?" She sounded—what? Indifferent?

"Yes."

"Good, you look so much better outside the office."

"I know what I look like, Sherry. So do you—remember?" He fumbled at his jacket pocket nervously. "Mind if I smoke?"

"Of course you know what you look like! Ashtray's

on the coffee table. Listen, Paul. Let's get one thing out in
the open. Your face is screwed up a bit." She looked
down and then back up at him. "Okay, it's screwed up a
lot. But there is a difference between being ugly and having a face that looks like . . ." She paused. "Let me put
it this way. Everybody has a good side. But usually they
have to tell you which one it is. You've just done away
with the guesswork."

"I was going to say a Picasso."

She laughed. "Okay, I might have chosen a different
artist. But, look, it's none of my business. You've evidently had a rough time, and your face really doesn't
matter to me. I didn't ask you here to analyze you, pity
you, mother you, or kiss your ass to get a better job."

"You said you had some thoughts?"

"Oh, that. It was a ruse." She busied herself rinsing
glasses that she had pulled from the cabinet.

"Why did you ask me here?"

"I asked you here . . ." She stopped making the
salad and looked at him. "Usually people skirt around a
bit before they get into the heavy shit. But since you want
to know. I asked you here because I'm attracted to you,
and I thought I could talk to you here."

Paul grimaced. Why did she want to talk to him?
What did she really want? Didn't she know his status
was temporary?

She laughed as though she had read the thoughts.

He nodded. "Could I have a glass of the rooster red
you spoke of?" he asked.

"Sure," she said. She poured him a glass of wine and
worked on the salad while he sipped.

"So what's the game plan? What do we talk about?
Montana game laws? That's about all I know anymore."

"Well, according to my overall plot I thought we'd
eat and drink wine. Then we can talk and see if there is a
mutual attraction. . . ."

Paul felt weak in the knees. "There is. I mean, I feel
an attraction to most beautiful women."

"But you've been in a cave in Montana. I'll bet you'd
be attracted to a . . ." She smiled. "Never mind. In that

case, saying it holds through the food and wine, then we can go into the next room and . . . you know."

"I know?"

"Well, we can take our clothes off and . . . like in the romance books."

"Just like that?"

"Normally I'd expect you to court me for the socially proper time. Flowers, candy, dinner out, and a few movies."

"Normally?" His mind was screaming that something was wrong with all of this. He fought an urge to run for it, out to his car and back to the hotel. But she compelled him with her eyes . . . made him want to stay.

"Paul," she said. "Relax. This operation may well end tomorrow or the next day, so I'm not sure we have the time or if I'm your type or any of that. I decided to reach out to you."

"It's been . . . I mean, I was expecting something altogether different."

"You haven't noticed me watching you? I thought you had. I've noticed you watching me."

"People must watch you all the time. You're a beautiful girl. This probably isn't a good idea."

"Normally I'm not this forward, and I've never jumped into bed with anyone on a first date, but I'm willing to make an exception because we're adults, and I've glanced at the Kama Sutra, and where this goes is up to you. But rules, now. We don't discuss the low points of your life, we don't feel sorry for each other. If the food stinks, you can lie about that. I hope you like lasagna," she said again as she picked up a pair of pot holders and reached into the oven for the dish. "If you want to leave after dinner, go. If you want to stay, stay. Okay?"

He managed a weak nod.

As she was passing him on the way to the table with the hot pan stuck between pot holders in her hands, she paused and kissed him on the lips, gently. She looked him in the eye and smiled, and he could see that she really didn't care about his ruined appearance. It almost eased his nervousness, but he hadn't been in a romantic setting with a woman he was attracted to in something like six years. And then it had been Laura. He had known her intimately, and he had had an unscarred face and the natural confidence of a bulldog. That moment seemed a million years in the past.

She lit candles and turned the electric lights off.

They bumped their knees together, under the table, through dinner. It started as accidental, but each time they brushed against each other, the contact lasted longer. Paul was a bit self-conscious; he'd forgotten what a first date felt like, and he felt himself getting aroused. He was flattered by her attention. He liked Sherry, but he was haunted by second thoughts. What could she be setting him up for?

"It can't be sexual harassment if it's my idea," she said, seeming to read his mind. "Maybe you can sue *me*."

"Your idea?"

"You'd better believe it," she said.

Dinner ended, and Sherry replaced the classical CD they'd listened to during the meal with a Nat King Cole disk. Then she poured them glasses of wine, led him to the couch, and sat beside him with her legs tucked up, her knees against his thigh, her hand behind his shoulder.

"Get enough to eat?"

"Yeah, but with Italian you're hungry again in a week."

"Comfortable?" she asked, laughing at his joke.

"I'm getting there," he replied. He reached up and put his hand under her chin and brought her in close for a long, deep kiss.

"Can we talk a little, I mean, before we retire to the other room? I know I've seen you every day for the last few days, but we never just talked before."

"You hardly know me," he said.

"Everyone hardly knows you. I mean, they know what they see . . . observe about you. Like people follow you without even realizing they've made a choice in the matter. It's something about your eyes—I mean your eye"—she smiled—"it has real depth to it."

"Like a dark pool in the moonlight," he said.

"Stop crackin' wise." She touched his scar so gently, he hardly felt it at all. "Even this. No one notices for long. Not after they hear you talk. They assume you've been there and given your all. Battle worn."

Paul sat up. "My all? I didn't give anything, Sherry. I stumbled into a wasp's nest and good people died. They died for sins they didn't commit."

"I'm sure you're wrong."

"See, Sherry, most leaders aren't shit. Just because you call someone Chief doesn't mean they are. Look at the pharaohs and the thousands of slaves they killed to build a tomb for their own remains. Little leaders, like me, are no different, really. People get promoted despite themselves. Look at T. C. Robertson, for Christ's sake. I was just as bad. Names became small tags to move around a board. Someone's getting too big for their own britches—move 'em to Alaska and let 'em wade through ship holds of tuna looking for a kilo of grass. Their families, too. Out of sight with the snap of a finger. Let's not get into what sort of leader I was. I don't want to remember those days."

"From what I know of you, you were a good leader, Paul. Rainey said you were the best and the brightest."

" 'Was' is the key word."

"Paul, none of that matters. I mean, people have died, but you had no way of knowing they would die. I don't believe that it was your fault for one minute, and I don't see how you can believe it either. You defeated Martin Fletcher fair and square, and he couldn't see his own guilt because he's narcissistic."

"Martin doesn't hate me because I defeated him. He hates me because he thinks that I violated the warrior's code he imagines he lives by. That I cheated and I wasn't man enough to come after him head on. That I was responsible for his collapse."

"Cheated him?"

"He thinks I framed him."

"Did you?"

"It would have been dishonest, against the code, and a coward's way out. But—"

"But?" she asked.

"But maybe sometimes things have to be done around corners. I mean, we make choices that seem better than the other alternatives." He looked at her to see if he was saying too much, or not enough. Why burden her with his personal cross? "Hindsight is twenty-twenty. But in his mind I'm a coward, and maybe he's right. I shouldn't have arrested him. I should have shot him between the eyes while he was sitting across a table from me. Eye to eye, man to man. *That* the man would have understood. But I just didn't have what it took. That was the right thing to do. Then I would deserve . . ." He stopped and looked at her. There were tears in his eyes. "I would deserve . . ."

"Everything you've thrown away."

Suddenly Paul began to tremble, and he looked distressed, as if he were going to vomit, but he just began to cry, silent tears streaming down his cheek. Sherry held him tightly while his arms hung limp, and he cried like a child. He cried for a long time as she held him.

When he stopped crying, she could feel the wall going back up.

"See what a leader I am? I'm sorry, I'd better go." He shifted his weight away from her.

"Why?"

"This really isn't a good idea . . . I mean the wine and everything. I guess I should apologize for . . ."

"I could quit the job. That's it, isn't it?"

"What?"

"Do I look like someone who can't find a job without making the boss? Plus you're temporary here."

"You're serious?" Paul stared at her, studying her, suddenly seeing her differently from the way he had before.

"Dead serious."

"Boy, are you setting yourself up for a disappointment." He managed a nervous smile.

• • •

Paul stood beside the bed while Sherry undressed him slowly in the darkness. He was almost embarrassed. She peeled off the shirt, the pants, and the rest, and as she did, she covered the skin she was exposing with kisses. She ran her tongue over the bullet scars as she found them, nipped at the skin with her teeth, gently. Paul shivered; his wounded leg shook involuntarily, and he felt as if he were going to fall down, but he remained standing until she led him into the sheets. Then, with her back to him, she lit a candle and removed her clothes and draped them over the dresser slowly as he watched from the bed. It was like some wonderful adolescent dream. She turned, and as she did, her softly contoured buttocks became a triangle of dark pubic hair, and her shoulders gave way to her perfect breasts with small, dark nipples. She knelt into him and pressed her body against his torso. He kissed her breasts and her neck and pulled her down. They embraced and rolled toward the center of the bed, and Paul trembled like an awkward schoolboy about to get his first taste of love.

Later they were lying beside each other—he smoking a cigarette, she tracing words he couldn't decipher on his chest with her finger. For the first time in five years he felt safe, if only for that moment. In a small apartment in Nashville, far from the stone walls outside his cabin, which he had assumed could shelter him. Even though she had said it didn't bother her, he put the cigarette out after a couple of drags.

"You have a beautiful body," she said. "For an old man, I mean."

"So how old are you?"

"Small talk?" she giggled. "You know how old I am. You pulled my file and read it. I saw it open on your desk."

"Sorry. I was just trying to . . ."

"Make conversation?"

"Something like that."

She snuggled against him and twirled his chest hair with her finger. "My turn to open up? Okay, fair's fair.

Let's see what my file didn't tell you. My father was a biology professor, and my mom was Amerasian and taught painting. Only child. Spoiled rotten. Good childhood. Believed in Santa Claus until I was in junior high. Boy, did I feel like an idiot. Betrayed by my own parents, by commercial interests, by the media. Now, tell me about your childhood."

"Boring stuff."

"After I finish, okay? Will you?"

Paul nodded.

"You're the fourth man I've ever slept with. That's due to a natural shyness, not lack of want. Bert, my high-school sweetheart and first husband, was the first."

"You've been married."

"Yes. It lasted through our freshman year, when he found his next true love. Then I had this year-long rebound with my western-civilization professor who looked like Mussolini. Then I had a long romance with an archaeologist in graduate school, and now there's you."

"It's been a while for me, too."

"I can imagine. Living on a mountain in Bear Butt, Wyoming."

"Montana."

"Same thing. What, they don't have girls there?"

"My wife, Laura, was the last. Been about six years, I guess."

The memory of the last time they had made love sank a shaft through his soul. It was something he had managed to repress. Was it sex? No, it had been something else. Anger, rage, and pain. God, had that been he? How could he have done that to Laura? He remembered her face, the tears, which had given way to a look of betrayal, hurt, and finally something close to blind hatred.

He felt as if he had been shot through, hollow, and there was a taste in his mouth that was coppery, acrid. He wanted to get up and run, but he was affixed to the spot. Later that same night there had been a terrible fight.

He remembered how it had started . . . it was too pain-ful . . . was that why he hadn't remembered?

"You all right?" she asked, shattering the thought.

He smiled as best he could through the curtain of pain and confusion. What else had he repressed that was crucial? What else? Why did he think of Barnett and Hill so much? He had hardly known them. Had he? Suddenly there was a swarm of memories swirling so fast that he couldn't see them clearly, but he had the sense that they were important.

"Hope this was worth breaking the fast for."

Paul laughed nervously—distracted and filled with anxiety and . . . fear. "It was, Sherry. This was wonder-ful for me."

"Your childhood. Remember?"

Not now! Jesus, not now. Something important is happen-ing.

Sherry sat up and looked down at him, realizing something was wrong. "Are you all right? What the hell is going on? Did I say something?" There was pain in her voice. "Paul?"

"I'm fine."

"You look like you've seen a ghost."

Several. He took a deep breath and lit another ciga-rette; the fingers of his right hand trembled. "It's okay, I thought I'd pulled a muscle for a second is all." He imi-tated a laugh.

"My story. Let's see. There was a father. He was a writer who published twenty paperback pulp westerns. He lived in Louis L'Amour's shadow. We got by, but his career wasn't much in the way of a living. My uncle Aaron sort of subsidized us with the store he owned— owns. I worked in his store from the time I was four or five."

"Hard labor?"

"Aaron's a great character. He makes everything an ordeal. Sees life as a very narrow path."

"True grit?"

"The truest. He's been more of a father than uncle. He was proud of my father—sold his books in the store.

He saved a complete set for me, but I expect they're dust by now."

"Were you close to your father?"

"I guess. He died of lung cancer when I was a small boy. Then a few months later my mom died, too. I was at the store one day, and there was a freak accident with a horse that kicked her, knocked her out, and she froze to death right there by the barn. So I stayed on with Uncle Aaron. When I was sixteen, I moved into a cabin he'd built."

"College?"

"College. This man with a lot of money and power had a cabin—hell, a log mansion he called a lodge—near our place. His boy fell into the water, and I was there and got him out, and so to show his gratitude, the boy's father paid my college fees. I found out later that the National Human Resource Foundation, which awarded me a full scholarship, was his. So the McMillans rewarded me with a degree. Good swap for a few minutes in cold water."

"Jack McMillan? The oil man?"

Paul nodded.

"Paul, he's the richest man in America, isn't he?"

"Well, I'd say he's right up there with the top ten or so. I don't think paying for my education was a drain."

"Was he . . . I mean, did he pull strings for you, after?"

"My career?" He tried to keep the edge out of his voice.

"I didn't mean anything by that."

"I never traded on our relationship." *Until recently, anyway.* "He's repaid me a hundred times over for something I would have done for anyone. I asked him to let me follow my own path. I didn't want to owe him my life."

"Your history's certainly a lot more impressive than mine. I met Captain Kangaroo once."

"See, you're one up on me."

"I only have three people to compare you to, but you're definitely in the top fiftieth percentile." She lifted the covers and peeked in. "Well, you old cowpoke, ready for another swing around the dance floor?"

Paul had to fight hard to gain consciousness, and as he moved into a state of awareness, he realized that he'd been drugged. His perception was way off, and he couldn't move his arms or legs. He could make out the shape of someone standing beside the bed. A dark hood shrouded the features.

"Who are you?" he asked.

"Who do you think?" Martin said as he moved into Paul's field of vision.

"Martin?"

"It's one of my names. It was Martin Fletcher you condemned with false evidence."

"No, I saved your life. The others wanted to—"

"You had Barnett, Hill, and Thorne Greer help you. You put the drugs and money in the wall behind the bookshelf while I was away. Like a thief in the night. And because I went to prison, the Company wanted me silenced. So my wife and son were murdered. I escaped alone, and I remained alone to be eaten by this cancer of pain."

Paul felt Sherry beside him.

Martin stepped closer. "So it is true. You set it up."

"No," he lied.

"Ask them. . . ." Martin stepped back to allow Paul to see that Barnett and Hill were across the room. They were standing at attention. "Tell my old adversary what you told me," Martin commanded them.

"It's true, sir," they said. "You killed us."

Martin stepped away from the bed and pulled his hood back. The face was familiar . . . it was the face of Paul's father as he had looked in the hospital. The skin was withered parchment-yellow and had patches of mold on it. "It was dishonest. You have brought this on all of them. It's on your head. You are hereby condemned. I have opened the gates of hell for you."

Paul's mind was on fire, and the pain was blinding,

excruciating; he knew, even through the agony, that this would last for eternity.

Paul screamed himself awake. As he opened his eye, he realized that Sherry's bed was on the top of a tower and she was gone. He sat up and looked down to discover that the structure, hardly larger than the bed itself, was a good eight or nine hundred feet in the air and was made from ancient bricks set in crumbling mortar. He looked down in horror and realized that the tower was breaking apart as it reacted to the breeze, swaying. Then he realized that there were other towers at different levels. The closest was lower by thirty feet or so. Laura and his children were standing on it, huddled together. They swayed close together and then away at intervals. He knew he could jump, but if he did, the towers might both collapse. He thought that they would collapse soon anyway. They moved like cobras being charmed, and bricks were falling from them as they moved. As his tower tilted crazily and snapped in the middle, he jumped. He caught the edge of his family's tower and realized that they weren't even on it, but on a third, farther away. The tower he had been on collapsed, and he watched the bricks scatter silently. They fell, and a dust cloud grew as the debris hit. He tried to pull himself up but the platform slipped and swayed. Laura swung her own tower toward him and grabbed his arm. Then she, Reb, and Erin pulled him up and onto the final platform. He hugged them, and the tower tilted crazily and collapsed. They fell screaming toward the ground. He tried to flare out and fly, but he was falling too fast. And he couldn't reach out to them. Somewhere inside his thoughts he knew he was dreaming.

He jerked awake in Sherry's bed, holding on to her tightly. "Laura! Laura . . . I'm sorry!" Then he realized that this wasn't Laura but Sherry.

"Are you all right?" she asked.

"Yes," he said. *No, I'm not all right. I'm dying.*

"You were yelling 'Laura.' "

"My wife. Ex-wife."

"Should I be jealous?"

Paul got out of the bed slowly and pulled on his pants awkwardly.

"Leaving?" she asked. "Please don't leave."

He sat down on the bed and kissed her tenderly. "I'm just not accustomed to sharing a bed. Besides, I have to get some work done."

"Are you sure? I was planning breakfast in bed," she said as she looked at the clock. "I can fix it now. It'll be light soon."

"Can I have a rain check?" He pulled on his shirt.

"Sure. I reckon I could stomach at least one more night of pure excitement beyond a human's pleasure measure."

33

Reid was snoring. Laura had lain awake for what seemed like hours before she took any action other than closing her eyes and trying to ignore the rhythmic sound. She nudged him and applied pressure until he rolled from his back onto his side. That usually worked. He snored when he drank, which was rare, and when the pollen count was high, or maybe it was something weather and plant related. She didn't want to wake him until she had to get him moving before the kids woke up. Once she had explained the relationship to them, they had more or less accepted it. She wanted to sleep, but she found that she had opened the door and allowed thoughts and anxieties to enter. She had to face the fact that sleep was not going to be rejoined.

Laura didn't know why, but since she had learned Paul was out of Montana, she hadn't felt the same about Reid. Some spark was gone, but maybe when this nightmare was over, things would return to the way they had been. But for the first time in their relationship she was ashamed that they were sleeping together. Maybe it was because of the danger. She thought of Paul more and more—all the time. Obsessed with the unobtainable. *The man abandoned us physically and emotionally. Or did we abandon his needs?* She wanted to feel angry, but she couldn't. She hadn't thought for a long time that she could still be in love with Paul. Was it possible?

She got out of bed without waking Reid, dressed for work, and left the room with Wolf leading the way. She would have moved past Reb's room except for the fact that there was a sliver of shimmering light at the bottom of the door, which signaled that the TV set was on. Reb often fell asleep with the set turned on. She reached in to turn off the television and found her son illuminated by the glow of a black-and-white western. He was perched on the window box staring out the window, hugging his knees to his chest.

"Reb?" she said. "Do you know what time it is?" She approached the child, who didn't move. "Reb, are you okay?"

"I don't understand why," he said, his lip quivering. "What did we do to him to make him hate us? I was just little."

She hugged Reb to her chest and looked out at the wall of bamboo where the sleeping blackbirds were staggered like musical notes. "Your father doesn't hate you or me or Erin either. He loves you and Erin very much. Your father is in pain, Reb."

Reb pushed away so he could look into Laura's eyes. "In pain? Why doesn't he take something?"

"His pain is beyond medicine, Reb. See, I think he feels guilty because his career is over, and because two of his men were killed when he got hurt. Two young men that he felt responsible for. He thought he should have been more careful. I think somehow he's punishing himself by keeping away from us. But he loves you guys."

"And you, too?"

"In his own way."

"And Mr. Greer was with him?"

"Thorne was there. In fact, he saved your father's life."

"Why does that man want to kill us?"

"Some people are just crazy."

"If Daddy doesn't hate us, why isn't he here? He could still be here—where they are. You know, across the street."

"He can do more where he is."

"One time you told me that he didn't get his face fixed because it would hurt too much. But Erin said Daddy didn't get his face fixed because he didn't want to."

"The doctors I spoke to thought he wouldn't get his face fixed because of guilt. They said he was using it as a way to punish himself because of what happened to two agents who were with him, the ones that were killed. He left us because he couldn't believe he deserved to be happy. So he deprived himself of the things he loved best. The people who loved him best he tried to drive away, too, and when he couldn't, he left."

"You believe that?"

"I believe he might have used his disfigurement to cut himself off from the things he loved. That could have been fixed, and he knew it. We loved him and he knew that, too. I know he didn't want to be loved." *But what about the night before he left? What did that do?* Laura pushed the thought back down.

"He said that?"

"No. But I know your father really well, and I think he covered up his real feelings. He probably doesn't know why he did what he did any more than we do."

"Maybe we should tell him that."

"Waste of breath. Your father doesn't see that he's selfish. He doesn't want to share his pain with us. Maybe time will heal him. But, Reb, one thing is certain. Your father doesn't hate you. He doesn't know you, and that's his loss, not yours. We have to go on with our lives. Put him behind us."

"What about Reid?"

"I don't know. Let's wait and see. Now, go to bed."

"Don't get me wrong," he started. "Reid's a nice guy and all, but it isn't the same thing. He could never be my own father."

Laura kissed her son on the forehead and went out. Wolf, seemingly pleased that a trip was in the making, licked her hand as they walked down the hall toward the staircase.

No, Reid couldn't be your father. Not any more than he could be my husband.

Reb climbed out of the bed and knelt beside it. He folded his hands on the sheet and closed his eyes. "Dear God, please bless Mama, Erin, Reid, Wolf, and the men watching. Please talk to my daddy and tell him . . . we love him very much. Tell him we want to be together again. I'll do anything you want me to if you'll help me just this once. I know I ask you for stuff all the time, but I won't bother you about other stuff if you'll let Daddy come back and let the bad man go away and leave us alone. Me and Erin need our daddy. I do so I'll know how I'm supposed to act when I grow up. And he needs us so he won't mind getting old and so his heart will stay warmed up."

He paused, thinking for a few seconds.

"God, I'm real sorry I was mean to him on the phone, but it was hurting my heart. He's my daddy and I just want him back, and I don't care if his face is all messed up or anything. Really. We all do, even Erin, and even if she won't ever admit it cause she thinks she's tough. I know how busy you are, so thank you for listening, sir. Amen."

Reb climbed into his sleeping bag and put his thumb in his mouth and lay there with his eyes open, wondering if the message had got through with all the millions of other prayers that were making their way to God's ear.

The agents had moved back across the street after Laura and Reid had returned. Thorne Greer was sitting with the earphones in place watching the perimeter of the Masterson house on the monitors as the camera views were alternated every five seconds. He wasn't aware that he was watching until something moved on a screen. He watched as a cat jumped over the wall, and then he tracked the animal's progress until it disappeared into the tall grass beside the path. Woody and Sean were asleep on the twin beds across the bedroom. As he listened to Reb's prayer again, he prayed silently for the son he had lost in the canal. A son who could never kneel and pray for his father. And he prayed that Reb's prayer be answered.

Thorne waited until Reb was back in bed for a few minutes to shift in his own chair. It was as if he thought he would disturb the boy by moving. Thorne poured another cup of coffee from the pot and sat back.

He looked over at Woody and Sean, who were sound asleep. How much help would they be when Martin came at them? This was their first job together. Woody was often silent, strange around the edges. His sense of humor seemed forced, as if jokes were something he saw as unnecessary. He never really got into the spirit of things the way Sean did. He was detached, observing and filing everything away in his mind for future reference or something.

Sean, the proverbial baby face, was another matter. With his game-show host looks, he didn't seem overly competent. He was short, but the women's movement and the relaxation of physical minimums had allowed him to enter the agency as an agent in the field. Maybe some disguised skills would show up when they were in a pinch, but by then it might be too late. Sean reminded him somehow of Joe Barnett, one of the rookies killed in Miami. It was then that Thorne realized that all of the agents on this job were single. As far as he knew, there wasn't a husband, a wife, or even a serious relationship in the bunch.

Woody and Sean had certainly never discussed girlfriends, beyond making boastful conversation about their conquests. Sean and his father shared a house on an island in Puget Sound and raised bloodhounds. Woody lived alone in Los Angeles but didn't have a California tan. The only person with a wife or kids was Paul. Thorne realized that Paul didn't want to have to worry about anyone's family except his own, and he didn't want anyone in the field to be worrying about any family other than his either. *Were better-qualified agents discarded for that reason?* It was a good question, and someday he thought he might confront Paul with it.

Thorne had serious doubts that he could take Martin in a fair fight. Not that there would be a fair fight, because it was against Martin's nature. But Thorne would certainly lose if things were within spitting distance of equal. At forty-seven Martin Fletcher would still be in fighting trim. Thorne wasn't, however he might look to the untrained eye. Fighting trim was a way of life—mental, physical, and emotional. Traveling with celebrities, watching party guests, playing volleyball, and working out with weights wasn't even a good start on it. He worked out at a gym three times a week, and he could run a few miles without passing out, but Martin was a different story. Martin was the sort that had to be taken by surprise, from ambush.

34

Eve Fletcher awoke to discover her small dog lying like a paperweight on the foot of her bed. She sat up and probed at his body with her toe under the sheet. "Puzzle? Mr. Puzzle?"

A block away, inside the DEA van, Larry Burrows sat with a cup of coffee watching the screen.

"Goddammit, Mr. Puzzle!"

"Hey, come see this!" Larry yelled. Sierra rolled from the bunk, rubbing her swollen eyes, her hair pressed against the side of her head. She looked at her watch. "What the heck, Burrows? It isn't time for my shift."

"Look, old Eve's got herself that fur-covered doorstop she's been praying for."

"Owww, her's gonna be in a foul mood today," Sierra said.

On the screen Eve had got out of bed and stood hunched over, punching at the stiff dog's flank with a pencil.

Sierra poured a cup of coffee and sat down in a swivel chair. "You taping this?"

"I'm going to send it to *America's Funniest Home Videos*."

Eve lifted the dog's leg with the eraser end and peered at his belly.

"What's she doing now?"

"Maybe she's gonna give him the fuck-of-life maneuver."

"Please, I haven't had my coffee yet. Mouth to mouth," she said, laughing.

Then, as Sierra and Larry watched, Eve rushed down the hall and into the kitchen. Larry switched the views so that they had the back of her leaving the bedroom, a long shot of her approaching the kitchen down the narrow hallway, and the top of her head and shoulders as she rummaged through the kitchen cabinets. When she straightened up, one of her sagging breasts came free of her gown.

"God, that turns me on," Larry said.

"Grief," Sierra said. "Have some respect for the bereaved. She just lost her sole companion and best friend. He was like her own child."

"Does she look like Jerry Clower in drag, or is it just me?"

"Who's Jerry Clower?"

"Country comedian . . . a hayseed Tip O'Neill clone," he said.

The camera shots changed as Larry turned the selector switch to maintain continuity. B: hallway south, C: kitchen. When Eve came back, she stopped and put her hands into sandwich bags for mittens. Then she used one to lift the dog by its tail and the other to open the dark, already partially filled, garbage bag. She dropped him in, removed the sandwich bags from her hands, and tossed them in. Then Eve pulled the drawstring tight and tied it into a knot. The roof-mounted cameras followed her back to the kitchen and out the back door, where she opened the lid to the refuse can, threw the bag in, slammed the lid down, and then went straight back into the house without so much as a peek over her shoulder.

"Nice service," Larry said. "But she wasted a bag that coulda held a lot more. Coulda used one of those little candy-sized bags."

"Forget what I said about respect. I hope she catches her tit in a drawer," Sierra said.

"I guess different folks deal with grief in different ways," Larry added. "Something tells me she'll get over this loss, somehow." He removed his wire-framed glasses and wiped the lenses inside a pinched fold of Polo shirttail.

He changed to an image of Eve's legs protruding from the closet in what had been Martin's room. The room was as Martin had left it when he'd joined the service. Twin beds with baseball players depicted on the spreads. A round braided rug and a chest of drawers with Martin's artifacts still displayed on the top, as though he could return at any minute to assume his previous life.

"What the hell's she doing now, looking for the dog's insurance policy?"

Sierra sipped at the cup of coffee. "Look," she said. "What's that she's throwing out?"

Rectangular objects were hitting the floor behind Eve's feet.

"Money!"

"Jesus, it's bills! Old bitch's got herself a stash of cash."

"If those are C notes . . . there's over a hundred thousand showing. She coulda bought the little carpet crapper a cigar box or something."

Eve finished and then started stuffing the cash into a large wicker purse that had been under the closest bed. Then she pulled three wig boxes from the closet and took the wigs out and lined them up.

"She's going somewhere as a woman," Larry said.

Sierra tapped his shoulder and he ducked. "Ouch!" he said, laughing.

"She's taking the money to Martin," Joe McLean said

over their shoulders. "Let's get ready. She's leaving for Florida. Fifty bucks says next flight."

He lifted the telephone and dialed Paul.

Larry and Sierra looked at each other and wondered how long Joe had been standing there behind them.

35

PAUL HAD LEFT SHERRY'S APARTMENT, GONE HOME FOR A SHOWER, and had taken Joe's call while he was drying off. He dressed hurriedly and drove straight to the office, pausing only then to call Rainey and Sherry on the cell phone to tell them to hurry over to the office without any explanation. Then he had armed the phone's signal scrambler to make sure the call was secure before he called Thorne in New Orleans.

"When you leaving for Miami?" Thorne asked.

"As soon as Eve leaves her house," he said. "I'm headed to the office first to make sure everything's in motion," he said.

"I wish I was going in with you and the boys," Thorne said.

"I'm depending on you to take care of things in New Orleans. No one else I can trust, Thorne."

"Okay, Paul," he said, not masking the disappointment. "See you after the shoe drops. Don't lower your guard for a second. Good-bye."

The telephone went dead.

It was quiet in the conference room. Paul made a pot of coffee, but he didn't need it—Joe's call had him wired. The dream was still haunting him. Maybe "haunting" wasn't the right word. Stalking him.

Paul spent the next hour trying to decide what Martin would do between the time he met his mother and the time when he returned to complete his revenge against the family.

Rainey came in and interrupted Paul's thoughts.

"Tried to call you last night," he said. "I was afraid you'd left without me. You wouldn't do that, would you?"

"No, Rainey. I had some thinking to do. What about the Buchanan kid?"

"He doesn't remember anything," he said. He shrugged his shoulders and sat in a chair, which he turned to the window. "It's October the first. That means it's going to come down real soon."

Paul nodded his agreement. "Sooner than that," he said, smiling. "Today."

"Thank you, Jesus," Rainey whispered.

The telephone rang and Sherry's voice came over the intercom. "Mr. Masterson, Tod Peoples on one," she said. There was a new, playful lilt to her voice.

Rainey stood and walked toward the door. "Want coffee?" he asked as he opened it.

Paul shook his head as he picked up the telephone.

Tod Peoples seemed pleased with himself. "Back from the dead? I must've called the Hyatt twenty times. Your cell phone was off."

"Battery was dead," he lied.

"I got some very hot news for you."

"Eve is flying out today," Paul said.

"Very old news, that. I'm talking about what our bad boy has been up to in the Crescent City."

"He was in New Orleans?"

"Oh, yes, he certainly was. And . . . he most definitely isn't working alone."

"Tell me what you got, Tod." Paul lit a cigarette and listened to the account of Lallo Estevez's murder and the finding of two other bodies, one a known hit man.

"There's no proof it was Martin," Paul said at last.

"No," Tod agreed. "No proof. But we both know it was."

"Okay. I've got some things to do." Paul was fighting the urge to scream out loud.

"Oh, by the way. Remember the prints you sent?"

"What? Oh, the envelope." He felt strange, lightheaded.

"I ran them against every known and unknown. Amazing. We collect prints from all over the world and—"

"Tod, please cut to the chase. I've got a lot to do." *Like get things in motion and figure out what these dead Latins mean.*

"Kurt Steiner's left thumb and index finger. Maybe he mailed it."

"You know him? Fax me a picture! Christ, that's great!" Suddenly Paul was ecstatic.

"Can't help you on that one, Paul. His prints came to me from a police ID card from Argentina. I only had it on file because the Colombian army came across a print or two on a weapon they happened across at a jungle training facility. One of those resorts for the cocaine barons."

Paul was squeezing the tennis ball furiously. "So you know who he is. But not what he looks like? I presume he isn't a mail carrier these days in Colorado."

"Yes and no. I mean, I know who he is . . . but nothing else."

"Tod. I hope you won't take this wrong, but if you had more information on this Steiner, you'd tell me, right? I mean, you wouldn't limit my information? I know you parcel out bits and pieces and that you have your own agenda. But, Tod. We're talking about my children. My wife." There was an edge to his voice that he couldn't control.

There was a strange silence for a few seconds.

"I've told you what I know. I wish I could do better."

Paul slammed down the telephone receiver, sat for a few seconds, and then lifted the phone and pressed a preset speed code.

When Rainey came back into the room, Paul was talking feverishly into the telephone. "I don't give a rat's ass whether she likes it or not. Get your people in that house and all around it. For the next few hours don't let them leave the premises for any reason." He listened for a beat. "Get what you need—agents, cops, the fuckin' Army and the SWAT team. If she gives you any trouble, you call me." Paul slammed the telephone down and lit a cigarette even though he had one burning in the ashtray at his right.

"Peoples?" Rainey sat on the table looking down at Paul.

"No, Thorne. Remember a Colombian coffee broker named Lallo Estevez?"

"Sure, the dapper coffee dealer."

"We knew he was connected with the Medellín cartel, but we couldn't pin anything solid on him."

"Yeah, I remember him. Influential pals in D.C."

"He's dead. A towboat crew fished a guy out of the Mississippi River yesterday ten miles south of New Orleans. No ID, but he had his throat slit from ear to ear with his tongue pulled through above the Adam's apple. Feds ID'd him by his prints."

"And it was Lallo Estevez?"

"No. Was a guy named Ramon something. I'm ahead of myself. The floater was a freelance Colombian hitter."

"Maybe it was a Colombian suicide," Rainey laughed. Paul smiled at the fact that Rainey had made a joke.

"He was an enforcer with Perez years ago. Lallo was reported missing by his wife about the same time this guy was surfacing . . . so to speak. The investigating cops found something on the coffee baron's desk—a list he'd evidently made the day he died, which they turned over to the feds."

Paul crushed out the cigarette that he had left in the ashtray before he continued.

"Estevez's wife called the police because he hadn't come home. The driver, his bodyguard, didn't come home either. The last thing on the list was an entry to meet 'M' at eleven on his company-owned dock on the Mississippi River. The cops snooped around the dock, and there was a place where there was a lot of broken auto safety glass and where something had scraped the edge of the pier. So they brought in a portable sonar, which picked up something downstream. They dropped cameras, and voilà . . . Cadillac with two corpses inside."

"Estevez?"

"The chauffeur was buckled in his seat belt with a round just behind the ear. Same gun as Mr. Necktie was killed with. Estevez was in the trunk."

"You said he had his throat slit?"

"The hitter did."

"Was it Fletcher? Martin has time to wander around killing *everybody* he's pissed at?"

"Peoples is ready to bet big bucks on it," Paul said.

"So he's been in New Orleans." Rainey had a far-away look in his eyes. "Could he still be?"

"For the moment I'm assuming that's possible," Paul said. "He's capable. Thorne's team is moving in with Laura until this is over. He'll meet his mother in Disney World and double back for the finale, but there is a slight chance he might be planning to escape to Florida *after* he attacks my family and meet his mother while we're running around chasing our tails."

"Or he might not be after your family. He said he wasn't going to kill them. Maybe he just wanted you to worry and commit a force to protecting them while he lounged around in Disney World with Mama."

"Possible." Paul allowed himself to smile. He lifted the cane and tapped it against his palm. "But I don't think so. He'll double back if he gets the chance. I don't plan to let that happen."

Rainey sat down on the edge of a chair, nervously tapping his hands on the armrests like a speed freak about to impart the truths of the universe. "Let's think this through for a minute. If Martin killed Estevez and his pals, he'd have to be pretty sure no one could put him on the scene. At least not this fast. What if the hit man was just there to take Martin out? Maybe Estevez set him up. Martin trained the Medellín boys' army, so maybe the hit man was working for Martin. Maybe the hit man dropped Lallo into the drink, and then he was killed in turn because he could finger Martin."

Paul squeezed the tennis ball. "If Martin is in New Orleans to hit my family, why would he take a chance of clipping someone else in New Orleans first? He would have to assume we could find out he was there. Or he's using the hits in New Orleans for misdirection . . . which is what it has to be. We look our asses off in New Orleans while he lies in the sun in Florida unmolested. Then when we're stir-crazy a few weeks down the line, he pops in and hits my family. I can see that."

"He wants to sucker us to New Orleans so he can be safe in Florida?" Rainey asked.

"We're going to nail him," Paul said. "This time it ends. One way or another." *He'll wait for me to be there before he acts. He wants me to see them die. Otherwise they'd already be dead.*

Sherry entered the conference room. "Mr. Masterson, you have a visitor."

"I wasn't expecting anybody."

Sherry handed him a business card, which Paul read. "A lawyer? Do I need a lawyer?"

"He says it's important. And highly confidential."

Rainey stood. "I'm going for an Egg McMuffin. Want anything?"

"No," Paul said.

Rainey walked from the room. Sherry smiled. "How you feeling today?"

"Great. Thanks again for last night."

"Thank you."

"I've been doing a lot of thinking since. You helped me, I just wanted to let you know. Sorry I left so early, but it had nothing to do with you or the night. I'll make it up to you, promise."

"Anytime."

"By the way—see if D.C. will send us something with real speed. The Merlin won't do. Ask for a Gulf-stream or a Falcon. We're going to Miami in the next few hours."

"It's drawing to a close?" Her voice shook a little.

"Looks like it. Let me know as soon as you hear from Peoples and"—he held up the card—"send this guy in."

Sherry left the room, and seconds later a young man dressed in an expensive suit and patent-leather cowboy boots came in. Paul gestured and he took a seat across the table.

"I'm Paul Masterson," he said.

"Ben Tackett."

"Sherry tells me it's confidential. I'm right in the middle of something, and I'm not doing drug investigations. You may want to see the—"

"This isn't about drugs. It's about Ed Buchanan."

"Buchanan . . . should I know who that is? Coffee, Mr. Tackett?"

"No. I'll do this fast." The attorney scrambled his fingers and locked his hands on the table surface. "Rainey Lee was in the Buchanans' home last night."

"One of the scouts," Paul said, remembering. "Sorry the name didn't stick. I sent him. He said it didn't produce anything."

"Sir, this is Tennessee, and there are specific laws in Tennessee to protect our citizens from out-of-control federal officers."

"What the hell are you talking about?"

"Are you not aware that Agent Rainey Lee threatened the Buchanans at gunpoint?"

"What?"

"Ed Buchanan is a client and friend of mine. He is aware of the pressure that Agent Lee has been under—what he has been through—and that's the only reason Mr. Lee isn't already under arrest. Ed says he isn't the same person he was before. Their sons were close friends."

"I know."

"In the kitchen. Evidently Rainey got verbally rough with the child because he couldn't recall seeing some accomplice this killer was supposed to have had. Betty Ann grew hysterical, and when Ed went to the kitchen to call the police, Mr. Lee took his gun from his holster under his jacket and aimed it at Mr. Buchanan." The attorney pulled out a pad and read the lines he had written on it earlier. "Then he told Mr. Buchanan to 'sit the fuck down and shut his fucking mouth and stop interfering in federal matters or all hell was going to break loose.' He told him if he 'said one,' again I quote, 'fucking thing he'd come back and bury him in the flower garden.' He told Mr. Buchanan he had nothing to lose. They said his eyes were"—the attorney looked at the paper—"feral." He pushed it away. "In a word, it scared the shit out of my client and his family."

Paul exhaled loudly and lit a cigarette. "Mr. . . . ?"

"Tackett. Call me Ben."

"Ben, Agent Lee is under a lot of stress, as you have said. Tell the Buchanans that they have the apology of the DEA and that Mr. Lee's firearm was not loaded. We have him under the care of the agency psychiatrist, and we are humoring him by giving him some busy work. Tonight I am flying him out of here. By tomorrow night Mr. Lee will have been committed to a facility where he can get the professional help he needs so desperately."

"Not loaded? The gun wasn't loaded." The attorney raised an eyebrow.

Paul shook his head. "I unloaded it myself. Rainey is an old friend. I didn't know he had done any of this. Please accept my deep and sincere apology."

The attorney stood. "Well, I leave this in your hands.

The Buchanans also ask that they be left out of this. They'd rather Mr. Lee . . ."

"I understand completely."

After the attorney left, Paul sat down and thought about what Rainey had done. It was irrational. It was irresponsible. It was, in fact, criminal. Rainey was a dangerously loose cannon.

Paul picked up the telephone and dialed.

"This is Paul Masterson. I need to speak to T. C. Robertson." He lit a cigarette. "A status report. Urgent. Yes, I'll hold for the director." *Acting director.*

"Hey, Paul. How's it going?"

"It's all coming together, but I've got a problem we have to discuss."

"God, you know how I hate problems. You assured me—"

"It's Rainey. I think we might have to put him on ice until this is over. He pulled a gun on a citizen. Man and his wife. Parent of one of the Cub Scouts. Looks like he's over the edge."

"What do you want me to do?"

"He needs a few months in the Barn." "The Barn" was slang for a facility in Maryland where troubled federal agents were sent for extended rest and rehabilitation. It was obvious to Paul, looking back, that he should have been sent there after he'd been released from the hospital, but it never came up. Someone near the top of the DEA had probably short-circuited normal procedures because they hadn't wanted him back in the picture for some reason. Politics, rivalry for a higher position, or maybe whoever it was thought they were doing him a favor by keeping him free. There was no proof, except that the Barn and intense therapy would have been a normal step in his rehabilitation. Maybe he had just been cast off because he was damaged goods, not worth the investment.

Something alerted Paul that he wasn't alone. He turned as he spoke and realized that the conference-room door was standing open.

"I'll call you back, T.C."

Paul picked up his cane as he went to the door. The hallway was clear. He went to Sherry's office and stuck his head inside. She was seated at her desk. "Oh, good." She picked up a pink message slip and held it up so he could see it. "The Falcon is coming later this morning."

"You seen Rainey?"

"He was just here while I was on the line. Isn't he in the conference room? I thought he was going there."

"Get on the telephone, Sherry. Tell security to drop the gate to the garage."

"Why?"

"Just tell them to do it. Now. Tell the door guards no one leaves the building."

"What's happening?"

"Just do it!" Paul cleared the door and ran for the elevators as fast as he could, given the limp. No telling what Rainey would do if he knew Paul had plotted with T.C. to lock him up.

Paul stopped short because Rainey was standing at the elevators with a McDonald's bag in his hand. There was a cup of coffee spilled on the floor at his feet. He was crying. Paul approached slowly and put his hand on Rainey's shoulder. "You okay?"

"It's embarrassing being out of balance," he said between the tears. "I am not in control, Paul. I'm sorry, God, I'm so sorry. Please . . . help me. I'll go to the Barn after Martin's down."

Paul embraced his old friend. "I will help you. I promise I will. It'll be fine again, you'll see," Paul said. "Now, I'll have your weapon," he said. He backed off and extended his left hand.

Rainey had overheard Paul planning his incarceration, turned, and made for the elevators in a momentary panic. But as he'd waited for the cab, he'd heard Paul's orders to Sherry and had known he couldn't get out of the building. Even if he could, where would he go? Nothing but Martin mattered, and he couldn't hunt Martin blind. He couldn't very well follow Paul on the chase from a distance, either. He knew he'd have to take another tack. It was easy. The tears were real as rain.

Inside he felt a calm. It was what God wanted so his family could be reunited. There would be a blood atonement. When the time came, the weapon for Martin's destruction would be at hand.

36

"WHAT NOW?" LAURA SAID AS SHE SURVEYED THE FIVE AGENTS who were standing on the porch. Reid, behind her, was looking over her shoulder.

"I don't want to alarm you," Thorne said. "Martin has been in New Orleans in the last few days."

"Oh, no," she said. "Come in. The three of you standing there like that, I was thinking you were going to tell me something had happened to Paul." She smiled nervously. *What a strange thing to think . . . to say.*

"I was just going to make some coffee," Reid said, turning and going off down the hall.

Thorne cleared the door, followed by Woody and Sean, leaving the two local agents on the porch. "Paul had ordered us to move in closer. In light of Martin's possible presence, nothing else makes sense."

"How about the porch? I could get a desk and some cots and a phone line."

"This isn't a joke, Laura. The man is—"

"Don't say dangerous, Thorne," Laura said. "Make yourselves at home. You don't have to sell me."

"More surveillance agents are coming on to watch the exterior. We're going to put a few uniforms around the streets near the house."

"There's Reid's room for your guys, and I can move Reb in with Erin, so that frees two more single beds. You can bivouac the national guard in the yard if you'd like, just keep them out of my studio." She turned and walked into the studio. "Make yourself at home. I have work to do."

"Laura. My orders are not to allow you or the children out of the house for the next forty-eight hours. We're going to start with the trip home from school today."

"Who gave the orders?"

"Paul." Thorne leaned close and whispered to Laura. "Martin is in Florida waiting for someone we know he's meeting with. But there's a chance a partner may try something to keep us off his trail. Kidnapping one of you is a distinct possibility—even killing someone."

"I see. Just forty-eight hours?" She tried to imagine her life back in her control. Forty-eight hours and she'd be free? She decided she could stand almost anything for forty-eight hours.

"Within forty-eight hours everything should be over."

"I suppose he wants to move us."

"Well, we feel we can watch you here just as well as anywhere. And we'd have to expose you while we moved you. We're going to have dogs go over the house and property to check for any . . . unusual things."

"I would have assumed the idea is for you guys to be conspicuous. At least I hope so. A few troopers milling around won't bother me in the least. I'll explain it to the children."

Thorne followed Laura into the studio. He stood and stared at the three large canvases on the far wall. One, the centerpiece, was of Reid standing in a mountain meadow at night surrounded by young sheep and illuminated by the light of a fire, which was out of frame to the right—based on the light fall and the shadows. In his right hand, held at midpoint, was a tall staff, carved over with scales, with the triangular head of a serpent at its topmost point. The base of the staff, which ended in the grass, was actually a gleaming spear tip, which reflected the firelight, a golden orange. Two freshly born lambs, their translucent skin accented with rivers of blue vein, were cradled in the hook of his left arm. One rested its head against Reid's chest and had a look of peace, while the other was in a state of wide-eyed terror. In the shadows of the trees, barely visible as lighter shadow shapes, were a pack of wolves, their eyes lit orange. One of the wolves, the one in the foreground, was very large, and his eyes were bright-yellow points on an otherwise featureless, and singularly sinister, form.

"Jesus," Thorne said. "That's one very amazing picture. Sure ain't Disney." Laura looked amused. "What does it mean?"

"Nothing much," she said absently. "Well, maybe that shepherd who bears some resemblance to Reid is protecting his sheep from wolves. It isn't so very deep."

"You got the idea from literature?"

"I got the idea from the way he was standing when he exited the shower one day and struck that pose. I thought . . . Am I embarrassing you, Thorne?—I'm divorced four years now."

"Oh, no—hellfire, Laura. I live in L.A. It's just the shock is all . . . I mean, seeing the man naked like that."

"That's strange. Naked, you say? Yes, must be some sort of coincidence. Maybe it's because he was naked while he posed." She laughed, and it was a full, relaxed sound.

"I didn't mean . . . Laura, I'm no judge of art, but—you got your kids here."

"Reb and Erin have both known the details of the human anatomy for several years." She fought the urge to laugh out loud.

"What would you do if Paul saw it?"

"Thorne! Paul and I haven't spoken in years. What makes you think he cares if I paint nudes?"

"He cares."

"About what?"

"About you, the children."

"How can you tell? Because I sure can't."

"I can just tell, that's all. You don't know what it took to get him out of that place. He almost had a nervous breakdown at the idea of leaving. Until we told him you and the kids were in danger, he wouldn't hear of it. Take my word."

Laura studied Thorne for a few long seconds. "You're telling the truth, aren't you? You believe it, I mean."

"Yes."

"How does he look, Thorne? How does he seem now?"

Reid entered with a tray of coffee and set it on the table.

"Thorne, coffee?" he asked.

"No. We were discussing the painting."

"They don't have male nudes in Los Angeles, it seems," Laura said, laughing.

"Sure they do, we have lots. No place more loose than Hollyweird. But, Reid, doesn't it make you nervous to have this up on a wall? I mean, in all your natural splendor, and all for the world to see? I mean, you're no mystery anymore."

"No. But I have to admit that the thought of this hanging"—he realized he was pointing at the genitals and smiled at Thorne—"this painting hanging in some Bavarian industrialist's great room and being stared at by strangers for the next three or four centuries is hard to handle. Maybe being the twisted fantasy of some young lassie not yet born. I'll be some dead and dusty memory, but this thing will be exactly as it is now. That's the strangest part to me. For the time that canvas lasts, I will always be thirty-something."

"Just like Jack Benny," Laura said.

"What do you think of the others?" Reid asked.

"I hope you won't take this question wrong, Laura, but what do you get for a painting like this?" He pointed at the picture of Reb in a toga with Wolf, standing on the steps of a ruined temple. Wolf was staring at the viewer, and there was a dead asp, belly up, under the dog's paws—blood-red where the serpent's flesh had been shredded by the dog. Reb's skin was translucent, like that of the lambs in the painting of Reid, the blue veins showing. The dog's eyes were crystalline blue, interchangeable replicas of his master's.

"I'm not sure," Laura said. "They're asking one hundred twenty-five for this series of three."

"That seems really cheap," Thorne said. "Maybe I can buy one of my dog, Sambo? Not this big, though. I wouldn't have a place to put it in my apartment. Maybe horizontal instead of vertical, and love-seat size instead of sofa. Is that about the same money, huh?"

"Or you could take a photograph of the dog and use the difference you'd save to buy a new Rolls convertible," Reid said.

Thorne's mouth opened, and he stared dumbfounded for a split second. Then he laughed. "You mean a hundred twenty-five thousand?"

Laura smiled. "I know it's obscene, considering the people you could feed with that."

"Jesus," Thorne said. There was a new respect in his eyes. "Could you teach me how to do that?" The light mood was broken by the sight of the two agents carrying boxes down the hall toward the stairs.

"I'll show them where to put that," Laura said, leaving the ballroom.

"She's very talented," Reid said. "They'll bring ten times that someday."

"A million dollars! Jeez."

"It isn't out of the question."

"Well, it's out of my question and answer." Thorne turned to look at Reid. "I keep thinking that we've met before."

"You've met all of me," Reid said, indicating the painting.

37

MARTIN HAD ALWAYS LOVED SPYING BECAUSE IT WAS THE SECRET sharing of information—information he wasn't supposed to have. And the more craftily it was taken, the less evidence there was of his having taken it. He found himself out in the open sunshine on St. Charles Avenue a mile from Laura's house collecting information. If those DEA fools knew what he looked like, he'd be dead. Martin Fletcher shifted in the driver's seat of his old Chevrolet so he could see down St. Charles Avenue and checked his watch. It was two P.M. Erin's streetcar would be arriving to pick her up any minute. It had been a long time since he had watched her, but today was important. Thorne and the agents had moved across the street and into Laura's house. There were agents on the perimeter, and police patrols had been tripled within ten blocks of the house. He had decided that he couldn't afford to drive by the house anymore until it was time to move in for keeps. He had a plan in case they stayed ensconced inside.

He was hoping they would move the family before his mother took the agents off on the annual parade. He knew that if he was in Paul's shoes that's what he would do. They assumed they could follow her to him. But they couldn't move the family too far, or to a place that was too well protected, because they wouldn't risk putting them completely out of reach of an attempt. They also couldn't risk losing a shot at him. No, that meant too much to all the people involved. Not even Paul could order them whisked out of sight completely. He knew what was in Paul's mind: that if they missed him with his mother, they thought they could get him when he came for the family. They would assume they had two opportunities at him. But he knew something they didn't know—that there was no way they could possibly succeed. He was on St. Charles Avenue to see how good the new stage of coverage was. So far it looked totally amateurish. Either they weren't taking him seriously, or they were completely incompetent. It didn't matter which.

Martin had not been at all upset that the agents had found his bug. He had anticipated it. He had figured correctly that they would then bug the house themselves, and when they had, it had just become a matter of frequency searching until he was able to apprehend the signals being sent to the DEA's receiver. The laser device didn't bother him; he'd figured that was the technology they'd use. He listened carefully to the morning's broadcast, which he picked up from a remote receiver carefully hidden three blocks from Laura's house in a boarded-up Sunoco station.

"She's very talented," Reid was saying. "They'll bring ten times that someday."

"A million dollars?"

"A million bucks, aw shucks." Martin mimicked Thorne's voice. "Ow fuck me runnin'."

"It isn't out of the question," Reid's voice answered.

"Once the bitch is dead," Martin added, "sky's the limit. Maybe three million."

"Well, it's out of my range," Thorne said.

"So's Lassie's IQ." Martin giggled.

"I keep thinking that we've met before," Thorne said.

"You've met all of me," Reid said.

"Not yet," Martin said.

Martin snapped off the tape and removed the earphones. He was watching the streetcar stop. He knew Erin's schedule as well as he knew Reb's. One day a few weeks earlier he had taken a seat on the streetcar beside Erin. He had been disguised that day as an older man and had spoken to her, turning his most disarming personality into several blocks' worth of small talk. He could have killed her but let the opportunity pass. The time just hadn't been right.

He watched as a woman in her late thirties passed, pulling a six- or seven-year-old boy along toward the corner. It triggered a flow of memories, and he closed his eyes and rubbed the sockets gently. He had liked to watch his parents—to spy on their secret world, starting at age four or so. He had especially loved it when they were arguing, because when they argued, they made up with an emotionally charged fuck that made the springs echo through the house, and they snorted and yelled things that were funny.

Martin remembered everything. He had been small, seven or eight, and his ears half again as large as his head as he moved down the narrow hallway toward his parents' bedroom that night. Martin had stood in the dark hall and peered into the well-lit room from the vertical opening between the jamb and the door's edge. The door would not close all the way because it was warped, and if he stayed well back in the darkness, he could watch their secret lives.

That evening promised a good making-up session because his father had himself worked up into a rage and he was screaming at his mother, who was sitting on the bed looking into her lap, where she had locked her fingers around some knitting. "We can't afford it!" he shouted, his face looking like a hot-water bottle filled with all but enough pressure to explode.

"He wanted it," she replied. "And we can afford it," she added calmly. "You're his father, and all the other kids have bicycles and far, far more than he has." She wagged the needle in his direction, and this further enraged him.

"He's a fuckin' pansy. He'll get hurt on it, and doctors cost money. More'n we got, the way we're goin'."

"You're a skinflint. Marty's a good boy. And he's your only son."

"Son of mine? That punk'll be trading blow jobs for baseball cards in a few years. And he's no son of mine. You fooled me, you slutty bitch. His father was more'n likely some clap-drippin', liver-lip, monkey-dicked nigger from—"

"Don't you dare speak about him like that!"

"He's a pencil-dicked fairy, and you're a dried-up sack of corn husks. You haven't felt a human emotion since the first time you felt hunger and wanted to suck your mother's tit."

"I'm warning you," she said flatly. "I won't let this pass if you say any more. That's all, and you know I'm good as my word." She might have been reading instructions off the back of a cake-mix box. "Don't talk about my Martin."

"Or you'll what?" He raised his fist over her head. "You cock-suckin'—"

"I'll kill you."

He dropped his hands and bent down closer to her face. "He's a little bed-wetting, turd-eating, cock-suckin' . . ."

From the hallway the motion Martin caught from his perspective was more like a sneeze than a thrust. Eve jerked her head down and then pushed up with both hands, and then she was standing with a knitting needle in her hand, the tip buried deep in his father's eye socket. Milton Fletcher's body lurched as if he had been electrocuted. He collapsed in a heap.

"Oh, dear, now look," she said. She reached down and tugged at the needle. Then she put her foot on his forehead and pulled hard, and there was a noise like a cork popping and she had pulled the needle out. She wiped it carefully on his pant leg before she put it into the basket on the bed.

"I told you," she announced. She pointed her finger at the body and wagged it up and down. "I warned you, mister. Don't say I didn't."

Eve turned and saw her son standing in the shaft of light with his hands covering his mouth.

"Come right in here." She pointed at her feet as if she was commanding a dog. He entered the room, his eyes wide in terror.

"Baby, it's okay. Daddy had a seizure is all."

The child looked down at the open eye, which had filled with blood.

"I saw . . . ," he said. "You stuck his eye with that. How'd you do it?"

"Were you spying on your mother?"

"No. I was just—"

"Spying. Well, when you spy, you never know what you'll see." She laughed and patted his head. "Did you hear me warn him?"

"Yes."

"See, you have to listen to Mother. It isn't who you know or what you know, baby. It's what you know about who that matters."

"Is he dead?" Martin had gone down on his knees like a prisoner awaiting interrogation and prodded his father's cheek with his finger. It came away red, and he inspected it carefully before he wiped it on his pants.

"Deader'n Kelsey's nuts," Eve said. "Help me. Lift up his feet and I'll pull 'em. Else he might snag something. Wait a minute, let me get a towel before he bleeds all over the floor. Nothin' harder to clear up as that."

Young Martin had followed his mother, who pulled his father through the house by his thick wrists. Martin had struggled to hold up the feet, using the cuffs of the pants as handles. He looked at the towel that she had wrapped around the head and noticed the spot growing as they went. They went through the kitchen and down the stairs and stopped in the yard, where she leaned him up against a tree.

"Are you cold, baby?" she asked.

The child shook his head. His feet were wet, and it was cool.

"Wait here," she said, and ran back into the house.

Somewhere a dog barked a promise. Martin remembered that. Three times. Then tires had squealed out in front of the house as a drunk in a large loud car stopped, one car door opened and slammed, and a shrieking woman opened up. "Youthinkyou'resoooo—hot! You sack . . . of . . . *shit*!"

The driver yelled something unintelligible that was muffled by the trees, and the tires squealed as the car turned the corner. Seconds later a house door slammed, rattling the glass.

His mother came out their back door and strode up holding a shotgun—naked except for her shower cap and reading glasses. She jerked the towel free from Milton's head and pushed the gun barrel hard against the pierced eye, resting the butt on the ground between his splayed legs. His father's hand made a fist in the grass beside his leg, and he made a noise that sounded like a fish being stepped on.

"He's not dead," Martin had offered. "Gonna stick him in the other eye?"

"Reflexes prob'ly. Go in the house so you won't mess up your good pj's. Now, if anybody ever asks, you were asleep and never heard a sound or nothin'. And Daddy had been drinking somethin' awful for days and crying about how he never did amount to nuthin'. Give Mama a kiss."

Martin kissed the cheek she offered. "Didn't 'mount ta nuthin'," Martin practiced. "Drunk all the time lately. Cryin'. An' didn't you warn him afore you stuck his eye out? You bet you did."

"No, Martin. Now, listen to Mama. You forget the warning and stickin' the eye part, because it didn't happen. You say that, you'll get us both electrocuted or hanged and put in the cold ground where the worms will eat our faces off."

"Turn us into old skeleton bones."

"Exactly."

Martin nodded to himself even as he had nodded to her that night. She had smiled at him, kissed his forehead, mussed his hair, and directed him by turning his shoulders facing toward the back door. "Go inside and say your prayers and get ready for bed. I'll be in to tuck you in." She pulled him to her and pressed his face against the furry place between her legs. He could recall the smell, a strangely comforting blend of musky perspiration and a hint of stale urine. Then she had pushed him off toward the house.

He had knelt on the braided rug, folded his hands, and begun his prayers as soon as he got inside. He always minded. He'd heard the blast, and it looked as though someone had fired a flashbulb outside. Before he was finished praying for all the things he had to keep up—now his father's soul going to heaven had to be included—he heard his mother turn on the shower and pull the curtain. Then he finished with the Lord's Prayer, climbed into bed, and listened to Eve singing her South Pacific song, which she usually did with the hi-fi on full blast.

"I'm gonna wash that man right outta my hair . . . gonna wash that man right outta my hair . . . gonna wash that man straight on outta my hair . . . and send him on his wayyyyy!"

The next morning he had awakened and had gone out to see if he had imagined it all. There was what had once passed for his father, the first stiff he'd ever seen, with half of his head gone. The sight would always remind him of a ruined picture, with the pierced-eye side turned to one gaping hole—the skull all but empty. The remaining eye bulged out a full inch at the end of the optic nerve bundle. It fascinated Martin, and he had crouched for a better look while minding that he didn't get any of the ick on him.

The shotgun had been placed so his father's thumb was hooked inside the trigger guard. The bark on the tree behind him was deeply gouged and stained deep rusty brown. The drying brains were coated with crawling blowflies, and a trail of ants entered the pajama-pant leg and fanned out through the opened shirt collar across the face and inside.

"Life is competition," his mother had told him, shocking him. "It's eat or get et. And never let anyone do you bad less you pay 'em back fivefold." He turned to find her standing on the steps with a cup of coffee in her hand and a cigarette pegged into the corner of her lips. She put a hand on his shoulder.

"Come, and I'll fix you some eggs like you like 'em. Then I better call the cops and say I found him. Maybe I'll say you found him and you can like stare at 'em with your mouth open and not answer their questions so you don't let nothin' slip out you shouldn't. Seems like nobody reported the shot. The hell is wrong with people these days?"

The police hadn't seemed all that interested, and the questions they asked had been met with Martin's straight face.

"Boy might best see a psychiatrist," one cop said. "This can turn a kid nuts. Turns grown men nuts."

He remembered how he had slept with Eve in the years after that night. He wondered whether he had instigated the bedroom play or had merely understood her needs. He was twelve at the time, maybe thirteen when the sex started. He remembered that he had had pubic hair and his mother had taken that as a sign to start his education. The first step was to teach him how to touch her in that special way—how powerful it had made him feel to be able to create the orgasms in her—control her breathing with the pressure and motion in his fingers. He loved to watch her lose control and flail and make the noises she had made only for his father before. She had never discussed it, but she had shown him how wonderful an orgasm could feel. She had rubbed his erect penis with warm lotion until it had throbbed—hurt, but hurt in a divine way, and had taken it in her hand like a bar of soap and rubbed her hands together vigorously until the thing erupted, squirting from his navel to his lips. It made him feel good—no, beyond wonderful. Martin felt blessed to have had such an understanding, giving, and strong mother.

Her love was an all-powerful and totally giving thing. It was instruction. A lesson for a better life. "This is what girls all want," she'd say as he started rubbing at her. "For a big man like you to get them to a special place. The place where the cat goes in his mind when he purrs."

He called up the memory of a black girl his mother had brought him for his pleasure. He had loved her skin, the ebony breasts with the hard purple nipples, the soft hair in her armpits, the narrow waist, the hard rounded buttocks, the muscular legs, the dark slippery-wet vagina that reminded him of an orchid. The smell of her breath, of her sex, their sweat and his semen. Eve called her their maid, but her real job was to please Martin sexually. His mother must have paid her well, because she was with them three days a week for a year or so. She told Martin that she liked fucking a lot better than doing house-work—in fact, she loved to fuck. Any way Martin wanted it. Any way at all, and she was eager to teach him new ways to please her. Martin spent most of their sessions experimenting, keeping copious notes, and when she was away, he would dream of what they would do next time and write it down in detail. She seemed to love it. Not that it mattered to him. She, the person inside that sleek, black, seallike skin, meant no more to him than a squirrel playing in the oak trees out-side the window. She was hardly more in his mind than a sock to toss off into.

After that girl came around, Eve's own lessons in physical love had ended. He missed them, but growth is change, and change is good. But the spiritual love, the undying gratitude he felt for her support and comfort, had endured. From his mother there were no secrets, only shades of the truth for her consumption. She loved

Martin's soul and he loved hers. They might be the only two people on earth with souls. He was truly content only when she held him against her and talked softly to him. No one could ever understand their love. No one.

Besides, he remembered her earliest admonition as she worked over his manhood with her oiled hands. "In nature a mother's love is a pure thing—a real thing. After all, what's a man but a tame animal? Animals in the wild do it with their mothers, so it's natural as anything."

A garbage truck blowing past interrupted his memories. He opened his eyes and glanced at his watch. He couldn't get back into the moment for a while, but with concentration he was back there as though it had all happened a week earlier instead of over thirty years. The evening before, Martin had seen the Cadillac on the news as it had been pulled from the river like some great fish from the depths, the driver's form a bloated shadow; his left arm caught in the rush of escaping water had waved like a flipper. PROMINENT LOCAL BUSINESSMAN SLAIN. Front-page banner. Even in a city as numbed to murder as New Orleans, it warranted celebrity handling. There were photos of Lallo Estevez with his young children, with the mayor, the present governor, who was the past governor as well. There was a shot of his chauffeur standing at attention while Lallo entered the limousine. The gangster with his extra smile who had been discovered by the towboat crew was buried in a lower column in section B. Martin had hoped that the car wouldn't be discovered before he had finished in New Orleans. But it added an interesting addition to the mix, and he couldn't have let that business lag or affect the mission he had devoted the last six years to. Add another variable into the complex equation. They would try to catch him with his mother in Florida—but had no idea of how slim the odds of their succeeding really were. He smiled at the thought of how he would make the DEA professionals look like what they were: dead clowns.

At two o'clock Erin walked through the school doors in the center of a wave of kids. She was barely able to contain her excitement. She exchanged looks with Eric Garcia and was sure she was blushing. They had spent ten minutes formulating a plan at recess. He had all afternoon to spend as he saw fit. She didn't, but hadn't told him that. She had told him that her father had bodyguards watching her—that he was a DEA agent and worried excessively. If Eric had been reluctant to date the daughter of a federal agent who put watchdogs on his daughter's tail, he didn't give any indication of it. In fact, the challenge of seeing her under such circumstances seemed to excite him.

Erin saw Sean standing beneath a tree in the schoolyard with his hands in the pockets of his seersucker suit coat. He was wearing dark glasses, but she knew his eyes were locked on her. He wouldn't approach her but would walk behind her all the way home. They had wanted to drive her from door to door, but she had refused flatly. Her mother had reluctantly taken her side, saying that they could cover her without embarrassing her in front of her friends. As she passed Sean, he started walking. She looked over her shoulder and saw Eric slide into his mother's gray Mercedes.

Erin walked the two blocks to the streetcar stop. She turned to find Sean standing three feet behind her, surveying the people nearby. He met her stare.

"Hi," she said.

He nodded. "Where's your Mace?" he said.

"Haven't got a refill yet. So where's my ten bucks, and I can go over to K and B for one?"

He reached into his pocket and started going through his wallet. He handed her a ten.

"Okay, we're even." She put it into the zippered compartment on her backpack. "It *was* your fault, you know."

"If you say so."

"Okay, so let's let bygones be bygones," she said. She handed him her book bag. "Least you can do is carry my books. They're heavy."

Erin looked out of the corner of her eye as the streetcar approached. There were maybe a dozen kids and a few adults waiting for the car. Sean took the bag with his left hand and placed the strap over his shoulder. The car pulled up, and the conductor opened the front and rear doors simultaneously. People started climbing in through the front while others exited through the rear doors. Sean and Erin were going to be last in.

"After you," she said.

He smiled and started to climb in. Then he realized something was happening, and he turned to see her running for a nearby Mustang that had pulled up crowded with young girls. Before he could close the distance, Erin jumped over the door of the car, fell in among the other bodies, and the tires squealed as the vehicle pulled away from the curb, the laughter of girls filling the air. Sean cursed out loud as he ran after the car until it was obvious that he was never going to come within a hundred yards. He turned in time to see the streetcar pulling away, leaving him standing in the middle of St. Charles holding her book bag. He was filled with dread as he fished the cell phone from his breast pocket.

A battered Chevrolet Caprice honked at him, and he stepped to the curb, cursing and feeling very small. He heard the car's driver laughing as it pulled by him, a loud barking that ricocheted around in the car's interior. The big automobile roared off in the direction the Mustang had gone.

Seconds later the prowl car that had been providing additional cover wheeled up beside Sean, and he jumped into the backseat. They gave chase, but the next light changed before they got there, and a line of cars began moving across the intersection immediately. The policeman turned on his blue lights, and the cars moved grudgingly aside. Sean cursed out loud, but by the time the prowl car had cleared the intersection, the Mustang had several blocks on them.

38

Woody carried the small nylon book sack as he escorted Reb to the red Volvo 850 that he had parked by the front doors. Children were scattering as they passed out of the doors of the buildings. Reb's bus was in the line, along with ten others waiting for their passengers.

"Why can't I ride the bus?" Reb asked as they reached the car. "And you follow like always."

"Not today." Woody's reply was flat, businesslike. Alton Vance, one of the agents who had spent the last few days watching over Reb's school, was in the rear seat, waiting.

Woody scanned the line of cars and buses for anyone who might be out of place before he climbed into the Volvo. Reb looked at the agent in the backseat. "Hi," he said. His eyes rested on the short black object beside the agent's leg. "What's that?" he said, barely able to mask the excitement.

"That's my water gun," the agent said, smiling.

"It's an Uzi, isn't it?"

"Belt in, Reb," Woody said.

"Can I shoot it sometime?"

"Get your hands wet. It leaks something awful," Alton Vance said.

Woody cut his eyes to the backseat, and the agent shifted uncomfortably. Then he looked at Reb. "Forget it," he said. He reached over and belted Reb into the seat. As they were pulling out, the cell phone rang. Woody opened it and put it to his ear. "Yeah?"

The agent listened for a few seconds and then put the telephone in his lap. The car accelerated rapidly and kept gaining speed until the needle was passing eighty. Alton's eyes met Woody's in the rearview.

"All *right*," Reb said, his eyes searching Woody and the speedometer. "Smoke it, baby!"

Alton's eyes asked the question.

"Sean dropped the package on St. Charles," Woody said.

Alton tensed and nodded.

Reb looked up at Woody. "That's code. A package means a person. 'Dropped' means 'killed'? *He killed somebody?*"

Woody cut his eyes over on a straightaway. "No. Dropped means dropped. Lost."

"Erin?" Reb's face had lost color.

Woody nodded.

"The killing man got her?" His voice trembled.

"No," Woody said, adding a reassuring smile. "She's in a Mustang with some girlfriends."

"That's Jessica's car. Jessica's a B."

"What?" Alton said.

"You know, beeotch."

"What?" Woody said.

"Bitch," Alton said, snickering. "Slang for bitch. Maybe it's a Louisiana thing."

"There's an APB out on the Mustang," Woody said.

Woody pulled the Volvo up in front of Laura's house. Thorne stepped out onto the porch with an Uzi in his hand and waved. "The car's been spotted on Canal Boulevard near the big cemetery. Go give Sean a hand."

Woody put his mind to remembering the main streets, the way the city was laid out. Canal Boulevard, not Canal Street near the river.

Woody waited for Alton and Reb to get inside before he did a rolling turn in the middle of the street and took off toward St. Charles.

The telephone rang as Woody turned onto St. Charles. It was Sean calling from a prowl car.

"There's a problem," Sean said.

"You got the Mustang?" Woody asked.

"Well, sort of. We have the car. It's just that Erin isn't in it."

"Where is she?"

"The girls are taking the fifth. They refuse to say anything. It's some sort of misplaced loyalty."

"I'll be right there."

Woody pulled around the prowl cars and slid to a stop, tires squealing. There were six city cops standing beside the car, swapping teases with the girls. Woody stepped from the Volvo with his hand behind his back and strode over to the driver's-side window. "Pretty boy's here," he heard a cop say.

A red-faced Sean stepped back from the car, and the girls laughed. He gave Woody wide berth.

Woody put his face even with the driver's. She was sixteen, had blond flyaway hair and wide, excited blue eyes. "You gonna take us in?" she said, putting her wrists together and holding them above the wheel. The other girls giggled their pleasure.

"Girls, this is an emergency. Where's Erin?"

"You gonna beat it out of us?" the driver asked coyly.

"Erin's life is in danger."

"From Eric?" she said, then put her hand over her mouth and laughed.

"I bet it is!" another said.

"Where'd you drop her off?" Woody was still smiling.

The driver shrugged.

"This is a nice car. I bet your daddy bought it for you."

"He sure did."

"I hope he insured it." Woody lost the smile, reached in and pulled the keys out, and threw them. They arced high, catching the sun as they traveled far into the cemetery.

Jessica crossed her arms in defiance. "I don't have to tell you shit. When my father—"

"Your father isn't here."

"You better get those keys . . ." Her face was red with anger and disbelief. She stopped talking because Woody was pulling a gun from the holster under his navy blazer. He aimed at the front tire and pulled the trigger, filling the still air with the explosion. The tire gave up its air in a whoosh. The cops were stunned, and their hands went for their holsters reflexively. Sean stepped between the men and Woody, his own gun in his hand. "No interference!" he yelled. They froze.

Woody took a couple of steps as he contemplated the car. Then he placed the muzzle of the Glock against the front of the hood and pulled the trigger again, punching a black hole and causing a waterfall beneath the car. A plume of steam rose from the curb as the hot water rushed out and searched for the gutter drain. The girls in the car began crying but were too frightened to move. Passing cars slowed, startled faces took one look at what was happening and sped away.

"She's in the Quarter!" Jessica yelled. "She's meeting her boyfriend."

"Name?"

"I dunno, Eric Garcia."

"Eric Garcia," Woody said.

Sean was speaking to the sergeant in charge, whose face was red. He ran to join Woody as the Volvo pulled away toward the Quarter. "He said he's gonna report this."

"What'd you say?"

"I told him to spell your name with an *e*."

"The French Quarter is a big place. She might not even be there still. We need the police on this. They found the car."

"What car? That's crap. Fuck that. I know where she is." He tossed Sean the partially empty magazine from the Glock and jammed in a fresh one, which he pulled from his pocket. "Fill that back up, will you? Shells in the glove box." He turned to Sean. "So, cute girls, huh?"

Sean started laughing. If Woody knew where Erin was, his ass was going to be safe—chewed raw, but safe. In the meantime, if anything happened to Erin, he was convinced that Paul Masterson would kill him. Literally.

Martin had followed the Mustang filled with girls across Canal Street and into the French Quarter. He kept far enough back so they wouldn't spot him, though he knew they wouldn't look back. He had been wary of the prowl car, but it was far behind them.

Martin wasn't certain why she had ditched the young agent Merrin, but he assumed she had a reason. He had wondered briefly if it might be a trick to flush *him* out, but he was fairly certain they believed he was out of state. He didn't see anyone else on their tail. Unless one of the girls was a ringer, an undercover cop, it made no sense. He didn't sense a trap, he sensed a fifteen-year-old runaway.

Now what would he do? What could he do? Tipping his presence wasn't in any of his contingency plans. He decided to watch and wait. He imagined himself, a large python sliding in the grass behind a grazing rabbit, hungry but not starving.

The Mustang pulled over after the car turned onto Canal off Carondelet. The door opened, and Erin stepped out onto the curb. The Mustang sped away, the girls waving and squealing as the car gathered speed. She started walking down the street into the French Quarter, and Martin passed her, pulled into a parking garage, and stepped out. He handed the attendant his keys and a five-dollar bill just as Erin walked past the open door. *What if Paul is in town? What if she is going to meet him? No, she hates her father. Or does she really? Probably not.* He let her go a block before he started following her.

Erin had never been to Roscoe's. It had been pointed out to her by friends who knew underage people who'd been served in the place. She stopped and gazed across Iberville at the sad front of the place as she gathered her courage. The sign had been neon, but vandals, or patrons, had put an end to that part which flickered blue. ROSCOE'S TAVERN. She looked at her watch. Two forty-five. She had told Eric she'd meet him there at three.

Erin walked to the front door and tried to open it. It was locked. She pressed her face against the window, using her hands to cut the extraneous light so she could see inside. There was movement inside the room, like a ghost moving in a dream. She tapped on the glass, and the form moved closer. Then the door cracked open at the seam, and she was staring into the eyes of a boy who couldn't have been much older than she was.

"Yeah?" he said.

"You closed?"

"Open at six," he said. His eyes didn't move from hers.

"I was supposed to meet a friend here," she said. "At three."

The boy leaned up against the doorjamb and wiped his hands on a towel. "You can come in. It's hot out there," he said.

"Not if you're closed." She smiled.

"You could wait inside. I'm just cleaning up."

"You work here?"

"My old man owns the place. It's okay."

"Your old man Roscoe?"

"Roscoe was a bulldog. Died before I was born."

"I'll wait out here." She turned and saw that the man who had been on the corner was standing across the street in the window of another bar, staring at her. When she looked into his eyes, he averted them. She opened the door to Roscoe's and slipped inside.

"Lock it back," the boy called from behind the bar.

"You have a phone?" she asked.

"Sure," he said. "Pay phone."

My purse is in my book bag! Erin reached into her pocket, but it was empty. She heard the sound of pool balls clicking in a back room and laughter. "Aren't you closed?" she asked.

He turned his head toward the back room and then back to her. "My brother and some of his friends. Waiting for my dad for a handout. He's gonna kill me for letting them in. They're assholes." He placed a quarter on the bar, and she took it. "I'll pay you when my boyfriend gets here."

"No prob," he said.

She dialed the number Eric had given her. It rang and then a woman picked it up.

"Hello," she said.

"Is Eric there?"

"Eric is taking his music lesson."

"Where?"

"In the den. Who is this?"

"This is Erin Masterson. I'm a friend of Eric's."

"Might I take your number and have him call you after the lesson?"

"Could you get him to the phone for a second?"

"Sorry, Erin, I can't interrupt."

"How long is the lesson?"

"It's over at four."

"He must have forgotten the lesson, I guess?"

"No, the lesson is every Tuesday and Thursday. Is there a message?"

"No. Wait. Yes." She thought for a minute, anger building at the betrayal. "Tell him he's a liar. No, tell him he has no honor."

Erin hung up, and when she turned, there was a beer on the bar between her and the boy who was busy cleaning glasses.

"You want the beer?" he said.

"Sure," she said. "But I'm presently undercapital-ized."

He looked at her and tilted his head slightly.

"Broke."

He smiled crookedly. She took a swallow, and her eyes teared from the cold, alien bite.

"He ain't coming, huh?" the boy said. "It was me, I'd come."

She thought he was sort of cute except that his head was all but shaved, his ears were big, and his unevenly spaced eyes were slightly different sizes. But he had a nice way about him. He was a boy with adult responsi-bilities.

"I don't think so. Screw him."

"Jaaaaackieee rat!" a voice boomed from the other room. The bead curtain parted, and a large man in his late thirties dressed in a black leather vest and jeans came into the room. His chest was filled with thick black hair. "You fuckin' punk. Bring us a round. Well, well, well, little brother. You want to introduce me to your sweet-heart?"

"This is my brother. He's not really a doctor, he just looks like one."

The man laughed out loud. His hair was black stub-ble. His skin was blue-white, and there were numerous homemade tattoos on his arms and chest. He moved up to stand beside the stool Erin was seated on, his un-focused eyes pinned on her.

"Buy you a drink?" he said.

"No, I have to go," she said. He was scaring her.

"Stick around."

"No, really. I have to go." She moved.

"Come on, I insist. One little drink and you can go."

Erin watched as the bottle arrived. The boy started to pour a jigger, but the man slapped it away, reached over the bar, and picked up a freshly washed mug. He poured three inches into the bottom and pushed it to her.

"I'm tellin' Dad. That shit's like forty bucks a bottle, wholesale."

"I don't drink whiskey," she said.

"Leave her be," the boy said.

"That's a solid suggestion," a voice said.

Erin looked up to see Woody standing in the door-way that led to the back room. The two other men who had been playing pool were standing behind him hold-ing their cues. He walked out into the room. The two men followed menacingly, their eyes blurred by drink and drugs. Woody stopped three feet from the bar. The taller of the men behind Woody had a large ring through his nose. The agent didn't even look at them.

"She's old enough to do what she wants," the biker said.

"Actually, she's only fifteen," Woody said.

The men moved farther into the room.

"He came straight in through the back door like he owned the place," one said.

Woody crossed to the front door, unlocked and opened it for Sean. The agent walked in, glaring at Erin.

"What you guys want with her?" the biker at the bar asked.

Sean opened his badge case, and the biker looked at it.

"I don't want to go home," she said.

"Oh, DEA! Nice badge, but there's no drugs here and the kid don't wanna go. No tellin' what you got planned for her. I know how you feds operate." He put his hand behind his back as though he was reaching for something. Sean put a hand on the butt of his weapon inside the jacket.

"I'll bet you do," Woody said. "Why don't you just sit on your hands? If you're thinking about pulling what-ever you got back there, I have to warn you that I'm going to disarm you."

The other two had moved up beside Erin and the biker.

"We don't want any trouble," Sean said.

"I'll go," Erin said weakly.

"You don't gotta," the biker said. "These cheese dicks got no authority here. This ain't a federal deal."

Woody moved to Erin, his face inches from the biker. "Erin, get up and walk to the door."

The biker at the bar cut his eyes at his friends, and as he did, he swung his left hand, which held Erin's mug, toward Woody's face. With one fluid motion Woody caught the man's wrist and allowed the swing to continue until the man was off balance. Then, using the man's weight and the motion of the swing against him, he reversed it and there was a sickening pop as the bones in the wrist broke. The biker was left holding his limp hand in his right one like a sleeping puppy.

The other two men stepped back with their pool cues upraised defensively. "Jesus!" the larger one said, stumbling.

"Jesus!" Erin repeated.

Then Woody turned to the biker, slapped him hard across the face, and when the man turned from the blow, Woody lifted the large hunting knife from behind his belt. Woody looked at the blade for a second, then lifted the knife over his head. The biker collapsed against the bar as the blade came down in an arc and was driven so deeply into the bar's surface that little more than the handle was showing.

"Hot damn!" the boy behind the bar said, amazed. He reached out and touched the handle tentatively. Then he gripped it with both hands and pushed and pulled for a few seconds with everything he had, but the knife wouldn't waver.

The other two men had backed up all the way to the door leading to the pool room.

Woody looked at the boy behind the bar and smiled. "Keep trying, King Arthur. Who knows?" He put his hand on Erin's arm and led her to the door.

Sean stepped out into the street first and scanned the sidewalks and tops of the buildings until Woody had secured Erin in the backseat of the waiting Volvo. A pair of police cars had parked one at either end of the block.

Martin had seen the cars approaching, the Volvo leading, and had stepped into a small rare-book shop located diagonally across the street from Roscoe's. He stood inside the shop's window with a book of poetry in his hands, looking up casually as the agents loaded Erin into the waiting Volvo. Sean Merrin climbed into the driver's seat, and for a brief second Martin's eyes met Woody's as the agent paused before entering the car's passenger door. Martin dropped his eyes to the pages of the book, and when he looked up again, the Volvo was gone. He glanced at the book's spine as though he were checking the condition of the cover and then set it back on the shelf.

39

THE DEA JET, WHICH HAD BEEN CONFISCATED FROM A CAPTURED drug lord, had been outfitted for the trip with sandwiches and drinks. The interior was done in what Paul referred to as "Splendor de Latinos," which to Rainey explained the red leather, crushed velvet, and gold-plated chromium strips on everything. The bathroom had been marble with gold fixtures, but the agency had taken it all out so the plane would be able to take off with full fuel on board. They had left the crushed velvet and wall coverings and the chrome-plated trimmings. "Only a Latin drug lord who had grown up in a hut with hard dirt floors and tin walls would consider marble and gold trimmings worth cutting the airplane's range in half for," Paul said. The two agents had the entire cabin to themselves, but they sat together in overstuffed leather seats. The plane took off and turned south.

Paul looked at Rainey, who was staring out the window at the carpet of cloud that stretched unbroken for as far as he could see. He had debated whether he should allow Rainey to accompany him, or send him on to the Barn immediately, but decided it was better to keep him close at hand for now.

"Miami. It's been a long time," Rainey said. "Doris loved Miami Beach. It'll be great being back there."

"We're not going to Miami," Paul said. "Not yet."

"Where are we going?" Rainey turned to face Paul.

"New Orleans."

"Why? Martin's heading for Miami!"

"I want to see Thorne and take a look at the operation. Review the troops. We'll leave there when Eve makes her move."

"Tonight?" Rainey asked nervously.

"First you and I have to talk."

"What about?"

"You and this operation."

"What about me?"

"What happened at the Buchanan house?"

Rainey turned his head. "I know it was extreme, but I was afraid the operation was in jeopardy."

"You could have put it in jeopardy."

"I did what I thought needed to be done. I was swept up by my . . . zeal."

"Fortunately Ed Buchanan is going to forget it happened. At least for the time being."

"But you disarmed me."

"I had a talk with T.C. this morning. No change for you. Never was, officially. You're still on administrative leave."

"Until when?"

"Until there has been a psychiatric evaluation and you've got some much needed rest. You need help and you need time. I was wrong to let you come into this. I made a bad call."

"Oh, you made *a* bad call?" Rainey looked at Paul incredulously.

Paul turned his head.

"Your bad calls cost a lot of people, including me.

You know that? They cost me . . .'' Rainey started crying, slammed his hand on the arm of the seat, and leaned forward almost in Paul's face. "My family! *You* cost me *my* family."

"I didn't have any idea what would happen."

"Oh, you didn't have any idea. Well, then it's okay, Paul," Rainey said sarcastically. "Paul didn't mean to do any harm. He built a fire in a tank farm and it got to the stored gasoline. My, my. He got in a pissing contest with a polecat. Well, then all's well with the world. My daughter burned up in front of my eyes!" Rainey stood, hitting his head against the ceiling. He didn't seem to notice. "Burned up and died in agony. I watched that!" He slammed his chest and leaned down, placing his hands on Paul's wrists and putting his face inches away from Paul's. Paul didn't know how to respond.

"I was *there* while you were fly-fishing in the mountains. My son was thrown off a cliff onto a floor of sharp rocks. He exploded like a bag of oysters tossed out of a helicopter. He was spread over the . . ." He dropped his head. Tears were flowing freely. "And Doris—"

"I don't . . ." Paul felt numb. "Rainey, you have to believe me. I didn't . . ."

Rainey's eyes were like those of an enraged animal. "Fuck what I have to believe! And fuck you! You owe me. You have to answer for what you've done. And you will, by God, you will answer."

There was silence in the cabin except for the whine of the jet engines. Rainey let go, straightened his hair, and sat back down. He composed himself with two or three deep breaths, took a handkerchief from his coat pocket, wiped his eyes, and blew his nose.

"You going to cuff me, strait-jacket?"

"No. I've worked something out with T.C. When we go to Miami, you're going to continue on to the facility in Ashborne, accompanied by a Justice agent."

"To the Barn. You mean I'll weave baskets and vegetate with the other cows at pasture. Paul, I'll go. But, listen, I have to be there when it goes down. I have to be there, or I will never be able to live with myself."

"We'll take care of Martin."

"No. I knew that Thorne's family died. I knew that Joe's family died. I should have known what was happening. *I* should have taken the precautions to protect my own, no matter what Doris or anyone else thought or said." Rainey slammed his thumb against his breast for emphasis. "*I* was in denial and *I* failed them. I failed them and they're gone. Maybe you or Martin set things in motion, but I was in a position to see it happening. See, it's on my head more than yours. You were out of the loop."

Paul sat back wearily. His left hand was throbbing, so he put the cane aside and took the worn tennis ball from his pocket and began squeezing it vigorously.

"I can't live with it. You have my gun."

"I put it in the safe at your office," Paul replied. "Relax."

"Handcuff me, but let me be there when he's taken. That's all I ask. I beg you! No matter what either of us has done . . . just give me that. Let me see his body. Please? I'm begging you? That can be your atonement." Rainey got out of the seat and got onto his knees and looked as if he were praying to Paul. "I'm begging for my life. After, I'll go anywhere. I'll take retirement. I'll check into the Barn, anything."

Paul was collapsing inside with a thousand pains, aches, and confusing thoughts. He honestly didn't know what was right. Could he trust Rainey to stay back and let the A team handle Martin?

"All right," Paul said in a whisper. "You'll go to the Barn after this is over? And you won't get in my way or try to get in the middle of anything?"

"Word of honor," Rainey said.

Paul looked at his watch and then out the window.

"I just thought of something," Rainey said. "The date on my watch reminded me."

"What's that?"

"You know what tonight is?"

Rainey was facing Paul, but his eyes were looking out the window over Paul's shoulder. "Six years ago yesterday Thorne, Joe and I were standing in a hospital waiting room in Miami, covered with your blood."

Paul looked at Rainey. "Really?"

"Well, I remember because I missed Doris's birthday—we were in the middle of planning and executing the raid on the dock. Remember?"

"No, I don't."

"Funny what you remember and why."

"That's one anniversary I haven't been celebrating on a yearly basis," Paul said, frowning.

40

TWO FIGURES MOVED UP THE SIDEWALK, HOLDING TO THE SHADOWS. One moved ahead of the other and out into the sidewalk beside the curb. The other slipped over the wall and moved silently into the overgrown yard.

Alton Vance, dressed in slacks and a T-shirt with a London Fog jacket to cover the nine-millimeter machine pistol, was standing on the north side of Laura's porch, watching the bushes for a cat he had seen a few seconds earlier. He looked at his watch. It was early, but darker than normal due to the overcast sky. He heard footsteps on the street outside the wall and turned to watch for the approaching pedestrian. He wondered whether he should radio the house, but those people had been through hell.

They had arrived in the Volvo, Erin looking deflated, Sean shaking his head in some sort of signal to let Alton know something amazing had occurred, and Woody, Mr.

Stoneface, staring straight ahead. He couldn't wait to find out what had happened. He wondered if he should call the guy in to Woody, but the fellow was just a drunk. Thorne was a little ways down the street, walking the dog, and there were cops out on the perimeter at every intersection for two blocks. Sometimes drunks cut down Laura's street after the cops had checked them out. They couldn't very well close off the street.

Alton was thirty-one and African-American. He had been assigned to New Orleans straight out of training after law school. His wife had wanted him to practice entertainment law, but he'd been drawn to a life where there was a touch of steel and a badge and satisfaction that this would be a better world as long as he did his job well. He was tired, but this assignment was coming to a head hundreds of miles away. He was sure that Monday morning would find him back at home for a week's vacation. He needed it.

He saw the top of a head for a split second and heard someone fall and mumble. *Fuckin' drunk.* He checked the Uzi, which was shoulder strapped and hung under his right side, as he moved to the gate. As soon as he got to the bars, he saw the feet flailing as the man tried to get up. "Goddamned bitch," the man growled. "Tryin' to tell me somethin'. Fuckin' whore . . . I got money! Who she think she is?"

Alton relaxed his grip on the machine pistol, stepped through the gate, and stood above the man, whose face was to the ground. Alton reached over to lift the man, and as he did, a second man slid in behind him and pressed something against his back. "Don't move or you're dead."

The drunk flowed upright, looked up and down the street, then smiled at the agent. He tucked his head and said, "Inside, move it."

Agent Alton Vance moved through the gate with the ex-drunk before him and the unseen man behind. The ex-drunk stripped Alton of the Uzi and the SIG Sauer nine-millimeter. Alton felt something cold slide around his neck. . . . "What was that?" he said as he put a hand to his throat. In answer the man behind him said, "That, Mr. DEA, was Martin Fletcher cutting your worthless throat. Welcome to the end of the world."

Alton Vance had never imagined himself capable of such blind fear.

Laura was furious with her daughter. Erin had hit the door raging against Woody and Sean and all the baby-sitters who were ruining her life. Laura had almost slapped her but managed to hold back. Then Erin had collapsed in tears. Laura had been paralyzed with fear the entire time she had waited for them to return, think-ing that Erin had been grabbed by Martin Fletcher. Erin had made a passing reference to the fact that Woody had broken a man's arm in a bar while disarming him.

Now Erin had showered, dressed in clean clothes, and was lying on the couch in the sun room off the kitchen, resting her head on Laura's lap the way she had when she'd been younger. She had even apologized for her selfish behavior. Laura hoped that she had learned the kind of lesson that no one could have taught her. Kids all thought they were born bulletproof, tragedy re-sistant. Sean was seated across the room with an ice pack held to his neck. Reb and Woody sat at the counter, and Reid was leaning against the stove with a glass of wine in hand. Laura was a little miffed at him because he hadn't reacted with appropriate horror to the news that Erin had run away. "Kids, go figure," he had said to Laura's complete amazement. "She'll come home when she gets hungry."

Laura hadn't spoken to him until Erin had returned.

Reb and Woody were arm wrestling on the counter after the dishes had been cleared. To everyone's feigned amusement, and Reb's genuine amazement, he was beat-ing the agent. "See, using the breath-expansion technique works—when you take a breath and hold it and put the air power into your muscles," the agent said. Woody groaned as the boy pressed the backside of his hand against the cool marble countertop. He whispered to Reb so the women wouldn't hear. "A quick uppercut to the nuts is the only thing that works better."

"Is that what you did to the man that scared Erin?"

"If the breathing technique works so good, Woody," Reid said, "how come you don't use it yourself and beat him? Take a few minutes off, for Christ's sake."

Woody didn't look up. "What's eating you, Mr. Dietrich?"

"You. All of you guys. How many times a day do you have to be a hero?"

"We do what we're paid to do."

"The DEA? Does the DEA hire people with your demonstrated talents as agents?"

"There," Reb said. "It does work! I can feel the power." He growled.

"It's about the transfer of the power from mental to physical," Woody said. "Three out of four. So you know you didn't just get lucky."

"That's enough," Laura said. "Erin, run the dishwater."

Erin moved to the sink.

"So, Reid?" Woody said. "Want to try your luck?" He slapped his arm on the counter.

"I don't see what that proves," Reid said. "How about a game of chess?"

"That's just a game," Reb said. "This is real."

"I'm not much for arm wrestling," Reid said, dismissing the idea. "Wouldn't want you to snap my arm showing off for the girls."

"Whatever," Woody said. He smiled at Reid.

"What would it prove?"

Woody shrugged. "Probably nothing."

"You ever killed any people, Woody?" Reb asked.

The room went silent.

Woody turned to him and grew thoughtful. Then he looked at his hands and silently counted each finger twice. "Not so's I noticed."

"Really?" Reb asked.

"Nope," Woody said. "If I'm lying, I'm a professional janitor."

"But you beat the cold shit outta—"

"*Reb Masterson!*" Laura snapped.

"—the guys that almost hurt Erin."

"I imagine maiming is easier if you don't have too much intellectual interference," Reid said, smiling. "Anybody can maim, kill. Violence is the defeat of reason. Your brain is the ultimate weapon, Reb. I'm sure Woody will agree with that. Brains over brawn. Progress."

"You wouldn't say that if you'd seen that creep who . . ." she said, stopping when she saw Reb's face turned toward her.

"I wouldn't have been in a dive," Reid said smugly.

"Drop it!" Laura said.

"I see your point," Woody said. "Chamberlain reasoned with Hitler, Roosevelt with Tōjō," Woody said.

"Too bad you weren't there to talk sense to Ed and his pals," Erin said bitterly.

Reid looked at the ceiling. "Rabin, Arafat. Begin, Sadat. Mandela, de Klerk. Mahatma Gandhi, Martin Luther King. They won important peace treaties without resorting to guns. And I'm not talking about thumping a drunk redneck who would press his amorous intentions on a pretty girl. Erin, I'm thankful Woody's reflexes are as good as they are. But there are very few instances where professional warriors are needed in day-to-day life."

"That's naive, Reid. There are people who don't respond to reason. That's where violence comes into play. As defense and deterrence."

"And vengeance," Reid added. "That's a great one. This guy Fletcher is just a bully with a sharp mind and an unpleasant agenda. He needs to be locked up in a mental ward."

"I have never gone looking for trouble," Woody said.

"Well, that's your slant on the world? You can find exceptions to support any argument," Reid said.

"So can you, I imagine," Woody said. He smiled again, mockingly. "If Mr. Fletcher comes through the door, we'll let you reason with him."

The two men stared at each other like two dogs

standing across a filled bowl. Reid was smiling but his eyes weren't.

Laura stood and walked over to the sink. "Boys? Let's try to see if we can avoid the stereotypical cabin-fever flare-ups?"

She put her hands into the dishwater and jerked them out, screaming, "Dammit!"

"What?" Erin said.

"It's cold!" Laura said. "Ice-cold. Are you sure you ran the hot water?"

"Yes," Erin said. "I know one from the other. I bet we're the only family in America that doesn't use the dishwasher for ecology reasons."

"The hot-water heater must be out again," Laura said. "The pilot goes off," she explained to Sean and Woody. "We just have to light it again. It's in the closet right down the hall. I'll do it," she said. "I was supposed to remember to order a new one."

"I'll light it for you," Woody said, standing. "Matches, lighter?"

Reid looked at Woody and smirked. "That's okay, Woody. It doesn't take a karate expert to light a water heater."

Laura exhaled loudly. The animosity had been building between the two men since Woody had moved into the house, and she was getting tired of it. She couldn't believe that Woody's heroics angered Reid, but they did. Didn't Reid understand what Woody had done for them today?

Reid opened a drawer in the kitchen, took out a box of strike-anywhere matches, and went out into the main hallway. Woody followed. Reid opened the closet door and looked in at the ancient gas-fired apparatus. Woody moved inside first, and Reid followed him, irritated.

"You'll just get dirty," Reid said. "I'll do it. I've done it before. You'll waste time trying to figure out where to put the match. And you can't beat it into the hole. This isn't like fighting. Takes finesse."

"Oh, Reid. I know where to put the match. They just won't let me."

"Look, Woody, relax," Reid said. "This isn't a contest." He knelt down and looked at the pilot. "It's out. Give me an inch or two. Maybe you could step out into the hall?"

Woody moved against the wall and laughed. "I'm sorry, Reid. I didn't mean anything. Honestly, it's just my smart-ass side."

"There isn't room for both of us in this closet. No way either of us can light it unless one of us gets out."

"I'm going," Woody said as he tried to squeeze his bulk around Reid, their faces inches apart. "I've earned my points today. Maybe I should let you get a few . . . so you can justify your presence."

"You fuckin' cocky—"

There was the sudden sound of fast-paced footsteps against the wood floor. *Breached!* Instantly the professional baby-sitter knew several things. Someone, two or more someones—people alien to this environment—were moving up the hall from the front rooms, toward the family in the kitchen. He knew there weren't supposed to be any people inside the house who could come from the front quadrant. As he was assimilating this, he was moving for the doorway and reaching for his holstered gun. But Reid pressed against him and slowed the action.

Woody uttered a last warrior's curse because he knew that if it wasn't for some immediate miracle . . . there would be nothing left to do but die badly in a closet that wouldn't even allow for the two of them to fall down. *Dead-meat sandwich.*

Laura heard a sudden commotion from the hallway and voices, and before she could react, a man moved into the kitchen with a gun in his hand. Sean was drawing his pistol and moved across the nook to put himself between the intruders and the children. It all happened in a split second. Before she recognized the man, Sean's gun was already aimed at him, and she was horrified that he might fire.

"*No, Sean!* It's Paul."

"I know," he said, dropping the gun's hammer carefully.

Suddenly everyone froze. Reb and Erin hadn't even reacted and were still in conversation, facing each other. They turned at the same instant, and Erin screamed involuntarily.

"You're all dead, just dead as dead gets," Paul Masterson said angrily, his one good eye twice normal size. "I just strolled in past your outer ring of cops, killed the agent on your perimeter and two men who were stuffed into the water closet like a pair of lovers. If I had been Martin, I could have killed everybody in this room, gone out the back door, and been free to stroll off. What the hell is wrong with you people?"

It had taken Laura's brain a second to register that the man who had entered her kitchen was not the one she had expected, and then to realize it was Paul. The incongruity of his appearing at all had caused mental confusion. Not knowing how to react, her mind sent a message to her brain to giggle. She giggled.

Paul moved aside to allow Rainey, Woody, and Reid to enter the kitchen. The children were both staring at their father with their mouths open. Woody looked embarrassed but relieved. Reid looked confused, unsure how to react.

"Where the hell's Thorne?" Paul asked, looking at Sean.

"He's out . . . for a while . . ." Sean said.

Paul seemed to ignore his family as he spoke. "Agents Merrin and Poole, Rainey and I skirted two patrol cars with no trouble, took out Vance in front, walked right up to the porch, and opened the door. If I were Martin Fletcher, I'd be up to my ass in bodies! Is this how you follow my orders? The front door wasn't even locked, for Christ's sake. Do I have to do everything myself?"

Erin began crying hysterically, her face collapsing in on itself, and she ran past Paul, down the hallway, and up the stairs. He watched her out of sight but said nothing. His face might have been stone.

"What the hell's wrong with *her*?" he said. "It isn't her fault."

"We weren't expecting you," Sean said defensively.

"Oh . . . if it had been someone you were expecting, that would be different?"

"Sir," Woody started. "It was unforgivable."

"We just thought . . ." Sean started. "I guess we relaxed because the mother is on her way out today and we assume Martin is otherwise engaged."

Paul's lower lip was trembling. "If I had replacements available, I'd can the whole lot of you."

"No, sir," Sean said. "We'll torque up."

Woody nodded. Paul turned to Reid and stared at him. "You must be Dietrich."

Reid extended his hand, and after a pause that dragged on far too long, Paul accepted it, pumped it once, and dropped it. He focused his eye on the man and frowned.

"You don't know what she's been through today," Reid said.

"Who, Laura?"

"Erin."

Dear God, Laura thought. *If he finds out, we'll have another terrible scene with the kids. Let him find out later.*

"We're fine now," Laura said, her eyes burning a warning into Reid's. "Erin just decided to act like a teenager today."

"Mr. Dietrich, has anyone explained the kind of danger you're exposed to by being here?" he asked him. "I would advise you to find some other place for a few days."

"Paul!" Laura said. "Who the *hell* do you think you are?"

"Well, I don't think he's aware of the stakes."

"I am," Reid said. "Fully aware. And I am not going anywhere."

"What the hell do you mean storming into my house as if you own it? What gives you the right to speak to my friend like that? To come in here uninvited, waving a gun around."

Paul looked at his ex-wife and dropped his head a fraction of an inch. Then he looked at his son as if he had just realized he was in the room. He holstered the Colt and took his cane from Rainey.

"Sorry, Mr. Dietrich," he said. "Hello, son."

He turned to Sean and Woody, but before he could speak, the front door slammed shut. Paul whirled, launched down the hall, and the house was filled with the sounds of Paul Masterson's wrath and Thorne's muffled replies. The dog ran into the kitchen dragging his leash and cowered against Reb's leg. Rainey stood in the doorway and appeared both embarrassed and a bit amused. He nodded at Laura, and she walked over and hugged him.

"Don't much care for the company you're keeping," she said. "But it's really good to see you." She hugged him.

"When you moved inside here, the security should have been far more intensive," Paul said as he and Thorne entered the room. "Is this the way you watch your movie stars? By walking their dogs? Can't the animal water the plants inside the gate?"

"No—well, yes, Paul. It's . . . I mean, it isn't the same thing. We've been at it around the clock. We shouldn't have lowered our guard. I wanted to stretch my legs. It's just that we're so relieved we got Erin back . . ." He stopped. "I left four good men here."

Laura rolled her eyes skyward.

"Four?"

"Nelson's out back," Thorne said.

"Missed that one," Paul said. Then he realized what Thorne had said. "Got Erin back . . . back from where?"

Reb was still staring at his father, unsure what to say, his face blank. "Woody kicked the guy's ass and broke his arm," he said finally.

Paul looked at Reb, his face giving away nothing.

Laura was doing a slow burn; Reid stood with his arms crossed. "I don't want this Erin incident discussed now." She cut her eyes to indicate Reb's presence.

Rainey said, "Laura, could you take Reb and Reid upstairs for twenty minutes? Paul needs to talk to Thorne."

They filed out. As they passed Paul, Reb looked up at his father. Paul stared at him and winked. Or maybe he had just blinked. It was a guess either way, because he hadn't smiled at all. As Reb was led from the room by his mother, he turned so his eyes could stay locked on his father until he was led out of sight.

After the room was cleared of civilians, Paul sat on a stool and lit a cigarette. "What's this shit about Erin?"

As Thorne told the story, Paul listened carefully, alternating his gaze, and made no motion save a few shakes of his head in disgust.

After Thorne finished, Paul looked at Sean and Woody, and his tight mouth relaxed into a brief smile. "Thank you, Woody, for saving my daughter. Sean, shit happens and you fucked up, but you recovered nicely. I hope you've learned a lesson. You know how dangerous this operation is, and what happened had nothing to do with Martin. If Martin had been around, we'd be in mourning right now instead of celebrating the safe return." He crushed out the cigarette. "Are you all back to one hundred percent?"

The men nodded.

"Now, what makes you think Martin doesn't know everything we know?" Paul said.

"Even I'm not sure what we know. What do we know?" Thorne said. "We're like so many mushrooms here. In the dark."

"Have you swept the house lately for bugs . . . today?"

"No. We've had it under our control since—"

"He had bugs in place before you came in, right? So he knew you were here."

"We assume that," Sean started.

"Assume?" Paul said. "Who told you that you could assume anything?" Paul stared at Thorne and tightened the line of his lips.

Thorne's face betrayed the insecurity he felt. His status had sunk from ruler of the roost to advanced amateur in a heartbeat. He was embarrassed and trying to fight the urge to be defensive in front of his men.

Paul wrote something on a piece of paper and held it up.

It said: Kill our transmitters.

Paul turned and poured himself a cup of coffee. He didn't look up again until Sean had run the frequency-sweeping equipment through the rooms. Paul smoked a cigarette and dropped the ashes into the garbage can.

"Nothing," Thorne said after the search was completed. "Not so much as a blip."

"Our lasers?"

Thorne said, "Disarmed."

"Very good," Paul said. He patted Thorne on the shoulder. "Let's forget the lapse. It happens. I've been known to relax myself. Let's just make sure it doesn't happen again. We're entering the most dangerous time of the operation. Every single assigned agent is about to swing into motion in Charlotte and Miami. But for right now, when you feel safest, you have to be most alert. What we least expect may well happen. We're dealing with very crafty men."

Paul lit another cigarette. "Did you know that Martin can capture signals from bugs planted by others? He explained it to me once. Piggybacking he called it, and he said he had perfected it. Maybe he was just bragging."

"You mean, if he knew we were using the window readers, he could intercept the signal?"

Paul shrugged. "You turned off the transmitters, so we're okay now. Sorry I got so excited. It's my nerves. Martin probably wouldn't come in like I did. He isn't into suicide. He's too goal oriented." He looked at Thorne and smiled. "I'm telling *you*? You knew him as well as I did. In fact you were the first one at DEA who suspected him of being the leak."

Thorne perked up again, feeling adequately restored as leader of his team in the eyes of the agents.

"Martin's accomplice is a man named Kurt Steiner,"

Paul said. "My guess is that he's here in New Orleans. So even though we don't expect Martin to be in New Orleans tonight, Steiner may be. He might do something dramatic to draw us here. What he lacks in the sort of personal motivation driving Martin he will undoubtedly make up in some other compensation."

"Asshole buddies?" Thorne asked, laughing.

Paul frowned. "Agent Lee and I are flying out in an hour or so because I plan to be in Miami when Eve gets there. Whichever way she moves, we intend to have her covered. My people will be in place in Miami, Dallas, or Denver—wherever she heads. We have every confidence we'll find Martin. If we miss his friend, the game will not be over. When we take Martin, we have to take Steiner as well. All we have so far is a set of his fingerprints from an Argentine police ID."

"That'll be a trick. Any chance of a picture?" Thorne asked.

"Not clear yet," Paul said. "Have you swept the house for explosives like I asked?"

"Yes, sir," Sean offered. "It's clean."

"You mean it's clean as far as a dog could tell. I don't plan to take the chance that Martin doesn't know how to fool a dog's nose. My family has to be moved to a secure location unknown to anyone outside this house. Nobody is to have a chance to get through to Laura and the kids. They won't be able to resume a normal existence until Martin and his friend are neutralized."

"Force her into exile?" Woody said it before he had a chance to think.

Paul froze and looked at him. "Of course. Safe house somewhere until this is over."

"Sir, no disrespect intended, but what if she doesn't want to go? Mrs. Masterson doesn't strike me as someone willing to give up her life to Martin Fletcher or anyone else."

"Might want to discuss it with her," Thorne said. "You forget she doesn't take orders from us, and she hasn't been in love with the intrusion."

"She'll do what has to be done. For the kids." *For weeks, months, years? No, she wouldn't.*

"Maybe the Laura you were married to would have let fear rule her life. But I don't think we're talking about the same lady," Thorne said.

"She'll follow my orders," Paul said. "For Adam— Reb and Erin."

"I don't imagine Fletcher or his friend will follow your orders," Woody said.

Suddenly Paul wondered what else he was taking for granted. He began to feel anxious. The next few hours took on an entirely different cast in his mind. *Martin may act in or out of character. What if all of the scenarios I've anticipated are worthless? Why do I assume Martin will cooperate in his own defeat? How much of what I'm doing is based on what other people think? How much of our intelligence is inaccurate?*

Paul turned, wrote a note, folded it. "Thorne, have a word?" When Thorne approached the counter, he handed it to him. It said: *What do we know about Reid?*

Thorne folded the note and whispered. "Usual check when we started. Nothing out of the ordinary."

"You see yearbook shots from his high school?"

Thorne looked at Paul, surprised. "He's okay, he's been here for over a year."

Paul finished the thought. "Very firm handshake for a salesman. Hard calluses on his hands for a paper shuffler."

"He sails. That involves work."

"I see. Doesn't he travel a lot?"

"The man owns a business."

"Well, just to humor me, keep an eye on him. Keep Woody close to him."

Paul turned to look at the two younger agents who were talking with Rainey. "I'll be upstairs."

The doors Paul was certain belonged to the children were closed tightly, and he walked by, slowing only slightly to listen for conversation. He followed the sound of voices to what he presumed was Laura's bedroom. The door was cracked open, but he tapped with the ivory head of the cane.

"Come in," Laura said.

He opened the door and walked in. He had no idea what he was going to say.

"This was quite a surprise," Laura said. She sat on the end of her bed with her arms linked across her breasts defensively. Reid was standing by the window. Evidently their conversation had not been an entirely pleasant one. Reid looked relieved that Paul had interrupted. Paul noted a pair of loafers parked beside the bed. The side of the bed he himself had once inhabited. Laura's eyes met his as he lifted his gaze from the floor, and he knew she knew what he had been looking at. "If I'm interrupting, I'm sorry," he said. "Don't have much time."

"Not at all," Laura said. "I have to say, of all the people I didn't expect to see, you're at the top of the list."

"Sorry I couldn't announce I was coming. There was a chance Martin might have discovered the fact, and it could have spurred him to try something radical."

"Secrecy was always easy for you," she said.

"I was just telling Laura that I don't think we're safe here. I think the family should move," Reid said. "Laura disagrees."

"Why is that?"

"The house is large, fairly open, and this guy, Martin, has been in here before. Planted bugs, right?"

"I'd bet Martin knows this place as well as anybody. He probably knows *all* our strengths and weaknesses. I imagine he knows a lot about you as well." Paul locked eyes with Reid. *I wish I did.*

Laura spoke evenly. "We're perfectly safe in this house. I am sure Thorne's men will be careful from here on."

"What do you suggest, Reid?"

"Reid thinks we'd be safer on his boat," Laura said. "On the lakefront."

"I don't know anything about this boat," Paul said. "Fill me in."

"Thorne's seen it," Reid said. "It's a forty-eight-footer built in the forties. Three cabins. Docked at the yacht club. Solid wooden hull. All the amenities of home. I know little about guarding and defense, but it can be docked at the end of a pier, which can be covered from all around with a few men. No way to sneak up on it."

"Too much chance Martin might know about it. Vulnerable from underneath. Martin's at home in the water. Better to pick a hotel at random . . . home of a friend. He's had ears in here."

"That's the other thing. The boat's not common knowledge. I don't imagine we've discussed it in the past weeks, except possibly for the work that was being done on it. But it wasn't scheduled to be returned until next month. They finished early. We hadn't been on it for months until a few days ago, because it was in dry dock. I don't think your Martin or anyone else would imagine us being there. Plus, it sits high in the water. No one could slip on board without coming on from the dock. And there's a front coming through tonight. No one would think we'd be sitting on a boat in a thunderstorm."

Paul looked at Reid for a few seconds, sizing him up, this man who had taken his place in his family. A bolt of jealousy moved through him. *Her house—his yacht. Cozy.* Paul resented feeling like a man who had sold his old car for two hundred dollars and learned that the buyer had sold it a day later to a museum for a hundred thousand. That wasn't what had happened, and Paul was aware that he had no right to be upset. Nonetheless, the thought dug into him, and it wasn't a shallow trench.

It was hard for Paul to look into Reid's eyes, but Reid seemed intent on studying him as they spoke. He realized that Reid was sizing him up, too.

"I was hoping for a few minutes to talk," Paul said. "Alone."

"I don't want to see Laura upset," Reid said. "You seem to have a talent for doing that to people."

Laura turned her eyes from Paul to Reid and smiled. "How much more upset do you think I can get? I'm fine,

Reid." She kissed his cheek as he went by, and Paul noticed she didn't close her eyes as she did. "Go," she said. "And don't fight with Woody. He can kick your ass, you know."

Paul's heart sank. He had not imagined how painful it would be to see her kissing another man, even superficially. But he couldn't let his jealousy color his opinion of Reid. *Who is Reid?* He wanted to ask Laura questions but he didn't.

Paul and Laura maintained position and were silent until Reid had closed the door.

"I like the house," he said, making a stab at conversation. "Real nice . . . the furnishings are . . ."

"Paul, we aren't going to waste this time talking about decorating, are we?"

"No. So the kids . . . they've grown."

"Kids do that. They're like weeds—they grow whether you watch or not."

"I deserve your sarcasm," he said.

"As a matter of fact you do, Paul. All of our lives were very manageable before Martin started running about killing our old friends. Destroying the future. That's what he's doing, you know. He has no future, and he's refusing to allow you to have one either. He's evil but he's also pathetic, because he can't help what he is. Evil is easier than good. Want to tell me what you guys did to him that made him go to all this trouble? It wasn't arresting him, was it?"

"I framed him."

"You what?"

"I planted the drugs and money he went to prison for having."

"Dear God," she said. "You bent the law? *You?*"

"I guess you're upset and I—"

"*Upset!* Paul Masterson, you self-centered asshole! I've had people listening in on me while I'm making love in my own bedroom. My children are in danger of having their throats cut in their sleep because you dangle us as bait for God knows how long. Jesus, Paul . . . upset?" She sat on the end of the bed, stood, and then sat down again. "Even from Montana you've been ruining our lives."

"Reid seems like a nice guy," he said.

Laura looked taken aback. "He is. He has his own money, his own separate life, and we see each other when we feel like it. Perfect with me. I hope you've been seeing someone."

"One someone. A girl."

"I hope it's a girl." She laughed. "In Montana?"

"Nashville."

"Recent development, then. Nice girl?"

"Yeah. Really nice. She's studying anthropology." Paul wished he hadn't mentioned Sherry. "She's young. Too young, I think." *It wasn't a relationship, though maybe it could be.*

"She'll be at home in Montana?"

At home in Montana? No, I don't think it's like that at all. God, I wish I could grab her and things could be the way they were. Paul shifted his weight so the cane took more of it off the floor. His leg hurt. "Saw the paintings downstairs. Well, I didn't look close. I wanted to. I'm glad your career has . . . You've done so well."

"We get by financially. Hell, we do really great in that department. It's just hard because there's never enough time. The kids help out and don't complain too much, but I've been working seven days a week. The show."

"Germany. I heard. We always planned to go to Germany, remember?"

She dropped her arms to her sides. "I need to start getting the children ready if we're leaving. For the boat, I mean."

Paul caught something in Laura's eyes. Something soft. A memory passing through. *She has to feel something . . . deep inside, maybe?*

"Laura. I'm changing," he blurted.

"I'm happy for you," she said. "I hope we're all changing."

"The last time we were together . . . I seem to remember that we had a fight."

She laughed. "Had a fight? Had a fight? Paul, you have a talent for understating. The police came. You destroyed our bedroom. Threw a doorstop through the TV set. Slapped . . ."

"I hit you?"

"Yes, you did hit me. But I accept my share of the blame. Drop that weight here. That's the past and you weren't yourself."

"Your share?"

It was as if a curtain that he had been peeking under lifted to reveal a reality he had covered over in his mind to make it bearable. He remembered the way a drunk will remember the night before, in swatches, unpleasant swatches of humiliating moments. He remembered that he had made a sexual overture after a day of throwing temper tantrums and snapping at the family. He remembered pulling Laura close and kissing her. He remembered that she had pushed him away and started crying. "Don't touch me!" she'd said. "Who the hell are you? I don't even know who you are!"

"What's wrong?" he'd said.

"What's wrong? Look in the mirror. Tell *me* what's wrong. You aren't the man I married, the man who fathered my children. You're a mutilated madman who terrorizes my family. What makes you think I want to sleep with you?" She had turned to leave. "I'd rather take a beating."

He had seized her from behind by the shoulders and thrown her to the bed. Then he had pinned her and started taking her blouse off. And she had . . . she had . . . laughed. She had laughed. "Oh, please fuck me, mister," she had said, laughing. "It's my best fantasy. To be screwed by a monster."

Then he had taken her, and he had taken her in anger. He had torn her clothes off and had forced himself on her. *Had she resisted? Or did she give in?* When he had expended himself and collapsed on top of her, she had lain there, still, beneath him.

"Thank you," he'd said. *Thank you? Why not I'm*

sorry, forgive me? Help me because I hurt and I can't do anything to feel better.

"Get off me, you freak." Her voice had been a hard whisper, a hiss.

And he had slapped her, and she had fled to their bathroom and locked the door. He had wanted to apologize, he had wanted to take it all back. He had been ashamed beyond belief. He had flown into a rage that controlled him completely, and he had destroyed the house like a drunken vandal. He remembered sobbing and railing at the injustice of life. He remembered the police banging on the door and finally coming in with their weapons drawn. The image of Laura holding the side of her face, which was swelling, and telling them that everything was okay. Then, through the fog of emotion, Thorne arriving and explaining to the cops what Paul had been through in Miami. He remembered that was why he had left. Anger and shame and the sure knowledge that she and the children were better off alone. Safer alone. He had known that he wasn't good enough for them as he was. And he was haunted by a future that was lost.

He looked at Laura. *I love you . . . forgive me . . . God, please, Laura. I love you so much. I feel like I will die without a chance to start again . . . make up for what I've done to you, my children, to myself.* But he couldn't say any of it. "You still have that pocket gun I gave you?"

"Yes. In a box in the closet."

"I want you to get it and put it in your purse and keep it with you until this is over. I don't want you to tell anyone, and I mean *anyone,* that you have it. Not my people, not even Reid."

"Why not even Reid?" The softness in Laura died and was replaced with stainless steel. "Who the hell are you to tell me to keep something, anything, from him? He cares about me . . . us. I don't even know who you are. You can't even trust your own men. What's going on here?"

"You share everything with him?"

"Did I ever keep secrets from you?"

We weren't talking about me. Paul shook his head. "No. I don't imagine you did. I apologize."

"I won't mention it. I mean, if you really believe it's best. You're the professional. But I don't like it."

"I need to talk to the children."

She frowned. "Well, Paul, you've already talked to your son. You remember, don't you? I do. I found him staring out the window at three o'clock in the morning thinking about how wonderful the experience was. And Erin probably has a few things she wants to impart, but I doubt you want to hear them."

"I've made some—"

"Mistakes, you weren't really going to say mistakes, were you?"

"Yes."

"Well, let's make this the last mistake, shall we?" She stood again. "Let me see if they want to say good-bye. Then, either way, I want you to just leave us in peace. A bunch of false promises will just. . . . You've already done enough damage for a lifetime."

"I said I've changed."

"What, you just read *Embraced by the Light* or *The Road Less Traveled* or something? Had a spiritual awakening, have you? Oh, Paul, give me a break."

"No."

"Do what you want, you always have." She whirled and left the room, leaving only her scent lingering. Paul fought the urge to throw himself onto the bed and cry like a baby. Inside, where his heart lived, he did just that. He was sick with himself. Facing himself as she saw him was more painful than anything he had ever felt before. It was torture.

Erin was staring out the window when her father tapped at her door.

"What?" she said, her voice filled with irritation. "Is he still here?"

He opened the door and stuck his head in. "Erin, I wanted to say something to you. As your father."

"You aren't my father." She lifted the picture of her

on Paul's shoulders. He was smiling—her tongue was sticking out at the camera. "This was my father, but he's dead." She tossed the photo onto the bed, facedown.

"Erin," he started. "I'm leaving in a few minutes. I wanted to say that I know what I have done to you, what I've been, and I hope the future can be different from the past."

"It will. Because I won't waste time caring about you anymore. I wasted a lot of days and nights thinking about . . . feeling responsible for. . . . Never mind. Why don't you just get out of here? We don't need you."

Paul searched her eyes to see if she was serious or talking out of pain. He realized he didn't know how to read his child's eyes. He didn't know who she was. He felt as if he had walked into a world where things reminded him of something he had once known, but where he was a stranger. He felt unwelcome—was unwelcome. *Why shouldn't I feel like this?* he wondered. *These people don't know me. Why did I think they would?*

"Go away," she said.

"Erin, pack some things," Laura called from the hallway.

"I'm not going anywhere with *him*."

"We're going to the *Shadowfax*. Your f— Paul is going"—she looked at Paul, who didn't offer a destination—"someplace else."

Erin turned her back and stood with her arms crossed. "Erin," Paul said, "I . . . I hoped . . . Erin. I'm not very good at saying what I mean. . . . I . . ."

"That isn't what Reb said. Reb said you were *very* good at saying what you mean. If you have anything else to say to me, drop it in the mail with the annual package. And, Mr. Masterson, I don't play with dolls or stuffed animals anymore. Just so you'll know."

She turned her back on her father, dismissing him.

He left the room, turned, and stood with his back to Erin until Laura closed the door. "Want to see what Reb has to say?"

•　　•　　•

Reb was seated on his bed with his hands in his lap, a stern look on his face. He might have been waiting to take a spanking. Paul entered the room. Laura stayed in the hall.

"Hi, Reb," he said. "Can I speak to you?"

"Hi, Daddy," Reb said, smiling. "I didn't mean to call you. I'm sorry I did it. It was a real bad thing to do."

Paul walked over and sat on the bed beside his son. He looked at Laura, and she said, "I'll be in the studio." Then she closed the door.

"I'm sorry I went off on you, Reb." He put a hand on Reb's shoulder. "It was really, really mean of me. What you did was right."

"Why'd you do it? 'Cause you were hurt?" Reb looked at Paul's face, reached up, and touched the scar gently as if he thought a sudden move might frighten the tissue away. "It isn't so bad lookin'."

"It's not that, exactly. I did it because I felt guilty. Of staying away. Of hiding from you. Other things . . . adult reasons."

"You felt guilty all the time? Since when?"

"Since this happened."

"It hurt, Mama said. You almost died."

"Yes. It hurt. It hurt me worse inside than outside."

"I don't know what that feels like. Not at the same time, I mean. I know what guilty feels like, though. And pain, too."

"Reb. It's hard for me to say things . . . you know, personal things to people. Always has been. Sometimes I want to say the right thing and I can't decide what that is. I can't put my feelings into words. Sometimes even when I know the words, I can't say them. It's like there's this wall inside me that I can't make myself climb."

"I do that. I mean, like when I didn't have a daddy. Reid is a good daddy sometimes. He tries, but he isn't used to kids. I guess we make him nervous. He keeps my secrets, though."

"I want you to know something just between us, okay?"

"A secret?"

"Yeah, I think you might say that. Sure, let's call it a secret. Reb, I love you and Erin as much as I ever loved anyone or anything, and the distance between here and there and between us because I haven't been around doesn't mean I love you any less. I need to tell you that I think about you guys every day. If it hadn't been for the memories I had of you . . . before this happened . . . well, they kept me going. I can say that you saved my life more than once." *Your old man knows the sharp taste of gun oil.*

"We never wanted to be away from you."

"Well, Reb, you and I are going to be close from now on. I promise I'll be a better father to you. And Erin, too . . . when she isn't mad at me anymore."

"Will it hurt if that bad man kills me?"

"Reb? Don't be afraid of him. You have protection."

"I mean, I'm not scared . . . if he kills me. I'm a guy . . . guys die all the time. But Erin and Mama? Is it true that only a coward hurts women?"

As true as anything there is. Paul put a hand on Reb's shoulder. "Reb, only the worst kind of coward hurts women. I promise you. I'm going to make it a full-blown, big-sky, cowboy promise like my Uncle Aaron used to make to me. I swear by the stars that no hombre beneath 'em is ever gonna harm one hair on your head."

"You won't let 'em?"

"Hey, cowboy, that's a big-sky promise. He can't hurt you now, 'cause I won't let him. That's the truth."

"And you'll always tell me the truth? Promise?"

"I'll never lie to you." He crossed his heart. "I'll never lie to you again in word or deed."

Reb poured himself into his father's arms, and Paul hugged the boy, and once again it was all he could do to keep from crying out loud. He had never felt so empty and full at the same time. It was the most wonderful feeling along with about the worst. It was frustration and fear and love. He had forgotten what unconditional love was all about. But at that moment he remembered, and he knew something he had not allowed himself to think about. He knew exactly what he'd thrown away.

Paul dropped his voice to a whisper. "Reb. It's a secret, but I'm going to Miami. After tonight, if everything goes as planned, you will all be safe from the bad man."

"Promise?"

"I promise I'll do everything that can be done."

Paul found Laura in her studio, standing before a canvas holding a brush.

"Reb is okay," he said. "I mean, I think we can build a relationship. It isn't too late, I hope?"

Laura said, "I'd say that's up to you. Kids are forgiving creatures."

Are adults? "I'm leaving. Gotta get into the air."

Laura wanted to say something. She looked at Paul, and he knew she wanted to say something that she wasn't going to say. *What?*

"Anything else?" he said. "Anything?"

"Make sure Martin Fletcher can't ever hurt another child."

He nodded. "Martin Fletcher will never harm another child."

Laura turned and began painting even as tears blurred her vision. *I hate you, Paul, I love you, Paul.* She resisted the voice that told her to go to him and throw herself into his arms.

Paul was fighting the urge to turn her around and pull her close. He took a deep breath, turned, and walked out, the cane tapping the time of his steps. Rainey joined him in the hallway.

She heard the front door close and sat down in a chair and sobbed.

Outside, Thorne held Paul's door open as he climbed into the car.

"I'll call in a van to take them to the boat," Thorne said.

Paul fixed a gaze on him. "Forget it." He looked at his watch. "I'll do this. I have to check it out myself—nothing personal. You get back inside and guard them close. I'll get some help here in a little while. Stay put for now."

"But your flight."

"I'll take care of this before I fly out. I've got time."

Thorne watched the car until it was out of sight. The agent looked up at the sky where the clouds were being pushed northward at impressive speed by the incoming wind. It made him feel dizzy to watch them. He could smell rain in the air. Thorne saw a tight schedule lining up for the evening.

41

EVE WAS STANDING ON HER PORCH BESIDE A SUITCASE. THAT MORN-
ing Mr. Puzzle had been picked up by the garbage truck
as Eve had frowned at the collector through the kitchen
window. Larry lost the five dollars he had bet Sierra that
Eve would have a change of heart and get the animal out
of the can.

Eve was wearing a glen-plaid cloth coat. A scarf
printed with a violent fury of flowers, vines, and green-
ery covered her hair and shrouded her face like a hood.
She had the wicker purse locked to her chest when the
yellow cab pulled up in front of her house. The driver
stepped out and walked toward the porch.

"Airport, ma'am?" he said.

"Get this." She tapped the suitcase with her toe. The
driver lifted it and carried it to the car. She followed five
feet behind and watched as he placed the case on the
floorboard and pushed it in.

"Drive carefully," she admonished from the back-seat. Larry Burrows smiled to himself and pushed the ill-fitting cab-driver's cap back. He had watched her dress on a black and white, he hadn't been ready for the savage ferocity of the scarf and the effect of the rhinestone-encrusted cat's-eye glasses with deep green lenses. Her brilliant red lips seemed to float angrily in the center of the luminous white oval of face. The look was withered movie star fleeing the press after a scandal of epic proportions—or a deranged, over-the-hill geisha.

"Taking a trip?" Larry asked.

"I don't answer personal questions from servants," she snapped. "USAir."

Good grief, he thought. *Servants?*

After a ride conducted in complete silence, Larry pulled the cab against the curb under the USAir sign.

She handed him a twenty, which was worn almost white in places. He tried to hand her the change, but she waved it off. "That's for you. You drive okay and you're quiet."

She turned and handed her ticket to the porter while Larry climbed into the cab and drove away past the other airline entrances.

At the end of the next airline's entrances he pulled over, opened the trunk, and traded the knit shirt, golfer's jacket, and chauffeur's cap for a blue button-down, a navy blazer, khaki slacks, and loafers. Then he put on a pair of horn rims and slicked his hair down, using some cream from a tube and a thin comb. He lifted a briefcase, closed the trunk, and entered the airport. A police officer stepped from the curb and got in and took the cab, which had been borrowed from local vice's motor pool. Stephanie was waiting for Larry and hooked her arm in his. Minutes later they were at the gate a few feet away from where Eve sat clutching her purse and staring at the waiting airplane's tail section through the windows.

Eve boarded nearly last. Larry and Stephanie got on ahead of her and began to get nervous as the plane started filling up and she still hadn't come on board. Just as they were about to decide that she had other plans, she walked in and took her seat beside a man in a red sweater. The last people on board were, according to their uniforms, a pair of airline personnel.

The airplane taxied out and took off. As soon as the plane was off the ground, Eve pushed her scarf back until it was off her head and gathered on her neck. She busied herself with a flight magazine.

Two rows behind her, Stephanie smiled because she knew Eve couldn't be reading without her prescription glasses. Larry had a Scotch and water and fell asleep for the duration of the flight.

Stephanie was glad Eve was almost blind—or she might have recognized the two cable-repair agents who were sitting a few rows in front of her, trying to look inconspicuous. Joe McLean, boarding last in a pilot's uniform, walked back to the bathroom, passing her without so much as a sidelong glance.

42

PAUL PICKED UP THE PHONE ON THE SEAT AND DIALED THE LOCAL DEA chief's number. The call was forwarded to the man's home. Paul ignored the background noise—television newscast, kids yelling.

"Thad, Paul Masterson. I'm in New Orleans for a quick visit."

"Yeah, Paul. What can I do for you?"

"I just cracked the house, where I walked straight through two police patrols and one of the two best men you said you had. He's licking his wounds about now."

"What do you want me to do about it?"

"What? Well, Thad, if a crippled, one-eyed man and a red-headed Watusi can get in, what do you *think* you should do about it now?"

"Paul, I'm sorry about that, but Greer's in charge. I gave him my two best agents, but he's deploying them."

"Listen, Thad. If you want to cover your ass on this, I

mean if you want a career after this weekend, I'll tell you what you should do."

"Listen, Paul—"

"You listen, Thad. Turn off the fucking television or go into a quiet room and get on the horn to the chief of police and the Coast Guard. Here's what I want."

"But—"

"Butt's an ass, Thad. I've told you what's wrong. You don't want to see what'll happen to your career if anything happens on your watch. Anything happens to Laura and the kids, I'll bury you so deep you'll have to dig a hole to China to see stars."

"Okay, Paul, tell me what you want."

By the time Paul and Rainey Lee stepped from the car and started walking on the dock near the *Shadowfax*, cars filled with policemen and serious men in suits were converging on the yacht basin.

Within thirty minutes half of the New Orleans SWAT team was at three locations in the city. Sharpshooters were being briefed on the grass beside the yacht club. Others were near Laura's house and setting up in a grassy field across from Tulane University.

The Coast Guard had furnished their best diver, who was searching the piers around the *Shadowfax* for bombs. The bomb squad had dogs checking the dock lockers, the vessel's deck and interior. A Hatteras was pressed into service and moored within sight of the boat where snipers would be positioned. The dockmaster's people were towing away the other vessels on the nearby piers to rob any opposing force of cover. Paul spent an hour giving orders and making certain the security was as close to impenetrable as possible. He was beginning to feel a lot better about the situation.

Thorne was completely amazed. All he had to do, it turned out, was join a work in progress. Anyone coming in from outside had to pass through several police roadblocks. There were uniformed patrolmen, deputies, and highway patrolmen in evidence.

By eight-thirty it had started to drizzle a little, as if

the way was being prepared for the impending storm that was moving over the Louisiana coastline. The tropical storm had already weakened as it neared landfall south of New Orleans. Although there was little chance of serious wind damage to secured vessels, the Coast Guard had posted high-wind warning flags at the mouth of the harbor. There was a steady stream of boat owners who were checking lines and securing their vessels in preparation for the weather.

A forty-foot Coast Guard cabin cruiser sat like a mother hen, one hundred feet away from the *Shadowfax*, in effect guarding the channel. A group of seamen stood on her stern. One sailor had an M-16 on his shoulder and a pair of binoculars in his hands. The others were watching the diver preparing to drop into the water from the pier.

Paul and Rainey watched as the diver slipped the mask into place and slid into the dark-brown water. The flashlight came to life, and its white glow began moving down the length of the boat's hull.

Once Paul was certain the boat would be as safe as an open location could be, that it would take a platoon of fully armed Martin Fletchers to pose a serious threat to those aboard, he prepared to leave for the airport. He was certain the security could be no better were the President on board.

43

THE STREETS AROUND LAURA'S HOUSE WERE ALIVE WITH BLUE-lighted cruisers and armed patrolmen on foot. There were roadblocks on the corners. Two K-9 units were beside each other, the dogs standing in the rear seats, anxious and showing their tongues. There was a darkly dressed, black-faced figure standing on the porch roof with an automatic weapon held across his chest. A police Hughes 500 made a low pass over the side street and turned its powerful beam down into Laura's backyard, turning everything white as snow. The wind was picking up, and it was beginning to drizzle.

Thorne, dressed in a rubberized parka, stood in the yard talking to the police captain in charge of the forces that had descended on the neighborhood. He heard a loud beating of rotors and looked up to see a giant orange-and-white Coast Guard Sikorsky passing overhead. It was the signal to move.

Inside, Wolf was excited and barked every few seconds as another figure passed by the window. Reb entered the room in his slicker with the bird in the small traveling cage.

"Why don't you leave Biscuit here?" Reid said.

"No," Reb said.

Reid took a breath and exhaled. "This'll be quite an adventure."

"We aren't shoving off, are we?" Reb said nervously. "Going out on the lake?"

"No, we're staying docked," Reid said.

"Good," Reb said. He didn't mind sitting at the dock, but being out on the water was scary for him. When he was going for a sail, he wore a life jacket from the time he got to the pier until he got back on dry land.

Erin said, "He's terrified of drowning. You know he won't take lessons because he's afraid he'll drown learning." She rolled her eyes toward the ceiling. "Wears a life preserver in the pool."

"Well," Reb said. "People that drown always seem to be good swimmers. Sometimes they say how these great swimmers drowned. People who don't get in the water don't get drowned."

"He's friggin' impossible," she said, exasperated.

"He may have a point," Reid said.

"Nothing is impossible," Reb said. "So I won't learn to swim or take my vest off, and I'll be twice safer than you, Erin."

She stuck her tongue out. "And that stupid bird."

Laura came in with Wolf's lead, and the dog started jumping and spinning. "Okay, Wolf. Just a minute. Erin, got your slicker?"

"In my bag."

"Well, put it on."

"We're just waiting for the word," Woody said. He had a radio in his hand, which was alive with confusing, coded, and unintelligible official chattering. Woody had an earpiece, which he hooked up to silence the radio, calming the room.

Laura was amazed that he could understand anything coming over the air. It sounded like a grand and official stew of voices to her. She was grateful this pandemonium hadn't been a constant since the protection had started. To Laura this pitch of confusion was mind deadening. Her anxiety level over missing work, and being in limbo until Martin was dealt with, made it hard for her to stay cool on the outside, even for the children's sake.

"Maybe we should leave Wolf at home," Reid said. "And Biscuit."

"I'll stay with them, then," Reb said, poking out his bottom lip.

"But Wolf'll need to be walked," Reid added.

"I'll walk him if he needs to," Reb said.

"Someone will," Woody said. "Let's not worry over the zoo."

"I'd feel better if I had a gun," Reid said.

Laura almost said that she did but remembered what Paul had said. *Tell no one.*

"You know how to use a gun?" Woody asked.

"I fired a few guns in my youth. I know what you guys are taught in your handgun training," Reid said.

"You do?" Woody said.

"Sure, they go over it and over it until you get it right. They tell you that the bullet comes out the little front hole, so you should stand behind it when you pull the trigger."

Woody stared at Reid with bored eyes.

Reb and Erin laughed. Woody didn't.

"If you hear shooting, just do one thing we always tell civilians over and over," he said.

"Stand behind us?"

"No, kiss the dirt and we'll help you clean out your pants when it's all over."

The kids and Woody laughed. Reid didn't.

Agent Alton Vance stepped inside from the porch. He was carrying a shotgun with a flashlight bracketed under the barrel. "Okay, people, we're ready." Thorne was standing behind him with his pistol in hand.

Wolf was wild-eyed and had to be pulled along as

Reb led him toward the big orange-and-white Sikorsky helicopter where Thorne and Sean waited by the open door. There was a ring of heavily armed, flak-vested cops around the place, their backs to the helicopter. The craft was sitting in the park across from Tulane University, its rotors moving slowly enough so the individual blades were in evidence. The family climbed in through the large door and were buckled into the seats by crew members dressed in orange jumpsuits who were wearing handguns in nylon chest holsters.

Reb looked back out at the police cars with their blue lights echoing in the mirrors of wet pavement on St. Charles. "The rain won't hurt it?" Reb yelled at the man with the white helmet who fastened him in. The bird inside the cage seemed to be trying to fly in several directions at once. The guardsman placed a jacket over the cage. "This chopper'd fly underwater, Hoss, but we plan to stay in the air," he said.

"I hope so," Erin said.

The blades picked up speed, and the volume of the engines grew to a roar.

"Where's the parachutes?" Reb yelled. The man secured Wolf's leash to a ring set in the wall beside Reb's seat, and the dog skittered into a nervous half crouch, his head bowed. Thorne and Sean climbed in last, and the Sikorsky lifted off the ground, tilted, and rolled out to the north with its precious cargo. Reb looked down at the lines of stopped cars on St. Charles Avenue.

"Let's see Mr. Fletcher follow us now," Reid said, smiling.

Thorne nodded nervously as he dialed a number on his cell phone. "Okay, Paul, we're in the air. Good hunting."

As the Sikorsky traveled toward the lake, Paul's jet was taking to the air through the rain. The sky closed in on the craft, enveloping it in cloud as it climbed.

44

In Dallas, Eve held the wicker purse against her chest and seemed to be short of breath as she walked down the concourse. Joe McLean had changed out of the airline pilot's outfit and into a zippered jacket and baseball cap. The airport was thick with people arriving and departing. Eve was a mother goose with her five agent goslings, scattered but trailing along behind her, trying to look inconspicuous. They were all hooked into hidden radios so they could talk to each other. Larry and Walter wore Walkman look-alike transceivers. Joe, Stephanie, and Sierra wore small receivers that looked like hearing aids, with separate microphones in their lapels. Stephanie's microphone was clipped to her bra, between the cups.

Eve moved well behind the speed set by the flow of fellow travelers, and it was all that the agents could do to keep from running into her. She slowed and entered the ladies' bathroom. Joe waved Stephanie inside, and she almost tripped over Eve when she went in but veered toward the row of sinks and started fumbling in her handbag, watching Eve in the mirror. Then Eve was staggering toward the line of sinks.

"Are you all right?" a woman dressed in a flight attendant's uniform asked.

Eve whirled and looked at her. There was spittle on her lips, the lipstick smeared. Her eyes were dull where they looked over the dark lenses. "I'll be fine. I need to splash my face and freshen up before I get on the plane."

"Let me help you," the woman said, ushering Eve to the sink. Eve pulled the scarf free with one hand while maintaining the grip on the purse. Stephanie stood at another sink and played at checking her makeup. "Seems our girl is having a hot flash," Stephanie whispered. She watched out of her peripheral vision as Eve flooded her face, wetting the front of her dress as she did. "Let me get a sky cart to drive you to your flight," the stewardess offered.

"That would be nice. I feel kind of peaked all of a sudden. I'm not used to flying. The excitement."

Eve smiled a crooked smile, and the stewardess smiled back. Warning buzzers were sounding in Stephanie's head. Eve might have something up her sleeve. She could be trying to lose her tail or make them show.

Stephanie went out through the doorway behind the stewardess and waved at Sierra. She showed the stewardess her badge. "Police business, ma'am. I'd appreciate it if you'd call that sky cart and go on with your business."

The stewardess didn't ask any questions. She satisfied herself that the badge was real as far as she could tell and nodded her head. Then she walked toward a gate and spoke to the man taking tickets, who in turn nodded, eyed Stephanie, and spoke into the telephone.

"What's up?" Sierra asked.

"We need to get someone to the sky cart that's picking her up."

"What do you mean?" Sierra asked.

"She asked for a sky cart," Stephanie said.

"Okay, guys," Joe said. "Stay alert. Larry, watch for the sky cart. Stephanie, you tell her when it arrives."

Joe had taken a seat and was watching with interest. Larry and Walter were standing together acting like traveling partners. They carried small, stowable bags. Larry turned so he could watch for the sky cart.

"How'd she look in there?" Joe asked.

"Bad. She's either one ace actress or she's in some sort of physical distress."

"Think she's onto us?" Joe asked.

"I don't think so. She told the stew she's catching another flight and she wanted the sky cart, so she can't be going to Denver—that gate is close by. I'm betting the Miami flight. Tell the others. I think she was going to try to lose us and then jump the plane at the last minute."

Stephanie went back into the bathroom to discover that the room, though filled with moving people, was empty of Eve. She almost panicked until she moved down the line of stalls and saw Eve's leather orthopedic shoes under the door. She tapped at the metal door.

"Somebody's in here!" Eve shouted.

"The lady outside called you a cart. They'll be right here. Are you all right?"

"It's just indigestion. I'm feeling better now," she said. "Thank you so much. You're very thoughtful. Most people aren't, you know."

"I can see you to the cart," Stephanie said.

"No, I'll get there fine. Thank you again."

The sky cart was just stopping outside the door when Eve exited. All the passengers were agents. Walter Davidson helped her aboard, a Walter Davidson who had made sure he looked nothing like the way he had at her house when he and Sierra had installed the camera optics and transmitter. As Eve stepped into the cart, Walter dropped a beacon into the pocket of Eve's plaid coat. Now they could track her from over a five-mile distance by car and as much as twenty by helicopter.

"Where to?" the driver asked.

"Gate seven," she said.

The cart pulled away and Stephanie had to trot along to keep it in sight.

When the cart pulled up to gate seven Eve climbed down, toddled over to the counter, and presented her ticket. Sierra got in line behind her. The cart pulled away, went thirty feet, and Joe McLean and the other agents got out and grouped as Stephanie walked up to them.

"Stephanie, you're staying back here for safety," Joe said. "We'll go from here without you." He scribbled a number. "Call Paul that she's on the flight to Miami. Tell him we've got a beacon in place so they can pick her up at the airport."

Joe and the other agents slipped through the gate after Eve. Eve took her aisle seat in first class and didn't look up at any of the agents as they filed on board and went back into the coach section to their seats and settled in for a long flight.

As the other passengers were filing past, Eve slipped out of the outer plaid jacket, pulled another scarf out of the purse, and slipped it on over the one with the violets. She stood, looked behind her at the riot of bodies filling the aisles, tucked her head in, and hurried off the plane.

The flight crew were in the entrance. Eve stepped through the bodies and spoke to a stewardess.

"Dear, I'm in first class and I have decided I need more sessions with the doctor before I actually do it."

"Do it?"

Eve frowned. "Fly in a plane. It's all right to leave without me. I've done this before. I'll get the refund later."

She turned and started walking briskly toward the gate.

As the last of the passengers passed through the first-class section, Joe watched one of the stewardesses pick up Eve's plaid coat and take it toward the closet to hang. So she was getting comfortable. He exchanged glances with the other agents and smiled at Sierra. Great!

After the flight attendant went through the standard instructions, the curtain closed and the agents in the rear of the plane settled in for the flight to Miami. Larry Burrows looked at the dial on the tracking device as the plane taxied toward the runway and was pleased with the strength of the signal.

Joe took his cell phone out and dialed Paul to tell him they were on the way.

Stephanie had walked a few feet away and was lost in thought when Eve emerged from the walkway. She had left behind the plaid coat and was wearing a thin raincoat with a hood and a dark scarf over the floral one. Stephanie saw the reflection of movement in the window—someone walking from the companionway—and turned a bit, instinctively, but nothing alerted her to the fact that there was anything unusual going on. She was listening to the idle chatter that filtered through the microphones.

Stephanie watched as the plane was towed out to the tarmac and began its warm-up. "Have a good trip, guys. See you in Miami after the hammer drops. Call me, okay? Soon as something happens."

"Roger that," Joe said. "Thanks for everything."

"Good hunting," Stephanie said. As she removed her earpiece, she was starting to tear up. All that work and she was going to miss the payoff. She knew she might live her entire professional life and never get a shot at this kind of action again. People like Joe would always have her doing shit work, meanwhile taking the credit for her successes. Maybe they'd put her behind a counter or something. Maybe she'd leave the DEA and see if she could move into the FBI. She watched the runway until the plane sped down it, sailed up, and began its climbing right-hand turn. " 'Bye," she said sadly.

As Stephanie was passing the rest room, someone moved quickly into the corridor and bumped into her. Stephanie felt a jolt when she looked up and realized that she was staring into Eve's face. The white makeup was off, the sunglasses had been replaced with her thick bifocals, and she was wearing a different coat. Stephanie's mind seized for a second, and Eve glared at her, angrily.

"Watch where you're going," Eve snapped.

Stephanie's eyes were locked on the large woman's. "Well?" Eve said.

"Excuse me," Stephanie squeaked.

"I swear . . ." Eve turned and trudged off back toward the terminal. Stephanie followed.

Stephanie had to call Paul Masterson and warn him. Somehow Eve had slipped off the plane without anyone's seeing her. Stephanie had no idea how she had done it—not that it mattered now. They'd have to figure it out later. *Is Martin here in Dallas? What if he is? How will I know? I'm swimming in shit.*

Eve stopped at a bank of telephones, and Stephanie was smart enough to figure that she would look to see if she had a tail. Stephanie didn't know what Eve's long-range vision was like, but sure enough, Eve did take a sweeping look down the concourse. By then Stephanie had stepped into the doorway of a shop. While she watched, Eve put on her reading glasses, reached under a phone with her right hand, and retrieved something that had black tape on it. Stephanie couldn't see what it was. *A message? No, a car key. No, she doesn't drive.*

Eve glanced around as she pretended to look through the small purse she had hidden in the folds of her clothing. She waited a couple of seconds and took off again, with Stephanie following. Stephanie reached into her purse and felt the handle of her nine-millimeter. *I'll know Martin when I see him. I have to. I have to stop him. . . .* She remembered Paul's warning: ". . . *the single most dangerous man I have ever known. Do not engage him one on one. If he is identified . . . shoot to kill . . . shoot to kill . . . shoot to . . .*"

Eve stopped at a row of lockers and looked around again. Stephanie averted her eyes and quickly stepped into the cocktail lounge, taking a seat at a table. *What if Martin's watching me right now?*

Stephanie held her phone down in her lap and dialed Paul Masterson's number, which they had all memorized on Joe McLean's orders.

She looked up to see that Eve had opened the locker

door with the key she had retrieved and was staring right at Stephanie, her eyes huge through the lenses.

Stephanie averted her gaze again, took a count of six, and when she risked another peek, Eve was reaching into the locker, her attention focused on something inside. Stephanie tried to figure out what Eve was doing as she pressed the send button on the cell phone. At that instant there was a brilliant flash and ear-closing pressure—everything in the world went white as the wave hit Stephanie. She realized, in that euphoric and detached state of shock, as she was floating backward on the wave, that something wasn't exactly right. That Eve was vaporized. Then there was just darkness . . . and silence.

45

THE GROUP WAS GETTING COMFORTABLE IN THE LOUNGE OF THE *Shadowfax* while Laura set about checking the stocks and selecting a couple bottles of wine from the cabinet.

Alton Vance and Tom Nelson were standing in the galley door, which opened to the cockpit, in still-dripping rain gear. They had Uzi machine pistols hanging in plain sight under their arms.

"Woody, do you or the other men want a drink—a beer or a coke?"

The agents shook their heads.

Alton Vance turned to Woody. "We'll cover the pier," he said. "If someone made a pot of strong coffee, I imagine we'd drink it."

"It's going to be wet out there. I've got a couple sets of foul-weather gear in the hall storage closet," Reid said.

"These coats are fine," Alton said. The two agents disappeared up the ladder to the cockpit. Their feet could be heard as they walked aft.

"Hard shoes," Reid said, frowning. "They're scuffing the deck."

"Sorry," Woody said. "They weren't thinking they'd be walking on boat decks when they chose their shoes."

Reid went out to the hall closet and brought back a yellow rain jacket and a pair of pants. "Gore-Tex," he said. "If I need to go outside."

Woody waited for the coffee and then stepped out to deliver it to the guards on the pier.

Wolf sniffed at the door, then turned three tight circles before lying down at Reb's feet.

Thorne and Sean were in position across the marina, Thorne scanning the piers through binoculars and Sean waiting his turn at watch. He saw Woody hand the steaming mugs to the agents on the pier. The rain was falling harder, and Thorne turned up the collar of his coat to help keep out the wind.

"I guess we can relax a bit. I mean, there's a fucking army out here," Sean offered. "Man'd be nut cakes to try anything." He looked again at the sniper on the roof of a boathouse and at the one directly across, set up in the flying bridge of a fifty-foot powerboat moored less than one hundred yards away.

"The man *is* nut cakes, kid. The sniper on the boat there has a Winchester model seventy, looks like," Thorne said.

"A two-seventy you reckon?" Sean asked. "That's a flat shootin' round. At this range I'd imagine thirty-oh-six with a one-hundred-eighty-grain boat tail would be perfect."

Thorne exhaled. "For deer hunting, maybe. They use three-oh-eight, kid. Every sniper on earth uses a three-oh-eight. He can pierce your earlobe at five times that distance and not even make a heat line on your cheek."

"I used to hunt. Growing up, I mean," Sean said, trying to make conversation. "I used a thirty-oh-six."

"And one-hundred-eighty-grain boat tails, right?"

"Yeah."

"Was a sniper in Nam I knew. Marine Corps fellow.

Sheriff now in Utah. This guy took a VC's head right off his shoulders. Shot measured out to a quarter mile. VC never knew what hit him."

"You an atheist?"

"I'm a Libra," Thorne said dryly.

"It's almost like hunting from a stand."

"Right," Thorne said. He trained the binoculars on the diver who was surfacing beside the Coast Guard launch and the men on the aft, standing under the awning, looking miserable in their rain gear. God, I'd hate to have that fucker's job, he thought to himself. He watched as the diver said something to the guardsmen. One of them handed him a set of fresh tanks and took the old set up onto the deck. Then Thorne watched as the bubble trail headed toward the Hatteras where the prone SWAT sniper watched the *Shadowfax* through his scope.

All evening, swimming in that murky shit. Like being a friggin' earthworm.

46

THE FALCON WAS ABOVE TWENTY THOUSAND FEET MAKING A BEE-
line for Miami. Paul's telephone buzzed from inside his
briefcase. It was Tod Peoples.

"Where are you?" he said.

"Tod, we're over the Gulf, headed for Florida. My
shadow team should be landing there right before we
do."

"A bomb went off at a DFW terminal a little while
ago. Just getting the update. Looks like . . . okay, ten
dead, no telling how many wounded."

"Bomb? When?"

Rainey sat on the edge of his seat, the Bible in one
hand. "What?" he asked. "What bomb, where?"

"Went off fifteen, twenty minutes ago," Tod said.

"A diversion maybe?" Paul wondered if the bomb
was to help Eve lose her tail.

"What bomb, where?" Rainey repeated.

"DFW," he said to Rainey. Then he spoke to Tod again. "That was after Eve's flight took off—Joe called me on his cell phone when they took off for Miami. This is not good. Maybe the bomb was just late going off? Maybe it was supposed to be a diversion while Eve sneaked on the Miami flight?"

"Martin twenty minutes off with a bomb?" Tod's voice was full of skepticism. "Man's very accurate, but it's too coincidental not to be Martin."

"A bomb is too overt for a diversion with his mother in the place. Maybe the flight was originally scheduled to be loading later and he set the device before the schedule change. Can you check that original schedule from where you are? When he bought the ticket."

"Sure," Tod said. Paul heard keys clicking in the background. "Just a minute."

There was a click alerting Paul that he had another call coming in.

"Believe this shit? Hold on, Tod. Got a call on the other line."

"I'm not going anywhere," Tod said.

"Hello?"

"Paul?" The voice was light, the background full of static.

"Is that you, Joe?"

"Yeah. This is terrible."

"The bomb?"

"Bomb? What . . . no bomb. Paul, we can't find her!"

"What? Find who?"

Joe said, "Eve. She isn't on the plane."

"How the hell could she not be on the plane? Look in the can," Paul said, his heart sinking.

"We did. Larry's asking the stewardesses. . . . Wait a sec. . . ."

Paul could hear Joe talking with someone he assumed was Larry Burrows.

"She got off."

"What?" Paul shouted. "How can anyone get off a fuckin' plane?"

Paul listened while Larry mumbled something. The static grew louder, and Paul couldn't make out but a few words.

"At the terminal? In DFW?" He listened for a few more seconds, then clicked back to Tod. "Anything?"

"Regularly scheduled flight," Tod said. "That's strange."

"It gets stranger. Tod, that was Joe. Eve slipped them at DFW."

"Then she got another flight."

"Tod, see what took off in that window. After the Miami flight and right after the blast. Call me back."

The telephone went dead and Paul turned it off. He sat for a minute in silence tapping the phone against his teeth as he thought. Something had been nibbling at his subconscious all day. Something Rainey had said. *"Six years ago, the day you were hit. Thorne, Joe, and I were standing around in a hospital waiting room in Miami covered in your blood."* Then another piece, something Tod had said. The reason it had stuck in his mind. *"His only weakness is his mother. He has seen her every year on or near his birthday with one unavoidable exception six years ago."*

"Rainey, when did Martin break out of prison?"

"Day you were shot. Or maybe the day after that. I can't remember exactly. We didn't know it right off."

"Son of a bitch, that's it!" Paul yelled. Six years ago Martin had missed his rendezvous with Eve. It was when he was . . . *This is the anniversary of Martin's family's deaths!*

"What's what?" Rainey asked.

Paul picked up the phone and dialed a number.

"What's up?" Rainey asked.

"Thorne, it's Paul. She slipped them. Eve slipped Joe's team, but that doesn't matter. She's a red herring. Go red alert. Meet us at Lakefront Airport in forty-five minutes. Martin's still in New Orleans."

Dear God, why didn't I see it?

Paul dialed the direct number for Tod Peoples and screamed at the cockpit door as he pressed the final numbers. "Turn around!"

"You sure?" Rainey asked as he stood, then stooped to avoid hitting his head.

"I'd stake my life on it." Paul watched Rainey enter the cockpit.

The copilot came out into the cabin behind Rainey. "That weather's already covering the area. Airport's closed. We'd have to go to an alternate strip or wait a couple of hours to get in."

"New Orleans!" Paul said. "Now! To Lakefront."

"They're closed, I said. Am I not making something clear? There's no way to see the ground. There's a thunderstorm passing through with moderate turbulence. That means it isn't quite bad enough to twist us like a beer can, but enough to slap us out of the sky!"

"Then we'll open it!" Paul yelled.

"It's out of the question, sir." The copilot spoke as if he were certain Paul simply didn't grasp the situation. "Minimums won't allow—"

"Turn back and land at Lakefront, or I'll blow your fuckin' heads off and fly it back myself!"

"But it isn't possible. It's suicide! The turbulence will take us out of the sky."

"Don't call Lakefront till we get close and then declare an emergency and put her down. Don't tell me you can't—just do it. Not doing it is suicide."

The copilot went back into the cockpit, leaned over to speak to the pilot. The pilot turned and looked back over his right shoulder at Paul, who took out the Colt, held up it in plain view, and jacked a shell into the chamber. He let his arm down on the armrest, his wrist down, the pistol aimed at the floor. The plane banked sharply right and headed north by northwest for the Louisiana coast.

"We're flying back into the storm?" Rainey asked.

"Yeah, you want out? They do." He pointed absently at the cockpit.

"Where can I go?"

Paul smiled. "Say a prayer for us, Rainey. And for every one of our people in New Orleans."

"I never stop praying, Paul. I've never stopped, and I think the first set's being answered right now."

"I should have stayed with them."

Rainey nodded and muttered something about hindsight as Paul dialed Tod Peoples again. Rainey had never seen Paul so upset.

Rainey decided that if they landed, it was a sign from God. Then he would do what he had to do. He hoped Paul would not get in the way. But if he did, Rainey would walk over him and anybody else who got between him and Martin Fletcher. God was delivering Martin to him.

47

Laura loved the sound of the rain against the deck overhead, and she loved the hollow clanking of the scores of wind-driven halyards, their steel spring buckles against the aluminum masts, like some magnificent world filled with wind chimes. But the wind had become a wall of noise, and something sharp on the outside was catching the wind and had become a high-pitched whistle. Laura had drained two glasses of red wine to relax her nerves. Woody sat on the couch in his California-casual billowing silk shirt and white Italian pants. The shoulder holster looked completely out of place. Woody's eyes were cold, the lines around them tight. He seemed even more distant than usual.

"You play golf, tennis?" Reid asked him.

"Golf some. Ride horses. Work out."

"You must find this bodyguard thing boring," Laura said.

"No," Woody said. "Quiet is normal, but it's always quiet before—"

"The storm?" Reid laughed. "Absolutely."

Laura smiled. "I just hope it's as quiet after the storm as it was before. I wonder what's happening in Miami."

"What did you do before?" Reid asked.

"This and that," he replied.

"Where did you learn your violence? School or before? How does it feel to hurt people?"

"I don't go around hurting people unless they want to hurt someone I'm shielding," Woody said. "Someday you might have reason to be glad that I'm like I am. Thankful there are people like me so people like you can sleep safely."

"I'll just check on the kids. Reid, Woodrow, would you like a glass of wine?" Laura said.

"Glass of wine would be great," Reid said. "I need to walk Wolf, and I'll give the guards coffee while I'm out."

"Give you a hand," Woody said, standing.

"Don't be silly. No sense getting that silk shirt wet. I need to take him out."

Woody sat back down. "They won't allow you off the boat," he told Reid. "Orders from Masterson."

Reid raised his eyebrows. "What kind of gun is that?" he asked, changing the subject abruptly.

"Glock," Woody said.

"Could I see it? I've never seen a Glock up close. Never felt comfortable with pistols. Pistols are single-purpose instruments. I mean, they're only good for shooting people with."

"Well, as long as some people need shooting, I hope the guns'll be around." Woody pulled the Glock and stared at Reid.

"Would be a better world without them," Laura said.

Woody removed the clip and the shell from the breech and handed it to Reid, grip first. Reid held the gun and aimed it at the wall. Then he gave it back. "Interesting. I remember them as being heavier. You keep a bullet in the barrel? Isn't that dangerous?"

"In the chamber. We carry them armed so they'll be

ready to use. Sometimes a split second makes the difference between walking and being carried."

"Where's the safety?" Reid held the gun out to Woody between two fingers.

"These don't have a safety per se. They're like revolvers in that—"

"Please." The edge was apparent in Laura's voice. "I'd rather you keep that put away. I mean, it isn't really necessary to have it out armed, is it?" Laura said. "Paul never entered the house with a hot chamber."

"It doesn't matter to me," Reid said. "I'm sure Woody here knows what he's doing. But these walls are thin. What with the kids and all . . . I mean, if there was an accident . . ."

Laura went back toward the bathroom.

"No sweat," Woody said. He put the magazine back in place and the extra bullet in his pocket.

Reid filled two of the plastic, insulated coffee mugs, snapped the tops in place, and put on the rain slicker. "Wolf!" he called. The dog jumped up and followed him to the door. Reid put the leash on the animal, and they started out, the coffee mugs in Reid's left hand.

As soon as Reid was out the door, Woody took his gun out of the holster and slid the receiver back and forth slowly, careful that the action didn't make a loud noise. Then he slipped the magazine out of the gun and put the bullet he had ejected for Laura's benefit back into the chamber. He smiled to himself. *Civilians.*

Outside, the Hatteras's halogen spotlight hit the agents, who were standing on the dock covered by large umbrellas. Reid pulled up the hood and stepped over onto the pier. The guards walked up. Wolf sniffed at their legs and wagged his tail. Though the dog was hunched against the wind, he didn't seem to mind the rain. Reid looked back and saw Woody standing on the deck by the aft door, holding his telephone.

"Guys," he yelled. "Thorne says we're on a full red alert."

"Why?" Alton yelled back.

Woody shrugged. "Hey, you want to ask?"

Reid handed the two guards the coffee. "Thought you guys might be needing these. One of you can knock on the hull if you need anything else and I—"

"Thanks," Alton said. "Appreciate the coffee. This weather is a bitch."

"I was gonna take the dog for a walk," Reid said.

"I'll do that," Alton said. "We aren't supposed to let the group separate until we get an all clear. Now there's a red alert. I'll pass the word to the uniform guarding the gate," Alton added as he walked away down the dock behind the dog.

"All right," Reid said to Tom Nelson. "When he's finished, just put him on deck, he'll scratch at the door."

He looked up, and Woody was gone back inside. "By the way, have you worked with Woody before?"

The agent shook his head. "No, Thorne and Sean neither, though. Big organization."

"He's DEA, too, isn't he?"

Nelson laughed. "Depends on what *he* said he was. I haven't asked, myself."

Reid shrugged. "I guess he's the kind of guy who doesn't feel comfortable answering questions," Reid said. "Seems nice enough, though. He gets on well with the kids."

Reid went back inside, locked the galley door, and hung up his coat. "Brrrr," he said. "The wind drives that rain straight through you. I'm gonna take a hot shower." He looked into Laura's eyes and lipped, "Join me?"

Laura shook her head. "I'm going to see if I can get Erin to go to sleep. I think she's a lot more upset about Paul's visit than she's letting on."

Reid turned to Woody. "Woody, listen for Wolf. They'll turn him loose on the boat, and he'll scratch to get back in."

Woody opened a book that had been on the coffee table. It was a large photographic essay called *A Day in the Life of America*. "Back in twenty," Reid said as he went down the hallway.

"Take your time, asshole," Woody said to himself.

He watched Reid walk down the hallway. Then he waited for a few seconds, slipped off his shoes, drew his gun, and crept back to the aft cabin door. He listened there until he heard the shower running, then placed the gun back in the holster and returned to the lounge. He looked out the window at Tom Nelson's legs as he moved by in the blowing rain. Then he turned and walked back toward the galley. He removed his shirt and hung it on the back of a stool and ran a hand through his wet hair. A bolt of lightning illuminated him, casting a bright white rectangle of light across the cabin.

Alton walked Wolf to the grassy area at the end of the dock. He spoke to the armed policeman who blocked the pier from the parking lot as he passed. There were several small sailboats on trailers on the edge of the parking lot, and Wolf started nosing around the tire of one. The agent looked out and could barely make out the flying bridge of the sport-fishing vessel where the SWAT sniper was positioned. He could see only a hazy form where the Coast Guard boat was anchored. A man under an umbrella moved briskly toward the yacht club. Alton walked that way, hoping the dog would relieve himself so they could go back out on the pier. There should always be at least two men on the pier near the boat. But with all the firepower around the place he wasn't worried. The man was in Florida.

The dog led him to another pair of small sailboats on trailers and pissed against one of the tires.

"I have to go myself," Alton said, looking around. "Hold it here." He put the leash over a cleat on one of the trailered boats. He walked a few steps and, after checking again over his shoulder, opened his zipper.

As the agent began relieving himself, he heard something behind him and turned to see the policeman from the gate walking toward him, playing his flashlight on the ground in front of him. Then the uniform touched the brim of his cap and turned his back, unzipping his trousers to urinate. Alton looked down at the dog he was supposed to be walking. "Seems like we're the ones with weak bladders and you just stand there growling at our own people.''

The dog growled for a second time, and before Alton could turn, the cop locked an arm around his neck, pushed the round blade deep into the base of his skull, and with a quick wiper-blade motion ended the agent's life. Martin Fletcher held the agent for a second, then released him to the ground. Then Martin pulled Alton's coat off his body and put it over the recently purloined policeman's uniform.

Tom Nelson was glad to have the coffee. He hated the close lightning because the accompanying thunder was deafening. He wasn't concerned that he'd be struck, though. There were a thousand aluminum masts aimed at the sky, and his umbrella was a comparatively small target. He kept his eyes on the point where Alton and the dog would appear. "Red alert," he mumbled. He saw Alton coming, all but pulling the dog along. He tried to make out the sniper's roost on the Hatteras but couldn't. In fact, he could barely see the row of boathouses or the Coast Guard vessel.

Then he heard something and looked down to see a diver surfacing near the *Shadowfax*'s stern. Tom waved. The diver waved back and started swimming toward the pier. Tom dropped to his haunches so he could speak to the man in the wet suit when he broke the surface again. Nelson was vaguely aware that the diver he had been watching earlier was black, and this diver was white. He was staring at the man's blue eyes through the mask's lens and reaching for his Uzi when Alton and the dog reached him. "Alton . . ." He started to mention the diver's skin-color change.

At that point he saw that the man in Alton Vance's coat wasn't Alton and realized that the Uzi was in the wrong position. When Martin bowed to dispatch the agent, the dog seized the opportunity to pull free and ran off down the pier in a panic.

Martin wiped the blade of the ice pick and turned to make sure that the killing hadn't been witnessed. He was always amazed that men won't scream, not even when they face certain death.

Close overhead, jet engines whined as a plane passed on its way to the airport to the east. Martin and Kurt Steiner looked up reflexively, but neither could see the landing lights through the soup.

48

THE FALCON BOBBED AND WEAVED AS IT DESCENDED THROUGH AN envelope of angry cloud. Rain ran in rivers over the windows, and the jet engines roared back at the thunder as the plane banked hard over Lake Pontchartrain and the flaps engaged.

"See, it ain't so bad," Paul said. "I can almost see the water. Hope we don't see it up close."

Rainey said, "God didn't bring us all this way to drown us in a lake. We'll make it."

As the plane turned for final approach, the cellular phone rang. Paul was delighted because it took his mind off the impending zero/zero landing, coming in over the lake with no margin for error.

"Hello, Tod," he said loudly.

"Tell him I said hi," Rainey added, looking out the window at the passing whiteness. ". . . And 'bye."

"What's up?" Paul said. "We're trying to crash the

agency's plane in zero/zero. We're on final." Paul listened, his face growing paler by the second. He put his left hand against his brow. "Okay, I got it."

"What?" Rainey said. At that moment the plane pitched up violently, and Paul looked out to see hangars at oblique angles to the window.

"Looks like our boy blew it," Paul said.

Rainey's knuckles went white as he gripped the seat's armrests and the jet shuddered.

"This is what you call a missed approach," Paul said. "We'll go around and try again. I've got a good feeling about these pilots."

Rainey smiled at Paul's calm exterior. He was sure Paul was as terrified as he was. "What did Tod allow?" Rainey asked through clenched teeth.

"Martin played pop goes the weasel with his mommy."

"The bomb in Dallas?"

"Eve salad. Stephanie was forty or fifty feet away when it went off. Blast knocked her unconscious, but she'll be all right. Shock, cuts, blown eardrums, broken leg, and a concussion."

The plane's wings finally leveled, and it started gaining altitude.

"That's not good," Rainey said. "Martin's got nothing now."

"He's thrown his anchor into the drink."

"He isn't planning to survive."

"I bet they'll nail the landing this time," Paul said, pulling the telephone's antenna out again and dialing. "Let's see if our ride's here yet." The plane banked and bucked right as it entered the base leg over the lake.

"Everybody wants to live, Rainey. Even Martin Fletcher."

"Naturally," Rainey said without conviction. He knew firsthand that some people didn't care one way or the other. He felt excitement grow inside him as the plane bobbed and weaved.

●   ●   ●

Martin Fletcher crouched on the boat's stern against the cabin wall, reached down, and opened the plastic-wrapped bundle with his knife. He looked at the Semtex and the detonators to make sure everything was ready. He connected the detonators and handed Kurt the bomb. Kurt, being very careful not to make any noise, disappeared into the aft door and closed it gently behind him.

Then Martin lifted Alton's Uzi, checked the breech to make sure it was armed, and moved slowly toward the cockpit door.

As he walked silently forward on the port deck, the rain beat at him mercilessly. He poured the contents from a pair of white capsules into his mouth and shivered involuntarily as the awful taste hit his tongue. He was already a walking amphetamine vessel. It was a feeling well beyond the edge he was usually after.

He checked his watch. *Give Kurt time to plant the Semtex in the engine room against the fuel cells.* He had taken a dozen of the amphetamine pills over the past few hours. As he stood in the rain, waiting, he closed his eyes and followed a line of thought. He thought of his wife, Angela—his Angel—and his son, Macon. *Today is their day.* He thought about that night in the jungle when the rain fell in heavy sheets, washing the grave dirt from his hands, turning it into mud on his clothes.

It had been just after his escape from prison, and at that point in his life all he had wanted was to give normalcy a try. He had thought it might be possible for him to spend the remaining years of his life taking it easy—enjoying the fruits of his labors. He was healthy, wealthy, and wise, and he was tired of life on the edge. He knew he could no longer live as he had. Men like him usually ended up quick-dead or in prison, but almost never retired. He planned to retire because that's where the shortest odds were.

He had already struck out at Masterson and the team, and even though word had reached him that he had failed to kill Paul, the man had been marked for life, assuming he survived. Martin had decided that he had made one hell of a point. *Look in the mirror, Masterson, and you'll always think of me.* The others were just following their leader like hungry puppies.

Had it not been for the plans of others, he might have lived out his life differently, spent his golden years with his own family, safe and rich in South America. Angel's attention and the presence of his son had quenched his thirst for revenge on Masterson. Or so he had thought at the time.

The escape from prison had been masterful. Two freelancers, posing as the FBI agents who had been scheduled to arrive later that night to move him to Marion, had plucked him from prison and delivered him to a hangar. There a pilot whose normal cargo was arms for the contras and cocaine on the back haul had waited with an airplane. Angel had been waiting there with Macon in her arms and three suitcases at her feet. Angel had been with him since he had trained troops at the Democratic College. She was Latin, raised in New York. Small, almost boyish, and beautiful. Her skin was deep olive and her eyes the soft brown of a doe. She had been a dutiful mate. In fact, she had satisfied his requirements as no one else had. He could sit and look at her for hours. She moved like a ballet dancer, and she loved him beyond reason—just as his mother always had. He had dreamed of the day Eve would join them in South America.

The trip down was pleasant even if the plane was riding less than forty feet off the waves in order to skirt radar. It was a clear night when the Navaho touched down on the small strip hewn from the lush Guatemalan jungle.

The pilot had kept the props turning, lingered on the ground just long enough to see his charges handed over to the three young men who were dressed in T-shirts, sneakers, and baggy jeans. Then the plane turned amid a flurry of dust, took a loud roll to the end of the strip, turned again, built speed, and was up and stuck in a long, lazy curve toward the north. Martin and Angel and their son, Macon, stood against the canopy of trees, touching each other. Freedom had never held meaning for Martin before that moment.

The young men had lifted the suitcases into a battered Jeep Wagoneer, placed them on the rusted floor. The men were quiet, and their young faces quick to smile. They were like armed servants. Martin asked for a gun, but they protested that they were paid to watch over him and there was no danger. Martin relaxed. They were just kids. As the Jeep bounced along on the way to the compound, he and Angel sat shoulder to shoulder. The men, unused to female company, chattered like monkeys and took every opportunity to turn their gaze on Angel and the child. The jungle road was a rutted path, and the Jeep bucked like a young stallion as they sped along.

There were three houses among the storage buildings and power shed hidden in the lush foliage. The guards put the family in the largest dwelling, a low concrete house. It was dusty but comfortable. There were the normal sounds of jungle joined by a mufflerless diesel generator, which powered the ceiling fans, the refrigerator, and the electric bulbs. The refrigerator was well stocked with food and ice. The cabinets held bottles of liquor, but neither Martin nor Angel had a taste for anything but each other's company.

The men who'd sprung Martin had given him traveling money and passports. Macon, his son, was lightskinned, and his hair was curly and soft. Martin Fletcher had never liked small children, but Macon proved an exception. This child created something warm and real in Martin's heart. He saw himself and his mother reflected in the large blue eyes, Angel in the lips and nose. For the rest of that day they relaxed and became a family in the jungle.

Macon had been born after his father's arrest and was already toddling when Martin had held him for the first time. Macon liked him, or seemed to. Martin watched the child teeter around the small house that first evening—walking a few steps and sitting hard on the tiles. Then repeating the maneuver again and again without ever crying. After Macon tired, Martin and Angel made love for the first time since his arrest. As they made love, his son slept beside them in a drawer Martin had taken from the chest and padded with a bedspread. It began raining, and they had fallen asleep, locked on to each other, when the young bodyguards hit the house. Maybe they were emboldened by the storm or the money they had been offered for the job. Maybe it was the grass and the thought of rape after the man was dead. They never said.

Martin awoke to a loud crash as the louvered door exploded open under the force of a boot. Martin, whose reflexes were automatic, pushed Angel to the floor by the crib and rolled in the opposite direction, because a machete used for gardening was propped against the wall near the headboard. He moved toward the door as the tall man burst through the bedroom door and began firing at the empty bed. Martin put the heavy blade through the man's forehead, and he collapsed into himself, the thin blade locked into the skull to the bridge of the boy's wide nose. There were fast footsteps in the living room, and the second man hit the door expecting to find the room's inhabitants dead. The shotgun was half-lowered. As Martin had moved beside the door, Angel had grabbed up Macon and was heading for the window and freedom.

Martin wrenched the blade free as the man with the shotgun entered the room. The boy looked at Angel and then at his dead friend and was raising the weapon when Martin stepped in behind him and pushed the blade's wide tip down into the torso at the place between the neck and the collarbone, severing the blood pipes that ran into the right side of the brain and back out, as well as opening a lung and the heart. As he pulled the blade out, the big gun went off. The shotgun blast caught Angel in the back, and she fell hard, her head hitting the wall and then the concrete floor. There was the dull, wet sound of crunching bone and mashed tissue.

The guard who had been left to cover the window pushed the shutters open as Martin pulled free the nine-millimeter Browning Hi-Power that had been stuffed into the shotgunner's waistband. Martin opened up, and round after round hit home as the youthful guard stumbled backward into the foliage like a man who was being electrocuted. Then it was silent; Martin's ears were ringing, and clouds of cordite swirled like wood smoke in the air above the killing floor. Martin had moved across the room, dropped to his knees, and turned Angel to him. Her nose was bloody and strangely flattened. There was a strange smile on her lips and a look of abject terror in her coffee-brown eyes. She squeezed his arm.

"Martin, where's Macon?" she whispered, touching his cheek with a trembling finger.

"He's fine," Martin said of the still child.

"Take care of him for—" She gripped his arm for a second, went through a death rattle, and her body jerked itself stiff and then relaxed. Then Martin turned his attention to Macon.

The buckshot had passed through Angela's delicate frame, and the child's abdomen had been opened like a dropped melon. After what felt like a great deal of time had passed, Martin had wrapped Angela's and Macon's bodies in blankets and carried them one after the other outside. The rain fell in torrents, but he managed to dig a four-foot-deep hole and dropped them in as gently as possible. Then he knelt over the bulging mud and screamed his rage at the clouds. He was answered with thunder.

After he had dragged the dead *pistolero* inside, he set the house on fire using a jerrican of gasoline from the Jeep. Then he drove to the nearest town and left it there. He rode on a bus for hours and then caught another. It was days before he took notice of where he was.

The three men, who looked like boys, had been contract killers. Contra soldiers, probably. They must have been better than they looked, or they wouldn't have been given the task. Martin knew that old associates in the CIA had decided to make sure he was silent about what he knew about whom. That was a business decision he understood. He cursed himself for not seeing it coming. He had overestimated his value to people who never got close enough to the help to understand how lethal one man could be. It didn't matter in the least who had pulled the trigger, though. Paul Masterson and his Green Team had used manufactured evidence to take him down. If he hadn't been arrested, he reasoned, he would not have represented a risk to the people who had hired the three assassins.

The men who sent the assassins had done what they had to do. The assassins had been poor soldiers killing for money and a future. Paul, Rainey, Thorne, and Joe had sentenced his family to death, him to a loneliness beyond measure. They were the ones who had to pay.

He had used Angela for company, assistance, animal comfort, and for cover. For Martin that was the closest thing to love he could feel for a living woman. But in the space of a long day and an evening, he had loved Macon beyond the way an animal loves its own. Through their deaths he had fallen in love with them.

He had killed his own mother because he couldn't allow her to lead his enemies to him, or to live alone if he was to die. Now they would all know that he had killed the Mastersons, and the rules would change. After tonight he would be hunted like no other man in history. He smiled at the idea of what a challenge *that* would be.

She died listening to my voice. The recorded tape had started "Mother, I love you. Remember that I will always love you." Then the device's timer, triggered by the turning on of the tape player, had set off the Snickers-bar-sized block of Semtex inside the box. She could not have known what hit her. It was a merciful, kind thing he had done—out of love. Now she would be all right. If he escaped, he would be free; if he didn't, she would never have to grieve for him. He remembered what she had always told him: "There is nothing in life as terrible as having to bury your own child." *I have spared her what I had to go through.*

49

WOODY WAS READING WHEN A SHADOW CROSSED THE PAGE OF THE book in his hand. He got his hand on the Glock and brought the barrel around to find it aimed at a very surprised nine-year-old holding a red nylon sleeping bag and a cage with a bird inside. The cage had something white running along the walls. Reb had lashed Styrofoam blocks inside the bars.

"Reb," he said as he put the Glock in front of him on the coffee table and exhaled deeply. "You sneaked up on me."

"That was neat how you drew it out," Reb said. "I bet my daddy could do it faster."

"I know he could," Woody said. "Why aren't you asleep? It's late."

"The bed keeps moving me awake."

"The water's rough, that's all. The wind will die down in a while. But you're safe in a boat that was built for ocean traveling in rough seas. And, besides, I'm the Lone Ranger, kiddo, and Reid is Tonto."

"Reid doesn't know how to shoot," he said. "What's a Tonto?"

"We won't be shooting anyone." Woody smiled. "Go back to sleep."

"Where's Mom?"

Woody pointed to the teak door a few feet from where he was sitting.

"In there with Erin."

"I'm gonna sleep in there, too. I don't like the bunk cabin."

"I'm sure they'll be delighted to see you."

"See ya later," Reb said. "Where's Wolf?"

"He's walking. He'll be at the door any minute," Woody said. He looked up and saw the coated figure move by the porthole. *Glad I'm not out there*, he thought to himself.

"Reb, what's that in the cage?"

"It used to be an ice-chest lid. It's to keep Biscuit from drownin' if the boat goes under." He looked at the bird and shrugged. "I'll get him another chest cover. It was an emergency."

"Flotation? I see," he said, nodding and laughing to himself. "Wouldn't want a bird to drown."

He watched Reb disappear into the V berth. For a moment Erin's music filled the lounge with strains of hard-edged music. Then he started to open the book but heard a tapping at the door. He stood, picked up the Glock, and went over to it. "Yeah," he said.

"The dog," came the muffled reply.

Something's wrong! Woody pulled the gun from the holster and moved to the door with the gun ready. As he opened the door to the sight of a man he had never seen before, something moved behind him. *Shit! No hard shoes against the deck!* He was trying to bring the gun around when the man on his flank fired the Taser. Woody saw the lead wires stretching from his chest to the man's hand as he fell, helpless and twitching, to the floor.

"Hello, son," Martin said as he stepped in and

loomed over the agent. "Watched you do your stuff in the bar this afternoon—*nice* job." Martin stepped away and into the galley. "You too, Kurt," he said to the man in the rubber wet suit standing beside the couch with the Taser in his hand.

Steiner bent over and laid the Taser on the floor. He pulled a half-inch-wide nylon cable band from his back pocket, put the loop over Woody's wrists, and cinched it tight by pulling it.

"I got an idea you're gonna enjoy the fireworks show," Martin said.

Kurt got a second cable band and secured the baby-sitter's ankles. Then he took a small roll of duct tape from another pocket and sealed Woody's lips.

"If I hadn't had Kurt on board with that electricity rig, you woulda had me," Martin said. Then he dragged him easily down the hall toward the sound of the running shower.

Reb had come in and lain beside Erin on the bed, interrupting the mood in the room. Erin had been listening to Laura, who was seated across from her on the V-shaped bed.

"Reb?"

"Can I sleep in here?" He put the birdcage on the side table. The bird yawned and stretched a wing. "Pretty bird," it said. "Love the bird."

"Yes, we love the bird," Erin said, laughing. "Except when he shits on our clothes."

"Erin!" Laura said. "Poops, remember?"

"Except when the little shit poops on our clothes."

"Mama, remember the story about the little bird?"

"What story?" she asked.

"The one where the man has the bird in his hand and he asks the other man if the bird is alive or dead."

"Well," she started. "This war lord had a bird hidden in his hands, and he asked the wise man to tell him whether the bird was alive or dead. He planned to crush it if the wise man said it was alive and let it live if he said dead. Foolproof, right?"

"And he said?" Reb prompted.

"He said. You, great one, have the power to make the bird as you wish it," Laura said.

Erin said, "Blah, blah, blah."

Reb looked as if he were going to hit her.

"And he let the bird go?" Reb said.

"I think so," Laura said. "I can't remember. I believe he did."

"Sure," Erin said. "If he'd had Biscuit, he would have killed it because it would have pooped in his hand." She laughed.

"You should both try to get some sleep," Laura said as she finished her story.

"Okay," Erin said, tapping the magazine beside her. "Soon as I finish this *Vogue.*"

"You can read anytime. Sleep."

Laura sat with the children for a few minutes. Reb fell asleep immediately, but Erin seemed to be faking an attempt. Laura stood slowly and crossed the room. She closed the door behind her gently, noticing immediately that Woody wasn't on the couch. The heavy boat rocked under her feet as the swells rolled against it.

She lifted the wineglasses from the coffee table and started for the galley sink. She tripped, and one of the glasses fell to the wood floor and shattered.

Erin appeared at the door. "What was that?" she asked.

"Nothing, go back to sleep," she said. "I broke a glass."

"Where's Woody and Reid?"

"In the back, I guess. Go to bed."

"Where's Wolf?"

"G-O T-O S-L-E-E-P."

She turned. "You don't have to spell it, I heard you."

"I wanted you to think about it."

Laura collected the pieces of curved glass and dropped them into the refuse can in the galley. On her way back into the lounge she saw something on the floor near the door and knelt for a closer look. It was a

G-SHOCK wristwatch, with the strap broken; it looked like the one Woody wore.

"Woody?" she said aloud. "Reid?" *Have they been wrestling? Impossible,* she said to herself. There was no answer. She looked out the porthole to see what the agents on the pier were doing, but she didn't see anyone. She couldn't see the Coast Guard vessel. It was as if she were peering through a thick veil of moisture.

She started down the hallway. When she got to the bathroom, the shower was still running, and she tapped before she opened the door. The light was off and the room was filled with fog.

"Reid, how long does it take to shower? It's been a half hour. You're gonna wrinkle up."

There was no answer, so she turned on the light. She thought the room was empty until she looked into the shower and discovered Reid's naked form crumpled against the wall of the shower, facedown. The back of his head was swollen, and there was blood running from a long, deep wound. She could see a white river of skull in the valley of clean red.

"Reid!" she gasped. She knelt and picked up his head. It was warm. She turned off the water. Reid opened his eyes slowly.

"Reid, God, you're bleeding, what happened? Did you fall?"

"I don't know—I must have." Then his eyes seemed to clear. "No . . . someone was in here. . . . I thought it was you . . . then . . . Laura, I'm dizzy."

She turned his head slightly. He winced, but she had to look into his eyes. One was far more dilated than the other. *Concussion.* She said, "I'll get Vance and Nelson."

"Woody?" he asked.

"I couldn't find Woody. The guards aren't on the pier as far as I can tell."

"We've been breached. It's Martin." Reid closed his eyes and then opened them. "Laura, listen carefully. The bed frame on my side opens up . . . magnet inside the wood . . . Press at the top. It's a cubby and there are guns in there. Take one and lock yourself in the V berth.

When you get in there, there's a switch in the closet . . . it's an alarm. When you're safely in there, flip it. The troops will come running from all over. Don't open the door under any circumstances. If anyone tries to come in, shoot through the door. You'll have fifteen shots. Just keep pulling the trigger, and it'll fire."

"I'll help you get there, Reid. Can you stand?"

"There are two guns . . . get me one. Then get the hell to the V berth. Don't stop . . ."

"Reid, I can—"

"Don't fuckin' argue with me," he snarled.

"But your head—"

"My head is the least of our problems. The guns!"

Laura went into the bedroom. She located the cubby, pressed on the side railing, and it fell open. She reached in for the guns; then she ran back and gave one to Reid, who was up on an elbow. "I'll cover the hall. Help me out."

She grabbed his arm to help him. He could stand but was stooped and had no sense of balance. She was crying now. "I can't . . . leave you."

"He'll kill you and he'll kill the kids. He'll torture them first. He's a twisted deviate who has done horrible things to kids like Reb and Erin all over the world."

Her mind cleared a bit, and she seized on what he was saying. "How do you know so much about him?"

"I can't explain now. Run."

Confusion threatened to lock her reason. But she knew the children were more important than Reid was . . . than she was.

Laura left the bathroom and moved down the hall in an instinctive crouch, sweeping the gun from side to side as she went.

As she edged past the door to the crew cabin, she saw that it was cracked open, and there on the floor, tied hand and foot, was Woody. She started to enter but caught a bit of movement in the mirror and realized that someone was behind the door, waiting. Her mind, already filled with fear, pushed her on.

She moved rapidly to the door to the V berth, went in, and locked it behind her.

"What?" Erin asked.

The children stared at the gun with surprise in their eyes.

"Everything's gonna be all right. We've got to keep our wits," she said.

Laura was holding the gun tightly when she heard the galley door to the deck open and bang closed. Then she heard voices speaking in hushed tones. She prayed it was Vance or Nelson even though she knew it had to be Martin and someone else.

"Erin, Reb." She couldn't think of what to tell them. Her mind was all but frozen, fighting for a plan. She heard something that sounded like wet deck shoes squeaking on the galley floor.

Laura remembered that the hatch in the berth's ceiling over the bed was locked from the inside. She turned to the door and looked through the keyhole. She saw a figure silhouetted against the light in the hallway. *Martin.* He looked completely different from the way he had when she had known him, but she knew it was him by the way he was standing—the set of his powerful shoulders.

"Erin. Come here," she said in a whisper. She sat Reb down and cupped her hands. She nodded in the direction of the ceiling. "Come on, we're getting out of here," she said, unscrewing the latch.

Erin put her foot in the stirrups of her mother's hands and was lifted up into the cool rain. She looked around and back down as her mother started to lift Reb up, but her eyes caught the movement of someone entering the cockpit from the galley. The rain was beating cold against Erin's hair. She looked down at her mother and Reb.

"Someone's coming!" Erin whispered, and dropped flat against the deck. She was on the edge of panic, holding the hatch open a sliver.

Laura pulled Reb back. "Go—hurry—get help!"

"I can't," Erin pleaded. "I'm coming back inside."

"Go!" she said, and pulled Reb back. "Just run!"

Erin closed the hatch and Laura locked it. Then Erin scooted backward until she was at the railing, and she pushed herself under the rail wires, slipping into the water between the hull and the pier just as a wave slammed into the boat, making it lurch against the rubber bumpers over her head that kept the hull from striking the dock. *It would have crushed my skull like a grapefruit.*

As Erin paddled under the dock, she looked up through the cracks in the flooring and saw the figure step to the bow and secure the hatch from the outside. *He's locked it*, she thought.

She turned and had just started dog-paddling when she heard a siren scream to life. It was an earsplitting wail and seemed to be coming from the boat—the mast, maybe. Then the *Shadowfax*'s diesel turned over. A large searchlight came on, pointed at the sailboat from the Coast Guard boat.

"*Shadowfax!*" an amplified voice boomed. "Cut your engines immediately!"

Erin could make out the shapes of men moving on the deck of the cabin cruiser. She started to swim in that direction but decided to make for the yacht club a hundred yards away. She could see someone standing in the *Shadowfax*'s cockpit, shielding his eyes from the bright light.

Then, as Erin treaded water, it was if the world were ending in a brilliant finale.

The harbor went white several times in rapid succession at different locations. There was a deafening thud, and the Coast Guard boat was replaced by an orange fireball surrounded by water vapor. Then a boathouse across the way went up, and the cabin cruiser that she had started to swim for evaporated. The harbor was filled with debris flying into the air and raining down all over. Several pieces of fiberglass and metal clattered against the deck of the *Shadowfax*, then splashed all around her. Several boats moored near the Hatteras were burning. She watched as the *Shadowfax* pulled away from the pier and began running for the harbor's mouth, illuminated by the fiery maelstrom. The siren aboard the *Shadowfax* stopped blaring, and the only noise was the crackling of fire and voices yelling.

Within seconds Erin heard new sirens. Police cars on the outside perimeter had started in toward the devastation. Diesel fuel and gasoline from ruptured tanks caught, and the flames rolled across the harbor out toward the other fingerlike piers, where scores of boats waited to be added to the catastrophe.

As Erin swam for the nearest boat, something rolled under her hands, a form moved, and Tom Nelson's face turned upward into hers. His lifeless eyes were open far too wide. Then his clothes released the air trapped inside, and he sank slowly into the dark water. Erin screamed, but the sound was covered by newly exploding boats. Then she climbed onto the pier and ran, stepping over debris as best she could. Her teeth chattered loudly, the violence of the muscle spasms blurring her vision as she ran toward the lights of the yacht club, her nightgown clinging to her like wrinkled skin.

50

THE FALCON LANDED SUCCESSFULLY THOUGH VERY HARD, DUE TO A sudden downdraft. The engines reversed with a loud whine, and the pilot taxied off the runway as soon as he could, stopping just off it in a perpendicular attitude. Emergency and security vehicles were coming down the runways and taxiways, washing the mirror of wet asphalt with their yellow and red flashing lights. The vehicles rolled up to the Falcon and stopped in a semicircle, halting the airplane's forward progress. Men climbed down from the fire truck and out of the other vehicles. Paul dialed a number and put his phone to his ear.

"Thorne, where the hell are you?"

"Coming from the terminal. A taxiway, I believe," Thorne Greer said, sounding out of breath.

"Well, hurry. This is looking like a lynching party."

Paul stood and moved to the door with the cane pinned to his stomach by his left wrist. He held the telephone in his right hand like a weapon. He slapped the pilot on the shoulder and noticed sweat running down the faces of the two men in the cockpit. "Damned good landing, boys," he said. "You'll get a big bonus for this."

The pilot looked at Paul through his red-ringed crystalline eyes. "You'll go to jail for this," he mumbled, his hands still trembling. "You're fuckin' insane. What you did was air piracy, and I'll make sure . . ."

Paul frowned. "Let me do the talking, and maybe I can save your licenses."

Rainey opened the door, and he and Paul stepped down onto the taxiway's pavement. Thorne Greer's car pulled up in front of the men who had advanced on the two passengers. Thorne jumped out and ran to Paul.

A large man in a cheap suit who was sopping wet held up a badge. "National Transportation Safety Board," he growled. "What the fuck's going on here? You nuts? You were warned off . . . you could have made several alternate fields that are open. You've put a lot of innocent lives in jeopardy." Paul assumed he was referring to people in the homes around the airport, certainly not theirs.

Paul held up his own badge. "DEA. We have a national emergency, and I don't have time to explain it to you. Don't speak to my crew, or you'll all be in debriefing for weeks."

"DEA, so fuckin' what? I never heard of anything that would allow you—"

"National emergency, I said!" Paul yelled to be heard by all in earshot. "We're operating on direct orders from—"

The necessity for Paul's explanation ended when the western sky suddenly turned a brilliant red-orange once and then almost immediately three more times. When the sound arrived, it was as if lightning had struck a few feet distant. Boom! BaBoom, boom, boom. The shock wave was a wash of air pushing through, which fluttered the men's wet clothes like flags. "Holy fuck!" the NTSB inspector said, his fat face orange, his mouth like a crater.

"Yacht basin. Must be fuel tanks," someone said.

"Bombs," Rainey yelled in alarm. "It's going down!"

Paul, Rainey, and Thorne jumped into the car, leaving everybody standing beside the plane, staring off at the red pulsing sky. The DEA Chrysler fishtailed off silently and, when the tires caught purchase, shot straight down the center of runway eighteen, leaving a crowd of confused personnel standing with their mouths agape, sharp shadows dancing behind them, and the light of the great fire reflecting in their eyes.

51

When Paul, Thorne, Rainey, and the other agents got to the pier, the *Shadowfax* was gone and the yacht harbor was a disaster site of astounding proportions. Flames reached like fingers high into the blackness, and the base of the clouds was stained bright red for miles. The heat was blistering, evaporating the rain. In the distance fire engines were racing in from all over, and the basin's parking lot was filling with emergency vehicles, ambulances, cars, and trucks. There were onlookers from the boathouses and condominiums nearby, emergency personnel and uniforms moving about in the light and smoke like frightened animals.

Paul and Thorne made the end of the pier where the *Shadowfax* had been moored. Thorne lifted a cleanly severed mooring rope. It was here. He waved his hand where forty boats locked to a pier were creating a wall of flame two hundred feet high. "The Hatteras with a

SWAT sniper and his spotter was out there. That section of boathouses was where another SWAT guy was stationed. See—over there." Thorne bit his bottom lip in anguish as he pointed to a burning boathouse. "Sean was over there—and there was a Coast Guard vessel anchored right out there."

"Come on," Paul said, authority filling his voice. "Let's see if we can get some information." They ran down the pier. Paul, Thorne, and Rainey joined a flow of uniforms into the building.

"Who's in charge in here?" Thorne yelled as they entered.

A police sergeant, his face blackened from the smoke, recognized Thorne and rushed over. "Mr. Greer! There's a girl from the boat in the bar there. I'm trying to coordinate . . ." He stared out the window where the world burned.

Erin was in the club's bar, wrapped in a blanket and surrounded by a ring of policemen. There was an emergency medical team attending her as cops fired questions at her. She looked like a feeble old woman who'd been rescued from a flood. Paul pushed a policeman roughly aside. "What the hell . . . ," a uniform yelled, and grabbed Paul's jacket and twisted it. Paul whirled and put his cane against the man's throat, pressing the shocked cop against a wall. Two other uniforms grabbed Paul from behind. Thorne moved in and flashed his badge. "Everybody back," he yelled. "He's ranking here!" Paul knelt and looked directly into his daughter's face.

"Daddy?" She blinked and seemed to come out of her trance. Her eyes flooded and her lip quivered.

"Erin, it's all right, it'll be okay." Paul sat beside her and put his right arm around her shivering shoulders, drawing her against him. "It's gonna be fine."

"Daddy. He has them. I saw him. It was him driving the boat away."

"We have to know who was on the boat and exactly where they were."

"Mama and Reb are in the V berth. Reid and Woody

. . . I don't know. Woody was in the lounge, I think. Reid in the aft berth. Mama and Reb were going to get out, too, but the man was . . . the man came and . . ." She hugged him desperately and buried her face in his chest. "It was horrible! People were on those boats and they died—didn't they? They just weren't there anymore. Why, Daddy?" she asked. "He took Mama and Reb . . . help them. Please, please help them. He'll kill them."

"No, Erin," he lied. "He wants them alive. We'll get them." Paul turned his head. "Get a chopper here," Paul said curtly to the soot-faced officer now standing near the tight group.

"We have one," Thorne said. "All-weather giant parked on the quadrangle."

"We found a policeman dead near the fence and Agent Vance beside a sailboat in the lot," a policeman said. "A German shepherd was huddled against a fence near him."

"Wolf. It's our dog," Erin said tearfully.

"Bring the dog," Paul said, hoping that its presence would help calm her.

Paul spoke calmly even though he was panicking inside. "Erin, tell me everything you can remember."

"Mama helped me get out of the hatch—I guess Woody and Reid are dead—or they would have . . ."

"Okay, Erin." Paul looked at the medical personnel. "Can you give her something? To calm her."

The attendant nodded and started fumbling through his case.

"We have to set up communication with Martin," Paul said.

"Woody had a radio on board with him," Thorne said.

Erin nodded. "He had the thing in his ear to listen."

Paul turned to the closest policeman. "Can we get a fast boat?"

A Coast Guard ensign, standing beside Rainey, spoke up. "How fast y'all needing ta go?"

52

MARTIN HAD CUT THE MOORING LINES AND PILOTED THROUGH THE walls of flame out into the chop, the *Shadowfax* pitching violently in the swells as it entered the lake. He had set a course for the causeway bridge and in a few minutes drew up alongside it. Then he had set the boat's auto-pilot to hold a course parallel to the twin spans, figuring that the bridge would mask the craft's silhouette from radar detection. The wind was steady from the southwest with gusts to forty knots. The boat listed hard to stern as the rudder worked to maintain the heading toward the north shore some twenty-five miles distant.

Kurt had placed the scuba tanks, masks, and flippers on the deck behind the rear mast. He had also placed a pound of plastique against the gas tank and equipped it with a remote detonator. There were two remote triggers with an effective range of one mile; they were operated by depressing a button and then releasing the pressure, at which point there was a detonation. The Semtex would convert the boat into confetti, the water for a hundred yards into a vapor cloud. They had used far less on the hulls of the three vessels in the harbor and the boathouses Martin had wanted neutralized. Kurt thought about how he had lain in wait under a pier and had overtaken the Coast Guard diver and killed him silently beneath the murky surface, before taking his place.

So far the plan, hastily put together, was working like a charm. Martin was a true professional, he thought. He could think on the fly, and with less information than people with all the time and field intelligence in the world.

Reid, propped against the wall in the bedroom, heard someone moving in the hallway and placed the gun at his side, out of sight. He was too dizzy to stand and was lying there still naked, wet, and bleeding. He watched as a silhouetted figure filled the open door.

"You'd be who?"

"Reid . . . Reid Dietrich."

"Please, I know your name isn't Dietrich. What is it, really?"

Reid closed his eyes for a few seconds and opened them. "George Spivey."

"Spivey? Oh, yes. That was your setup on the pier?"

"I planned to have you there."

Martin laughed. "A nice practice exercise."

"I underestimated you."

"So, tell me—you turned Lallo. You had something on him?"

Reid nodded.

"His business partners were his weak spot. He didn't need that. It was the excitement. I liked him, but because of his disloyalty he died like a pig, squealing in the dark."

"And you won't?"

"I'm short on time, so I'll get to the meat of the matter. You're a professional. I'm a professional. I won. You lost. Stakes we play for are death."

"Aren't you curious? About my mission? Who sent me?"

"Hell, son, you were supposed to kill me. Am I wrong? Like Woody. Why didn't you join them on the dock? Prior engagement?"

George Spivey nodded.

"Okay, George. Who sent you in?"

George Spivey shook his head, pain filling his eyes.

"Well, George Spivey, in my day the word 'professional' meant something. That Woody—now he's a professional. Him, I had to outflank."

George Spivey managed to smile.

"Nice boat, George. Solid, seaworthy. Yours or theirs?"

"Rich uncle."

"Confiscated by the DEA." He smiled. "I'm gonna blow it up anyway. Your head must hurt. Kurt's excitable, he thought he'd probably killed you. Frankly, I didn't expect to find you so alert."

"My head feels like an asshole that's had a cherry bomb go off in it."

Martin laughed again. "Very descriptive. You should have been a comedian. Laughing in the face of impossible odds is an admirable trait."

Spivey nodded.

"Kurt had to neutralize you because I couldn't have so dangerous an adversary walking about while I was tidying up and getting under sail." There was a note of sarcasm in the word "dangerous."

"Dangerous? Wait until you see what's coming next."

"I'm terrified," he said flatly. "What are you, shadow man, CIA? Dark angel?"

"How did you know I wasn't Reid Dietrich?"

"It's elementary, my dear Watson. The Reid Dietrich living in Atlanta was seventy-five years old. His son, the one whose identity you absorbed, was killed in a car accident in college. The company you supposedly own consists of a girl with a telephone in a depressing building in Fort Lauderdale. If the phone rings, she says the name of the company. If anyone asks for you, she says she'll take a message. Very large woman by the name of Trudy Winters."

Reid tried to clear his eyes—his vision was blurred and he couldn't hear out of his right ear. "Very impressive." He readied the pistol, which was wedged between his leg and the wall. He could hit Martin, but he didn't know where Kurt Steiner was.

Martin moved to the dresser and sat on the edge. "Whose voice *do* you answer to?"

"I'm freelance."

"The CIA paying your expenses?"

"Pick any initials. They all want a piece of you."

"DEA?"

Spivey turned his head away.

"Very good. I underestimated them. What am I worth dead to Masterson?"

"Not Masterson. Robertson. Seven-fifty."

Martin stood and glowered down at his adversary. "Time is growing short. Where do you want it?"

Martin pulled out his Browning .380 and slowly screwed on the silencer. "Been too much loud noise around here tonight. Hate to alarm the children prematurely. You're a pro. Pick it—heads or hearts."

"Listen, Fletcher. There's no reason to kill me. I've lost the game because I didn't know how good you were, didn't believe it. But you are. Let me go. I can't hurt you now."

"What about Laura and the children?"

"The spoils of the battle. I'll do something else as a show of good faith. T.C."

"What about him? He's paying you to take me out."

"He expanded the hit."

"Yes?"

"He wanted me to take Masterson out."

"T.C. wants Masterson snuffed!" Martin laughed as he removed the magazine, checked it, then pulled the receiver back and peered inside as if checking for grime in the breech. He locked it, returned the magazine, and released the catch feeding the chamber. "That's rich!" he said. "Do you think he'd pay me on that contract?"

"Let me go and I'll do T. C. Robertson for free."

"I would love to but I just can't. Wouldn't be fair to the other people who've lost to me."

Reid swung the Glock up and aimed it at Martin's chest.

"How about you lose," he said as he pulled the trigger. There was a dry snap.

Martin smiled, his eyes coldly pleased. "Oh, George. And we were becoming so close. I'm afraid you're typical of the kids today. No loyalty. No honesty." Martin blew air through his lips and inhaled slowly. "Try again."

George Spivey cleared the round with difficulty as Martin watched with a look approaching boredom. The heavy nine-millimeter round fell to the floor, and he pulled the trigger again. Another dry click.

"Wet ammo? Like a bad dream, isn't it? No bullets, removed firing pin? Perhaps it happened when I was searching the boat and found your little cubbyhole. And the phony identifications. I guessed Spivey's was the real driver's license because that picture was the least flattering." Martin aimed the pistol at Reid's chest. "I know you were just doing your job. And I know you're as harmless as a Christmas-tree ornament. But I don't see where it is in my best interest to leave you sliding about on the floor like a seal. I might trip over you."

Reid closed his eyes, then opened them to meet Martin's, and nodded.

The sharp pop of the silenced pistol filled the small room, the shell casing bounced off the low ceiling, hit the paneled wall, and clic-clattered across the bureau. Reid's pistol, still clenched in his fist, tipped onto the floor. There was a small black hole in Reid's chest, which slowly filled with blood. The dark liquid bubbled out and ran in a thin line around his ribs and began swelling onto the carpet. Reid's eyes reflected the shock of his new situation, and then the lids closed halfway down and locked.

"How soon it all comes to an end." Martin dropped

the gun to the side of his leg, put a hand to his chest, and looked down at George Spivey. "It's so like poetry," Martin said. He stepped into the bathroom, looked in the mirror, and used a wet washcloth to wipe the splatters of Spivey's blood from his face. Then he turned out the light and closed the door gently.

Laura . . . it's Marty," he sang as he pressed the lever knob on the V berth's door. "I think we should talk now. How are those delightful children of yours? I've been thinking about you all for such a long time."

"I've got a gun, Fletcher!" Her voice was solid, determined.

"Oh, please don't shoot me through the door." He tapped again, harder.

He heard the dry click of the Glock and smiled. "I hope it isn't one of those guns from inside the bed. Reid had terrible luck with his. I think they must be of faulty manufacture. I can kick the door in, but I'd rather not destroy such a nice piece of wood. So you just come out." He sat down on the couch. "Take your time, within reason. . . . Waiting makes it better in the end."

Thirty seconds passed before the door was unlocked and the knob, a brass lever, made a quarter turn. The door opened slowly and Laura stepped out, closing the door behind her—her body forming a protective shield. There was the sound of its being locked again from the inside. She stood defiantly erect, her arms crossed over her breasts, her chin up.

He patted the couch cushion. "Please, Laura, join me. Let's catch up."

She looked around and saw her purse on the coffee table by Martin's foot. She had tucked her .38 into it before they'd left the house.

"What did you do to Woody?"

"He's worked so hard, I thought he deserved a nap. He is a feisty bastard."

"And Reid?"

"This is the life, Laura," he said. "The open seas—

something really exciting about this, don't you think? Brings out the swashbuckler in a man."

"We didn't do anything to you, Martin."

"That's true, Laura. But your ex-husband did."

"Your problem's with Paul, not us."

"How do you like my new face?"

She looked at him, studying the features. He looked like a man of forty-two or so. Nothing unusual or attractive about the face. The eyes were like the eyes of something dead, or something that had never quite been alive. He was well-built, muscles tense under the skin like spring steel. He was grinding his jaws between speech, and he seemed steady and fidgety at the same time. *Speed.*

"You look different."

"Better?"

"Fishing for a compliment?"

"Fishing. Interesting choice of words."

"What are you planning to do with us?"

"Sit down and we'll discuss it." He patted the couch again.

Laura swallowed and forced herself to sit beside this creature. He put his hand on her leg and smiled, revealing a set of perfect teeth. She willed herself to allow his touch. His hand was as hard and cold as marble. *Bloodless.*

"Last time I did this, you tried to slap me."

"I didn't know what you were then."

"Very good. Honesty. I admire that . . . in my fucks." The last word hung between them, leaving something fetid in the air, like a creature long dead and visited by parasites.

He moved his hand to the point where her legs came together—resting on the ridge between them. She shivered involuntarily but made no move to resist. *Let him have me if it helps Reb. I can take it. I can take anything for Reb. God, keep him behind that door.*

"Why don't you slip out of these?" he said.

"But, Martin, I don't think you—"

The sudden slap across her mouth brought white light to her mind, a dull ache to her lips.

There was blood on her hand when she moved it from her mouth. She could feel the lip starting to swell. But instead of frightening her, the strike set her resolve. She knew that if she could, she would kill him as easily as she wiped paint from a brush.

His fingers tightened around her arms. "Rather I fuck Erin? Or the boy, maybe? I don't mind young and tight, and gender is irrelevant. I'm doing you a favor. I'm offering you what I promised you years ago. Now, take 'em off, or I'll take 'em off my way." He pulled a folding knife from his pocket, opened it with a practiced flick of his wrist, and slipped the blade underneath her sweater, stopping at the neck. He pulled the knife, and the material parted under the blade silently, leaving her bra exposed to his view. "If you can satisfy me, maybe I'll leave the kids alone."

He doesn't know Erin is gone.

"Promise?"

"No," he said. "But I'll consider it."

Laura stood and removed what had been the V neck like a coat. Then he reached over with the knife and slid it under her bra, between her breasts, and pulled gently; the apparatus fell away, exposing her breasts.

He moved toward her and took one of her nipples between his fingers. He pinched it hard and let it go. Then he stabbed the knife into the beam behind the couch. He moved back and watched.

"The pants," he said.

Laura closed her eyes briefly, steeled herself, and then removed her slacks and then her panties. Slowly, deliberately, playing for time. *They're coming. I know they are.* Then she sat beside him, closed her eyes as he pressed her shoulders against the cushions, opened her legs. She waited for him to get it over with. Tears were streaming down her cheeks. He placed his cold hand over her vagina, manipulating the clitoris with a deft and delicate touch. As the finger moved inside her, she prayed she could stay dry as the only form of protest left to her.

The idea of giving him any lubrication made her furious, but despite her revulsion, fear, and anger, her body defied her as his finger became slippery with her juices.

"You like this, don't you?"

She bit her lip and tasted the new blood that came to her tongue. *No, no, no.* "Yes." *Kill me now.*

"Can I fuck you? Are you ready?"

"Yes," she said. *God help me.* Revulsion threatened to turn to vomit. She felt full of bile and fought the urge to throw up the way a child will—by lying very still, willing it away.

"Beg."

"Please, Martin. Please . . ." *You bastard.*

"What?"

"Please . . ." She knew what he wanted to hear, and she forced herself to lip the words like a curse from the depths of her soul. "Please, fuck me." She clenched her eyes and waited for him to take her, but he didn't move. Then he stopped massaging her and removed his finger slowly.

He stood and, instead of taking down his pants, wrenched the knife from the beam, folded it loudly, and slipped it into his pocket.

She looked up and realized that he was not sexually aroused at all. *Speed. Can't get it up.* She had to fight to make sure her overwhelming relief didn't manifest itself with laughter. Her eyes must have asked the question, though.

"You don't do anything for me. You're too old." He walked across to the kitchen. "I couldn't help but notice Reb has your ass."

She reached for her purse, grabbed it up, and knew from the heft that the gun wasn't there.

He said, "I'm disappointed in you. Go back into your hole, Laura. Tell the children I'll be coming for them soon. Tell them if they're really good, I'll share them with Kurt."

Laura was crying as she pulled her jeans back on, wrapped herself in a lap blanket that had been folded over the back of the couch. As she slipped back into her jeans, she saw something on the floor. It was a curved, lens-shaped piece of the wineglass. She reached down as if she were cuffing her jeans and cupped the glass in her hand. She straightened and looked at Martin.

Get him close. "If you touch my children," she said, "I'll kill you."

Martin laughed and walked over to stand in front of her. "You'll what?"

She moved her hand through the air between them and struck at his exposed throat with the shard of glass, coming down and across as hard as she could. He pitched his shoulders back and tucked his chin reflexively. The glass opened a line across his face from the right ear to his nose. She had the impression that the lens-shaped blade had broken all the way through his cheek, glass against teeth. He punched her hard, and she hit the wall and slid down it, collapsing onto the floor. She looked up to see the line open and blood find an escape route and pour down his face in a bright sheet. *Missed the artery.*

"You fuckin' bitch!" he growled as he gripped the wound. "You have any idea what I went through for this face?" Then he looked at the blood on his hand and laughed, pitching his head back. The sound filled the cabin. She could see teeth as the cut opened like some horrible second mouth. "You're going to get me excited if you keep this shit up. Go back in there." He walked to the sink, wet a dish towel, and pressed it against his cheek to stem the flow.

She stood and tapped at the door. "Reb, open up. Quickly."

If Thorne doesn't come . . . before I'll let that demon touch my baby I'll . . . do whatever I have to do.

Did he hurt you, Mama?" Reb asked. She fumbled in Erin's suitcase and pulled out a knit shirt. She turned her back and put it on.

"No, baby. I hurt him, though." She held up the hand showing the piece of glass, smeared with his blood. "I'll kill him if he hurt you."

"Kill him?"

"With this." Reb held up a metal file.

Laura sat back down on the bed and put her arm around his shoulders. "It's okay, buddy," she said. "They'll come soon. Thorne will come."

" 'Less he got killed in those bombs."

"I'm sure he didn't. Besides, there are other people watching out for us, a lot of people. They'll come. You'll see." She tried to project some confidence but wasn't sure she had managed it.

"Sure," he said. She picked up the disbelief in his small voice. It saddened her, made her realize how slim their hope of survival really was.

"Reb," she started. "We have to look around in here for anything we can use to fight him. Just until help comes."

"Like what?"

"Like a flare gun, anything." She opened the closet and started pulling things out. "Check under the bed—in the cabinets."

"The flare gun is in the cockpit," he said. "Under the seat. I think."

"Anything."

"So, like something I'd get in trouble for having normally?"

"Exactly," she said. "A weapon—something . . ."

"I got ya," he said. "Like I'll know it when I see it?"

"Exactly. Like something we can use. Like the file. Screwdriver, anything."

He opened the cabinets under the bed and looked in to see if he could find anything he shouldn't have. "Know what?" he said.

"What?"

"Your mind is the best weapon there is."

Laura was startled. Reb made perfect sense. My mind. A weapon. Let's see, now. She looked around the room and finally at the lamp. An idea started to form. What was it Reid had said about the lights? The lamp cord. *I've made lamps before. It's simple. . . . What can I make with a lamp?"*

"No weapons," Reb said, closing the cabinet. He opened the last drawer. "Some liquor and . . . you could use a bottle to hit him," Reb said. "It burns like the man does at the restaurant with those bananas."

Flambé. Bananas Foster.

"Matches?"

"Nope," he said sadly as the vision of a flaming Martin dissipated.

Laura looked at the vent in the wall. "Reb, is the AC on?"

Reb reached up and felt the vent in the wall. "Yes," he said.

"Okay, I have an idea," she said. "This is what we'll do."

What was it Reid told Thorne about the power?

53

THE YOUNG PILOT LOOKED TO BE HARDLY MORE THAN A TEENAGER.
He was constructed on the order of a series of rectangles
with a head shaped like a pineapple. The effect was completed with a flat-top hair style and small ears that
seemed to have been glued and pressed against the skull,
possibly in an attempt by the gene pool to lessen the
boy's natural wind resistance.

He was wearing a tight black suit that shed the water
and a cap that said HSSI in gold lettering, and below that
the word "Cheetah" was stitched in a script face. The
navigator–systems operator was short, and his matching
uniform was wrinkled, giving the impression that it was
too large and that he had slept in it. They both wore
nylon shoulder rigs with government-issue nine-millimeter stainless steel Berettas and polished combat boots.

As Paul, Thorne, Rainey, two black-clad NOPD
SWAT-team members, and the soot-faced policeman from

the yacht club followed, the young Coast Guard pilot led the way to the boathouse. It was located away from the privately owned boathouses on the harbor and had a steel door, which the man opened with a nine-digit combination pressed into a keypad. Prior to the explosions there had been guards posted inside and out.

Inside the main room, some sixty feet across and fifty deep, two vessels seemed to be standing on a floor of dark water. They were secured to the U-shaped interior pier and were aimed toward the roll-up steel garage door. The boat closest to the entrance was a Cigarette racer that had been painted dark green. The cockpit was open to the elements, and there was an airfoil bar just over that with a phalanx of blue lights mounted on it. There was also a searchlight with a twenty-inch lens mounted between the blues. That wasn't what they had come for, and Paul's eye found the other almost at once.

The HSSI on the far side of the cavernous space looked like a floating stealth fighter; the hull was all soft curves, the reflective surfaces making radar return impossible. It was thirty-five feet long and, except for a small section at the bow, accessible from the cockpit through a hatch, completely enclosed.

Two black-clad SWAT-team members, who had volunteered to go onto the *Shadowfax*, stood a few feet away checking their vests and gear. Paul hoped they weren't so filled with anger at the loss of their friends that they would let their emotions override their training. They had lost their captain, who had been aboard the Hatteras, and four other of their comrades in the explosions. They would be armed with MP-5, nine-millimeter machine pistols equipped with silencers and subsonic safety rounds. Paul knew that the guns sounded like musical spoons when fired.

Rainey was standing beside Thorne as they awaited the pilot and navigator to check the systems and otherwise make the craft ready. His eyes gave away the rage that burned within him like napalm.

"I'll need a gun," Rainey said to no one in particular.

He turned his eyes on Paul and tried to calm the tightened muscles in his face.

"You're staying," Paul said authoritatively.

"Bullshit!" Rainey barked.

"That's an order."

"I'm going and you can't stop me, Paul. God won't allow it."

Paul turned to the soot-faced police officer standing beside the Coast Guard pilot. "Captain Mullin, Agent Lee is under arrest. I am charging you with detaining him."

"What?" the officer said, confused.

"Take out your gun!" Paul barked. "Point it at him, *now*!

The policeman did as he was told, but the revolver's aim lacked conviction.

"If he tries *anything*, shoot him. Hold him at the yacht club until this is all over. Then you can release him. That understood?"

"What charge?" Rainey asked, his face betraying the rage and the panic of being left behind at this juncture.

"Obstruction of justice," Paul said. "I need calm heads on this one."

"You're under arrest," the policeman said.

Rainey lurched at Paul with his hands out, the fingers like eagle claws. Paul shifted his weight and, despite the unsure leg, stepped aside and brought the cane down on the taller man's head. There was a sickening crack, and Rainey collapsed on the dock.

"Now cuff him, goddammit," Paul demanded.

"Paul?" Thorne started. "It's Rainey. He deserves—"

"It's for his own good"—he waved a hand toward the lake beyond the open garage door—"and theirs. Get the medics to look at that knot." He turned to Thorne and lowered his voice. "We got too many wild cards and no plan. *Okay?*" His voice quivered with emotion. "Think I wanted that? I'm sorry about this, Rainey," he said.

The navigator appeared in the door of the boat and waved them in. Paul led the others into the vessel.

" 'HSSI' stands for High Speed Stealth Interceptor," the navigator said as he brought the control panel to life, filling the interior with orange and green lights. "It's strictly experimental but they've worked most of the bugs out over the last few months. It was christened the *Cheetah*. We only take it out between the hours of nobody's looking and nobody's up yet." There was a whir as the big engine started, then only the hint of vibration to announce the motor. "It uses the latest in noise suppression. For starters each sound wave is—"

"Let's go," Paul said. He didn't care how it worked. "Cut the tour and get this tub moving."

"Tub?" The pilot looked at the navigator, and his eyes said that he couldn't believe Paul's disrespect or lack of interest in the latest technology represented. The boat was still so classified that it was rarely seen in the daylight, and the interior was off-limits to all but the engineers who had designed it, and military test personnel. Had it not been for the deaths of their comrades on the Coast Guard boat, time would have been lost seeking the authorization needed to take the boat, with noncleared personnel, into a potential combat situation.

"Unless you have to jabber it into working," Paul added.

One of the SWAT members closed the door, the pilot pushed on the throttle, and the boat moved silently forward and out through the open doors toward the crimson light of the fires. At the channel's entrance the boat accelerated, and the men, who were not seated, were all but rocked off their feet by the sudden speed.

Captain Mullin watched the boat head off into the open lake and then turned and helped Rainey to his feet. He holstered his gun so he could perform the cuffing, which he wasn't convinced was necessary, given the state of the man on the ground.

It had been years since the police captain had been on the streets, and he was rusty. He reached into his belt and removed his cuffs. Rainey had his right hand on the knot on his head—he seemed woozy, uncertain of his feet as he was being helped up.

"You don't need those," Rainey said. "What can I do now? They're gone."

"Orders."

"The man on that sailboat killed my wife and two children. You have kids?"

The opening of the street door stopped the conversation, and Rainey and Mullin turned to the sight of an ensign walking into the boathouse. He stopped and stared at the doors open to the harbor and the spot where the *Cheetah* had been. Then his gaze turned to the two men near the Cigarette racer. He put his hand reflexively to the Beretta at his side but stopped when he realized that one was a police officer.

"Halt!" he yelled. "Where's . . ." he started. He approached and saw the gun and cuffs in the officer's hands.

"Gone fishing," Mullin said, turning back to Rainey. "No," he replied to Rainey's interrupted question as he clicked the cuff on Rainey's free wrist. "No kids."

Rainey turned as though he were offering the other wrist, but instead he brought his fist down into the side of the cop's face like a hammer. When the dazed man hit the deck, Rainey kicked him in the stomach twice, deflating him and leaving him immobilized. Before the young ensign could get to his gun, Rainey had picked up the .357 and turned it on him.

"You know how to drive that?" he demanded. The ensign nodded weakly as he stared at the gun, which was aimed directly at his chest.

"I'm Rainey Lee, DEA."

The ensign shrugged, not visibly relieved that the man holding the gun was law enforcement.

Rainey untied the lines at the bow and stern and stepped into a Coast Guard speedboat. "In here, son, and drop the gun belt."

The ensign obeyed, letting the web belt with the Beretta fall to the deck with a thud. He stepped gingerly around Captain Mullin and dropped down into the cockpit. Rainey glanced at his name tag. "Okay, Gleason, move it."

The young man found the key in the ignition and twisted it. The big motors thundered to life with a deafening roar.

Mullin came around with a moan, shook his head, spotted the ensign's gun, and pulled it from the holster. He stood unsteadily and aimed at Rainey's head. "Cut the engine," he yelled, trying to make himself heard.

Rainey frowned at him and shrugged.

"Give me the gun!" Mullin yelled. "I'll shoot you, Lee!"

Rainey moved his own gun up so fast the policeman didn't have time to react. He saw the first muzzle blast—frozen in disbelief even as he was pitched back—never thinking to return fire. Three shots hit him, two high in the right leg and one in the right shoulder. He collapsed, writhing, on the pier. The street door opened, and another Coast Guard ensign entered, pulling his gun out, but he stopped when he saw Rainey's pistol on him. He raised his hands.

Rainey looked as if he were waiting for a signal to fire, his eyes emotionless, reptilian. Then he turned his head toward the open door as the ensign named Gleason throttled the vessel. When the boat's engines caught, the bow rose out of the water and the boat shot out of the facility. Once in the harbor, the ensign aimed out through the channel, and then, in what felt like seconds, they were out into the lake where the *Cheetah* had gone.

Rainey took a stance beside the ensign and laid the gun on the control panel, his large hand all but covering it from sight. His head was extended over the windscreen, and he stared out before them.

"Gleason, you familiar with that HSSI rig?" he yelled to be heard over the engines.

"Yes, sir." Gleason nodded in case his nervous voice didn't carry.

"Find it!"

"I'll do my best," he muttered. "But it's cloaked."

Rainey used his thumb to cock the pistol's hammer

where it lay flat on the console. "This is for her," he said, smiling and pitching his head toward the seats at the rear of the cockpit.

"Her?" Gleason replied, trying to understand, assuming Rainey was indicating the harbor. Someone who had died in the explosions.

"My wife!" he yelled. *"Her!"* Rainey smiled, exposing a row of teeth all the way to the gums.

The ensign turned, halfway expecting to see a woman in the bench seat. He looked back into Rainey's eyes for a second and realized with shock that the smiling man with the gun wasn't seeing an empty bench.

The young ensign began saying a rosary in his head.

54

"Everything you could need is in the storage units," the *Cheetah's* navigator said.

Paul and Thorne sat watching the walls of water that were being spewed aside as the boat left the harbor and began skimming the tops of the waves, the props shooting a rooster tail of water high in the air behind the craft. There was almost no noise, even as the engine had powered up. The SWAT-team members sat on bench seats, facing each other and speaking in half sentences, trying to dispel the tension they were feeling. One of them kept removing the magazines in his guns and checking them as though the bullets were an illusion that might disappear if he failed to keep an eye on them. Paul realized he didn't even know the men's last names. He didn't want to know them. Ted, the bigger one, and Brooks, the smaller. Kids, really. Weren't they all?

The pilot was watching a small screen that broke everything outside the craft into small, colorful, seemingly three-dimensional blocks. "Virtual reality," the systems operator said proudly. "Like a video game or a simulator." Another screen showed the lake as it might look in the daytime through a red lens. There was a blinking beside the bridge, and a seven-mile readout at the corner of the screen. The bank of screens taken together gave 360 degrees of view. Ten minutes out, the navigator pointed to a small blue light on the radar that represented something behind them, just exiting the harbor.

"Someone's following us," he said. "Fifty, sixty, now sixty-five knots."

The navigator touched the earpiece in his right ear. He turned to Paul. "Sir, your arrested civilian is unarrested. He just took that cop's gun and the speedboat that was docked. The police captain's got three rounds in him. Nothing fatal, it doesn't sound like. He took an ensign as hostage."

"Son of a bitch," Paul growled.

"Rainey never did like people saying no to him," Thorne said, shaking his head.

Paul rubbed his eyes. "He have radar?"

"Yes, nothing that'll track us or find the *Shadowfax* as long as it hugs the bridge."

"So he can't find us?" Paul asked.

"We'll be a needle in a haystack," the navigator said. "In this soup I'd rather have lottery odds."

"Good," Paul said. "We'll deal with him after."

From five hundred feet above the wind-seared surface of the lake, and a mile behind, the big orange-and-white Sikorsky helicopter was also tracking the sailboat, because even though the *Shadowfax* was hugging the bridge, the sophisticated system was not fooled. The Sikorsky was also monitoring the thirty-five-foot-long *Cheetah* and the third vessel that had just come out into the lake. The craft's computers worked with the one aboard the *Cheetah*, plotting and replotting the estimated interception point, factoring in the speed and direction. According to their figures, the third boat, on its present northeastern line, would be off by a half mile in a few minutes. At the *Cheetah*'s interception point with the *Shadowfax*, the big Cigarette would be at least twice that.

Paul, seated in the control room with his hands gripping the cane, was relieved that Erin was no longer in harm's way, but worried that Martin might have caught the news of Rainey's escape and the shooting on the radio. The cop hadn't used Rainey's name but had just said that the man under guard had escaped in a speedboat. Martin would naturally assume he was being trailed. He might also think the report was a cover for launching a surveillance vessel. He was counting on Martin's believing that no one would move against him, not with a bomb likely, until they had better intelligence, a plan of action. But who could be sure? It was of little consequence, so Paul fought to keep his mind on the present. *What is, is.*

Paul and Thorne had changed into black Gore-Tex SWAT-team outfits. Once on board, they would be within handgun range and would use safety slugs so that if they missed, the bullets would, at least theoretically, shatter before they could pass through walls. Reb and Laura were in an unknown location on board, assuming they were still alive. Paul looked at the diagram Thorne had put together from his limited knowledge gleaned from his single visit to the *Shadowfax*.

"I want to try something, to gain us some time," Paul said. "Thorne, get on the radio and try to reach Martin. Tell him I'm on the way in. Tell him I want to negotiate. I have a hunch that if he knows I'm coming, he'll wait to do whatever it is he plans to do."

Thorne lifted his radio and keyed the transmitter button. "Martin Fletcher, this is Thorne Greer. Do you read me?"

There was silence for fifteen seconds. Then Thorne repeated the salute. Paul was standing with his weight on the cane's handle. Then, after a short wait, they heard the microphone being keyed, followed by Martin Fletcher's unmistakable voice. "What you want, Thorne?"

"I want you to let them go, Martin."

He laughed, the sound filling the otherwise silent cabin. "Laura and the young virgins? Or are they? Hard to tell with kids these days. We all know Laura is a loose woman. Surely you've had her."

He doesn't know! Paul thought. *They're still in the V berth.*

"Paul wants me to tell you that he's flying in. He wants a face-to-face."

"With what's left of the army?"

"No, alone. He said he'd come alone. He said for us not to press you. The weather is going to clear shortly, so he can land. No one's going to do anything until then."

"Word of honor?" Martin laughed into the transmitter. "You think I'm crazy, Thorne? I'm going to kill these people if anyone comes within a mile of this tub. I've got Play-Doh on board. Half again as much as I used in the little harbor display. I have the detonator with me, and there's another just like it with my friend."

"No, please, Martin. Don't do anything rash. I can get a boat and meet you so we can talk face-to-face. Give me a location."

"I'd like to see Paul. I'll tell you what, Thorne. I'll keep sailing, soaking up the atmosphere for exactly one hour. Then, if Paul isn't here, I'll set off the Semtex. Did you enjoy the Pearl Harbor re-creation we put on?"

Thorne gritted his teeth. "How did you manage?"

"Trade secret. Don't bother me again until Paul arrives. And don't try anything. Because, old buddy, if you do, I'll enliven the atmosphere on the old cruise ship with a little entertainment that will violate child-decency regulations, the laws of nature, and possibly the Geneva convention. I've never been much for rules. There's already blood on the walls."

Silence.

"Woody?" he asked.

"You in contact with Masterson?"

"Yeah."

"Get him on a hookup. I want to speak to him."

"But Martin, I'm—"

"Now, asshole."

"Just a second."

Thorne killed the microphone by releasing the button.

Paul took the radio and counted silently to thirty. Then he nodded at Thorne and held it up so he could speak into it. "Okay, go ahead."

"He's on," Thorne said.

Paul turned the radio to his mouth. "Yeah, Martin."

"Paul, long time no see."

"Wasn't my idea. I was kinda hoping we'd meet in the mountains before now."

"Been looking over your shoulder?"

"I had hoped it could be just the two of us."

"Wanted to die under the stars, huh? High pass drama."

"You that sure I would die?" Paul said. "You're awfully good at killing children, Martin. Been a while since you took on someone your own size."

"Ask Dietrich and Woodrow about that. I took out the two best you had. Now there's nothing in my way."

"You? I would have bet it was your pal Kurt Steiner who took them out. I hear he's pretty sharp. But you want me to believe you got it over on Woody Poole and George Spivey. Come on, Martin. I mean, you and I are both old men." When Paul mentioned Kurt Steiner's name, he heard an audible release of breath from Martin. *Good, put the son of a bitch off balance!*

"Old men, Paul?" he said. Paul could hear the anger in his voice. "I'm going to show you that I'm not getting older, Paul. I'm getting better." He laughed, and his laughter was a dark thing, filled with the energy of fury.

Paul wondered if making Martin mad was smart. *Yes, put him off balance.*

"Dietrich told me some interesting things before he died, Paul."

"That he was a pro who's been waiting for you to show for a year?"

"You know? I guess he was lying. But it amazes me

that T.C. knew what I was doing for that long. Gave Dietrich this boat, a Jaguar, and a big bag of DEA money."

Paul felt as if he'd been slugged in the chest. *T.C.?* He had thought Spivey was put into play by the CIA. It was what he had been told by Tod Peoples.

"You knew that, right?" Martin had picked up on the uncertainty as a wolf smells blood. "You didn't know he was hired by DEA? *You didn't know!*" He sounded truly excited.

Paul was silent for a second while he thought. "Spivey didn't know I knew who he was. I didn't know who hired him, exactly. It doesn't matter."

"If T.C. didn't tell you, how'd you know out there in Montana?"

"I know a lot of things. I even know about you and Steiner playing on the pier with Lallo Estevez."

"Good old T.C. Just like that spineless faggot to double-cross his own man."

"Spivey?"

"No, *you*! You know so fuckin' much—you don't know your director paid Spivey to do you, too," he said, laughing again.

Paul felt his heart lurch in his chest.

"That creep that your pal T.C. sent to do me, Paul— that guy has been sitting fat for a year, porking your ex-bride and waiting to drop the hammer on both of us!" He laughed out loud. "Now, that—*that's* ironic."

"You are truly one sick bastard, Martin. Tell you what I'm gonna do for you, Martin."

"What's that, Paul?"

"I'm gonna come out there and I'm gonna beat the cold shit out of you, Martin. And then, when I'm finished kicking your ass around the boat, I'm gonna kill you, man to man. You're one sick fuck. What kind of animal would vaporize his own mother?"

"Hmmm. Get any of your people, did I?"

"I'm coming for you, and my face is going to be the last thing you ever see."

"Maybe I'll entertain myself with the family until

you get here!" The voice was filled with barely controlled rage. "Maybe I'll love up on Laura."

"You should have kept Spivey alive if you wanted somebody to act jealous."

Martin calmed his voice. "I'll wait exactly one hour. We can open a bottle of wine, sit around, and shoot the shit like old times. Then you can watch me kill your seed, cowboy—like I watched my family die."

"What do you really want, Martin? What's your price?"

"My price, Paul? I'll tell you what. Give me back Angela and Macon, and we'll call it even."

"Was your pals did that, not me. I don't kill people, Martin."

"Not *you*!" Martin laughed. "Innocent and pure right down to the last drop, that it?"

"No. Not hardly."

"You framed me."

"I sure did, Martin. They wanted to hit you because there wasn't enough hard evidence. You burned some good people, and still I kept you alive."

"Well, Paul, you're a fuckin' saint. And I appreciate it. You hadn't kept me alive, I wouldn't be where I am today."

"I wouldn't have let anyone hurt your family."

"Hmmm. When you getting in?"

"Soon as I can get the wheels on the ground. Will you let them go if I come out there?"

"I'll be here. You think you can find the way, or should I turn Woody into a candle to light your way?"

"Stay put, I'll find you."

"By the way, tell your pals not to get too close, or something unfortunate might happen. Might get a case of premature eruption."

The radio went dead and Paul handed it to Thorne. He looked at Ted and Brooks, the two SWAT-team members. They had grease smeared over their features.

"Look," Paul said, "there's no sense putting any more people than we have to on board. I'll go on alone— I'm the one he wants."

Thorne said, "He'll kill them anyway, in front of you. You're the one with no business going. You limp, you never could fight or shoot worth beans, you're half-blind, and you might have a seizure and flop all over the place pissin' yourself. I'm the one should go."

Paul laughed bitterly. "Okay, I see your point." Paul was relieved they hadn't taken the out he had offered.

"Sir," Brooks said, "we're the best. I'm not bragging, just stating fact. We'll get them off the boat alive if they can be got off alive. The way I see it, there's two bad guys and they're professionals. Four of us will be about even odds. Less and . . ."

Paul thought over what the young man had said. "First thing we do is make for the forward berth while we cover the rear and cockpit. If possible, we extricate them before we confront Martin or Steiner. The woman and child go off into the drink at once. No talking or anything. On the deck, into the vests, and they go straight into the water. One of you, the closest to them, will accompany them. No matter what's happening. Fast and smooth. That's the straightest order I'll ever give. If they spot us, we have to keep them pinned and without firing blind. God knows where the bomb is or where the family will be."

Paul looked at the two policemen. He fought seeing the faces of Hill and Barnett. "When the family is in the water and Woody is located, you guys get off, because he'll blow the boat rather than be taken. Thorne and I will stay behind until Martin and Steiner are neutralized, or until the thing is ended. Whatever happens to us, those two do not get away. Promise me that."

Ted nodded. "We're square on that. That asshole killed a bunch of my friends tonight. He's toast."

"But one of you get the family on this boat and back to the dock first. That's an order."

"What about Reid?" Thorne asked bitterly. "I'm sorry I didn't check him closer."

Paul ignored Thorne's apology. "Most likely he and Woody are dead."

"What Martin said is true? About Reid's being a plant?"

"George Spivey's been under cover waiting for Martin to show here for over a year. Somebody who knew that told me when I was in D.C."

"A year." Thorne's face reflected the seriousness of what Paul had said. "Someone knew about Martin and what he was doing over a year ago? He said it was T.C.?"

Paul nodded, his lips tight together. "It's hearsay, at best. But, yes, I believe him. I don't think he's lying."

"That means T.C. knew he'd be coming for Laura and your kids a year ago. Knew it. Hard to believe a man could be that cold. Might be Martin said it just to fix T.C.?"

Paul didn't say anything for a few seconds. "Doesn't alter anything for us now."

Thorne sat. "Before Doris and Rainey's kids were . . . And you didn't say anything?" Thorne said, stunned. "You knew Reid was a plant and you didn't tell us? When did you find out?"

"I swore not to tell anyone as part of the deal for the other information we got. I only knew that someone was in place in the field waiting for Martin. I didn't figure out Reid was Spivey until just now. In case we failed, it was still the best chance to get Martin and save them."

"Who told you if it wasn't T.C.? Who else knew?"

Paul shook his head. He didn't want to put the spotlight on Tod Peoples. "It doesn't matter, Thorne."

"You didn't think we could take him?" Thorne sounded hurt.

"Woody Poole was my insurance policy. I never thought he'd show here before he met Eve. I was way off."

"Woody's another dark angel."

Paul nodded. "I think so. Someone from one of the other agencies, most likely CIA, wanted him included. He was pushed on me. I was only sure the team that's in Miami could take him. I didn't look far enough ahead."

Thorne grew silent for a minute as he assimilated the new information.

"We don't have anything to trade him? Maybe we could turn his friend Steiner with the right offer." Thorne said.

"No negotiating," Paul said. "We're going to kill them." He turned to the two policemen. "You know who the friendlies are on board?"

Nods from the SWAT-team members.

"Get a clean shot on *anyone* else, take it and make sure they don't get up again. We'll take the pilot out first, and silently as possible. That'll leave either Martin or his accomplice below."

Paul checked his gear and secured the forty-five he'd carried throughout his professional career. The cane stayed loaded. Walking without it would be difficult, but he had to refrain from using it on the deck and alerting the men inside.

The navigator turned around. "The Mae Wests—each is fitted with a beacon on it that we'll pick up. They inflate as soon as they're immersed or by pulling the strings. We'll be on the sailboat's stern in ten minutes. You'll need to get out on the bow. We'll hold it as steady as we can." Paul nodded and selected four of the inflatable Mae Wests.

He opened the rough sketch of the *Shadowfax* Thorne had drawn. He studied it. Going in would probably be suicide. Two detonators, a split second to trigger them. Martin would do it, would die himself, before he'd risk failing. Would the other man? Probably.

Five minutes later the four were wearing assault-style hoods. Paul turned to the pilot, whose face was demonically lit by the orange glare of the dials.

"I've got solo body-heat silhouette on the stern. Either the boy or someone seated," the navigator said as he inspected the red-orange form on the deck. The sailboat was a light-blue outline against a darker blue.

Paul thought about it for a second. *Reb? Martin's friend Steiner, watching for us?*

"Get us in close. When we get my family overboard, I don't want them wet good before they're in this boat. We're your second priority, but stay well back from the boat after you drop us. Do not approach the vessel under any circumstances once the family is aboard. No closer to the *Shadowfax* than two hundred meters until I have the bomb disarmed and Martin neutralized."

The pilot nodded. The four men went out the forward hatch and stood at the railing. There was a platform at the front that could be raised several feet to allow occupants of the *Cheetah* to board a larger vessel. The men wore Kevlar vests and goggles to protect their eyes from the rain—the speed of the boat drove the rain against them like BBs.

"Good luck," Paul said.

"Later," Thorne said. He smiled at Paul, and in that second Paul was swept with a feeling of loss and remorse. They would not all see dry land again. Maybe none of them would.

"If Reid is alive . . . if you get to Reid, and I don't, find out who sent him," Paul said. "And make sure people know."

Thorne nodded.

The *Cheetah* swung in from the east and pulled behind the sailboat. Ted held the figure on the deck in his binoculars as they swung in while Brooks kept his MP-5 trained on it. If it was Steiner or Martin, they would be full of holes before they knew what hit them. The cockpit was empty, which meant the vessel was on autopilot. The sound of the sailboat's diesel and the wind was far louder than the pursuit boat. Paul could make out the figure on the stern now. It was Woody. The agent was naked, leaning against the aft mast with his legs splayed on the roof of the aft cabin. His head was lolling, his chin against his chest. He looked unconscious, his head rocking with the movement of the boat.

As the boats fell into speed and directional sync, the

four men moved across the gangplank. They stepped quickly aboard the *Shadowfax*, their guns in hand. Ted led the group, with Thorne bringing up the rear. The *Cheetah* dropped back and veered away behind the veil of rain, then followed like a hungry shark on a blood trail.

55

KURT STEINER CAME IN FROM CHECKING THE COCKPIT, SHED HIS WET coat, and joined Martin, who was almost finished stitching his jaw where it had been opened. Kurt looked at the instrumentation on the galley wall, which included a compass with their present bearing displayed. Martin was seated at the counter before a small mirror as he used a curved needle from the boat's first-aid kit to pull a length of suture through and through, sealing the open wound in his cheek. He finished three, clipped off the extra nylon string, and wiped the oozing blood from his cheek carefully with a damp cloth. "That'll have to do," he announced. The white sutures reminded Kurt of the stitching on a baseball. The way Martin ignored pain never failed to amaze Kurt. It was as though he refused to acknowledge its existence and in doing so robbed it of any power it might have over him.

"What about them?" Kurt asked, pitching his head in the direction of the cabin door.

"Why, you want a little sport?"

"No," Kurt said. "There's no honor in—"

Martin's hand moved like lightning, and he seized Kurt's wet face between his fingers, the palm covering his mouth. "What the fuck do *you* know about honor? A bunch of claptrap you heard from a drooling old man who ran to South America with his tail tucked?"

"No, I mean . . ."

Martin's eyes flashed, and the teeth, between his tightened lips, were like white tiles set in a grout of blood. Blood flowed anew. Martin wiped at it, angrily or impatiently. "That little *mother* in there knows more about loyalty than either of us could ever understand." His face twitched and his eyes cleared. He released his grip and patted Kurt playfully on the shoulder. "Real loyalty, true devotion, springs from perfect love. Loyalty for men like us is a function of self-interest." The rose circles where Martin's fingertips had gripped Kurt's cheeks stood out as though painted on with rouge. Martin turned back to the counter, opened three of the white capsules, poured the powder into his mouth, and took a swallow of wine. He waved his hand in the air over the counter to dismiss the past few seconds as nothing significant.

Kurt hadn't moved a muscle. His expression did not betray the pain he felt at the rebuff or the fire of anger that was burning inside him. "I am loyal to you. I will die for you."

"So I am a cause worth dying for? I am an object for your perfect loyalty? Interesting." He searched Kurt's eyes with his own for an answer. "Hereditary anomaly, no doubt."

"My grandfather was loyal. To his leader."

"Yes, I'm sure he was. Even though his leader was a loser on a global level. I didn't mean to knock the old buzzard off his ragged pedestal. *Sieg heil* and all that shit."

"He was a great commander. He served in Russia. Lost two fingers and the toes on his left foot to frostbite," Kurt murmured.

"No fun tonight," Martin said absently. "We'll need

all of our energy for Paul. Maybe I'll draw it out for a long time so he'll have something special to remember. Think he'd deflower his own daughter to save the family? That is an interesting thought. That would be something for him to remember." Martin laughed out loud. "Oh, that's good! What a test of love and loyalty versus ingrained Christian morality."

Kurt frowned. "Let's just get it over with and get the hell out of here."

Martin looked at the man for a second, and then he backhanded him, sending him sprawling onto the floor. "*I'm* in charge here. *I* make the plans, *I* set the rules of engagement. The important thing *isn't* getting away. We'll get away if we deserve to. The important thing is teaching these fucking assholes about the limits of pain. If you want to go, get the fuck out now—take the tanks, I don't need them. If you're afraid to die . . . get the fuck out. Tell you what, you can have *all* the Lallo money. Live like a king in your country, marry some blond-haired, German-mix spick and bounce your own grandsons on your arthritic knees singing the praises of the Fatherland."

Kurt stood and pulled himself up into full attention. His face was twisted, red where he had been struck, and his lips pursed tightly together. "I'm not afraid, Martin. I *will* die if I need to—or if you order me to. My oath is my loyalty, my life. My life is yours to command."

Martin put his arms around the younger man, looked him in the eyes, and hugged him. "Then we'll live or die together. If we fail alive or dead, it's all the same. Without honor, what is there?" He took the detonator from his pocket and placed it on the counter. "I give you the honor of detonating the package when the time comes. Is the scuba equipment ready? There's a ten-minute delay. Enough time to get away," he lied. The delay after the button was released was thirty seconds. Martin had reset it.

Martin patted Kurt's cheeks softly, almost lovingly. "Let's go back and rig everything nice for our soon-to-arrive guests. And put a smile on that face."

56

THE FOUR INTERLOPERS CROUCHED AT THE *SHADOWFAX*'S STERN and stared at the sight Martin had constructed. Woody's mouth was covered with duct tape. His forearms were duct-taped together from the elbows to the wrists. His fingers looked like twisted oak limbs with the bark removed in places where broken bones showed through the skin. When he rolled his head up, Paul thought his eyes had been gouged out but realized that someone had packed the sockets as well as the ear canals with caulk.

"Dear God," Paul whispered. Woody was living in a dark, silent world where there was only pain for stimulation.

Ted crossed himself and pulled a knife out of a boot holster to cut the ropes that held the young baby-sitter to the mast.

Paul grabbed his wrist, stopping him as he started the first cut. Then he circled around behind Woody and saw what he had expected. A small, all but invisible trip wire led from Woody's waist to a coil of cotton rope. He looked into the coil and saw a fragmentary grenade wired to a chrome stanchion. The trip wire had been wrapped around the pin, and the pin had been pulled out so that only a small bit of the tip was still providing purchase and holding the device's spoon in place. Just to make sure it would come out easily, there was grease on the pin to kill any friction. *Hell of an alarm system!* He pointed it out to the others and pushed the pin back so that it was fully locking the detonator, then bent the metal slightly, using Ted's knife, so that it would take a hard tug to pull it out. Then he took the cop's knife and cut the trip wire. They lifted Woody and laid him on the deck. He was alive but mercifully unconscious.

Paul took one of the extra Mae Wests from its carry pouch and secured it around him. Then, with the help of the others, they dropped Woody into the sailboat's wake. He bobbed there, his head and shoulders out of the water, then disappeared into the wall of rain in their wake.

They began moving slowly and silently up the side of the boat. Thorne stopped to cover the aft cabin door; Ted knelt with his back to Thorne's and kept his gun trained on the cockpit door. From his position Ted could cover the cockpit and the door to the galley. He would see whoever was coming up before they could see him. Paul and Brooks moved slowly and quietly the length of the boat to the cabin in the bow.

Paul removed the snap buckle from the hatch's hasp, tossed it into the lake, and eased the door open. The music from Erin's radio escaped, and the first thing he saw was Reb's upturned face, filled with surprise. Paul put his finger to his lips for silence as he held out his other hand.

Laura looked up and beamed. "Paul!" she whispered. "Okay!" She grabbed Reb by the waist and held him up to his father like an offering. Paul pulled him free and into the rain, then reached in for Laura.

Brooks laid his machine gun on the deck and put a Mae West on the shivering child.

Paul pulled Laura up and into his arms. She kissed him hard on the lips. The policeman handed her a Mae West, and she started to put it on.

"Erin?" she whispered.

"At the yacht club. Fine. You two go on over the side. Brooks will stay with you. There's a boat behind us that'll pick you up in a minute or so."

"Where's Wolf?" Reb asked.

"With Erin. Safe."

"Biscuit!" Reb said. "Biscuit's in there!"

"It's just a bird, Reb," Laura said.

"He's not just a bird! Daddy, he trusts me and they'll kill him. I know they will."

"Where is he?" Paul asked.

"Down there by the bed. Please let me go get him."

"I'll do it, sir," the policeman said.

"No, I'll get him," Paul said. "You just do what I say."

The young policeman put the machine pistol's strap on his shoulder, grabbed Reb in his arms, and stepped to the railing. "Come quickly, ma'am," he said.

"Biscuit?" Reb said, fighting to get loose from the policeman's grip.

"Reb, trust me."

"You promise?"

"Yes."

"Cross your heart?"

"Promise. You take care of your mother till I get there. Can you do that?"

"Yeah."

"Ready?" Brooks asked.

Reb nodded and pinched his nose closed as the cop tightened his grip on the child's waist. Then, as Laura's and Reb's eyes stayed locked, the cop took Laura's hand, and they all three went over the rail and out of Paul's sight.

"Good-bye," he whispered. "May God keep you safe." He moved to where Thorne and Ted were.

"Okay," he said. "I want you two over the side, too."

"What?" Thorne said. "You nuts?"

"Thorne, I don't need you now. Take him and go. Follow in the *Cheetah* and make sure Martin doesn't get away if it goes wrong. Please?"

Thorne shook his head. "No. I'm staying until we drop the hammer on these assholes. You just want to have all the fun."

The policeman looked at his watch. "I don't have to be home for two hours yet," he said. "Let's put this franchise out of business."

"Okay, then," Paul said. "I'll go in from the V berth. Wait two minutes, or until you hear the first shot, and then come in. Thorne, the aft cabin. Ted, you come in through the cockpit. We have to take them by surprise, before they can think to set the bomb off."

"Good luck, Paul," Thorne said.

"I don't need luck," he said. "I got looks."

Paul went back to the V berth and opened the hatch. He tossed the cane down onto the bed. Then he followed it in. He looked around. The bird was in the cage on the dresser. He smiled at Reb's attempt at drownproofing the caged bird. But there was probably no way to save the bird, he decided. *Can't let it go—it can't fly with clipped wings, and it sure as hell can't swim.* He took the cage's handle and, using his cane tip, placed it up onto the deck in the rain.

"Friggin' two-dollar bird," he whispered.

He looked at what Laura had been doing before he'd interrupted, and once again smiled. She had peeled the end of the looted lamp cord, wrapped the frayed copper ends around the knob, and plugged it back into the outlet. She had planned to fry Martin. The cord, with its off/on switch, would fire up the door. She had a flowerpot filled with water, which he imagined she had planned to pour under the door when Martin came. Whoever opened the door could have been electrocuted. Paul imagined the circuit was on a ground-fault interrupter, which would break the current before any harm was done. So the effort would have failed, but he was damned proud of her ingenuity. He was sorry that he'd never get to tell her how proud he was of her, how much he loved her, and how deeply sorry he was that he had destroyed their happiness. Maybe she'd know anyway.

Then, as he was ready to move to the door, the knob lever turned. "Open the door, Laura," Martin said.

Paul walked over, held the gun up, unlocked and opened it. He wouldn't have recognized Martin, but he was delighted at the pure shock that was painted across the new face. He wondered fleetingly what had happened to Martin that had required a field stitching. Paul had the drop on Martin. His hands were at his side, empty.

"Paul!" he said.

"Surprised, asshole? You invited me."

Paul held the cocked Colt against Martin's head while he patted him down with the left. He removed the electronic trigger from Martin's pocket and used his teeth to open it. Then he pulled the nine-volt battery out, dropped the device to the floor, and smashed it flat with his heel.

"Where's your little pal?"

Martin shrugged. "Kurt? You know how hard it is to keep up with the help."

"Where's Reid?"

"You mean Mr. Spivey?"

Paul nodded.

"About now I imagine he's telling some convoluted tale to St. Peter. So T.C. really *didn't* tell you about Reid, did he?"

"That shouldn't matter to you, Martin."

"No." He smiled. "But the question is why he didn't warn the others. Might have got at me sooner, don't you imagine? Didn't warn *you* that your days were at an end, either, did he?" Martin laughed, pleased with himself. "He never liked you, you know," he said softly. "Politics at its most lethal. You gonna kill him for it? No, you aren't a killer, are you? I never have figured out what

you are . . . besides lucky. You should have died in
Miami."

Paul peered over Martin's shoulder into the empty
lounge, the galley, and the darkened hallway.

"Where's the little family? Upstairs? Gone? And I
thought they were enjoying the cruise." He laughed, and
Paul saw that there was no fear in his eyes. He looked
happy, even excited. Paul knew the time had come to
shoot him, but his trigger finger remained at rest.

"Okay, Paul, what's next?"

An alarm went off inside Paul's head. *He isn't worried. The bomb. There's another triggering device with . . .
Where's Steiner?* Paul's answer came by way of a flash
from the darkened hallway. Then he was falling backward, shot. It was almost as though he had simply lost
his balance, except for the pressure in his upper chest.

As he lay on his back beside the bed, he heard the
rattle of Ted's machine gun fill the lounge and the answering bark of another machine gun, unsilenced, deafening. He lifted his head and looked at the doorway
where Martin had been. The pain wasn't there yet, but
his left shoulder was shattered, useless. He tried to get
up, but he was like a flipped turtle. Then the pain found
a path through the natural defenses, and it was blinding.
Paul flailed at the bed, reaching for the cane, but it was
beyond his fingers somewhere.

There was a pitched battle being waged on the boat,
and he couldn't move. He cursed and reached deep
down inside himself for the strength he needed. Maybe
Martin thought he was dead. He raised up again to look
for his Colt, but it was gone. Either in Martin's hand or it
had fallen into the lounge. He tried to steady his
thoughts, concentrate, but the pain was searing his mind,
filling him with panic. Unbidden, a memory was flowing
back. Something that had been lost to him for six years.

He was remembering something he had not supposed he could ever recall—something the doctors assured him was lost forever to the trauma. He
remembered the dock in Miami, seeing the doors of the
shipping container opening, and he remembered seeing

the dark faces of the men behind brown sacks of sand. He saw the surprise on the Colombians' faces that they were alive, that the bomb had not gone off when the doors opened, the trip wire had failed. He remembered them bringing up their guns as Barnett or Hill pulled him back and both took position in front of him to protect him with their own bodies. He saw, over their shoulders, the flashes from the Mac-10s. And he saw, as he fell backward, a slow, silent ballet of blood and brains turning and falling through the air above him as he fell.

Paul lay there on his back against the carpeted floor with his mouth open, needing to cry but knowing there wasn't time, fighting his way back from the then to the now. Those two boys in Miami had sacrificed their lives for his, and no one but he had seen it. They could have stayed safely on the side, but he had been in the line of fire. Had they known they were trading their lives for his?

Was that why I kept seeing them?

57

KURT STEINER HAD BEEN COMING DOWN THE HALL WHEN HE'D SEEN Masterson holding the gun on Martin. He had drawn his own gun, taken hasty aim at Masterson, and had dropped him. Then Martin had picked up the agent's Colt just as a fusillade of bullets, fired at a downward angle from the cockpit, had ripped up the room around them. Martin had emptied the Colt and made it to the counter, picked up the Uzi he'd taken from the agent on the pier, and returned the fire, sending thirty nine-milli-meter rounds through the wall and ceiling, trying to hit the man in the cockpit. Then he had reloaded and emp-tied it, leaving the air in the galley thick with cordite smoke.

Kurt ran back toward the aft cabin immediately, where the Uzi was lying on the bed alongside the deto-nator. He made it to the bed just as the door opened, leaped across it, lifting the Uzi as he fell behind the bed.

Thorne Greer aimed his pistol into the room and began firing rapidly. Kurt waited for the agent to empty his magazine, then came up and returned fire, hosing the doorway. After the gun was empty, he realized that Thorne had moved away before he had fired. Kurt could see through the swirling cloud of smoke that the door, filled with holes and quill-like splinters, was rocking gently like a flag in the breeze. He tossed the empty Uzi onto the floor, took out his pistol, and put the detonator in his top pocket. He also took a fragmentary grenade from the open panel in the bed frame, just in case, pushing the lever into his web belt to secure it.

Kurt followed the extended gun hand. He went out onto the deck and swept it from side to side, ready to shoot at the agent. He saw a shoe, which he took for Thorne's, lying on its side beside the rail. "Gone over," he said. "Chickenshit." He looked around the mast to the starboard side to make sure; it was clear. Then he peered back around at the port side and it, too, was deserted. He saw that Woody was gone and registered without emotion the fact that they had discovered the trip wire. He moved toward the open cockpit and, certain the bow deck was clear, stepped up and aimed his gun inside. The policeman on the floor had been a casualty of Martin's Uzi. He had taken uncounted hits in the chest and head.

"All clear, Martin!" he yelled into the galley.

Martin appeared. "Where's your detonator?" he asked.

"Here," Kurt said, touching the breast pocket with the barrel of the pistol.

"Give it to me." Martin held out his hand. "We're going back."

"What?"

"The family can't be far behind us. Same boat that dropped the team off. We'll locate it and we'll take it out with the Semtex. Send 'em to the bottom."

Kurt reached into his pocket and took out the device. As he was holding it out to Martin, he was aware of something large descending on him from above.

•   •   •

Thorne had climbed twenty feet up the foremast, where he had clung on tightly, keeping himself as covered by the structure as he could. Luckily Kurt hadn't bothered to look up. When Thorne saw Martin reaching for the detonator, he had dropped. At the last split second of the fall Kurt had turned his head up, but he had only had time to look surprised before Thorne landed his feet squarely on his shoulders. Thorne had the gun in his fist and was braced for the hit, so he was able to fire at Martin before he stopped sliding on the wet deck. He tried to stand but couldn't because his ankle gave when he put weight on it. His fingers confirmed the bone was pressing skin out from the inside. He wanted to vomit.

Kurt was stunned, the breath knocked out of him, Thorne assumed. But he was quick enough to get out of the line of fire. Thorne hoped that he had at least broken one of Kurt's collarbones. Kurt had lost his SIG Sauer pistol, and Thorne picked it up and hurled it back over his shoulder into the water. He fired another few rounds at the galley door.

Thorne didn't know what to do next. He assumed Paul was dead—how could he not be? He couldn't walk, but he found he could lift himself upright and stand, balanced on the good leg. At least he could kill one of them, maybe.

Kurt, who had circled the cockpit, came at him from behind on the fly. Thorne turned, and when he put weight on the shattered leg, he started down, but he pushed hard against the deck with the good leg as Kurt hit him. The motion was just enough to allow him to change his attacker's balance, and the two of them pitched off, their legs hitting the rail hard and turning them on their axis as they sailed out into the darkness.

Martin was going to backtrack. Not to help Kurt, but to go after the family. They would be on the boat that had transported Paul's team. They'd be following, waiting for Paul's victory like wide-eyed groupies.

He went down into the galley to make sure Paul was

really out of the picture. Between the adrenaline and the speed coursing through his system, he felt invincible.

Paul had managed to drag himself across the room, leaving a wide smear of fresh blood. Martin saw that his enemy was breathing and had a cane clenched in his hand. Martin exhaled loudly. "Paul, Paul," he said. "No vest can stop KTW, you of all people should know *that*." He laughed. "You're lung shot, I believe."

Paul opened his eye slowly and focused it on Martin, who was grinding his teeth.

"You are something! But what on earth made you think *you* could take me? Couldn't even squeeze the trigger when you had me. Had to listen to me jabber. Paul, you don't *do* that. You take the shot."

Paul exhaled. "You're right, Marty. Never listen to a man you intend to kill."

"You've learned too late, but you've learned." He took the boot knife from his leg sheath. "Now I'm going to prick you with this. You'll go fast, if not completely painlessly. Then I'm going to sail back until I can see the boat that brought you. I'll set the course, jump into the lake, and make sure your family meets you upstairs. There's enough Semtex against the fuel tanks to take out anything within a few hundred yards. But I'll be far closer, Paul. If they escape for some reason, I'll be there, like a shark. I see a head bobbing, and pow." He held up the blade and admired it.

From where Martin was seated, the cane seemed to come from the side of Paul's right leg like a cobra rising from a basket. He saw the hole in the center of the tip and held out his right hand to ward off the inevitable. The heavy bullet passed through the hand, exploding the ceramic knife, and struck him dead in his chest, knocking him against the wall. He sat down with a look of complete disbelief in his eyes. Paul watched as Martin closed his eyes and his head dropped, chin against his chest, and he was still. Martin's thumb was the only digit on the knife hand that hadn't been destroyed outright by the heavy lead slug.

"You shouldn't have taken time to talk, you egotistical fuck."

Paul went up through the galley's open door, picking up the Colt and putting it into the holster. He stepped out into the rain and looked up at the mast, letting the water run over his face. He ignored the searing pain in his shoulder. He fought the urge to offer a primal scream into the heavens. He had saved his family, and he, Paul Masterson, had slain the monster. Then he removed the battery from the detonator and put the two parts of the device in a molded cup holder on the dash.

He lifted Woody Poole's radio and spoke into it. "This is Masterson, *Cheetah,* do you copy?"

"Yes," the voice said. "We're due south of your position, picking up Mr. Greer and someone else."

"Careful, that's Kurt Steiner. He's dangerous."

"Paul," Laura said. "What about Martin?"

"Daddy?" It was Reb.

"Yeah, son?"

"What about Biscuit? He okay?"

Paul looked through the windshield at the bird in the cage sitting by the open hatch near the bow. The creature was puffed up against the chilling rain.

"I'm bringing him home, like I said."

Paul laid the cane against the seat and disengaged the autopilot, swinging the boat around and closing the throttle a bit. He removed the Mae West, which was exerting pressure on the shoulder, reset the autopilot to 180 degrees, and went to get the bird. He walked over to the cage, reached down, and lifted it to eye level. He looked in at the gray bird, admiring the orange circles on its cheeks, which covered the ear canals.

"You ain't just a bird," he said, repeating what his son had said.

He saw something reflected in the small water-smeared mirror in the cage and remembered something his uncle had told him when he was learning to hunt mule deer. *Never approach a deer you've shot if the eyes are closed—if he's dead, the eyes will be open. Martin's eyes . . . were closed!*

He was aware of the hollow crack as something heavy hit the side of his head.

Martin decided the chest wound was fatal—he was blowing blood bubbles with every breath. If he was right, he had minutes, maybe as much as an hour, left. The bullet had passed through the lung. The important thing for the moment was that the old heart was still beating. He looked at the destroyed hand and decided he wouldn't need it again, anyway.

Martin struggled through the aft cabin and went out onto the deck with the folding knife he'd used to cut Laura's clothes away. The rain had almost stopped. He stood still when he heard Paul on the radio, and then the boat was turning to the south.

When Paul went to the bow, Martin moved into the cockpit and there, leaning against the seat, was the cane that Paul had killed him with. It seemed only right that the heavy cane which Paul had used to shoot him should also be the instrument by which Paul died. He laid the knife aside and moved to crush Paul's skull.

He hit Paul in the head with his own gun cane just above the ruined eye socket and watched as the agent fell over the side of the boat, still holding the birdcage in his hand, the bird within flapping about wildly.

"You lose!" Martin screamed into the darkness, and then laughed a long, staccato bark.

Confident Paul would drown, Martin went back to the cockpit. With the detonator missing, the bomb was useless. So he would ram the boat and sink them all. He laughed out loud when he saw the detonator *and* the battery where Paul had placed them. *Fool didn't toss it!* He replaced the battery, using his left hand. The cover plate was gone, and the battery dangled by the wires like a pendulum, but the green ready light let him know it was live. Paul had changed course, heading back to the boat. Martin left the autopilot engaged. When he could see their eyes, he would set it off. His own vision was starting to blur, to tunnel on him.

"Sir," a voice came over the radio. "You're headed

right for us. You should see us in a couple of minutes when you break out of the rain. ETA approximately two minutes.''

Martin smiled, pressed the button down, and maintained pressure on it as he began watching for the chase boat.

Paul broke the surface and began treading water with no idea which way he should swim. At first he assumed Martin would turn and run him down, but Martin was piloting the *Shadowfax* toward the *Cheetah*. And there was nothing Paul could do to stop him. Nothing he could do for his family or himself. He would die, too. He couldn't move his left arm at all. He had never been much of a distance swimmer in his physical prime, but with his shoulder shattered he knew he couldn't stay up long. His bad leg was already cramping, and the right side of his head felt as if it were going to explode. He would die right here in the shadow of a bridge where cars were whizzing past. He saw something white bobbing in the chop a few feet away, and he swam over to find out what it was. It was the birdcage, held out of the water a few inches by the Styrofoam packed inside.

He took a deep breath, rolled over on his back, placed the birdcage on his chest and floated there, waiting for the end.

58

Rainey Lee was feeling a blend of boiling fury and orgasmic excitement. He was certain now that God wanted to let him have his revenge, because there he was flying out onto the lake when he should have been shackled on the pier.

The ensign seemed competent but frightened. Fine, he decided, that would help motivate him. He knew that the young man couldn't see Doris's spirit, but there she was floating over the transom of the boat, her hair and clothes unaffected by the earthly wind and rain, her eyes scanning the horizon. He knew she was looking for the sailboat but so far wasn't able to communicate its location. She seemed to be waiting. Maybe until they were closer. Maybe *he* had to do more before she could help him. It was his quest. His family couldn't be reunited until Martin's blood had been shed, the atonement made complete. He knew that, and he was prepared to do whatever he could to make it happen.

Everywhere he looked, his vision was blocked by an impenetrable wall of rain. He could barely see the bow of the forty-foot-long racer. The fuel gauges read between three-quarters and full, but he had no idea how long the boat could run at almost full throttle. He was dimly aware that he had fired on a policeman and escaped, but that didn't matter; the policeman had merely been another obstacle to overcome. He had not fired on Captain Mullin to kill him, but he could have done so with ease. He would do what he had to do, and lives lost on the fringe of his quest were of no consequence, including that of the young ensign. If he tried anything, Rainey would kill him.

"Sir, we're lost," the ensign said. "We have to turn back."

Rainey allowed the words to filter into his mind. He looked at the dark screen on the dash. "That's radar," Rainey said.

"Yes. It's no good for looking for the *Cheetah*. It's invisible to this one."

The young man was trying to foil Rainey's search. "Use it to locate the sailboat," he said.

"I don't know how it works," he answered.

Rainey cocked the pistol and placed it behind the boy's ear. "Figure it out," he said. "Do I need to count to five?"

The ensign flipped a switch, and the blackened radar screen became an unblinking green eye that looked everywhere and saw everything. The shore was a slightly curving line, the bridge a straight one.

"They're either behind the bridge or against it, being masked," he said.

"Go to the bridge," Rainey said. "When you get close, if they're using it for masking we should be able to pick them up."

Within ten minutes they had closed on the bridge, and a blip lit up green as the sweep passed through it.

"What's that?" Rainey asked, tapping the screen with the barrel of the .357. "Son, I'd bet your life it's the sailboat."

Then there was another return beside the first one.

"I don't know. There's two. Can't be the *Cheetah*." He looked at it for a few seconds longer. "It moved east and then west, slowly. Then it sped up along a north-south line. Could be a false return."

"A false return? What do they teach you these days?" he said. "It's as plain as the nose on your face. It's the sailboat, and the other's a helicopter," he said, laughing out loud. "Aim for the first one, son. They're waiting for us."

Rainey moved back so that the rain lashed his face, and he stretched out his arms and screamed into the fury, "Thank you, God," he yelled, "for delivering my enemies!"

59

The *Cheetah* had located Woody by the auto beacon. They had taken him on board, planning to let the helicopter evacuate him. The navigator had removed the tape from his mouth and had cleared out his eyes and ears as best he could and given him morphine—for his broken hands. They had to wait for the family to hit the water, and they'd send Woody along with them to safety.

Minutes after securing Woody they picked up the signal as Laura, Reb, and Brooks hit the water. They called for the chopper to come in and evacuate Woody as they made for the signals being sent by the transmitters in the Mae Wests.

Thorne and Kurt had been in a Mexican standoff for ten long minutes when the boat found them. Thorne, still in his life vest, had been holding his pistol on Kurt to keep him at bay. Kurt was armed with a folding knife, sure

Martin would come back for him. The dark-green boat materialized beside him, startling him. Instinctively, he reached for the grenade on his belt.

The side door on the *Cheetah* opened. The navigator and Laura reached down and helped Thorne climb inside.

"Move it!" Thorne yelled at Kurt from the clamshell door.

"Fuck you!" Kurt yelled back. The rain had stopped, and Kurt heard the giant Sikorsky approaching low and from the south. He had to do something fast. He pulled the grenade free, held it up over his head, and pulled the pin while he kicked to remain above the surface.

Thorne fired twice as Kurt reared his arm back for the toss, and once as the arm came forward. The first two bullets went high, splashing ten yards behind his head.

Then he loosed the grenade, aiming for the open door.

Thorne's next shot hit Steiner full in the neck. He slipped under the dark surface without giving up so much as a bubble.

The grenade had been high. It hit the door's edge and bounced along the sloping roof, exploding as it rolled off the stern.

When the grenade went off, the pilot shouted, "What the fuck was that?" A red light on the console began flashing.

"Grenade," Thorne said.

"Props are damaged," the navigator said. He lifted his microphone. "Duster One, this is *Cheetah*, do you read?"

"Affirmative, *Cheetah*. We're right behind you."

"We're dead in the water. Need you to evacuate four souls, and we'll need a surface tow as soon as you can arrange it."

"Roger that."

The navigator looked at the screen. "Sir," he said. "We got a blip. The Cigarette is closing on us at sixty-nine knots."

"Duster One, we're ready when you are."

"Prepare your souls for a ride in the basket. Be advised we have the *Shadowfax* at zero-zero-one degrees and a quarter mile and eight knots steady. Be advised a second vessel is closing from zero-ninety."

Then the chopper was above them, the basket already hanging below its open door, two white helmets visible.

"*Cheetah*, this is *Shadowfax*." A voice came in over the receiver speakers.

"Please identify," the pilot said.

But Laura and Thorne knew the voice. "It's Martin," she said, fear filling her eyes.

"*Cheetah, Cheetah*, this is *Shadowfax*. Bang, you're dead."

Then, as they watched in horror, the sailboat appeared out from the curtain of rain like a ghost ship making a beeline for their bow.

60

Martin dropped the transceiver to the floor of the cockpit. The rain stopped suddenly, and the lake to the south opened up to him. He reached down to the console and turned on the tape player. The large speakers that were mounted on the deck, designed for people's entertainment while they sailed or sunbathed, filled the air with an orchestral rendition of "Danny Boy." In the distance the giant Sikorsky was hovering. Below it, in the circle of spotlight, there was a strange craft, a speedboat. The chopper was raising its basket. Inside was a prone body, which Martin assumed was Woody Poole's, and the boy, Reb, was seated in there as well.

His heart soared and he checked to make sure the engine was operating at maximum power. Then he laughed and squeezed the detonator. He could arrive before the cot was back in the belly of the helicopter. Maybe he could take out the boat *and* the helicopter! If it remained anywhere near where it was, it was as good as down in flames. The boy and Woody might be killed even if they managed to swing away to run for it.

Martin felt the button, knowing that when he let go, the Semtex would turn the lake for a hundred yards around into vapor. As he watched, an orange-and-white Cigarette boat broke from the curtain of rain and turned to intercept him. He stared in disbelief as the boat closed. He saw someone in a white uniform fling himself off the side and into the spray.

"Fuck you!" he yelled. The boat was moving at a seemingly impossible speed. It was a bluff. No two-hundred-dollar-a-month swabbie would ram him. He laughed, and blood ran from his open mouth.

As the Cigarette boat closed, he realized that the pilot was Rainey Lee, and that he was screaming something Martin couldn't make out, though he imagined what the gist of it would be.

As Rainey corrected the long boat's course to slam into the side of the *Shadowfax*, Martin released the button and closed his eyes for the short wait, cursing his luck.

61

THE HELICOPTER PILOT REACTED TO THE IMPENDING COLLISION BY rolling off and flying south with Woody and Reb swinging in the basket under the Sikorsky. Laura, certain Reb would be safe, turned and watched. It was at that moment that the Cigarette boat burst from the wall of rain and aimed directly for the sailboat. She saw the racing boat close the distance between itself and the *Shadowfax*. It slammed into the sailboat slightly in front of the cockpit, the impact rolling the sailboat a few feet up on its side—the larger vessel was impaled. As she watched in horror, there was a white flash followed almost at once by a deafening, superheated blast wave that pitched the *Cheetah*'s bow high into the air. She felt as if she'd had her ears slapped, and her eyes watered from the impact. The brilliant white ball turned red as it rose into the sky, leaving a floor of white vapor. Above them the chopper tilted crazily back and forth and then straightened as the shock wave passed. Then Reb and Woody disappeared into the chopper. Finally Laura was pulled up into the helicopter and took her son into her arms. Both of them were crying.

Thorne was the last one in the basket. The pilot, the navigator, and Brooks would stay with the *Cheetah* until a vessel could be sent out to tow it back. The helicopter moved over and picked up the ensign who had fled from the Cigarette boat.

"We're heading in," the man who operated the basket said.

"My daddy!" Reb yelled. "He's out there!"

The man's face reflected what they had all known when they had heard Martin's voice on the radio. Paul Masterson was certainly dead, his body most likely vaporized along with Rainey Lee, the young policeman, Reid Dietrich, and Martin Fletcher.

"Son," Thorne said. "Your father is gone."

"No, Thorne!" Reb screamed, grabbing Thorne's Mae West and shaking it. "He's not! I know he's not." He looked up into Thorne's face and the tears streamed down both cheeks. "He'll die if we go away! He promised!"

Laura tightened her grip on him, but he twisted free. "He promised me he'd save Biscuit! He would never lie to me again. You look for him!"

"I'm sorry," the man in the orange suit said. "We have to get this man back." He indicated Woody, who was lying on a cot, conscious now, being given first aid.

"Do it," Woody said through his pain.

"Look for a few minutes," Laura said. "Paul's a hard man to kill."

They followed the *Shadowfax*'s reverse course for several minutes, the spotlight a white plate floating on the propeller-beaten surface below them.

"He's not here," the guardsman at the open door said. Reb was beside him, looking down, Thorne holding the boy back by the shirt gathered in his fist.

As they started the turn for home, Reb screamed and pointed. "Look!"

There was something just outside the spotlight beam, bobbing and waving. When the light moved a few feet to the east, it became Paul Masterson floating on his back with Reb's birdcage propped on his chest.

"Well, I'll be fried," the man in the orange suit said to himself.

62

THORNE GREER FOUND PAUL IN HIS HOSPITAL ROOM SURROUNDED by flowers. Paul's left shoulder was wrapped in plaster, and his arm was immobilized so the collarbone could heal. Thorne was carrying a long white floral box.

Sherry Lander, seated in the room's sole chair, was reading a magazine.

"Agent Greer," Sherry said. "How are you feeling?"

Paul opened his eye and smiled. "Thorne, come in," he said. "Excuse me if I don't get up." He had a bandage covering the right eye and the damaged brow. The plastic plate had absorbed the deadly blow, but the covering skin had been split wide-open and had taken ten stitches to close. He also had a plaster cast covering the shattered collarbone from Kurt's bullet.

"Anything on Rainey?"

Thorne shook his head. "Nothing large enough to identify off the bat. Just pieces they'll have to tissue-type and Martin's right index and middle finger attached to a bit of hand almost to the wrist. Divers found something that will interest you." He put the floral box on the bed beside Paul, who opened it and pushed aside the tissue paper. Inside was what remained of Aaron's cane gun. The ebony that had covered the barrel and the ivory handle were gone. The chamber and trigger were there, but the barrel had been bent twenty degrees by the force of the blast.

"Uncle Aaron'll have my ass."

"The breech and handle are fine. I think you can get a smith to make it good as new." Thorne looked out the window and took a deep breath. "Joe's on his way from Miami. Looks like Stephanie is going to get a promotion for hanging with Eve. President called Sean's father personally."

Sherry stood and put the magazine on a table. "I'm going for a cup of coffee."

"I'll get some brought up," Paul said.

"No," she said, "I need the walk." She kissed his cheek as she passed.

The men watched her out the door. "Nice girl," Thorne said.

"Think as long as I'm here, I should get something done with my face? I mean, the plastic's cracked and they'll have to replace it anyway."

"Couldn't hurt," Thorne said. "I'm leaving for the Coast this afternoon." He looked out the window. "T.C. is working up a press release to plug the successful operation, the deaths of two of the world's most dangerous men and the *Cheetah*'s successful role. We won't be mentioned, naturally. Except for our dead who died valiantly."

Paul gripped his shoulder because the movement hurt him.

"Bastard'll get the director's title for sure now," Thorne said sadly.

"I wouldn't put money on it," Paul said. "T.C. has a lot to answer for."

"T.C.'s a political animal, Paul. He won't get

splashed. Any evidence vanished with Martin and Reid . . . Spivey, I mean. Had Spivey lived, he would have gone silently into the night."

"There's no proof," Paul agreed. "But I won't forget. And neither should you."

"I've had all the reality I can stand for a while. I'm out of here for La La Land this afternoon. My boss is going on location in France, and I'm planning to go along for R and R. Next time something like this comes up . . . don't call me."

"Call *you!*" He laughed and winced from the pain. "You can't find this sort of excitement watching your celebrities sign autographs."

"Money's better, and I don't need to be shot again to feel alive. My idea of excitement is gonna be tight swimsuits on the Riviera. I'll leave the blood-and-guts excitement to guys like you."

"I'm so good at it," Paul said, smiling.

"Hey, you did all right . . . for an old man."

Paul nodded.

"Well, so long," Thorne said, squeezing Paul's right knee. "As long as you're going under the knife, why not have an extra lift to get those little wrinkles around the eyes out? Hollywood is always looking for rugged, handsome types. I know some people."

Paul laughed. "Get outta here."

Thorne paused at the door, seemed to remember something, patted his pocket, then took a minicassette player out and tossed it onto Paul's bed. "By the way, I wanted you to hear something. Keep the Sony. I stole it from the DEA."

After Thorne had cleared the door, Paul picked up the tape recorder and switched on the tape. It was recorded via laser beam aimed at a window. There was static for a second, then his son's small voice talking to God about his love for his father.

Paul didn't want to cry, because the movement made his shoulder throb.

•   •   •

Sherry saw Laura and the children as she was coming out of the cafeteria and knew at once who they were. Reb had the lion's share of Paul's features. Riding up in the elevator with them, she found herself staring at the boy. He noticed and smiled at her.

"Hello," he said. "We were in the lake bombs."

"You must be Reb," she said.

"Yeah, how'd you know that—newspaper?"

"No. I've been working with your father in Nashville. I'm Sherry Lander. I was Rainey Lee's secretary."

Laura smiled at her, and when their eyes met, Laura knew exactly who Sherry was. "When did you get in?" she asked.

"Early this morning," Sherry replied. "I'm glad you all are okay. It must have been really terrible. I've been reading the coverage. Good Lord!"

Laura looked down for a minute as the memory of Reid and the fact of his death slammed home. "Yes," she said. "Terrible."

"I wasn't scared," Reb said. "Not really. But did you know there are sharks in Lake Pontchartrain? They come up the river. Could have eaten us all. We were lucky."

Erin rolled her eyes.

"How's Paul this morning?" Laura asked. Her eyes were kind and playful, and Sherry was relieved that she wasn't going to have to play the secretary.

"Fine. Thorne was there when I left."

Sherry stopped at the arch to the waiting nook, where a man was watching a game show. "I'll see you later, maybe," Sherry said.

"Don't be silly, join us," Laura said. Sherry shrugged and looked at the floor, suddenly embarrassed. Uncertain.

"Go ahead, kids. It's room five-twelve," Laura said. "Down the hall and to the left." The children went down the hall and turned the corner.

Laura spoke to Sherry. "Come on. Let's go see the old man."

Sherry hesitated. "You need to have a visit without me in there. I'm leaving in a little while, anyway."

"Don't be silly." Laura put her hand on Sherry's arm and gripped it lightly. "I'd feel better if you would. I have nothing at all to say to Paul that I didn't say last night. He's told me about you. Not by name. Said there's been someone in his life. I'm glad."

"But I thought that maybe you and Paul . . . I mean, he's better, and what he feels for me isn't anything like the way he loves you."

"He told you that?"

"He's been in love with you since he first set eyes on you. Besides, I can't possibly love him enough to fill in for his family. I just want to see him happy. He won't be happy until he has you guys back."

"He said that?" Laura smiled.

Sherry shrugged. "I'm a kid. I'll find someone else—I don't think I could be saddled to someone so set in his ways. But there won't ever be anyone but you for him, and that's a fact."

The women hugged briefly, and the tension, if there was any, was gone for good.

"I'm glad, Sherry. I'm really glad he has someone like you in his life."

Laura touched Sherry's shoulder for a second, smiled, and the two women walked down the hall side by side.

63

Thackery Carlisle Robertson, looking every inch the conquering hero, stood at the podium, illuminated by a phalanx of television lights. A wall of cameras, both film and still, gathered footage for the world. T.C. was introduced by the attorney general and spoke in artfully constructed sentences that had been written by his assistants and approved, word by word, by his yes men. The operation had been called Dropkick for the press's consumption. ("The public loves a classic military-code name," T.C. had said.) Newspapers, magazines, and television news had played and replayed the death, destruction, and drama in New Orleans. Martin Fletcher and Kurt Steiner had been tagged narco-terrorists. Since the Oklahoma City bombing, the word "terrorist" had guaranteed attention. The biggest news had been the list of the DEA's top-secret devices that had been used to bring him down and would be used in the future against others of his kind. There were also hints of other advances too sensitive to name.

Paul Masterson's name was absent from the text.

T.C. began by congratulating everyone (too numerous to mention) who had been involved. But even though he named a few people, it was clear he was taking full credit.

A veteran network newsman, a tall, narrow-shouldered man with acne scars and hair like a black tortilla glued to his head, raised his hand and stood when T.C. pointed to him. "Sam?"

"Mr. Director, are we to believe that all of this, including the bombs that killed"—he looked at his paper—"let's see . . . twenty-two people—civilians in New Orleans, members of the New Orleans police, DEA personnel, the United States Coast Guard, twelve dead civilians in Dallas—that all this was the work of just two men? The same two men, Mr. Martin Fletcher and Mr. Kurt Steiner, responsible for up to some thirty other homicides over the past six years? And any number of other crimes, including drug trafficking, bombings, and contract killings, and—well, the list is staggering."

"That's correct, Sam. We're not sure of the exact number in all related cases, but I'd guess that estimate is low, if anything. Martin Fletcher was the most dangerous terrorist we"—he looked at the attorney general, who stood smiling uneasily with her assistants on one side of the riser, and nodded at her—"at the Justice Department have ever taken out of action. And let me say that every effort was made to take Martin Fletcher alive."

Robertson smiled. He felt the hero—hell, he was a hero. He had managed to capture most of the credit for taking a nightmare terrorist out. Inviting the attorney general to join him was an ass-kissing exercise, since she had not been in on the loop. The operation had been expensive in lives, but the public loved the drama of it. He was certain that no one could keep him out of the director's chair now. Maybe there would be an even bigger payoff. He had been thinking that he could actually be

President, or at least attorney general, in the not too distant future.

"Mr. Robertson," Sam went on, "I have had certain information brought to my attention that you also hired a man by the name of George Spivey, known to sources in the CIA as a cleaner, or hit man, to help in the capture of these two admittedly dangerous men. He was killed aboard the *Shadowfax*, a boat owned by the DEA."

T.C. wondered how much Sam knew. He couldn't risk stonewalling. "True. I can't discuss this sensitive . . ." *The boat's ownership traced back to us?*

"Isn't it true that he was put in place in New Orleans over a year ago and you paid him with DEA funds?"

"Mr. George Spivey was a military-trained professional and a patriotic American. These men he was after were"—he smiled—"terrorists. I have done nothing illegal, Sam. Sometimes it takes tough, not altogether palatable men to catch the sort of monsters who are threats to our national security, our citizens. I hired him as soon as I had identified these men, and paid his expenses. He was the best available to us."

T.C. noticed the attorney general was fidgeting.

For the first time since the floor was opened for questions, no other hands were up in the room. All eyes were riveted on the veteran newsman and the acting director. The pros smelled blood.

The attorney general was physically moving away from Robertson—distancing herself. She seemed to spot someone in the wings, raised her hand, and then walked off the riser, followed down the hall by her assistants.

"Sir?"

T.C. tugged at his collar and smiled nervously. "Sam, maybe we should let someone else ask—"

"One more question, sir. Can you explain why, when you knew these two men were killing the family members of former agents of the DEA, you neither alerted them, specifically Special Agent in Charge Rainey Lee or the recently reactivated Special Agent in Charge Paul Masterson, nor any members of their families, that they were targets of these two maniacs who you yourself have described as the most dangerous men on the face of the earth? Maniacs who, *after* you had identified them, still killed the entire family of Rainey Lee and a Cub Scout leader and mother of three. Didn't you, in effect, sentence a large number of innocent people to death by your actions?"

"Sam . . ." T.C.'s face suddenly looked like bleached bone. "I . . . I . . . I resent that insinuation! You have no proof for this allegation and I resent the implications."

His assistant, a young attorney with a glued-on smile, covered the microphone with his hand, and he and T.C. had a few words.

"Sir," T.C. said, "on the advice of counsel, and considering the question of national security, I must respectfully refuse to answer that question."

"On *what* grounds?" Sam asked incredulously.

"On the grounds that . . . on the . . . because," he stuttered, and wiped at his brow. Then he said, "Gentle . . . ladies and men, this press conference is over."

The room exploded; flashes illuminated the dais, a hundred voices were raised in an attempt to get another question answered, and print reporters went running from the room to capture a telephone as T. C. Robertson bolted.

64

THE EARLY-MORNING SKY WAS FILLED WITH SOFT, BILLOWING clouds. An eagle, her wing tips splayed like fingers, flew effortlessly just above the stream's surface where the cold water was rushing over the smooth rocks. Above the cabin, patches of snow clung to the sides of the mountains, seemingly anchored by the quill-like trees.

Paul stood on the grassy slope in the blue shadow of the mountain with a steaming cup of coffee in his hand. His unlaced boots were planted as he stood watching a great bird at hunt over the rushing water. On the right side of his head there were delicate rose-colored lines etched where the stitches had been removed. The black leather patch had been retired when Paul's damaged skull plate had been corrected. The socket had been perfected and fitted with a glass eye, which, except for an inability to track, was a perfect match with the left.

Paul turned toward the porch where Reb sat on the

railing with his back against the upright support, spooling green line onto the fly-fishing reel. Wolf sat and watched him anxiously. Reb, his young face illuminated by a shaft of sunlight, turned and beamed at his father.

"There's your eagle on her morning run, Reb," Paul yelled, and he pointed at the bird as it dived, flared for a split second over the stream where the water roiled white against the rock, and plucked a trout from the water. Wolf barked and watched cock-headed as the majestic bird soared off over the trees with the gleaming curve of gray locked in her talons.

Reb waved that he'd seen it. Paul waved back. He could see motion through the kitchen window as Laura busied herself with breakfast and Erin watched. Laura had joined them the day before for the final two days of their children's visit. Paul hoped the kids would spend more time in Montana and grow to love it as he did. Laura, too.

To say her paintings had been a hit in Germany was an understatement. The German critics had embraced her, the show had sold out, and she was anxious to start another series. In fact, it seemed the most important thing in her life, aside from the children. Whatever hope he had held that they might pick up where they had left off before his accident six years earlier had been put on hold. He was welcome to visit New Orleans as much as he liked, but whether or not he and Laura would share the master bedroom was up in the air. That move, if it ever came to pass, would take time.

In the shadow of danger, during the days waiting for Martin to move, and in the glow after it was all over, both had seemed to believe that they could start up again. But with the sense of crisis gone there had been a shift. Now she had had several months to reflect, to think about her life. They had talked it over in the hospital as he was going through the surgeries and the recovery. Before, he had been her protector. Now she didn't need him in that role. Truth was she didn't know where he would fit in within the parameters of her life. She realized that she didn't truly know him anymore. Laura was independent, certain. Defining a relationship would take time, he decided. If there was to be a relationship, a commitment for a future as a family, their connection had to be built on new ground. After six years alone he had learned to be patient.

Unlike Laura, he wasn't sure what he wanted next. He did know he couldn't stay hidden on the mountain as he had before. He was ready to live again.

Paul took a deep breath, tossed the last drops of coffee into the air, and walked back up the slope toward home with the cup rocking gently from his trigger finger.

About the Author

JOHN RAMSEY MILLER'S career has included stints as a visual artist, advertising copy writer, and journalist. A native son of Mississippi, he now lives in North Carolina with his wife and sons and writes full-time.

"Hunter passes almost everybody else in the thriller-writing trade as if they were standing still . . . worth every extravagant rave."—Daily News, *New York*

STEPHEN HUNTER

POINT OF IMPACT
____56351-3 $6.99/$8.99 in Canada

"Suspense that will wire you to your chair. Hunter is damn good."

—STEPHEN COONTS

"A novel that will keep you turning the pages long after you should have turned off the light . . . great entertainment."

—*Milwaukee Sentinel*

"Stephen Hunter has done for the rifle what Tom Clancy did for the nuclear submarine . . . score it a bull's-eye." —*St. Louis Post-Dispatch*

"Gripping . . . the tension of POINT OF IMPACT never lets up."

—*The New York Times*

THE DAY BEFORE MIDNIGHT
____28235-2 $6.99/$8.99 in Canada

"A breathtaking, *fascinating* look at what could happen—given the possibility of an atomic 'given.' A wrap-up you'll never forget."

—ROBERT LUDLUM

"Rockets toward a shattering climax like an incoming missile."

—STEPHEN COONTS

"Nonstop action and mounting tension."   —*The New York Times*

"The one to beat this year in the nail-biter class . . . an edge-of-the-seat doomsday countdown thriller."   —*Daily News,* New York